DARKSHADOW

The Chronicles of Eldershire - Book Two

PAM B. NEWBERRY

J. K. Brooks Publishing, LLC
177 Stone Meadow Lane
Wytheville, VA 24382

Publisher's Note: This is a work of fiction. Names, characters, places, and incidents are a product of the author's imagination. Locales and public names are sometimes used for atmospheric purposes. Any resemblance to actual people, living or dead, or to businesses, companies, events, institutions, or locales is completely coincidental.

Book Cover Design ©2019 Julie Kay Newberry
Book Layout Design ©2019 Vellum

DarkShadow/ Pam B. Newberry. -- 1st ed.

ISBN-13: 978-1-941061-09-1

❀ Created with Vellum

For my readers

"Think of me as your soul angel. I will be with you always, by your side, holding your hand. I am your spirit guide."
~ Mr Scruffy

CONTENTS

WHERE IS THE LAND OF
ELDERSHIRE?

THE FICTIONAL LAND OF ELDERSHIRE is a mystical world, unaffected by time. Most only get to visit Eldershire in their dreams, but it is readily available within the blink of an eye, if one believes. If a traveler were to visit Eldershire, it would be found beyond the rainbow and its boundaries are further away than the Polar Express can travel. The best method to reach Eldershire is through the assorted and multiple portals that are easily found within the realm of possibilities but most often are only stumbled upon through luck, magic, or mysticism.

Eldershire flourishes and vanishes depending on the needs of the inhabitants, the Elderians, much like Brigadoon. Elderians represent many sentient beings that reside in multiple shapes, forms, and species—tree spirits, nymphs, elves, and talking animals—to name a few. The forests of Eldershire make up the spirit of the land, interwoven with mountains, hills, rivers, lakes, oceans, flora, and fauna. The main forest, the Wild Woods, is in the heart of Eldershire and was ruled by King Elder and Queen Esmé for many ions. As the rule of Eldershire ebbs and wanes, the mystical guidance of Mother Elder and Yggdrasil, the Tree of Life work together to protect the beings and the land.

The Chronicles of Eldershire documents the lives and times of the Elderians—their encounters with evil beings—and the story of human, Kay 'KC' Carson, whom acknowledges the portents of things to come.

To see a Map of Eldershire visit https://pambnewberry.com, and then click on Books from the top menu.

CHAPTER 1
PAIN INFLICTED

Months after returning from Eldershire and a successful quest to retrieve the Efil Stone, her mind began to play tricks on her. KC Carson would notice a movement off to her side, only to turn and find nothing there. Or she'd hear a sound, and swear there was someone or something in the house with her, but she was alone. Each time, her head would pound with pain that would rage from deep within her.

Once, she swore she heard a voice speaking to her from a far distance. She had her hearing checked only to learn her hearing was fine. She couldn't forget the words—

Life is full of dark shadows. Some linger, others come when least expected. With a sense of purpose, one can overcome the dark shadows that threaten to take you away

Who said that to me? She wondered.

THE LAST HEAT of summer was seizing its every chance to make

August the hottest month. Walking into the kitchen after being outside for hours harvesting the last of her garden's bounty, KC was trying to fend off the latest head throb in hopes another migraine didn't materialize. Pork ribs were cooking in the crockpot, and now she needed to fix the sides for a home cooked meal for the family. She was tired, but happy. Her head throbbed.

The counter was full of her harvest—cucumbers, onions, tomatoes, and the first summer corn. She sliced some onions for a cucumber-onion salad. A sharp pain surged across the left side of her temple. With each slice, more pain came, but she brushed it off; she justified it was because she'd gotten too much sun.

KC wanted to sit and relax, but food had to be prepared. She hoped she'd have some quiet time after dinner. Ever since her return from that trip she could not fully remember, she felt her life seemed always to turn on a dime. She wondered what forces hated her so much. *When will I get to live my dreams?* Another sharp pain shot through her eyes. She held onto the sink while it slowly released its grip on her.

"Hey Mom," Bill said walking into the kitchen with Marie and Boomer following behind. He looked so much like his dad, Jack, same muscular build, same red hair.

KC put on a smile. "Hi, son. Hi, Marie." She wiped her hands and reached down to greet Boomer, their black lab, ruffling his head. As she went to give him a quick hug, Boomer reacted strangely toward her. He backed away, and began to growl and started to bare his teeth.

"Boomer!" Bill said. "Stop that!" He turned to KC. "Are you okay?"

"Yes. I wonder what's wrong with him? He's never acted that way before."

"I don't know. I'll take him outside. Maybe he smells those ribs and wants some. I know their sweet smell makes me hungry. I can almost taste them."

"I guess so." KC watched Marie set a large container down on the counter. "What do you have there?"

"It's my first peach cobbler. Bill said that you and Jack love cobbler. So, we got some peaches from the farm down the road from our cabin and voila," Marie said while taking a step back, and then opening her arms—her face radiant, her body starting to blossom as the second trimester of pregnancy began. She was due to have the baby in about six or so months.

"You look beautiful!" KC smiled at her daughter-in-law. Her long blonde hair curled naturally around her face highlighting her deep blue eyes. She was dressed in a sweet, cool jumper that emphasized she was carrying their first grandchild. "And your dessert will be perfect! A nice finish for our dinner." KC took a drink of water from her insulated bottle. The ice-cold liquid made her body feel refreshed as it slithered down her throat—the pain washing away.

"What are we having?" Jack, KC's husband, walked up to Marie and Bill and gave each of them a hug. "Where's Boomer?"

"He's outside. We're having ribs with corn-on-the-cob, homemade bread, sliced fresh tomatoes, cucumber slices with onions, and baked beans."

"A feast for the masses," Jack said. "Need me to do anything?"

"Why don't the three of you go into the den and visit while I set the table? Give me some room." KC's eyes twinkled. She was blessed in so many ways. And soon they would have a grandchild. Having her family all together made her forget for a few seconds the pain.

Then, the pain hit her again. If I could get this headache to leave me alone, she thought. She opened the oven to get the baked beans, and jumped back. She thought she saw eyes looking back at her. Thankfully, she didn't drop the Dutch oven. Setting it on the counter, she grabbed her head. The pain was becoming unbearable. She went to the bathroom to get some aspirin.

"Is something wrong?" Jack asked, walking up to the bathroom doorway.

KC moved over to him, and then wrapped her arms around his trim waist. She didn't want him to know she was having another headache. Each time he found out, they got into a disagreement about what she should do.

"I don't want to ruin our day, but I've got another headache. Thought I'd better take an aspirin so I can enjoy our time together. No worries. It'll pass." She walked over to the bathroom cabinet. The pain surged. She grabbed the counter of the bathroom sink. She looked to Jack. His forehead wrinkled with his eyebrows drawn together. He cleared his throat.

"What?" KC said feeling her throat closing up with tightness in her chest. "You don't believe me?"

"Of course, I believe you. I'm worried about you." Boomer walked up, but stood closer to Jack and pawed his leg.

KC reached to pet Boomer. He growled again, and then ran back toward the den.

"That's odd," Jack said.

KC shrugged. "My life is full of oddness anymore."

She walked past Jack and into the kitchen. Jack followed.

"There's no need to worry." KC said putting food on the table. "It'll pass. It's a simple headache. I thought I'd heard something at the door. Did you hear it?"

"No," Jack said helping place the dinner dishes. "You've been having headaches for months now. And, you keep hearing and seeing things that aren't there."

"How do you know?"

"I'm a detective. Observing people is what I do." KC gave him a quizzical look. "What? Did you think I hadn't noticed?" he said.

"Shh. We don't want the children to hear us. We can talk about this later."

§.

FOR THE MOST PART, dinner was uneventful, though at one point, KC thought she would run out of the room. Several times, she had the notion she saw an owl—a horned owl at that—flying around the dining room. It turned out to be a moth hovering around the ceiling light. She could have sworn otherwise. They had a good laugh about it when she shared what she saw.

With the food put away, Jack was off to a public safety meeting, and Bill and Marie headed home with leftovers and a bone for Boomer. KC looked forward to being alone with her thoughts and sitting down to relax.

Her headache had gone away about the time they finished dinner. Now, she wanted to put her feet up and sit in the quiet. By the time she finally was able to settle into her chair, an hour had passed since the family left. Her legs felt heavy from working a long day putting their garden to bed for winter. Moments like these, she savored—she also worried how long they would last. It seemed her sixty-six years proved one thing over and over—something always interrupted her plans. And, it was always forces outside her control. There were times she wished she could hide from the world.

As a kid, she had that thought often. One time she confided in Kitty, her mother, how much she wanted to run away.

"Kay, you need to think about what it would mean for you to run away from the world. You know you have to live here, don't you?" Kitty said. "It's the only planet we have." Kitty smiled.

"Mom, really?" Kay replied.

"Sit down there, young lady and listen to me. This is important."

Kitty pointed to the kitchen chair. She moved about the kitchen working while she talked.

"There was this princess who managed to hide away from the world. While she was gone some thirty years, her world changed without her. She was not there to see the changes happen. When she finally returned to her world, all those she knew were gone—they had passed on. The princess learned that she could no longer rule. She was alone." Kitty said.

"Mom, seriously, is that supposed to mean something to me?"

"It *will* young lady. Mark my words. One day, you will be old, like me. You will be sitting in your house all alone. You will find out what life is all about."

KC PICKED up a nearby picture of Bill and Marie taken right after they were married. A couple years later, Bill, 38, and Marie, 36, were expecting their first child. KC thought back to when she and Jack first married. In a few weeks, it would be their fortieth anniversary. She was thankful to have Jack safely home from serving his country and working for their hometown as a public safety official.

Standing up, KC walked over to the davenport and replaced the picture. She moved to the kitchen as she thought about her life with Jack. Time with Jack seemed to have flown by. For over twenty-five years, he was a pilot in the Air Force, and he also worked as a volunteer firefighter.

KC went back into the den and looked at the pictures again. She picked up one of Jack in his Air Force uniform. She remembered he was proud when he retired from the Air Force.

Then, after working for the town for fifteen years, he was promoted five years ago to Public Safety Director for their small community. He attended several schools to acquire his police certifications and detective designation. He worked hard to solve several mysterious cases since then.

Last week, Jack told her that this coming July he would retire. I am lucky to have Jack in my life, she thought to herself. *Why am I so selfish with my wants with him and the family? All that Jack and I have built could all vanish if I take it for granted. Mom was right. I need to cherish my time with him.*

Placing her drink on the side table and her cell on her desk, KC settled into her comfy recliner. She looked out through the large windows that formed the sitting porch of their veranda. She studied their property before her.

For the last twenty years, she and Jack had worked the land, toiled the soil, and cleaned the debris after many storms. She smiled at the thought of how wonderful it would be when Jack retired. When he could sit with her, they could talk about their dreams—enjoy the time they have left. They would have evenings together and they would travel to Ireland and go on a Viking River cruise through Europe. She knew she needed to try harder to be content. Her head throbbed. She got up to get another aspirin, returned to her chair, and washed the aspirin down with her cold drink.

The evening sun cast rays of light through the late summer sky. A squirrel frolicking in a nearby walnut tree caught KC's eye. She watched two more squirrels join in the romp, climbing over branches, and then chasing each other at high speed. Out of the corner of her eye, she caught sight of a large bird. It was a wild turkey. It yelped. The sound made KC think the turkey was assembling her family for a gathering. Then, she saw little baby turkeys scurrying out of the tall grass nearby.

KC retrieved her camera from a nearby desk and focused it. Through the lens, she caught a glimpse of the turkey stepping in behind some tall grasses next to a patch of woods that stood along the riverbank. While looking through the lens to get another shot, KC saw a squirrel that suddenly appeared bigger than life in front of her eyes. She jumped back startled. Looking at the camera settings, she did not realize the manual focus had moved to a close up view.

She looked back through the camera. The squirrel pulled a ripened walnut from the tip of a branch as his little back feet held on with all he had. He dangled the length of his body to reach forward for his prize. Clutching it with care, he sat down on the branch and began to chip away at the dull green covering.

Pieces dropped slowly as he rotated the green-covered delicacy around and around, chewing off the covering to get to the rich insides. Finally, it was revealed. KC continued watching him. She could have sworn the squirrel looked up at her and grinned. Then he sat back on his haunches and held the nut up close to his face.

KC watched him slowly begin to shake the hard shell that contained the meaty food. His speed picked up. He shook and shook it, and then he cried out a screeching sound that gave KC the impression he was frustrated. She giggled when she saw him bang the nut on the branch, rub it hard against the bark, trying to weaken the walnut's hard covering.

His front teeth dug, scraped, and chipped away at the covering. He held the nut up, and then it appeared he looked into the new gap he created. Time passed. KC continued to watch. The squirrel went back to scraping. Scratch, scratch, scratch. The sound of the nut being rubbed on the tree echoed through the window. In the distance, she heard the hoot of an owl. Odd, she thought. It was daylight.

Moving closer, KC peered through the screen of the window to see if she could eye the squirrel scraping away. Suddenly, the walnut fell to the ground. The squirrel screeched again. Then, he scrambled down the tree to the ground to find his lost treasure. She giggled to herself at how funny he was. He had worked so hard; much like she had that day. But, he dropped his nut. I feel like that too when I drop my nut, KC thought.

"You do!" KC heard a voice, but when she looked around, no one was there. "No worries, you aren't going crazy yet," the voice said aloud.

It had become a pattern. Every time she thought she was starting to feel better, she became conscious of the fact she was only feeling good temporarily. She looked down at her camera. Pushing a button, she flipped through the many pictures she had taken over the summer. There were at least a hundred or so. And then, there was an odd photo.

Remembering when she took it, she had played with the settings, dabbled with the black and white versus color affects. But, this image was different. It looked out of this world—bizarre—like an extraterrestrial. The photo was blurred, yet she could almost make out the outline of something, or was it someone? *I wonder what I saw when I took that image.*

"You saw me!" the voice said aloud, with a cackling laugh.

A cold chill traveled down KC's spine. She shook it off and went back to looking at her photos. She told herself to take some time to move the pictures to Jack's computer before the shots were lost, but she didn't want to deal with complicated processes right then. The simple thought of organizing the images made her feel sick inside. She didn't want to think. She didn't want to question. She didn't want to do anything but sit. Mostly, KC wanted to sit without having a headache.

She started moving toward her chair, and then thought maybe if she went to her workshop, she might tinker with some glass. Making stained glass was a passion KC enjoyed. Earlier in the year, she created a new studio for her stained glass projects and supplies, but she hadn't set foot in her shop for over two months.

Tonight is the night, she thought. She went to the door, picked up her sweater, and put it on, and then strolled to her workshop that was housed in a nearby shed. Jack built it for her the summer before. She was elated to have her own shop space she could leave as messy as she wanted.

The door opened with ease. It was not locked. They never locked anything around the property. Yet, for some reason she half expected it to be locked. The familiar touch of the knob reminded her it had been a while since she visited her shop. *Why have I not been in here before now?*

Stepping into the room, her knees felt weak. KC decided she better go back. She shouldn't be in the shop alone. She probably should wait on Jack. Closing the door behind her, a tear formed in her eye and flowed down her cheek. A painful tightness gripped her; she felt frail. She wondered when she would step back in her workshop again.

KC entered the house and felt a chill run down her spine. She shivered. She put the teakettle on, got out a mug, and placed her favorite tea inside—Lady Grey. Then, settling into her recliner, she sat back to wait for the water to boil. After a few moments, she began to feel warm, then her hands felt like they were on fire. Looking down at them, she saw her fingers change shape. They were long, withered, and covered in dark brown gore. She screamed.

CHAPTER 2

SAMHAIN

Two days later, KC still had not shared with Jack what she saw happen to her hands that night. It wasn't that she was trying to keep something from him, as much as she was nervous to tell him. She hadn't had a headache since then, which relieved her. *I keep seeing dark shadows.* KC didn't want to think the worse—a brain tumor.

The shadows linger. *I feel something is with me; I'm never alone.* She looked out over their farmland. She reasoned that the best way to deal with the strange visions and mind throbs was to ignore it.

She stood there looking at the rolling hills; the patches of tall trees intermingled with a bouquet of yellows, oranges, and tan fall flowers signaling the coming fall. KC took in a deep breath. The unusually cool air of the late afternoon felt good. The smells of burning firewood from garden and yard cleanup woven with the odors of warm cinnamon, apple and pumpkin cooking in neighbors' ovens brought a feeling of calm to KC. She loved the fall of the year.

The flames of the fire licked the debris. Jack was raking the dry leaves, vines, and twigs gathered from their summer garden into a higher pile causing the fire to grow with intensity. The bonfire roared to life casting shadows on the first September evening of the year.

Samhain. The word echoed in KC's mind.

"That's funny," KC said.

"What?" Jack replied.

"Did you hear someone say *Samhain*?"

Jack snickered. "Sam what? Uh, no. What does it mean?"

"That's the weird part. I know this. It means 'end of summer.'" She stared at the fire. "How do I know that?"

"I don't know. You tend to know some pretty weird things." Jack laughed.

"That's not so funny. You know weird stuff too."

"I do, like what?"

"Bet you know how hot this fire is?"

"Sure, I do. Well, sort of." Jack snickered. "I guess I know how to find out, but I don't know off the top of my head. So, see. You do know weirder stuff than me."

"Oh, really. Are we having some kind of challenge being thrown down here?" KC smiled.

"Sure. I challenge you to find one weird thing I know."

KC chortled. "That is the funniest thing you've ever said. You can't be serious. It'd be harder to find one weird thing you don't know." KC laughed more.

"Funny. Real funny. Don't give up your day job," Jack quipped.

KC threw more of the dried garden debris on the flames. Jack raked the crackling leaves closer together. The flames rose again with new vigor. The smell of the passing summer moved through the evening air.

"We better step back a little. It's getting hotter." Jack moved a bucket out of their way, and they stepped aside. KC leaned closer to Jack.

"What are you doing?" He asked.

"Don't you find this romantic?"

"I do," He leaned his rake on their garden vehicle, a John Deere Gator, and turned toward KC, pulling her closer. "Come here."

ॐ

KC WATCHED THE FIRE. She went into a havey-cavey state, tittering between life and death. She felt queasy, uneasy, almost ill wavering between what she could or couldn't do, watching the dragon swoop down over the crowd, flames engulfing them all.

After a few moments, she said softly, "It's like *Beltane*." The words flowed from her without thought. "It will purge the last chill of winter. It is a charm against sickness and disease." KC stood staring at the fire in thought. "Did you know that the sun and moon were thought of as symbols? Fire is an emblem of the sun while water is an emblem of the moon."

"Where did you hear that?" Jack pulled more sticks and leaves from the back of the Gator and piled them onto the fire.

"I don't know. Maybe I read it somewhere." KC continued to stare at the fire another minute. Then she said, "The serpent was worshiped also as an emblem of wisdom and eternal youth, since it renews its skin every year."

"That's interesting," Jack said while still raking debris into a pile.

"Yeah. It's casting off all symptoms of old age when it sheds. Wish we could do that."

"You've been doing that a lot."

"Doing what, shedding?" KC smirked.

"No. Spouting facts. What novel are you reading that is giving you those strange ideas?"

"Hmmm. I'm reading *The Library of Lost Souls* by Ransom Riggs. It's the last book of his peculiar children series. But, I don't remember facts like those."

Jack grinned. "You are one peculiar child, that's for sure." He handed some debris from the Gator to KC. "We better get back to burning or we'll be out here all night."

Her trance broken, she picked up her rake after dropping the debris on the fire and began to rake the pile tighter. The fire crackled. She continued to move the debris helping the flames along. KC looked around and didn't see any more piles from clearing the garden.

"I think we might be about ready to stop," KC said. "Is there anymore in the back of the Gator?"

"Nope. I think you're right." Jack moved the empty bucket and placed it in the back. He closed up the tailgate, then got in the driver's side. KC continued to stand and stare at the fire. Jack revved the diesel engine. "Are you coming?" he called.

"Yeah, give me a minute." She pushed a pile of ash upon the fire. It flamed up.

"What did you do?" Jack asked.

"I don't know." KC stirred the ash and the flames died back down. She took a second to reflect on her life. She looked back at Jack. He looked happy. She was happy. She loved the sounds of their property—especially the quiet.

Noticing that Jack was patiently waiting on her, she knew she'd always love him, though she feared he wouldn't always be with her. She turned to look at the fire and stared. Time appeared to stop.

Watching the flames, lost in her thoughts she heard someone calling her name—

"WATCH OUT!" he called.

"Where?" KC cried out. "Where are you? I can't find you?"

"I'm here. Be careful," then the large, horned owl walked up to her, talking.

KC stared in disbelief. "Ish, who is that?"

"Why, he is Mr Scruffy. Remember?"

THE SOUND of a motor roaring caused KC to jump back into the present. She turned and saw Jack waving to her.

KC placed the rake in the bed of the Gator. "What's the rush?" she said leaping into the seat beside him.

"No rush, just hungry." Jack bantered, and then drove toward the garden. "It's late and I'd like to get dinner. Why don't we grab some food and come back with some chairs to watch the fire?"

"I have an idea. Want to roast some wieners?"

"Sure. Can we put a pot of beans on the fire?"

"That sounds great. We haven't enjoyed camp fire eating in a long while."

Jack pulled into the garage and turned off the engine. "We haven't. I wonder why?"

"When you found out you had hemochromatosis, you said I couldn't cook with cast iron anymore."

"I forgot about that. We used to use those cast iron pots and all kinds of different utensils. That reminds me," Jack said getting out of the Gator. "I should get the ones we used to cook the wieners. They'll taste so much better cooked in those."

"Great idea. I can use that old pot we have with the lid. We can put it in the ash of the fire to cook the beans."

"You'll need canned beans, right?" Jack said as he stood at the door.

"Yep. That'll be perfect. Will you want a couple of beers?" KC asked, placing the basket of tomatoes they had picked earlier on a nearby chair. "These will make a great batch of canned Minnesota tomato sauce when I mix them with peppers, onions, and garlic— good eats this winter."

"Yes, on the beer. And, I'm not so sure I can wait until winter to taste that sauce!"

KC grabbed her head and collapsed to the concrete floor.

"KC!" Jack said running to her side. "KC?"

THE BLACK SOW licked the face of the still body. Seborn Armenius, Snowquidian Pack Leader, stepped closer. He peered through the dark mist. The bonfires on the nearby hilltops cast shadows. Many Snowquidians were blowing horns and dancing. Soon it would be time for the throwing of stones into the blazes to escape the mysterious spirit *Hwch ddu cwta*.

"Let each try to be first and the tailless black sow take the hindmost," voices cried out from the hills in unison while shadowy figures continued to dance around the flames. Seborn bent down and touched the lifeless body. He looked around and saw Arrington Balam and Eri walking toward him.

"What's that before ye?" Arrington asked.

"It appears to be human. But the Black Sow won't move away. I had hoped the cries of the revelers would cause her to move on, but she continues to lick."

"I'll get my cart," Eri said.

"What good will that do?" Seborn asked.

"Well, we can't leave it here. If it is dead, it will spook the spirits on this night. If it is alive, we should try and save it." Eri replied.

"We don't know what or who it is? Won't we be inviting trouble?" Arrington said.

"If that is true, then why do we need the cart?" Seborn said.

Flaying his barbed javelin, Arrington moved closer to the body. "Even my gae bolga doesn't seem to faze the Black Sow."

"Throw your gae bolga and see if that chases it away?" Seborn said.

Arrington threw with precision and the Black Sow was mortally wounded. The magic powers of the gae bolga pulsated the ground. The body moaned.

"It is alive!" Eri said walking up with his cart. "We must save it now. It is a sign of Kei. The Black Sow must have been a brave warrior. She gave her life for this being before us. We must give thanks and praise on this night of renewal. Ankou has been thwarted."

The Snowquidians reached down and lifted the body upon the cart. In doing so, the body moaned and long, blond tresses fell away from the face.

"I can't be certain, but I think I know her! We must find Mylo!" Seborn said repositioning the girl lying on the cart.

THE AIR on her face felt cool. Her hand moved to her head, and then she moaned. KC thought she was lying on the concrete garage floor.

"There you are," Jack said leaning over her. "How are you feeling?"

"I don't know. What happened?"

"I was hoping you could tell me."

"What?'

"You went down hard. I was worried you hit your head. How did you fall?"

"I didn't know that I fell. I was talking and now I'm here."

"I was about ready to call 911 when you moaned."

"I don't think I'm hurt." KC looked down at her body.

Jack said, "No, you don't seem to be. Can you stand?"

"I think so." KC took her time while Jack held her hand to help her up. KC rubbed the side of her head. "I wonder if I tripped over something."

"There's nothing on the floor. Let me help you inside." They walked into the den. "You sit down." KC sat down in her recliner. Jack continued, "We don't need to go back to the bonfire."

He went to the kitchen sink and continued, "I'll fix dinner." He brought her a glass of water. "Drink some of this. It will help. Do you hurt anywhere?"

"I've got a throbbing headache."

"I'm thinking we should go to the emergency room."

"What?" KC shook her head. "I don't need to go there. If anything, I can see Dr. Crowell tomorrow. It's Sunday. I'm okay except for this headache."

Jack left the den and came back with two aspirin. "Here, take these. Then sit back, and try to take it easy."

"Thanks!"

Jack sat down in the recliner next to hers. KC picked up the stereo remote and turned on some music to help her relax. She reached up and wiped her face. "That's odd!"

"What is?"

"My face. It's damp. Did you wipe it earlier with a wet cloth?"

"No. You were barely out a minute. By the time I thought about getting a cloth, you started to come around."

"Strange. It didn't feel damp earlier. There are weird things happening."

"Strange is you suddenly passing out."

KC repositioned herself. Her head throbbed. She grimaced.

"Are you okay?"

"Yes. It's a sharp stabbing pain along my temple." KC rubbed the side of her head.

"Maybe we *should* go to the ER."

"Jack, honestly, I don't think it has anything to do with the fall. I don't have a concussion, if that's what is worrying you."

"How do you know? Has this happened before?"

"Not like this, at least not that I remember. Besides, if it had, I would have told you." KC smiled at Jack.

"Yeah. Sure, you would have."

"I would have if I thought it was serious. I will say I've had a few sharp pains, but I thought it was like a migraine or something."

"I think it's time you get this checked out." Jack got up.

KC swung the recliner down to stand up and felt dizzy. She grabbed hold of the chair to steady herself. "I guess I do need to go see someone."

Jack grabbed his cell phone. "I'm calling Dr. Crowell. We're going to get you better."

"Thanks, Honey."

"I'm going to take care of you if it *is* the last thing I do."

"At the rate I'm going, I'm going to need you."

While Jack made the call, KC thought about Dr. Crowell, who had been KC's and Jack's family physician since they were first married. Years ago, the doctor shared she could see the scar tissue from when Jack had a major injury from which, by all rights, he should have died; but he didn't. His heart was not fully functioning as a result, and thus he could die when doing strenuous work if he didn't stay in shape and watch his diet.

KC's memory of feeling weak and fragile when Jack was reported missing during the war and presumed dead was coming back to her. Back then, Dr. Crowell had helped her avoid going into a deep depression. During the time when Jack was missing, KC would doodle evil images mixed with horror of Jack being tortured. The fact he crashed in enemy territory was never revealed to anyone except the doctor under orders of the military.

For some reason, KC knew that Jack had no memory of those events, yet she was put through hypnosis to remove her vivid recollections and visionary experiences. She never understood how or why she knew and saw visions of what Jack faced when his plane crashed during the war. Her fears mounted when she felt a surge of pain. She watched a bird fly into her window and break its neck, landing on the ground, the last signs of life fluttering away. *It was like that when the Elderians died.*

A tear formed on her cheek. Her memories were returning.

CHAPTER 3
BLACK SOW

"It's obvious from your description of what you are feeling and how you are reacting to the headaches that we need to do some tests." Dr. Crowell said while she placed her stethoscope around her neck, then pulled her white doctor's coat down by the bottom of the hem. "At this point, we need to determine what could possibly be going on with you. I'm going to do some preliminary mini-tests of your reactions. Please use the step here to get on the examination table. Okay?"

"Sure." KC stood up. She felt unsteady on her feet. She hoped the doctor didn't notice. She climbed onto the examination table while Jack stood nearby.

"Are you unsteady like that often?"

KC looked at Jack. Blast, she thought. "No. Not that I'm aware of." KC lied.

"First, I'm going to look you over." Dr. Crowell used a light to check KC's eyes, ears, nose, and throat. "With this next part of the exam, I'm going to use a pin to touch you in various places. You let me know when you feel something."

KC felt the pin touch her face, but she noticed along the left side of her face and across her forehead, she felt only one or two pricks. She tried to relax, but anxiety mounted. *That's not right.*

Dr. Crowell said, "This all looks good. Please hold your arms out in front of you and close your eyes. I'll let you know when to open them."

KC held out her arms and wondered how long it would be before they knew what was happening to her. She feared that a dreaded disease, like Multiple Sclerosis or Parkinson's, was tormenting her.

Dr. Crowell continued with her examination and after about ten minutes, she pulled up a stool, sat on it, and looked up at KC. "I don't want you to be alarmed about what I'm thinking is happening to you. After we talk, I'm going to get my colleague to give his opinion. Based on what I'm seeing, I think you are having little TIAs."

KC looked confused. The doctor continued, "Transient ischemic attack or TIAs are small mini-migraines that causes your blood vessels to pop. They manifest themselves in brief episodes of cerebral ischemia that is usually characterized by temporary blurring of vision, slurring of speech, numbness, paralysis, or syncope."

Sitting impassive, KC listened. "The part we must be concerned about is the fact that the TIAs are often predictive of a serious stroke. We need to determine if your vessels and arteries are in good shape or if anything you are eating or doing has caused the development of your symptoms." Dr. Crowell stood up. "Please wait here. I'll be right back."

She closed the door and Jack moved over to KC. "How are you doing?" KC studied his face. He looked as worried as she was at that moment.

"I'm terrified. What if it is Parkinson's? Dad had it you know."

"I know, but you don't worry until we know something for certain.

Besides, she didn't mention any specific diseases. She said she thought you were having TIAs, but she was not certain. They will do tests to determine what is happening. Until then—"

"Not yet." KC said interrupting him. The door opened and in walked Dr. Crowell with her colleague.

"KC and Jack, this is Dr. Paul Harris Doar. He is my immediate supervisor and our expert on TIAs and its related symptoms. I've consulted with him on what I've found, but he would like to take a look at you too."

"Hello, KC." KC took his extended hand and shook it.

"Dr. Crowell explained to me what you've been experiencing. We're here to help you find out what is going on. We need you to remember and to focus on the fact that an imagined threat is often greater than any actual threat you may encounter, simply because of terror. Your distress will intensify if you allow a phobia, a fear, to take you over. Do you understand?"

"Yes. I do." KC rubbed her forehead, "My concern is not my fear, but the fact I might be imagining what is real. Does that make sense?"

Dr. Doar continued to check KC for her reaction to stimuli while he talked. "What do you mean?"

"I hear a voice in my head as clear as you are talking now."

"*And that voice is not going away any time soon,*" the voice said.

"Your eyes just doubled in size. Did you hear something just then?" Dr. Doar asked.

"Yes. It told me that it wasn't going away any time soon." KC said.

"Why did you whisper?" Dr. Crowell asked.

"I don't know. I didn't realize that I whispered. Did I, Jack?" Jack looked at KC.

"That is my point about allowing your phobia to rule your mind," Dr. Doar said. "Jack, please wait to talk with KC after we are finished here."

"*They are such amateurs. They don't know who they are dealing with,*" the voice said.

"Do you?" KC replied.

"Do I what?" Dr. Doar asked.

"Oh, I spoke out loud. I'm sorry."

"Is the voice talking with you now?" KC nodded. "Okay, let me try this." Dr. Doar looked into KC's ears. She giggled.

"Did that tickle?" KC nodded. Dr. Doar continued with the examination. When he was finished, he asked his colleague to join him. "We're going to discuss your case. Please remain here."

"Sure, I've got nowhere to go."

"*Not yet,*" the voice said.

"KC, are you doing okay?" Jack asked.

"Why are you worried? I'm fine. I wanted the doctors to know the voice is always present within me. Was that wrong?"

"No. But, you could have at least warned them and not blurted it out. It made it look like you were making it all up, especially when you giggled."

"I couldn't help laughing. After all, it is a voice I'm hearing. Did he really think he'd see the voice in my ears?"

Jack smiled. "I hadn't thought of it from that point of view. I'm going to go to the bathroom. I'll be right back. Will you be all right?"

"Sure. Go ahead. I'll lay back here and rest a little."

☙

KC STRETCHED out on the examination table. She closed her eyes and took a deep breath. It had been a long day already. She wondered how much longer this would take. The time was two forty-five in the afternoon. They've been there since nine that morning. KC had gone through a series of tests. She thought about all she wanted to do when they got back home. It was at least a four-hour drive. She hoped this would not take much longer.

She looked at the clock on the wall, and without warning, she heard the crashing of ocean waves like you hear when visiting the beach. Rising up on one elbow, she looked around. The sound of the waves was vivid. She felt a cool mist of water on her face. She turned to see what was behind her. Nothing. She looked toward the door, but instead of a gray metal door, she saw an ocean scene.

Off in the distance, KC saw a plane floating in the water, an arm hung out of a window with blood marking the deep gashes. The water lapped, and then fell back in the ocean washing the blood away. KC noticed the Air Force logo. A sense of horror engulfed her when she recognized she was looking at Jack dead in his cockpit.

Before she could react, another memory came rushing into her mind's eye; one she had put away and never thought of again. The wicked-witch dragon, Nukpana, the one who had caused her harm —the way she revealed she killed Jack before was in the form of the Drakein, the purple dragon. There were long, purple tentacles slithering over her family's car. A vivid scene of her family dying in the truck wreck washed over her.

KC felt heat rising up in her body. Her heart began to pound like she was running. Sweat poured off her forehead. She wiped her hand across it and saw her arms and legs had changed to a purple, snakeskin color. A smeech, foul smelling smoke, rose in the air. She was lying on sand. The water lapped at her feet.

"How did I get here?" She said siderated.

"That's what I'd like to know," said the voice of a tall being standing before her, casting a shadow over her body. "You're not dead, are you?"

KC looked up, but the glare of the light shone brightly in her eyes. She used her hand to shade her eyes. "No. I didn't think I was." She studied her arm. "I'm fearful of what's happening. Why am I different? I'm no longer human, am I? What's happened?" She looked up and saw the being's face. She remembered. "Ish! You died! How am I able to see you?" The fear in KC mounted.

"I do not know. You do realize you are on the Isle of Donn—the Lord of the Dead's homeland. All beings, human included, eventually pay Lord Donn homage before they move on to the Otherworld. His magic cauldron holds the most sacred forms of wisdom gathered from the dead. Notice, as the sun sets at night, it too descends into Lord Donn's shadowy land."

"But, isn't the sun the source of all life?"

"That it is. It also provides the cadence for the rhythm of time. Therefore, the sun must spend its time by night in the realm of the dead. Sometimes, as a result, dark shadows appear."

"Ish, how is this possible? I remember you. I remember Nukpana!"

"I don't know. It is."

"How do I get back home? Back to Jack?"

"I don't know how you got here."

"How long have you been here?"

"Too long."

"KC? Wake up." KC felt a hand shake her.

"What?" KC opened her eyes and saw Jack standing beside her. "You're alive!" She reached up and pulled Jack closer to her, giving him a strong hug. "I thought I'd lost you. I thought I'd died too. I thought all was lost. Ish and Nukpana! Oh, what is happening?"

"What? KC, I wasn't gone five minutes. You must have had a dream. Who are you talking about? Who is Ish? Who is Nukpana?"

The door opened and the doctors came in. Dr. Crowell began wrapping a blood pressure cuff on her arm. "Are you okay?" KC nodded. She continued to take KC's vital signs while she explained what would happen next.

"We've decided we want to run detailed tests. Due to the time it takes for two of the tests, it will require an overnight stay. We're working with our schedulers now. Today is Tuesday. You will need to come back on Thursday evening with plans to stay in a local hotel. We anticipate we can get you in a room and prepped for the tests on Friday morning. We can check you in early on Friday morning, and we'd be able to have the tests completed by late that evening. You need to spend the night in the hospital on Friday for observation. You can plan to go home on Saturday morning. Will that work?"

"Yes?" KC looked at Jack. He nodded. "Yes, we can do that. Will we need to find the hotel?"

"No. We will set all that up for you. We could have you stay the night here Thursday night, but we thought you might want to be with your husband. It's not always pleasant staying in the hospital."

"That works out fine, the hotel that is. What time will you want us checked in here on Friday?"

"Early. 7:00 a.m."

WITHOUT DISCUSSING what had happened while she was alone in the examining room, Jack and KC walked back to their car in the parking garage. KC worried about what she said to Jack when he found her in a state of fear. *What is happening to me?*

Opening the car door, she thought about her conversation with Ish and all she had seen. It seemed so real. Was her experience in Eldershire real before? Or was it all in her imagination? The voice in her head was starting to jumble her thinking. *I can't worry about that now.*

Yet, she was more worried about who the voice *was* in her head. Could it be Nukpana? How would she be able to explain Ish and Nukpana or, for that matter, a talking owl to Jack? He's having trouble believing me now. She was mystified. How can I make him understand that all of it *is* real?

CHAPTER 4
ELECTRIC DREAMS

KC woke up early. She had tossed and turned all night. Her head throbbed and she felt like she'd be sick if she looked at any food. Sitting in her recliner, she flipped through her Kindle looking for something to read. It was four in the morning and Jack wouldn't be up for hours.

She found a novel she purchased months earlier and hadn't read. Opening the eBook, she scanned the pages. It was by Phillip K. Dick. A series of short stories that recently were used as the basis for an original dramatic series entitled *Electric Dreams*. Jack and KC had enjoyed watching that series. Reading the stories would be entertaining to her. She started to read the first story, *Exhibit Piece*. Gradually, her eyes felt heavy, and then she fell to sleep.

*

"KC," Jack said as he touched her hand. "Good morning."

KC jumped up suddenly, flailing her arms and swinging her fists with all of her might. She connected Jack's jaw with a strong right. He went down.

"Oh, God! Are you all right?" KC scrambled down beside Jack and lifted his head. "What should I do?"

"You can try out for the local women's boxing team. Where did you get a right-hook like that?" Jack sat up. "Gees, woman. I'll send out a white flag in the future before I come around you in the morning. What were you thinking?"

"I wasn't thinking. I was in a battle."

"You were what?" Jack stood up. KC tried to help him. He pulled away. "I don't think you should touch me. Gees, my jaw is killing me."

"Do you want to see a doctor? I didn't break it, did I?"

"No. Just like you, I don't think I have a concussion. But, you need help. I'm your husband. You don't need to fight me."

"I told you, I wasn't here."

Jack turned around and looked at KC. "What do you mean you weren't here? Yesterday, I didn't say anything about your imaginary voice or your friends, Ish and Nukpana. But. This. This right here has got to stop! You were sitting right there in your chair. You weren't *gone* anywhere. What *is* the matter with you? You are starting to alarm me. You need to get professional help. You're acting mental."

"Seriously? You think I'm acting mental? I've told you for weeks I'm hearing voices. Don't you think I know I've got something wrong with me?" Why is he doing this to me, she wondered. Doesn't he understand? "I don't think I know you any more," she said and walked out of the room.

KC began changing out of her pajamas, anger boiling up in her. She couldn't believe he thought she would purposely hit him. *I wasn't even here.* KC stopped dressing. "What am I doing?" she asked herself. Half dressed, she ran to the kitchen.

"Jack? Jack?" She didn't see him. She went to the garage door.

Opening it, she yelled, "Jack, are you out here?" No answer. She looked for his truck. It was gone.

Walking back to the kitchen, she grabbed a knife. She thought long and hard about what she would do. She opened the utensil drawer where the knives were stored and placed it back in the drawer. Next, she walked into the bathroom, found the bottle of aspirin, and took four. Her head was pounding. The headaches were coming more often and lasting longer.

Turning on the bedroom light, KC continued to change her clothes. It was only Wednesday, she thought. I've got to make it to Thursday. What if I don't? What if I can't hang in there? I'm scared. KC sat down on the bed. Tears flowed.

She thought about how she was acting and knew she hadn't been that livid since she went after Nukpana the first time. The image of Ish and Princess Derryth came into her mind's eye. She thought about Princess Istar and the look on her face when she realized her parents were gone from her life forever. KC thought about her own children. Soon, she would be a grandmother. Fear engulfed her. *I can't be like this around my grandchild!*

JACK WATCHED Bill and Marie walk into the local café. They sat down in the booth across from him.

"Where's Mom? She loves to eat at Grayson's," Bill asked.

"I needed to talk to you both about KC without her here."

"What?" Marie replied. "Is it serious?"

"Yes. Very serious."

A waitress walked up, "How may I help you folks?"

"I'd like a cup of coffee and a slice of coconut cream pie," Bill said.

"I'll take the same," Jack replied.

"I'll have coffee with cream and a bowl of fruit," Marie said reaching for the sugar.

"I will be back with your coffees."

"You were saying, Dad?" Bill said.

"Your mother is ill. I'm not sure what is going on with her, but she needs professional help."

The waitress set the coffees down. "It will be a few minutes and I will bring over your order. Do you need anything else?"

"I think we're good. Thank you," Marie said and put sugar in her coffee. "I wondered about her the other day when we visited. She seemed lost or in another world."

Jack removed his hand from his chin revealing a large bruise. "She did this to me this morning."

"Mom hit you? You're kidding, right?" Bill looked at Marie. "I mean Mom is a pacifist. She won't even kill a spider."

"She takes them outside in a napkin, even in the dead of winter," Marie added.

"Listen, I know that. Remember. I'm married to her. But, she is not well. I've got to get the doctors to do more. She says she keeps hearing voices. This morning, I went to kiss her and she reared back and slugged me. It was a brutal punch."

"Aren't you already going to see them this week?" Marie asked.

"Yes. We're supposed to travel there tomorrow. The tests are on Friday. I'm thinking we need to insist they keep her longer than one night for observation."

"You're not thinking of committing her, are you?"

"Yes."

"Dad, are you sure you want to do this?" Bill asked clinching Marie's hand.

"I've got to do this for her well-being."

KC WALKED around the kitchen clinching her fists and tried to figure out what to do. How could she be so stupid to hit Jack like that? What was she thinking? *Am I going mad? No one hears the voice but me, yet I know I'm not crazy. I can't be.*

She heard a snicker and turned quickly to see who was in the room. No one was there. She walked into the den, sat in her recliner, and tried to think. *What keeps happening to me? First, I seem to be doing fine, and then all of a sudden, a horrible pain shoots across my head. I must be dying.*

"Not yet!"

KC felt her heart race. The voice was clear as if a person was sitting in the room with her, but she was alone.

An evil laugh and a foul smell enveloped her. "I told you I'd get you. You are mine. I'm ready to make you think you are crazy. I'll prove you are crazy. No one, not even your precious Jack will believe you. That stupid son of yours and his fat wife won't believe you either. You are mine. All mine. And I'm not going anywhere."

KC grabbed her head and ran from the room. Out on the front porch, she sat down on the steps. She wanted to run away until she could no longer hear the voice, but she knew that would be impossible. She smelt the foul smell again and wondered why it was familiar.

"You can't escape me. I'm with you always!"

"Go away! Get out of my life! What do you want from me? I don't even know who or what you are!"

"Oh, My Pitiful One, you do."

KC froze in place. There was only one being in the universe that ever called her by that name. "You? It can't be. You dissolved into a million pieces!"

"No, My Pitiful One. You only destroyed a part of me. It's good to see you've got your memory back. You do remember me after all. I was beginning to worry. I've been with you ever since you took that lock of hair."

"This is crazy." KC looked around. "It can't be you. I gave that lock of hair to Lorne." KC ran back into the house slamming the door shouting a cri de cœur, "Where can I go? What can I do? This is not right. Oh, God, someone please help me!" Fearful of what she might have to do to save herself and her family, KC crouched against the hallway wall and prayed.

"You can cry out for help until the beings of Eldershire try to come help you, but they won't. They are in their own peril."

KC was a feckless weakling. She placed her head in her hands. "This can't be happening. Lorne has the lock of hair."

KC began to cry. The past months of emotions and her fear that what she was hearing was Nukpana flowed over her. Several minutes passed, and then she said, "How is that you were able to stay alive inside of me? How are you here with me now?"

"The lock of hair didn't keep me alive. It was you. You did!"

"What? Never!" KC looked out into emptiness. She couldn't see anyone. Horror and fear crept over her. The hair on her arms lifted. Cold sweat came out all over her. Her lips and chin trembled.

"My Pitiful One, you did. When you reached to cut my hair, you breathed in some of my essence. I've been dormant in your body all this time. Now, I want to return home."

KC thought back to that moment. She remembered she was angry and wanted to kill Nukpana—

KC MOVED into a crouched position while images flashed before her
—her first husband, Jack, dying with purple tendrils holding him
under water after his military plane was forced into the sea; the
tractor-trailer forced into her car, killing her entire family while the
purple tendrils were slithering away. KC felt her blood warm; her
insides twitched; her heart raced.

"I told you I control every aspect of your life. Yes. Even your first
husband's death. Your family's death. And, now I'll own your life. I
own YOU!" Nukpana's voice roared in KC's mind. "Causing the
death of your family while you stopped to help someone couldn't
have been more fortunate for me. You were always a sucker for
someone needing help. Look where that got you, My Pitiful One."

KC's rage boiled over. She maneuvered her hat onto her head,
positioned Fea to where the tip of the blade was aimed at
Nukpana's side. Looking down at the Efil Stone hanging from her
neck, KC recited Mother Elder's verse —

> *"Release! Release! Your desires will come forth.*
> *From neither joy nor sorrow be*
> *Like the old man's beard from the Fringe tree—*
> *This blade will release thee!"*

At the same time, KC shoved the sword backwards into Nukpana up
through her belly. She stood and watched Nukpana's image in the
mirror dissolve into millions of particles. Suddenly, a mix of black
and purple smoke enveloped them. KC quickly removed her sword,
turned to face Nukpana, and severed a lock of her hair.

KC stood back and watched what was left of Nukpana dissolve into
a black malodorous mist. Coughing and sneezing in reaction, KC
looked around the room for any of Nukpana's army coming
through the door. None came to the rescue.

§&

KC NOW KNEW she'd inhaled a part of Nukpana. KC also

remembered she had to show Nukpana she was strong. The fact she saved her family from Nukpana's grip and that despite Nukpana's best effort, her family was alive and well, it meant KC couldn't let Nukpana see any fear.

"That's impossible. There is no way. No Way! You're not real! You can't be. Get out of here! I HATE YOU!" KC screamed, picked up her water bottle, and threw it at the wall.

"KC what is going on?" Jack said standing in the doorway.

"Jack! Oh, Jack, help me!" KC ran to Jack and collapsed in his arms.

"*Bwahaha! I'm going to win!*" Nukpana's voice echoed in KC's mind.

CHAPTER 5
MOONLIGHT

The moonlight of the Two-Moons shone through the branches of the trees casting shadows on all who were walking into the cave. Mr Scruffy stood at the entrance encouraging the band of loyalists to move further into the inner cave.

"We must hurry before the second sign comes from our watchers. The turncoats are looking for us. Hurry. Move along."

"I believe we're ready to begin," Lorne said, walking up to Mr Scruffy.

"There are a few stragglers. We'll wait a bit longer."

"I'll inform Gavin and Iolair you'll be right in."

"Thank you!" More beings moved into the cave.

Mr Scruffy looked out beyond the trees over the rambling hills that stretched for nigh two leagues. A vivid memory reminded him of the last time he stood here. He and KC had escaped a surge of the Grey Menace. They found this cave near Mushroom Alley for refuge. He was wounded, she was eager to fight but scared. Mr

Scruffy looked up at the night sky. *It seemed like yesterday, but it could be over two seasons since she was here.* He wondered how she was doing in her new life with Jack. He missed his friend.

Iolair said, "Mr Scruffy, are you coming in? They're waiting."

He turned. "I guess we need to get this going." They walked into the meeting area.

"Mr Scruffy, please sit here. We are ready to begin," Gavin said. He turned to the gathered group of loyalists that united once word spread that King Elder was on his deathbed.

Gavin continued, "Beings of Eldershire, we welcome you. You have heard of the illness of King Elder. It is because of the sure passing of our leader we gather here this day."

The beings murmured. Mr Scruffy noted that from their excitement and reaction to the news of King Elder's grave condition, many did not understand how ill he was, let alone that he might not survive.

Fergus said, "Mr Scruffy, we call on you to explain why all the secrecy? It has put us in a dubious state. The idea the King would be tottering between life and death and we not hear about this until trouble is afoot!"

There was a loud agreement from the others. They hit their spears on the ground and recited in unison, "Yes. Tell us!"

Mr Scruffy motioned for them to quiet their voices. A few others said, "We are here for you!"

"Shan't we have a fire?" asked Gavin.

"The dark is best. We mustn't cause anyone to wonder from where the light comes at this hour." Mr Scruffy walked into the center of the inner cave.

"Gather closer as what I'm about to say all must hear. Fergus, you are right. But, King Elder's illness came on without warning. That is what makes what is happening so hideous."

Mr Scruffy paused. He opened his wings wide and used the tips of them to motion to his confederates to hunker in closer. "We must be ready to pledge ourselves. We are *now* fellow conspirators."

The group of rebels raised their weapons. "We're with you!"

"Your enthusiasm is well noted. But, none of us know what will be asked of us. We meet here to plan a deed that gives me sadness. We shall need to think through our plans before we begin our long journey—a journey to overtake our King."

A hush moved through the cave. The sound of breathing was so soft, if a feather were dropped on the dirt floor, one could hear it.

Mr Scruffy opened his wings again. A breeze moved through the still air. He looked to each one sitting or standing before him. All eyes were staring back at him. Each rebel seemed transfixed.

Gavin brought the silence to a close. "The King is not dead, yet."

The Rebels began talking at once as the murmur grew into a crescendo.

"Silence!" Mr Scruffy had grown in size. He was not to his full size, but larger than most beings present. "Sit down! I have important news for you that cannot wait."

There was a rustling of noise. The Rebels returned to their seats. "I'm sorry, Mr Scruffy. I didn't realize—"

"Gavin, you are one of the best, even with your weird ways, in spite of being a white hawk. Relax. We are in need of making plans."

Looking at his confederates, Mr Scruffy then looked down, and then into the dark space before he continued. "Yes. We need a well thought out course of action. For our quest to be successful, we must think about the means, policy, and devices we will need."

Fergus, the head of the Dryads said, "You are right. We must be careful because we don't have everything in place."

Mr Scruffy nodded. "And, before, with the first battle with Nukpana

—" A rumbling of voices giving discontent moved through the room.

"You said her name as though she is *still* alive. Is she?" Fergus said.

"She might be," Mr Scruffy reduced in size, then continued. "We don't know. There are signs. Mother Elder and Yggdrasil are concerned. This is why we must be protective of the identities of each of us. We must be wary of any new being that comes amongst us. We must be of the mind that we trust *no one* we don't rightly know."

The room seemed to move in closer to Mr Scruffy. He flew to the top of a nearby large stone.

"Let me explain why the concern, some might say fear, is growing. Six setting Two-Moons ago, I visited a camp on the path to Snowboro. At this camp, I heard strange news—news that gave me pause. This camp that I thought was in support of King Elder—retaining power and passing his reign to Princess Istar upon his death—was no longer with such a mind."

"That is heresy," said Gavin. "King Elder has always ruled the Wild Woods from here to Emerald Mountain. We've prospered under his rule, and will do so under his granddaughter."

"Aye," the others said. "Hail, King Elder!"

"As ye should be. But, there is a force at work here. This is what concerns Mother Elder and Yggdrasil. This force is causing beings not to trust and believe in those who are currently governing. The beings are falling for the idea that they should be profoundly at odds with what is generally accepted. They said they refuse to read and to listen to anyone they consider to be an outsider. They don't want to wait. They only want to react. This, my friends and compatriots of Eldershire, is dangerous."

Clasping his wings behind his back, Mr Scruffy paused. Then, he gazed down to the Rebels when he said, "The beings of this camp are not informed of everything they should know. They hear news that is not stated in fact—it is partially true—just enough truth to cause the beings to react, most often with anger and innuendo. Then, when someone questions the information or thoughts they repeat, these poor, misinformed beings are made to feel that their own sanity is being brought into question. I first saw this form of manipulation used on Earth, when I was there training to be a leader for King Elder. It was called 'gaslighting'."

A murmur amongst those gathered rippled through the room, and then grew louder. "Please. We must hear all Mr Scruffy has to say." Gavin sat back down.

"There is something you need to know. This camp is run by an owl of the Ninox family. And for those of you that know, you might be told that it is because of him that I'm leading this group of fellow conspirators. But, you must know, it is not."

"It is Camlann, then! The traitor!" cried out Gavin. "He swore he'd get his revenge on you. He always liked dressing in finery."

"It be him. But, he is the way he is due to no fault of his own. My Mum always said to her owlets, 'Dressed in finery doesn't make your feathers any more fine or a better owl.' What she meant was that just because some being is prideful of appearances, speaks a good word, or even does a good deed, doesn't mean that being can't be treacherous or evil. We must fight Camlann's lead in this tyranny—this tyranny of false information and greed. We must seize the power that is being built through manipulating our fellow Elderians. We must force it from their grasp, if need be. Protection of our beings, of Eldershire is paramount!"

Cheers of support bellowed forth as all those gathered came to their feet, yelling they were ready to stand and fight.

§

"Jack?"

"Hmmm?" Jack was reading on the couch in the outer room of the double room suite of the hotel. KC sat down beside him.

"Do you have a minute?"

"Sure." Jack closed up his magazine. "What do you need?"

"Have we traveled much in the past?"

"That's a strange question. Don't you remember?"

"Sort of." KC leaned forward placing her forearms on her knees, then clasped her hands. "I'm not sure about this, but I remember this wooded camp area. The trees were huge, like redwoods, but taller and bigger. Do you remember anything like that?"

"No. Not really. Where was the camp?"

"That's just it, I don't know. The place has a name; I'm sure of it. I just can't think of it."

"I don't remember a specific place like that we ever visited. What trees are bigger than redwoods?"

"Elders."

"Elders? Where do elders grow?"

KC smiled. "In Eldershire." She rubbed her eyes. "That's it. Eldershire!"

"Eldershire? I have never heard of such a place. And, if I did, I'm sure I wouldn't know where it is located."

"Sure you do. We were there just three years ago."

"KC, I have never been to a place called Eldershire. And, unless you've left me when I didn't know it, neither have you."

"But, there were these strange beings around us and we had some friends, Ish and Princess Derryth. Sadly, they later died. The funny part is we had a pet owl, Mr Scruffy. He could talk." KC smiled thinking of her feathered friend.

"KC." Jack stood up, turned, and looked at his wife. "Really now. You're pulling my leg, aren't you?"

KC looked up at Jack with stern eyes. "No. No, I'm not." She got up and walked to the bedroom. She stretched out on the bed and began to ponder. How on earth can I convince him that Eldershire is real?

"You know you can't," the voice said.

"Leave me alone. You can't help me." KC said and rolled over onto her stomach and pulled the pillow up under her chin.

"My Pitiful One, don't you want to know about Eldershire, King Elder, and your old pal, Mr Scruffy since you left?"

"What do you know about it? Would you leave me alone?" KC said out loud.

She got up and walked to the counter in the hall between the bedroom and seating area of the room. When she picked up the ice bucket to fix herself a glass of water, she saw it was empty.

"*You don't want to know how they are doing?*" the voice said. "*I'm shocked. Shocked. How can you not want to know?*"

KC picked up the room key, the ice bucket, walked to the door.

"Where you going?" Jack asked.

"We need ice. I thought I'd get some."

"You okay? I thought I heard you say something from the bedroom."

"Yep. I'm fine. I was humming." KC walked out into the corridor and looked down the hall to figure out which way to go for ice. Turning to walk right, she began to hum.

"*Clever, you are. Your humming will not keep me from talking. It won't make me leave you. You're stuck with me until you die. You hear me. I can tell that you do. You see, your blood pressure is getting higher,*" the voice sneered.

In a few quick steps, KC found the ice machine. The rattle of the ice hitting the bucket seemed to calm the sounds in her head. She walked back to the room and thought about how she would explain the voices during tomorrow's tests.

"You can't do anything that I won't know. You do realize that, don't you?"

"Great! Now, I have a live-in ghost I can't get rid of." KC opened the room door and saw Jack standing before her.

"What's going on?" Jack said as he walked beside her to the counter.

"Ah, nothing. I was talking to myself."

"Yeah. I know. I could hear you. You do realize you've been doing that a lot lately."

"Really? No. I hadn't realized. Sometimes I like to think aloud."

"This is more than thinking. It's like you are having a full conversation with someone."

"Hmmm. That's odd."

"I think we'll have to share this with the doctors. You didn't mention this before and I didn't think about it. Maybe the doctors will want to visit with you longer when we go for the tests. Maybe they can find out what exactly is going on."

"Sure. Whatever you think is best, Jack." Jack turned and walked back to the couch. KC walked into the bathroom, shut the door, and looked in the mirror. For a split second she saw Nukpana's face and the voice jeered, *"I am going to win. I am."*

KC slammed her fist into the mirror, breaking it.

CHAPTER 6
FACE IN A MIRROR

Jack opened the bathroom door. "Are you all right?"

KC turned with tears streaming down her face. "I'm scared, Jack. I'm really scared."

Jack walked over to her, put his arms around her, and pulled her close. They stood like that for a few minutes. Then, he lifted her head. Looking directly into KC's eyes he said, "It doesn't matter what is happening. I'm here with you. We will get through this together, like we always have." He picked up her hand and looked at it. "It doesn't look like you cut yourself. What happened?"

"The voice. It won't leave me alone. I keep hearing it tell me things that are impossible. I think I'm going crazy."

Jack eased KC toward the door. "Come. We can talk more comfortably in here." Jack led KC to the couch. They sat down beside each other. KC felt foolish.

"I'm sorry, Jack. I didn't mean to break that mirror. It's just when I saw Nukpana, I don't know. I freaked."

"You saw who?" Jack sat back in the couch. "Tell me what happened."

"This is going to sound crazy," KC said; she saw Jack grin. "Okay. It's been crazy for months. I know that. I don't even know how to begin."

"Tell me, who is Nukpana?"

"She is an evil witch that lived in Eldershire."

"Eldershire?"

"Yes. Remember, I told you I had been there."

"At a camp." Jack nodded. "What kind of camp?"

"It's nothing like you can imagine. It was a camp of tree beings and other animals and creatures."

"Are you sure you're not dreaming this or having some kind of hallucinations?"

"I hope I am. If this is real, it is worse than I thought it was."

Jack stood up, walked over to the counter, and turned back to KC. "You do realize that none of this makes sense even when you agree you hope you are having hallucinations."

"Yes. There is so much I need to explain. How I tried to kill Nukpana, how Mr Scruffy saved me, how we brought you and Bill and Marie and even Boomer back to life."

Jack stared. He shook his head, but didn't say a word.

"Jack? What's wrong?" KC stood up and walked over to him. She put her arms around him. "You have no idea how important it is for you to believe me. You do believe me, don't you?"

"Of course. I'm having a hard time. I'm trying to understand. Why haven't you said anything before now?"

"I didn't remember it all before."

Jack nodded. He walked passed KC, and then sat back down on the couch. "Come here and tell me what you remember."

"It's patchy. But, I'll try. And, I don't want you to think I'm crazy." KC smiled.

KC began with when she transported from her Jeep after Bill, Marie, and Boomer were killed in the car wreck. She decided not to mention that Jack was presumed dead or that she had married Jay-H. For some reason, she felt that might be stranger than telling him about Eldershire and the beings there. Watching his eyes when she told him about Nukpana and the fact she was an evil-witch dragon made KC feel panicky that he might think she *was* crazy.

"And, Jack, when I hit the mirror with my fist, I had just seen Nukpana's image in the mirror. I wanted to kill her, for real this time. I'm worried she may kill me."

"I won't lie to you. This sounds crazy. And, I'm worried about you too." Jack looked at his watch. "It's past midnight. We won't be able to solve this tonight. We've got to be up early in the morning. I need to process all that you've told me."

He put his arm around KC, and said, "I appreciate you trusting me enough to share this with me. I want you to know, we will get to the bottom of this. What do you say we get ready for bed? Maybe after you get some rest, and we get the tests over and see the results, we'll know more about what we're dealing with."

"You're right. I need to get some rest. I haven't slept well for weeks now." KC got up and walked into the bedroom to where she had placed her suitcase. She pulled out her pajamas. She said, "I'm sorry I broke the mirror."

Walking into the bedroom, Jack said, "It's okay, Honey. We need to figure out what is happening."

After cleaning up the broken glass, they settled into bed and snuggled. KC wondered how long before she would hear the voice again.

❧

THE MIST SURROUNDED HER, causing KC to think she should feel cold, but she wasn't. She rubbed her arms and they didn't feel damp, yet the mist was thick. She could see only a few feet in front of her as she walked down the path. A large pine tree came into view. The branches were outlined in the light that passed through the mist. KC thought she recognized where she was, but then she wasn't sure.

"Oh!" she jumped when a hand touched her shoulder. "Who's there?"

"It's me," Jack said. "I thought you'd like a cup of coffee."

KC opened her eyes and saw she was sitting in her library with a magazine in her hands. "Huh? I was walking in the mist of the trees. How'd I get here?"

"You've been sitting in the library for about an hour, at least."

"How strange." KC took the cup of coffee and drank. The coffee gave her a warm feeling as it went down. "I needed that. I didn't realize how cold I felt."

"Cold?" Jack said walking over to the thermostat. "It's 75 in this room."

"Well, I'm shivering. I must've been dreaming that I was walking in the mist of a forest, but I swear, I feel damp and cold. This coffee is good."

"Would you like something to eat?" Jack said.

"Sure. Anything you fix would be good."

"Okay. I'll go fix you a bite to eat, but I'll need to run to the store first. You want me to pick up anything special?"

"No, unless you can find some good cookies."

Jack bent down and kissed KC. "I'll be back in a bit. You enjoy relaxing." He turned and walked out of the library door closing it softly behind him.

KC looked down at her magazine and continued to read.

ॐ

"LOOK DOWN THERE," the voice said.

KC looked down and saw a vast area of trees that stretched for miles. She looked back to see who spoke. Standing before her was a strange being, he looked like an elf. "Who are you?"

"I'm Ish. KC, don't you recognize me?"

"No. I don't. How'd I get here?"

"You've always been here."

"What?"

The scene before her changed again. KC was watching a fight take place between several beings. She screamed in horror seeing the body of Ish lying before her. Then, she saw the image of a girl being burned to death by a dragon. The horror of the scenes caused her to feel shock and fear coupled with anger. She wanted to fight back, to save them, and to save her friend, Mr Scruffy.

"I'm in Eldershire! How'd I get back here?"

"You aren't really, my friend." Mr Scruffy stood before her in the mist.

"I don't understand. What is going on?"

"Mother Elder and Yggdrasil sent me. I'm here to tell you—"

ॐ

THE SCENE CHANGED ONCE MORE. KC was no longer in the forest, but back in the library. She stood up and looked around. "What is going on?"

"I don't know. I just came to get you for lunch. Are you all right?" Jack said walking through the door.

"No. I'm not." She sat back down and started crying.

ॐ

"KC! Wake up, honey." Jack was shaking KC as she came out of a deep sleep. "Are you okay? You were crying out."

KC sat up and wiped her eyes. "Gees. What a strange dream." KC looked over at Jack. "I don't think I've ever had a dream within a dream."

"Why were you screaming?"

"It was horrible what I saw. Two people I had forgotten about died in front of my eyes."

"Who were the people?"

KC thought to herself—I say people, but I guess I should say beings. But, if I did, Jack would be more worried I didn't mention them to him last night. He probably already thinks I'm going crazy. I can't tell him the truth. Not yet. *Not until I know what is happening.*

"Oh, that's just it. I don't remember meeting them."

"But, you said you saw them die in front of you. What happened?"

KC looked at the clock. "It's almost four thirty. We need to go back to bed. I'm going to go to the bathroom first."

"No, you don't. I think you need to tell me about your dream."

KC got up and walked over toward the bathroom door. "Not now, Jack. Besides, you want me to have those tests don't you? We need to get some rest. We'll have a nice long ride home and I can tell you all about it then." She smiled at Jack, and then walked into the bathroom closing the door behind her. I've got to figure out what Nukpana is doing. Mr Scruffy never got to say. I wonder when I'll be able to talk with him again.

MR SCRUFFY LOOKED at his companions. "It almost worked. She saw me. That much I know. I didn't get to tell her anything. She doesn't know what we're planning, so she will be on her own until we can talk with her again."

"What will we do about Camlann?" Gavin asked.

"Camlann is not your worry. When I visited his camp, I didn't know he was made their leader. We will work out those issues later. Right now, we must put our efforts into helping King Elder and Princess Istar."

"Won't Mother Elder and Yggdrasil know how to get word to KC?" Iolair stepped forward. "KC must know what is happening."

Appearing in the room, Mother Elder said, "Not before she arrives. We could try to reach her one more time, but the events in play are near. I'm not sure what will happen if we talk with her too close to the initiation of our plans. We must be careful. Her spirit is fragile right now."

"There is one thing we can do," Iolair said while reaching up to his neck and removing the red plaid collar he wore. "Can we place this on her somehow?"

"Now that may work." Yggdrasil reached for the collar and looked it over. "Yes. That is what we'll do. Mr Scruffy, will you be willing to try one more time?"

"The honor is mine. I do worry if we will cause more harm if she doesn't remember me."

"She'll remember you. She will be fine." Mother Elder said with confidence.

"When do I go again?"

"We'll wait. We must check the alignment of the Two-Moons calendar. Muin is ending and Gort begins in a few suns. Fading will soon follow and will be a time of ending and settling accounts. We must make sure we have all things ready before the start of the Five Dark Days," Yggdrasil said handing the red plaid collar to Mr Scruffy. "Be sure when you place this with KC, it is placed where it will not be lost. It is imperative she has this at the right moment."

"But, how will she know? I won't be able to tell her anything. I'll be lucky if I'm able to return without being harmed."

"She will know. She is the Chosen One. All will be as needed when it is needed. Faith is our one strong weapon. We must use it with all of our strength and being." Mother Elder walked over to Mr Scruffy. "Kneel before me. Yggdrasil and I will send you forth with blessings."

Mr Scruffy knelt and the ritual began.

Release! Release! I call to thee
On Earth across the Air
Let another on narrow times,
Come to me,

Seek the Efil Stone! Mark it Well,
She succeeded with a sign
That the One who shall follow

May the Red Chestnut bring
Healing and remove fears and

Apprehensions,
Fast darting, winged brother, come,
Message bearing, active being, come.

❧

May you be Safe in Peace and Love
Thank you, Red Chestnut!
Thank you, Efil Stone!
Thank you, Mother Earth!

❧

MR SCRUFFY STOOD up and grew in size. "May the summer solstice haven blend into the autumn equinox, Elved with grace and love. Peace to all."

With those words, he took flight.

CHAPTER 7
TIME PASSAGES

Putting the lid down on the toilet, KC sat down. "Go ahead. You've kept me awake all night. Tell me what you want me to know about Eldershire."

"I'll do one better. I'll show you," Nukpana said. The mirror that KC had broken earlier reappeared repaired. KC stared at images of Eldershire moving across the mirror like a slide show—Emerald Mountain, Mushroom Alley, the Wild Woods, Stones River, and Graves Mountain. Each as she remembered seeing when she rode on Mr Scruffy's back. He took her on that flight to introduce her to the beauty of Eldershire—the lush green of the forest, the majesty of the mountains, the beauty of the blue water. Then, the scenes changed. Nukpana began narrating and showing images of Eldershire since KC left—

"YOU'VE BEEN GONE ABOUT six years Earth time. The same tinne in Eldershire is merely four or five seasons. You'll find many things have changed."

"Tinne? I don't recall hearing that word before," KC said.

"Tinne is used to describe the passing of events—past, present, and future. May I continue?" Nukpana asked.

"I should have my head examined for letting you do this, but I'm tired and fearful of what would happen if I don't. Go ahead. I'm ready." KC worried what she might see. Nukpana was too eager to show her.

"Look at what has happened to your beloved Eldershire."

Before KC, she saw the landscape of Eldershire scorched in multiple places. The lush forests destroyed in large numbers. "What happened?" KC murmured.

"Barnabus' Trebbians did their duty for him," Nukpana said with demonic glee.

"Barnabus?" KC was repelled at what she saw. "Why?"

"To get what he needs. It is his way. You lost in your quest to save Eldershire. Taking me away didn't do anything to protect Eldershire." Nukpana's voice sounded wickedly cheerful.

"You are tormenting me. But, you are wrong. My quest was to retrieve the Efil Stone to prevent you from becoming a tyrant in power. That, I did do."

"Yes. In doing so, you managed to bring me back here with you to this uninviting place. I find your world destructive to me. There are too many humans who seek the light to avoid the shadowy underbelly of what is real."

"Then, I hope my world wipes you from my mind," KC said. "I've had enough. In less than two hours I'll be leaving for the hospital. Enjoy being miserable on your own."

❦

KC walked out of the bathroom and directly into Jack standing by the bed.

"Whom were you talking with? And, don't tell me no one. I heard you, as if you were talking with another voice," Jack said while holding onto KC. "I need to know what is going on."

"Seriously, it *was* me talking with me." KC removed herself from Jack's grasp and walked over to the bed. "I had a nightmare and was trying to convince myself I could go back to sleep for the little time we have left before we head to the hospital."

"I don't know what to believe any more," Jack rubbed his eyes.

There was a long pause. KC wasn't sure what to do.

Jack continued, "You tell me the most incredible story I've ever heard. We go to bed. You wake me up screaming. And now, you calmly leave the bathroom to go to sleep after I hear you talking with a different voice like someone else responding."

Jack shook his head and walked into the bathroom. "There is no one here!"

KC knew it was too much for him. It was too much for her—*and I'm living it*. She got back in bed and tried to settle back to sleep.

KC woke and looked over at Jack. His snoring was out pacing his CPAP machine. It helped him get the oxygen into his lungs he needed—a result of his life as a pilot and his plane going down in the ocean while on a training mission. She remembered how he was reported dead. He wasn't. In reality, it was Nukpana messing with her life then. KC wouldn't let Nukpana cause her family any more pain, not this time, if she could help it.

She reached over to wake him.

"What's up?" Jack said rising up on his elbow. "What time is it?"

"Time to start getting ready."

"It's so soon. I was just getting to sleep."

"Me too." KC moved her legs to dangle over the bed. "Sure hope these tests will help us find out what is going on with my head."

"Me too," Jack laughed. "At least, we are thinking alike this morning. I could use a good night's rest. And, I know you could as well."

"We probably should get ready so we can eat something before we have to be at the hospital, don't you think?"

"No. The doctor said you weren't supposed to eat this morning. Remember?"

"Well, boo. I'm hopping in the shower; I won't be long."

KC walked into the bathroom, stripped, and started the shower. She chose not to look toward where the mirror hung. Strangely, she had not heard from Nukpana since they talked earlier. As she went to get into the shower, she looked down at the floor drain. Two eyes peered back at her. She screamed.

"KC, what's wrong?" Jack called, rattling the door's handle. "It's locked. I can't get in. KC, answer me!"

"Yes, sir. I understand. We'll pay for the damages. Thank you, sir, and your people for helping me. Yes, sir. We'll be heading to the hospital in about an hour. Yes, sir. Thank you, again." Jack hung up the phone.

"Who was that?" KC asked sitting up. "Oh, boy. My head hurts." She grabbed the top of her head and lay back down on the bed.

"It's a wonder it didn't explode. Your head hit the shower floor when you fainted. I had to break the door down to get in. You'd locked the door." Jack walked over to KC and handed her a glass of water. "Here, drink this and take this aspirin."

"Can I with the tests?" KC asked taking the water.

"No need to worry. The tests are postponed until tomorrow. We are to go to the hospital and see the doctor in an hour. Let me look at your head."

Jack waited for KC to turn her head. He said, "You've got a good knot there. Surely, whatever was in your head was knocked out. I thought when I broke in the door and saw you that you were dead. I felt the floor jar when you collapsed."

"I don't understand; I didn't lock the door." KC reached for the aspirin and took it.

"You had to have locked it."

"But, I didn't."

Jack tilted his head, then said, "Thankfully, you are okay. I called the hospital after we got you out and let them know what happened."

"Who helped you? I was naked, you know."

"I covered you up with the bedspread from the bed. It was the staff here. I couldn't break the door down without their help, and then you were so tangled in the shower, I was afraid I'd break a leg or arm if I tried to move you myself."

"Thank you, Jack. You have suffered through this ordeal as much as I have. I am so ready to see the doctor and get whatever is in me, out of me."

"I'm with you there. Let's get our stuff packed and get to the hospital so we can get this fixed." Jack reached down to help KC stand. "Do you think you can stand on your own?"

"Yes. I do. I'm ready to do this." KC looked up at Jack and they kissed. "Thank you, again. I'm so glad you are here with me." But, KC was worried.

❧

JACK PULLED the car away to park and KC stepped upon the sidewalk to wait for him. He didn't have to drive far. "You were lucky," she said as he stepped up to her.

"I was. Maybe our luck is changing. Are you ready to go in?" Jack said putting his arm around KC's waist.

"Yes, I am—"

"Are you okay?" KC had doubled over. "Honey, can you walk?"

She looked up at Jack and said, "Oh, it's killing me. My head is pounding like it is going to explode. Get me inside. I'm going to faint." KC went limp in Jack's arms.

ॐ

"*I TOLD YOU, it would not work! I won't let it happen!*" Nukpana was screaming in KC's head.

KC kept squirming and mumbling.

ॐ

JACK WATCHED Dr. Crowell check KC's vital signs.

"What is going on?" Jack asked.

"We're not sure," Dr. Crowell replied. "We're looking for everything we can before we determine how to proceed. You said she hit her head this morning."

"Yes. There is a good size goose-egg bump on the back of her head where she hit the tile floor."

"I see it. She is definitely in distress. Her heart rate is up. We'll need to stabilize her before we can do the MRI." Dr. Crowell directed a nurse to get some medication. "Tomorrow, we'll use the Upright MRI. If she doesn't come around by the time we're ready to perform the test, we'll move her into the chamber using a wheel chair."

"When will you perform the test?"

"In her state, we'll wait to see how she is doing tomorrow, and then decide. We'll keep her in this room tonight. A nurse will be assigned to her case, along with two other patients. This way, KC will receive close care."

"May I stay with her?" Jack asked picking up KC's hand. The nurse finished administering the medicine and KC seemed to quiet down.

"Good. Her heart rate is normal now. She's much calmer. You may stay until eight this evening, and then you should go back to your hotel to get plenty of rest while you can."

"Oh, a hotel. I guess I need to get one. We checked out of our hotel room earlier. We stayed several miles away. Is there one closer to the hospital?"

"Yes. You'll need to go down to the registration desk and they will help you. Go ahead. She's not going anywhere. We'll keep a good eye on her," Dr. Crowell said with a smile.

Jack bent down and kissed KC. Finally, she was not fighting those demons in her mind, he thought.

"WELCOME BACK," Jack said walking into KC's room carrying two Styrofoam cups. "Are you thirsty?"

KC looked up at Jack and smiled. "Yes, I'd love something. What ya got there?"

"Iced tea. It's good and cold."

"Thanks," KC said taking the cup. "It's good to be with you."

"And you. You had me worried there, for a bit."

"I was too. The pain was awful. Did they find anything?"

"You've got a brain." Jack winked.

"You're not funny. Well, you are, but anyway. Did they?"

"Not yet. They have to wait until tomorrow."

"Oh. I hadn't been told. I thought they'd knocked me out and done the test already."

"No. They were waiting for you to stabilize. I went down to see about getting a hotel room. Dr. Crowell wants to wait before she conducts the test to make sure your blood pressure and heart are stable."

"I guess that's good. No need to die from some unrelated issue." KC sneered.

"No. We don't want you dying at all." Jack moved a chair closer to KC's bed. "Now, do you feel like talking?"

"Not really. I know you want to know more, but honestly, Jack. I'm washed out."

"It's not natural all this that is happening to you."

"I know. That's why the thought of what is happening frightens me."

A nurse walked in. "Hello, I'm here to give Mrs. Carson a shot to help her rest."

"Okay. Will you give it to me in my arm?"

"No. I'll use the IV here." The nurse inserted the syringe and KC watched the medicine go in.

"What will it do?"

"You will be fast to sleep in about five or so minutes. I'll check back in on you in a couple of hours. Mr. Carson, please call me if anything changes."

"Yes, ma'am."

"Thank you," KC said. She looked at Jack. "Where were we?"

"We were talking about what is and isn't natural. You know what you told me about Eldershire and the tree beings. That's not natural either, but your description seems so real."

"Not to make light of this time with you, but maybe I should write a story."

Jack tilted his head and grinned. "Maybe you should."

"There is so much good about Eldershire I want to share with you. My time there was magical."

"I know you said you are washed out, but before you go off to dreamland, tell me about it."

KC said, "I don't mind talking with you about Mr Scruffy. He is a smart owl and he was my very best friend."

"Are there other talking animals?" Jack was trying to be supportive of KC, but he felt kind of foolish talking seriously about this world that KC thought she once visited. KC adjusted her position in the bed. "Are you feeling more relaxed?"

"I am." She looked up at Jack, and then grinned. "I'm glad you don't mind me telling you about Eldershire. It is a beautiful—"

Jack stood up and walked over to KC. "Are you all right?" He touched her hand; she was resting. Her breathing was slow and steady. "Thankfully, she can rest."

CHAPTER 8
MIND OVER MATTER

A couple of hours passed. Jack sat at KC's bedside. He read a couple of magazines. Looking at his watch, he hoped KC would wake soon. He wanted to learn more about what she said she had been experiencing. It was about three-thirty.

"Hello!" KC said.

"There you are. How are you feeling?"

"Rested. I slept hard."

"Any dreams?"

"No. Thankfully."

"Want to watch some television?"

"Sure. Maybe we can find a good movie or two," KC said.

Jack felt some relief. She was getting rest. Even sleeping apart tonight will be worth it, if we find out what's going on.

They watched television, and then played cards. Time passed. About five, dinner was brought in for both of them. They enjoyed their meal. Jack had decided earlier that he would not bring up Eldershire to KC.

They had had such a relaxing time; he didn't want to spoil it. After dinner, they found another movie to watch. KC giggled like her old self. Jack was beginning to relax and thought that whatever was going on with KC might be fixable after all.

JACK GOT up and visited the bathroom, and when he walked back into the room said, "I guess it's close to time for me to leave?"

"Leave?"

"The Doc said I couldn't stay past eight. It's pushing that time now."

"I've got to sleep here alone?" KC looked up at Jack. "I don't want to stay here by myself. Can't you do something?"

"I'll try. I'll go see the nurse at the desk. You sit here and watch TV. I'll be right back."

KC watched Jack go out the door. "Leave it open," KC called after him, but he didn't hear her. The door shut.

"You're all mine now, My Pitiful One." KC placed her hands over her ears. "You fool. Don't you know I'm not in the room? Covering your ears won't stop my voice."

"It might not stop your voice, but it makes me feel good I am doing something, no matter how small."

"You poor, poor pitiful thing. Life is so hard for you. You have to make up little games in order to feel important. Good luck with that!" Nukpana laughed a hearty laugh, like that of an ogre pleased he'd eaten an elf.

KC looked at the door hoping upon hope that Jack would walk in. She felt she was going crazy, but she was worried that she wasn't.

It meant the voice was truly Nukpana and Nukpana was not dead.

"You're right. I'm here with you, and will be for a long time."

How is this possible, she thought? It can't be happening. "You wouldn't be driving me insane if you thought you had to stay with me forever. You're up to something. You always have a plan. You know something. Don't you? Nukpana, why aren't you answering?"

The door opened and a nurse walked in. "Hello, KC, I'm Gay Lynn. I'll be your nurse for the evening. The afternoon nurse filled me in about your case."

"Glad to meet you, but where is my husband?"

"Your husband?"

"Yes, Jack. Jack Carson. He should be out at the nurse's station. He was going to talk with a nurse to ask Dr. Crowell if he could spend the night."

"I didn't see him there."

"Oh, I wonder—"

"He may have gone to the Doctor's office."

"Yes. Yes, that's probably it."

The nurse picked up KC's hand and put a thermometer in her mouth. "I'm going to check your vital signs. Then, I'll go see if I can find him." KC nodded. "Your blood pressure is a little high, but your heart rate is good. No temperature. Anything upsetting you? Do you need anything?"

"No. I'm fine. You might want to see if you can find Jack."

"I'll go do that now." The nurse walked out and shut the door behind her.

KC reached for the pad of paper beside the bed. She picked up a pencil and began to draw. The images she drew seemed to flow freely from her mind's eye to the paper. She had sketched several when there was a knock at the door.

"Yes?"

"It's me, honey," Jack said. "I knocked to see if you were still awake. How are you doing?"

"I'm doing well. I'm even sketching again."

"May I see?" Jack reached for the pad.

"They just popped into my mind. Do you like them?" KC looked at Jack and saw his frown. "Is something wrong?"

"These images. Did you mean to draw such horror?"

KC took the pad from Jack's hands. "What do you mean?" KC looked down at the images and caught her breath. "What have I done?" She saw that the images were of Ish and Princess Derryth right after their deaths. Mr Scruffy was hurt, and blood was flowing from his damaged wing. "I can't believe I drew these."

"Neither can I," Jack said. "Who are these people?"

"I can't say. I would have sworn I'd drawn a beautiful scene of a forest. We were talking about Eldershire earlier. You remember when we toured the John Muir woods. It was a scene like that. I was trying to capture how beautiful it was. At least, that's what I envisioned. I have no idea how these images got on this paper. Jack, what is happening to me?"

"He doesn't know, but I do," Nukpana's voice rang through her ears. KC dropped the pad and grabbed her ears.

"I'm getting someone," Jack said leaving the room.

"Come back!" KC called.

"I never left you," Nukpana laughed. "I never will."

"Oh, you go away. I don't want you in my life. Get out of here, now!"

"Why so soon?" Nukpana said. "I've got more to show you. Eldershire has changed so much and has suffered greatly in your absence. Don't you know that King Elder isn't as young as he used to be? He's dying, you know."

"You're crazy. He's a tree being. They don't up and die."

"He's old, older than you can imagine. He is also sick. He ate some candy that was not good for him."

"How do you know? You've been here on Earth with me."

"There are some things I can do you'll be surprised to learn that I managed to do before I left Eldershire. Your presence in Eldershire was an extraordinary dimension. After being here on Earth, it seems to me that from what I've seen in your mind Eldershire resembled an earthly paradise."

"Eldershire, the Land of My Heart's Desire," KC said in a dreamy voice. Then, she became stern. "What do you mean it *was* that of an earthly paradise? It still is. Mother Elder and Yggdrasil would never let anything happen to it."

"Oh, My Pitiful One. It is not. It is all but gone and once my rule becomes the law of the land it will never be as it was."

"What?"

"When King Elder dies, the rule of Eldershire is there for the taking. Anyone with the right ideas will become its new ruler. Princess Istar has no chance. Mark my words what I tell you. It is your fault Eldershire and its rulers are so vulnerable. You left them."

"You know I had no choice. My family was here. I did what I needed to do."

"But, you didn't finish your job. You even told Jack that last night. I was still there. I'm still here."

"Only because you hitched a ride in my body. If only I knew what I needed to do to get rid of you. That one thing would make it better because I bet if you left me now, you would die. Wouldn't you?" KC looked down at her pad of paper and began to sketch. "You don't reply? You know I'm right. You would die."

"It is unknown what would happen. But, I'm not going to leave your body. You're stuck with me, now and forever. I will always be with you. That one thought is driving you crazy."

"You're the one that is crazy."

"Am I? Who's sitting in a hospital ready to be locked up?" Nukpana chided.

"They're running tests. What do you mean locking me up? They aren't." KC rebuked.

Nukpana laughed manically. "You do understand the nature of time warps—"

The door opened. KC looked in anticipation. It was Jack.

"There you are," KC said. "Where have you been?"

"It's been a chore trying to find someone to help. I found Gay Lynn and told her you were worried about what was happening to you. I had to wait on Dr. Crowell to return to her office."

"Gay Lynn?"

"Your nurse."

"Oh, yeah. So, what's the story?" KC looked at him hoping he would be staying with her.

"Dr. Crowell said she wants you to spend the night here without me."

"You can't be serious. I need you. More importantly, I need you here. The voice has returned; it is with me." KC pointed to her head. "I am afraid to be alone. Please, you've got to stay here with me."

"You do realize that a voice can't hurt you. It is what you are hearing in your mind."

"No, Jack. It is more than that. She possesses me. She is part of me. I am doomed if I spend the night alone. You've already seen what she can do to me."

"It is true, you've told me about Eldershire and you talked about what happened with your quest." Jack looked at KC. She saw in his eyes doubt.

"The doctor got to you, didn't she?" KC slammed her fists on top of her legs. "You're going to leave me here. After everything, I'm going to lose you for real this time!" Jack moved to put his arm around KC. "Don't you dare touch me unless you're going to stay here."

Nurse Gay Lynn walked into the room. "I'm here to give you another shot." She paused, looked at KC, and then at Jack. "Are you both okay?"

"No. Jack said he couldn't spend the night here." KC moved from the bed and reached to pull the IV from her arm. "If he can't stay here with me, then I can't stay here alone."

"Whoa! KC give me a minute," Nurse Gay Lynn stopped KC's hand from removing the IV. "There is no reason to be this hasty. Give me a second. Please get back into bed. I'll call Dr. Crowell and explain to her how serious this is. She'll understand you want Jack to spend the night. Okay?"

KC looked at Jack. He nodded. She got back into the bed.

"Good. I'll be right back."

Jack turned to KC. "I can't believe you just did that. How are we going to find out what is going on if we don't give your doctor a chance? The Nukpana woman, you honestly think she is going to kill you?"

"Yes. I do."

"Consider that if she was going to kill you, what is she waiting for?"

KC looked at Jack and realized he was right. "She is only trying to scare me into thinking she is going to kill me!" Jack nodded. "I can't believe I allowed her to trick me."

Nurse Gay Lynn walked back into the room. "Dr. Crowell said for me to give you this shot. It will help you sleep. She said you would sleep all night. The other two nurses on the floor and myself will check on you every fifteen minutes. This will give Jack the chance to go get some much needed rest too."

"Jack, please don't leave me. Please…ouch!" KC reacted to the shot the nurse gave her. "Why didn't you use the IV? That hurt!"

"You'll be to sleep before you know it. We'll wake you early to prep you for your test. Now, settle down, and get some rest." Gay Lynn said. "Have a good night, Jack."

"It is for the best, KC," Jack said. "Let me move this pad of paper back over on your night stand." He stood beside her bed moving the covers.

"What are you looking for?"

"Your pencil. Where did it go?"

KC rose up and looked under the covers. "That's funny, it fell down here." She handed it to Jack.

"Oh, my. I'm getting sleepy. The nurse was right. That shot is starting to work," KC slid down in the bed, and Jack positioned her pillow and the covers up around her. "I may fall to sleep faster than she thought." KC yawned heartedly.

Jack yawned in response. "Oh, keep that inside. You're making me do it now. I still have to go to the hotel."

"Hmmm. You do that now. If this med does the good job it appears it will do, I won't be awake much longer, and that voice won't be able to bother me."

Jack bent down and looked at KC. She looked like she was already in a deep sleep. He kissed her good night. He realized he still held the pencil and set it down on top of the pad of paper. As he did so, he noticed that on the top sheet there was a new drawing.

He stared at it in disbelief. His eyes scanned the picture and a chill came over him. The drawing was of KC looking in the mirror as though she was studying her reflection. In the mirror image was the face of an evil looking witch with a scar on her left cheek beside KC's face. The evil woman held up a wicked looking scepter that glowed. Jack discerned KC *is* not alone.

CHAPTER 9
SKETCHING

"Good Morning, KC," Nurse Gay Lynn said walking into the room. "I see you are up already at seven and sketching." She walked over to the window and opened the blinds. "It's going to be another sunny day. Did you sleep well?"

KC put her pencil down and laid the pad on her side dresser. "I slept okay."

"I need to take your blood pressure and temperature. You won't be going down for your test for a few hours, so Dr. Crowell has ordered you a light breakfast." The nurse picked up KC's hand and placed an oxygen-pulse meter on her finger.

"Did you hear that?" KC asked.

"Hear what?" Nurse Gay Lynn recorded her readings. "You may have heard my stomach growl. I haven't eaten yet." The nurse smiled, and then walked over to the door closing it. "Let me help you up to visit the bathroom. I'll be right here waiting to help you back in bed."

KC came out of the bathroom feeling refreshed. "When will Jack be here?"

"He'll be able to come up to your room after nine. I'll be back in a few minutes with your breakfast. Don't get up without me with you, please."

KC watched her leave. Why do people leave me when I ask them not to do so? Don't they know I'm not alone in this room? She reached over to the table, picked up her pencil and sketchbook, and began fiddling with them. She looked at the doodles she drew since waking. They looked like rosebuds and other parts of flowers. The sketches gave her a sense of calm. At least, I drew something pretty this time, she thought.

The door opened to her room, Nurse Gay Lynn walked in with her breakfast. "This looks good." She set the tray on the bed table. "I may have to go down to the cafeteria and get me some."

The nurse moved the bed table with the food tray closer to KC, and then she removed the covers of the food.

"It smells good." KC picked up her sketchbook and pencil.

"Here, hand those to me. I'll put them over here on the night stand for you." The nurse took the book and pencil to place on the nightstand when she paused. "What's this?" she said. KC saw the nurse staring at her drawings.

"Oh, do you like them? I so enjoyed sketching those scenes. It reminded me of happier days." KC went back to eating.

Nurse Gay Lynn said, "Do you mind if I show your art work to my friend at the nurse's station?"

"Not at all. Feel free to show them to whomever you wish. You were right; this food is good. I'm starving." KC went back to eating.

OUT IN THE HALLWAY, Nurse Gay Lynn moved quickly to find Dr. Crowell. She knocked on her door.

"Come in," Dr. Crowell said.

"Doctor, I hate to bother you, but I think you should see what I found in Mrs. Carson's room." Gay Lynn showed her the sketches KC had completed that morning.

"I don't understand. How did she know?"

"I'm not sure, but she is showing clear signs that she is becoming aware. What must we do?"

"We must wait twenty-four hours. We've got to have time to seek guidance."

"What? Postpone the test again?"

"Yes. We'll make up some mumbo-jumbo that would make sense to a layperson. We've got to buy ourselves some time before she goes into that machine."

"How about I explain to her husband that we accidentally fed her and she wasn't suppose to eat before the test? By the time he explains it to KC, it will seem like a normal course to take. Anything else for me, boss?" Gay Lynn said while moving toward the door."

"That should work. Keep your fingers crossed we're doing the right thing in waiting. It could mean the end for all of us if we've chosen poorly."

❧

"OH, THERE YOU ARE?" KC said when Jack walked through the door. "I wondered if you were coming back to me."

"Sorry, it took me a lot longer than I thought." Jack walked over to KC, bent down, and kissed her on the forehead.

"What? No kiss on the lips?" KC looked up and smiled.

"Sure." Jack kissed KC again. "I'm anxious to talk with you."

"What about?"

"Dr. Crowell has an idea of what is going on." Jack pulled a chair up beside the bed.

"Really?"

"As you know from our first visit, she thinks you might be having TIAs. She wants to make sure the tests you'll be having tomorrow will show that clearly. Then, they'll know how to proceed from there."

"Tomorrow? I thought the tests were to be later today?"

"Dr. Crowell said that there was a mistake in feeding you. We'll need to wait so you can have the tests safely. It is something about the dye they use to check your blood flow."

"I don't understand. How could they mess this up? I thought I'd be in and out. Now, I'm here another day." KC threw the covers off of her legs and got up. As she did, she became unsteady on her feet.

"Whoa, there," Jack said standing up to steady KC. "Grab hold of the bed and sit down."

KC grabbed her forehead and could feel her feet moving without her. "I'm going to fall—"

Jack caught her and lifted her up into his arms, and then placed her on the bed.

Nurse Gay Lynn walked in. "What happened?"

"When she learned the test had to be postponed, she got up in a huff."

"She wasn't supposed to move without me helping her. It is the effect of the shot she got last night."

"Why are you both talking like I'm unconscious or something? I've heard everything you've said. Now, what is going on?"

"That is true. I'm sorry," Jack said and walked closer to the bed. He took hold of KC's hand. Nurse Gay Lynn said, "After what the we have observed the last twenty-four hours, Dr. Crowell is even more convinced that you are suffering from TIAs. Before, she was speculating."

"It seems to me she is still speculating until the test results come in, right?"

"You have a point," Nurse Gay Lynn said. "She wants to get more observations of you when you have your episodes. Together, she and Dr. Doar felt it best to ease you into the prep for the MRI. The medicines she needs to use are rather strong. And, with you being served food, we need to be extra careful. Therefore, we need to wait until tomorrow."

"What medicines?"

"Besides the shots we've been giving you. There will be dyes that will be put through your veins for contrast. Dr. Crowell wants to be sure you will be ready for the test so you won't have an adverse reaction to the dyes."

KC felt a surge of nervousness come over her. She felt herself getting anxious and restless. "I wish I knew what was wrong with me."

The morning hours changed into afternoon hours and soon it was early evening. KC and Jack walked the hallways of the hospital, watched television, and played cards. Late evening began to show its signs of night. The day had gone by with no appearances from Nukpana. KC was beginning to wonder if she had imagined it all along.

"Are you nervous about the MRI?" Jack asked while replacing the deck of cards back in the box.

"A little," KC nodded. "I'm not sure how well I'm going to do with the test. I don't like tight places. And, to be honest, I'm worried about how I might react to the dyes or if they'll postpone again. What if I'm as severely claustrophobic as my Mom? She was horribly so, you know."

"You have mentioned that every time someone talks about a tight situation."

"Tight situation?" KC looked at Jack hoping he was teasing her. "I don't recall us ever being in a tight situation."

Jack smirked, then said, "I don't think we have together."

"What did you mean?" Watching Jack's face cringe, KC took Jack's hand into hers. "I guess I'm on edge. I didn't mean to snap at you. I remember reading some horrible stories about what you went through. You never really talk about it. How did you learn to deal with claustrophobia when you were a pilot during the war?"

"It was different at first. The first time I put on my face mask, I seemed to be okay. It was when I had to put on the rest of the suit, and then they zipped me into it from the back. At that moment, just as the last of the zipper went up to the back of my neck, I thought I would explode. They had taken several days preparing us for a similar situation. They had prepared us for how to react. They said to take deep, slow breaths. I started breathing very slowly. Then, they turned on the oxygen. When it hit my face, I relaxed."

"Did you have the same reaction every time?"

"No. After a bit, I learned what to do that worked for me. I came to understand that all I needed to do was to wait for that burst of oxygen. I was always fine. Not everyone was, though."

"But, suppose there had been no oxygen?"

"I would have had much worse things to think about."

"Like what?"

"Dying."

"Oh. Jack, did you hear that?" KC looked around the room.

"Hear what?"

"That evil laugh."

"No."

KC got up and walked over to the bathroom door. She turned around and said to Jack, "I hear it all of the time."

Jack replied, "I tell you what. Why don't you go ahead and get ready for bed? Your supper will be here soon. I'm going to go see if I can find some food. When I get done, I'll come back to say goodnight. Will you be okay?"

"Yes. It probably is a good idea. You go on. I'll be fine here." The door opened as Nurse Gay Lynn walked in with a tray.

"Are you ready to eat a little food? We have some Jell-O, some ice cream, and a nice cup of tea. Not much food for you tonight."

"Oh, my! A royal feast." KC smiled. "I had a big lunch. It'll help me with my girly figure not to eat too much." She moved around the bed and sat down in the chair.

Jack bent down and kissed KC on the forehead. "I'll see you in a bit. Nurse Gay Lynn, don't take any grief off of her. She's been rather feisty this evening. I'll be back in about an hour."

"Feisty?" KC said mocking him.

Jack blew her a kiss, and left the room.

"He's right, you know." Nurse Gay Lynn set the tray down on her bed table, and then adjusted it to fit over the chair.

"About what?"

"You need to get plenty of rest. And, you're right too."

"I am? About what?"

"You'll be fine here. I'll take good care of you."

"I won't be difficult." KC said. "Maybe this test tomorrow won't be so bad, after all."

Nurse Gay Lynn patted KC's hand. "I'll check in on you in a little while." She walked over to the door. "Would you like this left open or closed?"

"Feel free to close it. I'll be fine." KC looked down at her tray. I hope I'm right, KC thought.

You have no idea how it will be, now do you? Nukpana said.

CHAPTER 10
MRI

KC was awake before the sun rose. She sat and stared out the window of her hospital room. *Today. I'll finally find out what is going on with me.* She looked down at her locket and opened the oval shaped pendant. She remembered the day that her mother, Kitty, gave it to her. KC thought back to the last time she and Kitty talked about the necklace that her mother always wore—

"I gave you that precious locket before you married Jack to serve as 'something old.' Do you remember?" Kitty said

"Yes. You said it was from the old saying 'all brides must wear something old, something new, something borrowed, and something blue.'" KC winked at Kitty while removing the locket and handing it to her.

"I've forgotten. It was also for the something blue, wasn't it? Your dress was the something new."

"The forget-me-not flowers in my bouquet too. The open filigree design interlaced with tiny diamonds with the diamond-cut blue stone made the locket standout with its beauty. I've received many compliments since." Kitty held the locket. "Tell me more about it, Mom. You've not spoken much about it except that I must take care of it. I don't think I have a single memory of you that you weren't wearing it until you gave it to me."

"You've worn it with pride. It came to me from your great-grandmother Chen before she left this world. She told me it would serve an important purpose, and it must be kept close and safe."

"I have done my best to do both."

"That, I can see." Kitty handed the locket back to KC. "It will serve you well when you need it. Always remember its secret."

KC took the pendant and clasped it into place around her neck.

Absentmindedly, she rubbed the striking blue stone. The light glistened off of it. Then, she turned the locket around, opened it, and with a flick of a small latch, revealed a hidden area that could hold something as large as a lock of hair.

KC LOOKED DOWN at the golden tresses that lay in the secret compartment of the locket she held. She had no memory of where the lock of hair came from, but she knew in her heart she must hold onto it and protect the locket with its unique necklace.

A soft knock at her door caused her to quickly close the locket and slip the locket attached to the red plaid collar under the neckband of her nightgown.

"Come in," KC responded to the knock.

"Good morning," Nurse Gay Lynn said carrying a small tray. "Hope you are ready for the big day. You'll have a little time to relax before we must prepare you for the test."

"What time will I go for it?"

Nurse Gay Lynn set the tray on the nearby nightstand.

"Oh, it could be in the next hour or so."

"That soon?"

"It might be earlier. We have a sedative for you to take. An orderly will wheel you down to the second floor."

"Will Jack be here before I go?"

"I don't know. He should be."

KC felt a little annoyed at all of the rush. They had already kept her here an extra day. She wondered why they couldn't wait until she was sure Jack was going to be nearby. She didn't like the idea of the MRI. And, she didn't like the idea of taking medication that would make her confused before she was sure he was near.

"Can we wait? At least until Jack arrives?"

"Well, I don't know," the nurse was listening to KC's heart. "Your blood pressure is a little high."

"What is it?"

"147 over 79. Have you been up long this morning?"

"A little while." KC looked toward the door and watched Jack come through. He carried a large bouquet of flowers in beautiful fall colors. "Oh, how beautiful!"

He bent down and kissed her on the cheek. "Are you ready for this?"

"To leave." KC paused, and then nodded.

"I'll put these in water. Good morning, Nurse Gay Lynn. I didn't mean to interrupt you, if I did."

"Good morning, Mr. Carson. You didn't. We have a patient here who was glad to see you walk through that door. Now, KC. Let's have you take this medication so we can get this show on the road."

The drowsiness that KC felt didn't stop her from being aware of where she was while riding in the wheelchair. She looked behind her at the man pushing her down the aisle.

He looked familiar to her. She wasn't sure. She looked up at him. Her mind raced. Was it Gavin, the white hawk? His white hair and peachy complexion, and his blue eyes gave her a sense of comfort. He smiled at her, and then she turned to see them go through the double swinging doors of the MRI room.

The magnetic resonance imaging machine was larger than she expected, except for the opening where it looked like the table would move her body inside for the test; it was very small. She felt her blood pressure climb as fear of closed in areas began to envelop her.

KC tried to keep her voice soothing. "Where's the upright MRI?"

Pressure began to build as KC felt her chest tighten. She hadn't even gotten out of the wheelchair.

"I thought the meds I took were going to reduce my anxiety. I don't have control of my fear." She thought she was going to burst into tears. She considered getting up and running away, but she heard the voice of Nukpana.

"Oh, the scaredy cat has got to take a test. How awful for her. She's such a baby. Nurse? Doctor? Can someone please help this poor thing? My Poor Pitiful One. You are so weak. How can Mother Elder or Yggdrasil even think you could beat me?"

An evil laugh echoed and KC thought for a moment she saw Nukpana standing at the entrance to the MRI machine.

"What is she doing here?" KC screamed.

The orderly pushed an emergency button and two staff came running into the room.

"What's going on?" Dr. Crowell said.

"Doctor! I can't go through with it. She's here! Doctor! She's standing right there!" KC looked over and Nukpana was standing with her arms folded.

"I don't have to do a thing," Nukpana said and laughed again. *"You're proving to them you are crazy. Oh, this is glorious! My Poor Pitiful One!"*

KC began to whimper and cry.

The orderly turned KC's wheelchair back toward the door. "Gavin, good idea," Dr. Crowell said. "I should have thought of that. You stay with her. I'll be right back."

He pushed KC into the outer room.

"The idea of not facing that machine helped. Did I hear Dr. Crowell call you Gavin?" Gavin handed her a tissue and KC wiped her eyes.

"Yes."

"That's interesting. I used to know a Gavin. He kind of looked like you," KC thought his voice sounded like a bird's song. "But, not human."

"Not human?" Gavin walked in front of KC and knelt down in front of her. He looked up into her eyes.

"No. He was a hawk—a white hawk, and the leader of his people. A good friend."

"Where did he live?"

"Eldershire. Have you ever heard of it?"

Gavin shook his head. "What's it like?"

"Have you ever walked in an old-growth forest made of redwoods or other large trees where it is so quiet you could hear a pin drop on the moss covered floor? Eldershire is like that and more. There's a sense of calm that is hard to describe to someone who lives in this world where every second something is moving, changing, and there is high anxiety. Simply saying the name of Eldershire gives me a feeling of reverence and immerses me in tranquility. I think you'd love it there."

"It sounds like I could love it as you do. It sounds like you would like to return."

"It's funny, but I would; yet I'm fearful."

"Fearful?"

"Of what awaits me."

"There's no need to fear this test," Dr. Crowell said, walking beside Gavin as he pushed KC back into the MRI room. Nurse Gay Lynn walked behind carrying a tray. "Do you feel calmer now?" the doctor asked.

"Yes. Gavin helped me think of something different."

"Good. We're ready to get started."

KC looked at the three people standing before her and hoped she could get through the test without fear swelling up within her soul.

"I thought we were going to use the upright MRI?"

Dr. Crowell said, "As fate would have it, the upright machine is not available."

From the time she got upon the MRI table to the insertion of the IV for the test dye, and then finally moving the table into position to scan her head, the prep for the test took about twenty minutes.

KC thought the table moved into the tube at a snail's pace. The fear of claustrophobia did not immediately grab hold of her while the table moved inside the tube. But, once the table stopped moving, KC felt an urgency to get up and move.

"You've got to take me out! Now!" KC said. She knew if she didn't get out soon she would explode. The table moved out quickly. KC moved her hands up to the faceplate to move it away.

"No. Don't touch the plate." Dr. Crowell could be heard over the intercom. "We'll come move it for you."

KC put her hands down. "Please hurry. I'm not sure how long I can last here."

Nurse Gay Lynn moved to KC and removed the faceplate when the table stopped. KC immediately rose up.

"Wow! I'm not sure I can do this. The meds you gave me are not helping me relax. Isn't there anything stronger I can have?"

"We can't. You must be awake enough that we can ask you questions and give you directions you can follow. If we knocked you out, you wouldn't be able to respond to us."

"I'm not sure I can do this. I was beginning to panic before. I just don't think I can do this without something."

Dr. Crowell walked into the room. "KC, may I ask if we try another drug that won't put you to sleep, but makes you more relaxed, would you be willing to try that for us?"

KC looked at the nurse and Dr. Crowell. She studied their eyes. Her fear of not knowing what was wrong with her and why she heard voices caused her to want to overcome her fear of claustrophobia. "Yes. I'll give it a try."

"Good. Nurse, get Lorazepam intravenous 4 mg, and we'll administer it through the IV.

"May I also have a fan to blow on my face with a cold wash cloth I can place on my forehead?"

"We can do that." Nurse Gay Lynn walked into the test room with the medicine. "Gay Lynn, would you call down for the fan? I'll get the wash cloth," Dr. Crowell said.

Another ten minutes went by. Nurse Gay Lynn walked in with the fan and began to set it up. Dr. Crowell handed a cold washcloth to KC.

"Thank you," KC said taking the washcloth. "This is an interesting plaid pattern. It reminds me of something," she said, folding the cloth, and placing it on her forehead. She thought of her locket with its plaid collar in the pocket of her pajama pants. She hoped having it on her wouldn't cause some catastrophe with the test, but she had to have it close to her.

Nurse Gay Lynn said while turning on the fan, "How does this feel?"

"Wonderful. I didn't realize how hot I was. This cold cloth helps too. Thank you."

"Excellent. That cloth should help you as you transition. Do you think we might begin again?" Dr. Crowell asked.

"Transition?" KC said.

"When the table moves into the chamber," Nurse Gay Lynn said.

KC nodded. "I'm willing to give it another try."

"Are you beginning to feel the effects of the Lorazepam?"

"I might be. I know I'm not nearly as anxious or nervous as I was."

"Good. We'll try again." Dr. Crowell said, walking out of the testing room. The nurse checked the IV while KC tried to relax. The table began to move.

Nurse Gay Lynn said, "Before I leave the room, is the cloth on your forehead okay?"

"It is."

"And, the fan?"

"Perfect." KC could feel herself relaxing. The cool air was helping. "I think I might be able to do this now."

The table moved into position and Dr. Crowell said through the intercom, "How are you doing?"

"So far, so good," KC said.

"We're about ready to begin. When we ask you to hold your breath, you will only hold your breath for a short amount of time. Please try not to move. Do you have any concerns or questions before we start the test?"

"No. I think I'm ready."

"Good. When we start the machine, you'll hear a pounding sound. It uses a strong magnetic field that results in making a loud sound that may startle you. I'm going to start the machine for a short bit to align it properly with your head. Are you ready?"

"Yes."

"You will be fine. I'll see to it," Nukpana said.

KC felt her breath leave her as fear engulfed her.

CHAPTER 11
LARISSA MAR'S CABIN

"I commend your fighting spirit in the midst of what we face. Yet, we must not forget the lessons of the BlueStones," Mr Scruffy said, beginning his plea for his companions to take up the fight against Barnabus. "Give pause as I share the news of late. Our BlueStone is at the heart of who we are. It is at the heart of our history and of our being."

Mr Scruffy walked to the front of the gathering. He continued, "Where the Efil Stone is at the heart of our existence, the BlueStones are used in the essence of our lives. Our BlueStone—its dark blue-gray color—belies its strength and impact upon each of our souls. The BlueStones came from the heart of the deep seas where sunlight could not penetrate and rose to form the mountains that surround the lands of Eldershire. Each BlueStone serves as the natural foundation of who we are as beings in this land. Our BlueStone shaped our lives forming stout structures that we grew to depend on for its endurance to instill upon us the need to be strong and sturdy."

Gavin raised a wing. "You may speak," Mr Scruffy said.

"Is it not also true that our BlueStone has medical powers for us as well? My great-great-grandmother speaks of its healing powers in water."

"It does. It is said that when water is poured over a stone, the water absorbs the healing powers of the stone. It is thought our BlueStone can pass other virtues on to us beings if we care for the stone properly."

"Aye. That is true," said Iolair. "I might add that many believe some of the BlueStones have the property of lithophones, being musical stones, when struck giving off the sound of a bell, gong, or even a drum, but my beings believe it is actually the sound of the spirit inhabitants we hear. It is the 'Power of the Stone' many have said cause us to gravitate to our BlueStone."

"You speak for why we must remember the BlueStones. They will tell us what we need to do when the time is right. I have one here and we must consult it when the time is of most need. Mother Elder and Yggdrasil believe if we pause and wait, bide our time, our BlueStone will reward us. I worry we cannot wait too long. Only when we know where she is may we proceed. The time is upon us to stand up and fight."

All those gathered stood up in unison and cheered, "We will fight together!"

SEBORN MOVED AHEAD of Arrington and Eri being careful not to crowd Eri while he maneuvered his cart. "Try not to disturb the human. We don't want her waking before we can get her hidden away. We don't need anyone seeing us now. It will look like we've attacked her."

"This is true," Arrington said. "We need to be extra careful. Where are we taking her?"

"I don't know," Eri said, "I hope one of you has a good idea. We can't use my cabin. I'm not married. It is up to you two to decide."

"What about we take her to Larissa Mar's cabin?" Arrington said. "We could take care of her there until she either dies or we are able to find out more about her."

"That may work," Seborn said. "We can't risk Mylo finding out about her until we are able to explain how she was found. To do otherwise would bring trouble upon us all."

"Agreed," Eri said.

"With you, my brothers," Arrington said and picked up the yoke to help Eri move the cart. "It is getting dark. We should press on."

"GOOD TWO-SUNS, LARISSA MAR," Seborn said walking into her cabin. "How is our human doing today?"

"She still has not stirred. It's been three days and I worry."

"That she will die?"

"Yes. No food, no drink, and no bodily functions. You don't even know how long she had lain there when you found her. She must be on the verge of death. Why else has she not come around?"

"Have you used the BlueStone?"

"No. I thought I'd wait. To begin to use it will draw the attention of Mylo. You said you didn't want her to know anything until we knew something. We are no better off than we were when you brought her here. I am getting fearful of what may happen. What will we do if she dies?"

"We'll bury her and that will be the end of it."

"Seborn, you can't be serious?"

"Why not? No one knows she is here. She is just a human. What difference will it make?"

"It may make the difference of our lives." Eri walked into the cabin.

"I was just in the center of Snowboro. Word is about that a human is in our midst. Mylo returned from the gathering with the resistance. She is calling all leaders to a special meeting this evening. We must tell her what we have here."

"You are right, Eri. I must let Mylo know. But first, I want to give Larissa Mar one more chance at being able to awaken the human. Can you do it?" Seborn looked at Larissa Mar.

"I'm not sure. I'll try using the BlueStone. It is risky."

"Do it. Eri come with me. We will find Arrington and be back. Do what you can."

Larissa Mar watched them leave, and then looked at the human.

"I wish I knew if what I'm about to do is the right thing." She rotated the human slightly more onto her back. In doing so, a sparkling piece of metal moved. "What is this?" Larissa Mar said picking up a metal amulet hanging from a plaid like collar with a chain around her neck.

She studied the object and rotated it around in her fingers. In doing so, she saw the sparkling stones encircling a deep blue stone. Then, she noticed a piece of metal stuck out slightly. She used her finger to pick at it and it popped up revealing the inside. Larissa Mar continued to look at it closely, and noticed the center of the inside seemed to give off a blue glow that began to grow brighter.

"No!" The human rose up and grabbed the object, slamming it shut. "You can't! It will kill us all!" The object clutched in her hands, the human stared, and then collapsed without another word.

Larissa Mar startled by what she witnessed tried to figure out what to do next. Seborn, Arrington, and Eri returned.

"You didn't touch her, did you?" Seborn asked, walking over to the cot that held the human.

"No." Larissa Mar looked down to her hands.

"Did you use the BlueStone then?"

"No."

"What is wrong?" Seborn asked.

"She just woke up, but seems to have fallen back into a deep sleep."

"What? You did it?" Arrington said, walking closer to the human.

"No. I didn't do anything. She raised up and spoke, and then laid back down again."

"What did she say?" Seborn said. "She had to say something."

"I don't know. I'm not sure what she said. I couldn't understand her."

"What do you mean?" Eri asked.

"It is hard to explain. She rose up, said some words I didn't understand, and then laid her head back down as you see her now. That is all. I didn't do anything else and you came in."

"Well, do something now!" Seborn said. "We must get her awake to question her."

"I'm not sure it is wise at this time. I'm not sure. I can do it." Larissa Mar ran crying from the room.

"What will we do now?" Arrington said.

"Go after her. We need her." Seborn left the cabin, Arrington followed. Eri stayed behind.

The human rolled over and looked around the room. "Do you want to try to steal my necklace too?"

"What? You're awake!" Eri ran to the cabin door and called for his friends. "Come Seborn, now!" He looked through the woods and could not see anyone. He looked back at the human and made the decision to run after his friends. "You stay here. I'll be right back."

Not knowing where she was, KC raised up on her elbow to look around the room. Through the open doorway, she could see the landscape blanketed in white, snow-covered, and glistening. An occasional dark shadow peeked through leaving an impression of a deep ravine. *Where am I?*

She remembered enough about being moved to know she was with Snowquidians. *But, where is here? I'm no longer where I was.* She listened for any noise. A faint sound of water cascading over rocks came to her ears mingling with the crackling fire in the fireplace of the cabin, which gave off streaks of dancing light. The smell of sweet falling snow waft up her nose.

Her skin tingled. She looked down and realized she didn't have on clothes. *Where did they go?* A hide covered her. Standing, she wrapped it around her and began to explore the one-room cabin. It was simple enough.

Nothing stood out to her until she caught a glimpse of something flickering from the firelight. Lying on a nearby cabinet top was a crystal. The brilliant blue color was mesmerizing. She picked it up. Then, looked at her locket. The blue stones matched.

"Hmmm," she said. "I wonder." She saw out of the corner of her eye some clothes, beside the cabinet, on the dirt floor. They weren't the pajamas she was wearing. Quickly putting them on, she walked to the doorway and looked out.

Reaching into the back pocket of the jeans, she felt a fabric. Pulling the object from the pocket, she realized it was the red plaid cloth Dr. Crowell had placed on her forehead. "Good," she whispered. She returned her treasure to the pocket to keep it hidden. She listened.

The water continued to flow; no other sounds could be heard from the still forest covered with snow. Her feet were bare. *What can I do?* She looked back in the cabin and caught a glimpse of boots under the cot.

Putting them on, they were large on her feet. She decided to use them anyway because they would keep her feet warm until she could find out what had happened. She moved toward the doorway.

"You won't be going anywhere," Seborn said walking in and pushing her back.

"You can't! I've got to get out of here."

"Why? Who are you and why are you in Snowboro?"

"Snowboro? In Eldershire?"

"Yes. How do you know about us?"

"I was here before. I'm KC. Mr Scruffy is my friend."

"Seborn, you realize what this means?" Arrington said. "We've got to take her to Mylo now."

"Mylo, the Snowquidian?"

"Yes. Do you know her?" Eri said pushing Arrington into the cabin.

"She taught me how to fight. I was with her when her husband, Seif was killed. Nukpana, where is she?"

"Whoa! Nukpana? She is dead." Seborn said.

"No. She is not!" KC said. "She's in my head. At least, she was before I arrived here. How long have I been here?"

"Six full Two-Moons. We found you on the other side of the forest. Near—"

"Mushroom Alley?" KC asked.

"Yes."

"Take me to Mylo now. I must get to Mr Scruffy."

"We can't." Seborn walked over to the table and sat down. "You must tell us how you got here first. We must protect ourselves from shame."

"Shame? What do you mean, shame? We're talking about Nukpana. Life. Death. What has shame got to do with me being here?"

"I told you. You wouldn't listen to me. Oh, my lanta! What are we going to do?" Larissa Mar said walking into the crowded room.

"We're going to take her to Mylo and let Mylo sort this out," Arrington said. "I've had enough of trying to know what is best when we don't even know what is going on."

"You're right," Seborn said. "It is a full late Two-Moons walk from here. Where did you get those boots?"

"I found them under the cot."

"Take them off. You'll freeze your feet off without more protection. Larissa Mar, find her some protection for her feet."

Larissa Mar walked over to the cabinet. "Here, put these in-liners on. They'll give you warmth and protect your feet from hookworms."

KC took them. "Thank you." She looked at Larissa Mar and decided not to mention how Larissa Mar tried to take her locket. She pulled it out from under her shirt while sitting down to put on the in-liners. "How quick will we be able to see Mylo once we reach her camp?"

"I'm not sure. She should be back from being with Mr Scruffy," Seborn said.

"Mr Scruffy? He's here?"

"Not here. They were at a gathering on the other side of Mushroom Alley."

"How far to the gathering?"

"Two Two-Moons run. He'll be long gone by the time we get there. It's best to go to Mylo. She'll be able to help you faster," Arrington said.

KC remembered how Mylo and her other Snowquidian friends would pop in and out of any place. "Why can't you pop me to them now?"

"We don't have those magical powers. We are limited in what we can do until we've earned the right."

"I'm ready. Let's go." KC looked around and checked the cot she laid on. "I didn't have anything else with me?"

"Only that piece of metal around your neck," Larissa Mar said.

"Thank you. You were the one that undressed me?"

"No. You were already undressed when you were found." Larissa Mar looked slightly embarrassed and turned away. "Wait! Where is my BlueStone? I left it lying right here. Do you have it?" She said looking to KC.

"I do. I wasn't sure what it was. I took it in case it proved useful." KC handed it back to her.

When their hands touched, a spark ignited between them, and then KC could no longer see the Snowquidians.

CHAPTER 12
POSSESSION

What happened when I was in Eldershire and Nukpana was struck down? How did she get into me? She said it was at the moment I cut her hair. Is that possible? I don't believe it. She said something strange to me that Blazewing, her scepter, still worked and each time she used it, she felt weaker. I wonder. Do I feel stronger?

I remember that when I cut her hair, her essence was not yet fully purple. How then did she send a portion of herself into me? There is something else, something else that I'm missing. It's small. It's close. What is happening?

KC twisted and turned, and then she felt her body slump into darkness.

JACK STOOD LOOKING from the observation room into the MRI test room where KC was on the table not moving.

"What do you mean she is in a coma? How?" He sat down hard on a nearby chair and cried, "Nooooo!"

Dr. Crowell and Nurse Gay Lynn were silent.

Gavin calmly walked out of the room and down the hall. *She knew. She knew I was sent here to oversee her transport.* He marveled that she recognized him. He saw it in her eyes, yet she didn't say a word. *Good and faithful servant. She must be with my colleagues now. I pray she is.*

"WHERE IS SHE?" Mylo asked Seaborn, Arrington, and Eri along with Larissa Mar; they stood in her cabin. "Why didn't you bring her with you?"

"It's complicated," Seborn said.

"Uncomplicate it for me," Mylo said. "Where is she?"

"We don't know. One second she was standing there handing the BlueStone to Larissa Mar, the next she was gone."

"The BlueStone?"

"She had taken the BlueStone off of my cabinet top. When I asked where it was, she volunteered she had taken it." Larissa Mar said. Mylo watched her wring her hands.

"Why do you look like you are lost? You never came across as stupid, but you are acting that way! Leaving the BlueStone out for others to see it? Are you insane?" Mylo began pacing back and forth across the room. "No, you're not insane. You are daft! Plain and simple. Daft! Daft! Daft! Ugh! I could scream at your silliness. Why didn't you come to me immediately when you found her?"

"We thought it best to find out more about her first," Seborn said with vexation.

"This boggles the mind. How is your plan working out so far?" Mylo shook her finger at each one standing before her. "Don't answer. I can tell you. Not very well! Not well at all! Actually, terribly!" She stormed out of the room.

"What can we do?" Arrington asked the others.

"Nothing. We don't even know where she went. Where would we start?" Eri said. He crumbled into a nearby chair. "We tried to protect our own interests only to have that human disappear on us. We're doomed. She was the Savior. Mother Elder and Yggdrasil will have our heads!"

"Eri, you know you get excited at the least little thing. We can find her. We only need to figure out where she went," Seborn said.

"Ohhhhhkay! Now, we've got a plan. Everything will be oojah-cum-spiff. Wow. I've never felt so good about anything in my life," Arrington said mocking Seborn. "Just really, what are we supposed to do? She's gone! She disappeared before our eyes. You can't deny what you saw. Yet, you stand there before us and act as though this is an easy fix. It isn't. Now, tell me what we *are* supposed to do."

"Calm down, Arrington. I don't have a plan. Do you?" Seborn said, walking to the doorway. "I don't have any more of a clue than you. Except, I have this." Seborn held up the locket that KC *was* wearing.

THE TWO-SUNS WERE STARTING their descent into the low-lying valley. The yellow hues blended with the cool fall air giving off a feeling that a fight was about to take hold in the sky, as summer would struggle to give way to the change of season. She, like summer, was eager for a fight. Nukpana wanted her revenge. She looked out and felt she had done all she could do to secure her place in Eldershire. She poisoned as many as she could against King Elder. It was now up to Barnabus.

She walked over to her throne chair, looking Barnabus straight in his dark blue eyes. She studied his face. He looked a little annoyed. *I wonder how much he knows about me and my powers.* He is not afraid. I'm used to seeing weaklings come to my throne room. She gazed about the room. Graves Mountain hadn't changed too much while she was away. *I'm home.*

Nukpana got up, then walked back to the window to look at her land. "What news have you for me?" she asked.

"Nothing of importance," Barnabus said flicking the edge of his coat and switching his feet. Nukpana stared at him. She observed his hand jerk when he reached to rub the back of his neck.

"Tell me, are you nervous or agitated?"

"Why do you ask? Are you?"

"You are impertinent. I would strike you down right here if I didn't need you." Nukpana's voice rose. "Watch yourself or I might forget that important piece of information."

Barnabus turned his head away from her eyes.

"Are you going to explain why you do not have any news?"

"There is nothing to explain. The Elderians in King Elder's Camp are not talking; they're just going about their day-to-day work. Nothing has changed since you came back." Barnabus picked up the silver pitcher on the table and poured himself a drink into a silver goblet. "You have beautiful things. Fine things. Very fine things."

Nukpana walked over to him, wrenched the goblet upward from his hand, and then slapped his face. "My things are of no importance to you. What is of importance is whether you will live longer than the next five minutes. What do you plan to do to stir the Elderians into a frenzy? We need them riled and angry with King Elder. This is your problem to fix. How do you plan to do it?"

Barnabus stepped forward. He looked at Nukpana. He furrowed his brows. "I'll get them worked into a frenzy. Just as you want. I'll do my job. You have no reason to doubt me." He turned, and then walked out.

SEBORN SAT BEFORE THE CRONE, Baba Elli. He came to her as a last resort, but he had to know if what he suspected was true. She held KC's locket with the red plaid collar in her arthritic hands, twirling it around. Her long, dirty blond hair covered a large portion of her thin body. A ring was in her nose, and a feather held part of her hair back off of her eyes. She looked up at Seborn.

"Well?" Seborn asked.

"I'm studying it. You think there is something inside?" Baba Elli said while placing the locket on a nearby table, then standing up.

"Yes."

"I'm not so sure you should find out. You came to me because of my wisdom, my age, and the fact I can be a protector. You, I don't need to protect. But this—" She picked up the locket, and then held it high. "It does not belong to you. This is needed by The One, *She*, whom you took it from. You are trying to deceive me."

Baba Elli walked up close beside Seborn, bent down, and put her crooked finger on his nose. "You do know my name means witch," she smiled. She took a step back. "As an old grandmother, I can protect you, if I choose. Or, I can doom you to the Otherworld?" Seborn nodded. "Good. Then, why are you sitting there lying to me?"

"Why do you say I am lying?"

"Why do you answer my question with another question?" She looked at him sternly. "Your effort to deflect my intentions does not go unnoticed. You will reap the rewards of your efforts upon your death." Seborn's eyes grew large. "And, you should be fearful of my anger. Mine is minor compared to that of the being whose wisp of hair is hidden within this locket."

"What?" Seborn said.

Baba Elli held the locket up close to his eyes. "See it glow yellow? It knows it is not with its rightful owner. This is a powerful talisman. Your quest for power and riches will be your undoing. You," Baba Elli's lips turned in with displeasure, "are a fool!"

"How do you know? You never opened it." Seborn sounded incredulous to the old Crone.

"You speak the truth finally!" Baba Elli laughed wickedly. "Ah, you aren't as slow as I figured. The fact the locket glows tells me to be careful. Inside is the power of a maleficent spirit. It was most likely placed there to hold power over the wearer. Since you are not the intended target, it does not harm you, but beware. It doesn't mean it *won't* harm you."

"What do you mean it holds power over the wearer?" Seborn began twisting the end of his cloak with his fingers.

"You are afraid." Baba Elli nodded with a smile of contentment. "You know you've taken this from someone important. This locket was meant to be worn by that soul and that soul only. It was designed to have power over that soul. If you wear it, you will die. The power of the entity inside is strong. The longer it is away from the rightful owner, the glow will change from yellow to orange and finally to red. Red will not be good for you."

Baba Elli handed the locket back to Seborn. Once her hand fell away from it, Seborn heard a faint sound.

"What did you say?" he asked.

"I didn't speak. The glow is changing now. Do you see?"

Seborn looked down and saw a faint orange color and the locket felt as though it throbbed in his hand. "I must go."

"Yes. You must. Your time is limited now."

Seborn rushed out of the hut and down the rickety steps. The forest before him was darker than when he arrived. He began to run back to their camp at the edge of Mushroom Alley.

"YOU HAVE NO TIME." Seborn heard the voice, stopped running, and turned to look back at the Crone's hut. She was not there. He looked down at the locket he carried in his hand and saw a red-orange glow.

"Please. Don't do anything. I'll do what you need. I promise. I'll get this back to KC. I promise."

Evil laughter echoed through the forest. A flock of ravens flew out of the treetops. Seborn began to run and looked up to see the ravens were following along with him. His fear mounted. He prayed. The ravens' croaking calls grew louder upon reaching the edge of the encampment. "Oh, please!" Seborn begged. "I will give her the necklace. I will."

"STOP! GONIFF!" the voice said. Seborn halted his steps. "GOOD. YOU WILL NOT GIVE THE LOCKET TO KC WITHOUT HELPING ME BRING HER HARM."

"What?" Seborn looked down at the locket. Its glow was turning back to a brown-yellow.

"YOU WILL NEED TO FIND KC, CONVINCE HER SHE MUST GO TO GRAVES MOUNTAIN. YOU WILL GIVE HER THE LOCKET, AND YOU WILL ALSO GIVE HER THIS PACKET."

A raven flew by and dropped a packet at Seborn's feet. He bent down, picked it up, and brought it to his nose—a whiff of noisome vapor greeted him.

He looked down at the locket. "What do I do with this?"

"WHEN YOU ARE ALONE WITH KC, TELL HER YOU RECEIVED THIS PACKET WHEN YOU VISITED BABA ELLI; TELL HER SHE MUST DRINK IT. TELL HER BABA ELLI SAID IT WILL SAVE HER.

"I'm to tell her I saw Baba Elli? What about the locket?" Seborn looked around trying to find the voice.

"MAKE SURE SHE HAS THE LOCKET IN HER POSSESSION. THEN, YOU WILL TELL HER TO DRINK THE POTION IN THE PACKET TO SAVE HER LIFE."

"How will drinking that save her life? She doesn't even know where she came from. She keeps speaking of this place I've never heard of."

"IT IS OF NO WORRY TO YOU. YOU ONLY NEED TO MAKE SURE SHE HAS THE LOCKET IN HER POSSESSION WHEN SHE DRINKS THE POTION MADE FROM THE PACKET."

"But, what if I can't get her to drink it?"

"YOU BETTER OR YOU'LL PAY THE ULTIMATE PRICE WITH YOUR LIFE!"

"I don't understand."

"YOU WILL. BWAHAHA." The voice laughed.

CHAPTER 13
COMA

M r Scruffy walked solemnly up to Mother Elder and Yggdrasil.

"It is good to see you," Mother Elder said holding out her hand. Mr Scruffy took her hand, kissed it, and knelt in her honor.

Yggdrasil motioned for Mr Scruffy to rise. "No need for extended formalities now. We have much to discuss." Yggdrasil nodded toward the sitting room. They walked beside Mother Elder. Once seated, Yggdrasil said, "What news have you?"

"KC is lost. Gavin said she went into the MRI, but something happened and all of her did not transport. She was split into two beings—both fully functional. The portion of KC that remained behind on Earth is in a coma. We do not know where the other portion of her was transported. By the time Gavin got into the room, there was nothing he could do to change things. He tried to go through the same portal. Nothing happened." Mother Elder looked worried Mr Scruffy thought. He looked at Yggdrasil and asked, "What would you have us do now?"

"Gavin has split. Part of him must stay with the part of KC that remained. When she comes out of the coma, we will manage rejoining her in Eldershire. Have you talked with all beings in the far reaches of Eldershire?"

Mr Scruffy nodded. "All but Snowboro. Mylo will be with us later today to tell us what she found when she returned home after our gathering."

"Good," Yggdrasil said. "Let's get down to business about King Elder. What is his status?"

"He's dying. With no male heir, his granddaughter, Princess Istar, is having a fight on her hands for the other leaders to allow her to replace him on the throne."

"Who is her competitor?" Yggdrasil said.

"There is a new charismatic life form that came to camp. He is making a big impression on the Elderians with his flamboyant approach." Mr Scruffy said.

"What do we know about him?" Yggdrasil said.

"Understand, I've not seen him. This description comes from our scouts. He appears at times in the form of a vilde ravn, a supernatural raven, but is most often seen as a large, strong humanoid. His black, oily hair is worn tight in a ponytail, revealing his thin, sinister face. His expressive black eyes are set concealed within their sockets with large bushy black brows. Smooth skin compliments his cheekbones and leaves a satisfying memory of his fortunate looks. This is the face of Barnabus. He stands high among the others who may seek King Elder's throne. We have little information about him—where he came from or his history. He always wears black and is attractive, which makes his ability to turn heads problematic."

"Princess Istar's troubles stem from what?" Mother Elder asked.

"It is not clear. She is loved by the Elderians of the camp. King

Elder is still revered. We do not know how Barnabus is able to sway the interest of the various tree-being species. Some Elderian leaders are fearful Princess Istar may fall victim to his charms, if she hasn't already."

"Troubling." Yggdrasil got up and walked over to the mantel at the center of the far wall. "We have other worries. I'm having a difficult time picking up KC's presence in Eldershire. Many seasons ago, we gave her a locket by way of her Mother to keep an enduring connection with us. The necklace was in KC's family for many eons. It is not clear when, but each direct descendent was charged with protecting it. Only when the BlueStone was needed, would the keeper of the locket be required to use it. And, before she was lost, we verified she had it. Now, I sense the locket is not with her. What could it mean?"

"Are we sure she is in Eldershire?" Mr Scruffy asked.

"We're positive she made it here. Both of us felt her presence, but it was weak. With the news she only partially transported, it explains why her presence felt was weak." Mother Elder pointed to herself and Yggdrasil. "Two Two-Moons ago, it weakened further."

Mr Scruffy stood up. "You don't think she was harmed, do you?"

"It is more likely the locket was taken off her being. We must find her quickly. We do not know the power this Barnabus has. It seems he is working with someone, but we have no idea who it might be. If I thought for one minute that Nukpana was still alive, I'd be worried." Yggdrasil picked up a book off the table near the mantel and walked back over to the others.

"What is this?" Mr Scruffy asked.

"Unyore there was not much known about the Great Scrolls of Life. Nukpana saw them when she was a young girl, but Lug Elder has only heard about them from the teachings of his father. It is not clear if Nukpana destroyed the Scrolls at some point, or if she holds them in protection. However, we believe this book I hold is what is left of the collection of The Great Scrolls of Life," Mother Elder said.

"Where did you find it?"

"Fergus of the Dryads and Lorne of the Foxes found it during one of their expeditions north of Snowboro. They brought this to us a few seasons back. Having Fergus serve as Dr. Crowell gave us early notice that Nukpana was alive and starting to make changes." Mother Elder paused. She took the book and placed it back on the mantel.

Yggdrasil said, "Upon learning about Nukpana making her moves toward KC, we tried to get the book translated. We have not been able to do so. It appears to be in an old language of Earth, maybe that of Ogham. We hoped KC would look at it when she arrived."

"Why did you think she would know how to read it?"

"We didn't know if she could read it, but we did think she might be able to make out a few words or know whom we could speak with on Earth about being able to read it," Mother Elder said.

Mother Elder stepped forward. "Ralph, the Counselor of the Wolves, shared Eldershire lore about the Scrolls. He said that if the Scrolls were to come to harm for whatever reason, whether to make something happen in the offender's favor or to prevent something from happening that was prophesied, the damage to the Scrolls would be for naught. The Scrolls would be destroyed yet the prophecy would come to past."

"Is Ralph with King Elder?" Mr Scruffy was starting to worry.

"I'm beginning to think we leaders are being separated on purpose by some unknown force," Yggdrasil said. "Worry can cause undue stress."

Mr Scruffy said, "Wise words."

Mother Elder said, "And, what says Mylo?"

"Mylo told me earlier that Gavin would see to it that the part of KC remaining on Earth would transport to Eldershire safely. While serving as a go between with Jack, Gavin would communicate with Mylo every Two-Moons. When Mylo joins us, we should learn more." Mr Scruffy wrinkled his head feathers. "I hope."

Yggdrasil tapped his foot and looked at Mother Elder. "Ralph joined King Elder Four Two-Moons ago. He is to report to us Early Two-Moons."

"Good. Mylo said she'd be here about that time." Mr Scruffy got up and walked over to the opening, which offered a view over the valley below leading to Mushroom Alley. "Should I fly down to greet them? The Two-Moons and Two-Suns are beginning to align?"

"Yes. We need to find KC." Mother Elder said. "We need *all of her* here. The sooner she is here, the faster we can rejoin her. The quest she must complete will determine if Eldershire can be saved from the grips of the manipulative powers of Barnabus and his followers."

"DAD, what do you mean? What happened?" Bill asked giving Jack a perplexed look.

"Like we told you the other day, KC was brought here to find out why she continued to hear voices no one else hears and to see images of things no one else sees. Dr. Crowell believed your Mom was having TIAs. The MRI was supposed to help us learn what is wrong." Jack got up and walked over to the window and stared out. After a minute, he turned, and then went back toward his chair.

"That's the crazy thing," Jack said. He looked at Bill while sitting down on his chair that was near the doors leading into the hospital testing area. "No one knows what happened. She's in a coma. That's all they would tell me." He placed his forehead in his hands and began to cry. "She kept telling me the voice she heard was not fake—that her head hurt. Oh, God! Why didn't I listen?"

Bill pulled a chair near his father, and sat beside him. "But, Dad? That's not your fault."

Jack nodded. "I know in my head it's not. But, in my heart—" His voice trailed off. "I don't even know what—."

Bill put his hand on his Dad's knee. Jack swallowed, then said, "Dr. Crowell said a technician was operating the MRI and the test was about to begin. Without warning, KC's heart began to go into AFib. Then, she stopped breathing. They rushed in and were able to stabilize her, but she was in a coma."

Bill stood up. He paced up and down the hallway. He slapped his thigh. "Dad, I'm wondering."

Jack looked up at him with tear stains on his cheeks. Bill sat down beside him again. "Did you mention that Mom said the voice told her she would be taken away?"

"Yes. We didn't get to talk about that much," Jack said.

"Maybe her brain was playing tricks on her and this coma is her 'being taken' away. Was Dr. Crowell able to get any MRI pictures before Mom went into a coma?"

"I don't know. Why?"

"We might be able to—"

Marie walked up to them. "I'm so sorry it took me so long to get here. What's happened?"

Bill gave Marie a hug. "Mom's in a coma. It happened during the test."

"What?" Marie set her purse down on a nearby table. Bill pulled a chair over for Marie to sit near them. "Where is she now?"

"We don't know," Jack said. "Dr. Crowell said they were in the midst of trying to determine what happened and why, and they are running more tests before they move her back to her room."

Stunned silence seemed to echo in the hallway. The double doors to the testing area opened and Dr. Crowell, Nurse Gay Lynn, and Gavin walked up to Jack and his family.

"Mr. Carson, we're glad to see you have someone with you."

"This is my son, Bill, and his wife, Marie." Jack said despondently.

Dr. Crowell extended her hand to Bill and Marie. "This is Nurse Gay Lynn, and Gavin is the MRI technician. We would like for all three of you to come with us. We need to speak with you."

Bill stood up. "You **are** going to tell us what happened!"

"We understand your concern. If you will come with us to my office, we will be able to explain what we know at this time and our recommendations."

Jack stood up while trying to keep his emotions in check. He put his arm around Bill's shoulders and took Marie's hand. "I'm not sure what else we can do. Let's see what can be done."

ONCE EVERYONE WAS SEATED, Dr. Crowell explained what she and her colleagues believed happened to KC while she was in the MRI tube.

Jack listened intently. Fear was crushing him. His heart was breaking, but he tried to listen to the technical explanation of what they thought happened to his beloved wife. She must be so frightened stuck inside her brain.

"My darling," he whispered. Tears flowed down his cheeks.

AFTER MR SCRUFFY MET with Yggdrasil, Mother Elder, and Mylo, he and Mylo joined up with Fergus, the bear; Iolair, King of the Bald Eagles; and Lorne, the fox at the border between Mushroom

Alley and Snowboro. A fire in a pit was keeping the cold at bay; they sat nearby.

"We're pleased that Fergus could rejoin us in Eldershire as a split being. Your work with KC at the hospital is helping us stay informed with what is going on. Since Gavin is also split between the two worlds, Yggdrasil suggested Fergus come as a split being to this meeting to aid us in our discussions. Mother Elder said she was sure the area we just combed was the place where KC initially crossed over into Eldershire. It was the last location they felt KC's presence with certainty."

"Has anything happened around here in the last Two-Sun-Two-Moon cycles?" Lorne asked.

"There was the harvest *Samhain* celebrations," Mylo replied.

"What did the leader of this sector of Snowboro have to say?" Iolair asked flapping his wings to move some heat from the fire closer to the group.

"Careful," Mylo said moving back from the group. "I can't take the heat like you."

"Ah, dear lady, my apologies," Iolair said.

"Seborn, the Sector Leader, said that when KC touched the BlueStone, she disappeared." Mylo looked to each of them. Their faces were stern. "She still had on the locket that was supposed to help us know where she is located. At least, they think so. We are at a loss as to why she can't be sensed. If she is alive, there is no reason why we shouldn't be able to connect with her."

"Unless some other force is stopping us from sensing her," Mr Scruffy said. He got up and walked to the edge of the fire, picked up a stick, and began to poke at the flames. "Something isn't right. Something has happened that everything is out of balance. KC was supposed to transport intact. There was no reason a part of her would have stayed behind."

Fergus picked up a stick and joined Mr Scruffy in poking the fire. "I wonder," he said. "I wonder if there isn't more evil going on here than we anticipate. What would Barnabus do if he knew KC was back? Does he have the power to reach beyond this world?"

"You might have hit onto something there," Mr Scruffy sat down, rested his head on his wing tip. "Suppose we are looking at this all wrong? Suppose KC is hiding from us out of fear. Mylo, what is the promise of the *Samhain*?"

"Its meaning is glossed as 'summer's end.'" Mylo said. "*Sam* meaning summer and *fuin* for the later *'hain'* as end. It is a time of gathering. It is a time when the doorways to the Otherworld open allowing supernatural beings and the souls of the dead to come into our world. It is the festival for the dead. *Samhain* promises regeneration at a time of death, which means it is easier to communicate with those who have left this life. That is *Samhain's* promise."

"Where would KC go then?" Mr Scruffy mused. "Where?"

CHAPTER 14
BARNABUS

Barnabus and his Trebbians gathered in a large area of the Wild Woods. Below the tree canopy they talked of what they wanted. The Two-Moons, high in the sky, cast a light down on the topmost platform. Barnabus stood before them, and then held his arms up. The Trebbians became silent, and looked up to him.

"I stand before you now, more confident than I've ever felt before. More proud than all those who ruled the Land of Eldershire. I am here for you. I am the best leader you will ever need. I hate what you hate. I, alone, can fix it." The crowd cheered him on.

"We, together, can rule them all. We can be the One Group. We can make Eldershire all we want it to be in our way!" Barnabus said looking out over the lectern. He looked with a proud grin at the crowd, *his* Trebbians.

"We're for You! We're for You!" The Trebbians roared.

"Here we are. In this time. In this place. At the base of Red Bluff's Divide on the banks of Stone's River. We will cross, and then make our way to the Elder Camp. We will take them by surprise. They are fools. Idiots. Weaklings."

The Trebbians yelled, "We. Hate. Weaklings! We. Hate. Weaklings!

Barnabus walked along the platform raising his arms up and down encouraging them to continue. Back at the lectern, he said, "You sound so good! Together we will rule!"

The Trebbians cried out, "We. Will. Rule! We. Will. Rule!"

"Yes! We will! Together!

Barnabus turned, walked over to the edge of the platform, and took a running leap into the crowd of Trebbians standing in front of him. The Trebbians held their arms out and caught him, lifting him up into the air. Barnabus went sailing back upon the platform, landing on his feet. The Trebbians went wild screaming their support. Barnabus knew he held them in his palms.

Barnabus said, "You are my Trebbians. Elderians. You know. Some are allies. Some are enemies; some don't deserve to be here. Will you help me?"

The Trebbians chanted, "Kill! Kill! Kill!"

"Okay. Okay." Barnabus stared at his crowd. "I've never done this before. I hope you will stand with me." Barnabus waited and looked at the assembled crowd. Each section cheered in support when he pointed toward them.

"Okay. This is good." He shook his head. "Now, let's do a pledge. A swearing. Raise your hands." He waited. "I do solemnly swear." The crowd repeated him. "No matter how I feel. No matter what I must do. We will stand with you! We will fight for you! We will be loyal for you!" The crowd repeated his words.

Barnabus looked at the crowd, and then said, "Thank you." He smiled. His plan had begun.

The crowd broke out into a resounding cheer of support.

Barnabus looked toward the dark horizon. The Two-Moons were high in the sky. He saw her staring back at him. She was there. He was pleased.

🐌

THE METAMORPHOSIS SEEMED to KC like it lasted for a long time. Either that, or she was dreaming. She had time to watch what was happening around her. The lack of light in front of her didn't remove her ability to see the Snowquidians in the distance with a halo surrounding them.

They were moving away from her. *Am I falling?* She looked to her left, and then to her right. Images were moving past her with a kaleidoscope of color. Or, was she moving past them? She couldn't decide. She looked down to see if she was falling, but it was too dark to see. She looked back to her left. The images were moving by her at a slower pace. She knew what each of them was; she could even smell some of them—like fresh baked bread. She looked up. It was too dark to see. Looking back at the Snowquidians, she saw what was left of them, a tiny dot, closing out like a light bulb being turned off. They were gone.

KC reached out to touch an image. One stopped. "Oh, what have I done?"

She looked around and realized she was casting light; she had stopped moving or falling. She could see to her left and right, but not above her or below. The image before her was that of bookshelves. On one shelf was a door.

Reaching in to the image, she grabbed hold of what she thought was a book. It was a map, folded into many folds the size of a small notebook. She rotated it around. Nothing looked right at that moment. She refolded the map, and then decided to put it into her back pocket. She reached back into the image. This time she pulled out a jar. She rotated it around. There was no label. She held it up to try and determine what was inside. The glass, opaque, did not reveal its contents—liquid, solid, or even gas. She moved to place it back on the shelf.

"I wouldn't do that," the tiny voice said.

"What?"

"I wouldn't do what you are about to do. It would be an insult." The tiny voice squeaked at the end.

"To whom?"

"To what." The tiny voice replied.

"To what, then?"

"To me." The tiny voice boomed in KC's ear.

She jerked around and looked in all directions—up, down, left, right. She saw nothing. "Where are you?"

"I'm right here, beside you."

KC looked down, and to her right. It was what she thought was a tiny mouse; yet he looked different from the mice she'd seen before. It was dressed in what looked to KC like a musketeer costume straight out of the Renaissance. He wore a wide-brimmed hat with a feather plume, a draped tabard royal blue, trimmed in gold embroidery accented with the Tree of Life with a light blue background where the typical fleur-de-lis would be, a silver ankh dangled from his neck on a silver chain, a silver sword hung from his belt buckle, and of course the black leather high boots finished off its look.

"I can't believe my eyes. Have I imagined you?"

"No. I'm quite real. Let me introduce myself to you." The tiny creature grew to the size of a small dog.

"Oh, my!" KC wanted to scream, but covered her mouth instead and held in the scream. She wasn't sure where she was, and what effect it would have. "Who are you?"

"If you would calm down, I plan to introduce myself. I told you that, didn't I?"

"Yes. That you did," KC scoffed.

"Well. I see there is no reason to be of service to you." The larger, tiny creature reduced in size.

"Where?" KC swallowed. "Where are you going?" The tiny creature looked up at her. "I'm sorry. But, you did startle me."

It regrew this time to the size of a large dog. KC leaned backwards; his size started to crowd her space.

"May I ask what you are? You seem to grow and shrink at will."

"You may ask, but it is much more polite to know my name first."

KC extended her hand. "Excuse me. I am Kay "KC" Carson. Human from Earth."

The creature extended its paw, shook KC's hand, and said, "I am Sir Lafayette de Marquis, but most just call me Lafayette. I and my three brothers serve as the guards for Mother Elder and her designate, Princess Istar. I, in particular, am their secret confidante."

KC looked around. "Are they here? Can they see me?"

"No. I came to meet my brothers and stumbled upon you. Where did you come from?"

"Your brothers. You're not part of the Three Musketeers are you?" KC muffled a giggle. *I shouldn't laugh, she thought. I don't want to offend him any more than I have. I wonder what he is?*

"You haven't offended me. And, I'm not a mouse as you supposed. I'm a lemming. We are special rodents with special talents. My brothers and I are the Four Lemmketeers!" Lafayette bowed and came to attention. "We service Mother Elder!"

"Oh, dear."

"Yes. I read minds too." The larger lemming shrunk down to a smaller size. KC felt free to move and turned toward him.

"Look. You've got to realize how bizarre all of this is to me."

"Why? You've been in Eldershire before. Mother Elder told us you might be somewhere near. Mylo and the others don't know where you are. Why did you take off the necklace Mother Elder gave you?"

"I didn't. Somehow it was lost when I transported to wherever I am now. I don't even know how I got back to Eldershire. Besides, I didn't meet you before did I? And, I don't understand how I got here. Where *is* here?"

"If you mean where we are right now, nowhere."

"Do you talk in riddles?"

"Yes. No. Sometimes."

"Where am I going then?"

"Nowhere right now. This is the outer band of Eldershire. You've gotten yourself into a worm. How did you get here and not know what you were doing?"

KC scoffed. She looked at Lafayette and realized he did not see the humor. "That was an important question. I guess, I should ask. How do I get out?"

"You can come with me."

"That works."

"Hold your hands out and we will tumble to the next location." The lemming reduced in size, held out his little arms, and he was gone. Suddenly, he poked his head back in and said, "Aren't you coming?"

KC held out her arms and she was standing beside Lafayette in a field of blooming mushrooms. "Mushroom Alley!" she said.

THE TWO-SUNS WERE high in the sky when Lafayette turned to KC. "We've walked a good ways since we left the worm. You've not said a word."

"We were in Mushroom Alley. Now it appears, we are not far from Snowboro, straight ahead and past the great mountains is the Oak plateau that takes us to Mother Elder."

Lafayette smiled. "Good. Don't you want to know where we are going?"

"I imagine we will see Mylo. Will we go on to see Mother Elder and Yggdrasil? I'd like to know more about you and why I didn't meet you when I was here before."

"You are a strange one, you are. We'll be meeting up with my brothers on our way to see Mother Elder. They should be coming through that clearing anytime." Lafayette grew up to large dog size. "After they meet you, I'll tell you what you want to know." Lafayette looked toward the clearing. "You stand there behind that tree. I'll need to explain who you are to them or they won't be friendly. Eldershire isn't the nice place you left."

KC moved behind a large tree whose bark reminded her of the great redwoods of home. Realizing she did not carry a weapon, she crouched down and prayed Lafayette would keep her safe.

A BLOOD-CURDLING CRY came from the pus-covered face that stared into the mirror. Her skin, covered in warts, opened lesions bleeding, her crankiness growing with her hatred of KC.

"She is to blame for this! She caused the transformation of me when we split during the transport through that Earth machine!"

Barnabus cleared his throat.

Nukpana turned and Barnabus gasped in horror upon seeing how ravaged her face had become. He stepped back fearful.

"Why are you here?" A murderous rage grew in her.

"I come to give you news."

"You come to gloat!" She wished to berate him, but turned back to the mirror instead. "This must be undone," she whispered. Nukpana turned back to Barnabus, "My time is short. What news have you that I've not already acquired?"

"Our plan is working. With the help of my most loyal, the Trebbians are growing in number. More of the ruthless Elderians from King Elder's Camp are joining our force."

Nukpana turned back to the mirror and stared into its reflection.

Barnabus cleared his throat.

"Is there more?" Nukpana turned to him with her anger in check.

"The Earthling, KC, is making her way to see Mother Elder. Her guard is protecting her. We can't get to her without someone knowing our plans."

Nukpana walked down from the platform where the mirror was at a tilt, reflecting the back of her body. She watched Barnabus' eyes. She could feel him staring at her. She saw in his eyes what she knew she looked like—ragged and disheveled. She thought she might be dying; a slow death. *How much of it was due to her separation from KC?* She didn't know, but she would find out soon.

She turned and flashed anger, "You know NO ONE must learn of our plans! Be gone with you. I must take care of me!"

"At your will," Barnabus took a deep bow and backed out of the room. He walked a few paces, turned back, and saw Nukpana lost in her own hideous image.

WALKING DOWN THE DEEP, dark corridor, he thought how he must use her weakness while he could. Barnabus was pleased with his prowess.

Leaving Graves Mountain, he walked up to Olaf the Flashy, his right-hand comrade, and one of a few he trusted.

Slapping him on the back, he said, "She hasn't long. The damage to her from separating from that Earthling is starting to show. Our power is growing. It scares her."

Olaf grinned. "When Boss? When can I have her?"

"Time. Time is ours." Barnabus walked with Olaf out to his waiting entourage. He said to Olaf, "We must be careful to whom we give our trust. With our plans to kill KC over Nukpana's wishes, we will seal our control of the Trebbians. We can then begin to thwart Nukpana. Power will be yours and mine."

Olaf grinned, removing his pristine sword causing it to glisten from the Two-Suns' rays; the rays bounced reflections in multiple directions.

CHAPTER 15

THE LEMMKETEERS

"My three partners in crime," Lafayette intoned.

KC saw what were three more lemmings dressed like Lafayette. Their tabards are emblazoned with the Tree of Life with one difference—each tabard was designed with different color combinations, all striking and commanding attention.

"Let me introduce you handsome gents to my new friend." Lafayette turned and looked back at KC. He motioned for her to step forward.

KC took a step from behind the tree, at the same time all three lemmings pulled out their swords, grew to the size of a large horse, and yelled in unison, "On guard!"

KC shrunk back behind the tree.

"Whoa!" Lafayette ran over to KC. Pulling on her arm he said, "Come on. I should have prepared them first. They were startled seeing you." He pulled her away from the tree, and then turned to his brothers. "Seriously! You guys can reduce your size. This is KC. She's our charge. Mother Elder asked us to protect her. Remember?"

"KC?" One of the brothers said, reducing in size. He walked over toward KC. "I beg your pardon. We thought you were an evil foundling who might have tricked our brother." He made a deep bow. "My name is Sir Frederick O' Tomhrair, the descendant of Tomer at your service." He rose back up to his full height of about six inches. He then grew to the same size as Lafayette and said, "My friends call me Tonner not to be confused with Tomer, my family name." He smiled.

KC considered whether she should say something. She looked to Lafayette for guidance. He was motioning to the other two brothers to come closer. KC looked back at Tonner. "Glad to meet you." She decided not to courtesy or bow. Tonner nodded at her.

Lafayette said, "This is Sir Logan Ó Ayrshire De Auchinleck. He goes by Logan. And, he doesn't say much, but he is very observant. You'll find he'll protect you when you least expect it." Logan bowed with a royal flare.

KC acknowledged him and said, "Glad to meet you, Logan."

Lafayette whispered to KC. "He is paranoid about everyone and everything."

"Oh? Good to know. Is he often right?"

"Yes. That's why we don't mind his overactive imagination. His concerns tend to prove worthy of our concern."

"Who is that?" KC pointed to the one lemming still standing back away from her. He had what looked like a scowl on his face. "Can a lemming be mean?" she whispered to Lafayette.

"Yes." Lafayette turned toward his brother. "This is Sir Gareth de Claytor. We call him Crab."

KC stepped toward him. "Glad to meet you, Crab."

Crab looked at her, tilted his head, and said, "Why are you here? You are wasting our time." He turned and stormed off into the forest.

Tonner said, "Don't mind him. He is crabby all the time. We mostly ignore his temper, but he is a master at using his sword and protecting those that need protection whether they know it or not."

"Let's make our way to Mother Elder," Lafayette said. "She'll be expecting us before Early Two-Moons."

They had walked a fair distance when KC said to Lafayette, "Do you mind if I ask you a question while we walk?"

"No. What do you want to know?"

"I guess I should say several questions." KC raised her eyebrows, and gave a questioning gaze. "Tell me more about you and your brothers. Why are you called Lemmketeers?"

Lafayette laughed. "Did you hear her?" The others stopped and Logan walked back toward KC.

"You said Lemmketeers, but you were thinking musketeers." KC nodded. "You don't see our muskets, do ye?" KC shook her head. "That's because we keep them small until we need them." Logan turned to Lafayette. "Are you sure she isn't a plant from some evil witch?"

KC moved in front of him before he turned to walk away. She pointed her finger at Logan's chest. "Evidently, you don't know about me. I'm the one that retrieved the Efil Stone. I did away with Nukpana. At least, I thought I did. That is until I came back here. I didn't ask to do so. And, I don't need you giving me a hard time just because you are paranoid. I'm not in cahoots with any witch." KC pushed past him and walked toward the Oak Plateau.

"KC, wait!" Lafayette said jogging to catch up with her. "You shouldn't go off on your own in this part of the forest."

KC walked past Crab. He grunted. She turned to him. "You got a problem with me?"

"No." He replied.

"Good." She turned back to Lafayette. "Why can't I walk through here on my own? I never had an issue in the Mushroom Alley before."

"I mentioned things have changed since you were here. We have many Elderians that have turned to spying for the one who wants to be ruler."

"Who is that?" KC asked looking at each of them.

"We can't say his name here," Tonner replied. "It is best you wait and speak with Mother Elder. The forest has ears."

"If you namby-pambies have had enough of this jibber-jabber, let's get a move on. The Two-Suns are starting to set. Or are you too busy chatting to notice?" Crab pushed past KC.

Lafayette walked beside KC. "Tell me, Lafayette. Are you all really brothers? I mean, what are you really? You said you had a pack. What about it? Will we see King Elder? And, why is Princess Istar not the heir-apparent to King Elder?"

"You were right."

"About what?"

"You do have several questions." Lafayette said. "Your last two questions will be answered by Mother Elder. The pack you ask about, well, let's say that it was assigned to us by birth. We *are* all brothers. I'm the oldest. Crab is the youngest. We follow in our parents' path in service to Mother Elder and all of Eldershire. Once a Lemmketeer, always a Lemmketeer."

"I had no idea. By birth." KC pondered his words. "Why is he so mean?"

"Who?"

"Crab."

"He likes to have his tea in the morning. This morning, because of us having to go to Mother Elder, and running into you, he didn't get it."

"I get it. I'm not so good without my coffee in the morning."

Lafayette and KC began to move along the path. She said, "I read a quote by a wise man from Earth who lived during the Roman times, Marcus Aurelius. He said, 'The soul becomes dyed with the color of its thoughts.' Is that why Crab's cloak is colored red with black while yours is blue with gold, Tonner's is orange with yellow, and Logan's is magenta with green?"

"You, my dear, are wiser than your years. The branding of us is indeed through our souls. More will be revealed." Lafayette looked overhead. "It is getting late. We must move quickly. Will you run?"

"Sure." Her initial running steps caused KC to think back on the last time she ran through a forest. Smiling, she remembered her time with Ish running through the Wild Woods the first time she was in Eldershire. "Life seems to always cycle around, doesn't it?"

"That it does," Lafayette said growing to a horse size. "That it does."

HE WALKED BACK AND FORTH, pacing in front of the huge picture window that looked out over Snow Valley, and the forest toward King Elder's Camp. While waiting in Graves Mountain, he had time to recognize the fact that he had become a willing pawn of Barnabus. Worse, when he fell for his proposal, he had no idea how narcissistic, evil, and guileless Barnabus was until that moment. *What have I done?*

The door behind him opened. He turned with fear rising in his throat.

"You look nervous, Isicaranon, my trusted counselor. What bothers you?" Barnabus said, walking toward him with determination.

Isicaranon turned around and faced Barnabus. He knew he had to think quickly. He must not let Barnabus know his decision or it would mean certain death.

"I've been thinking about your plan. I'm wondering if you shouldn't adjust your timing slightly. Princess Istar is growing in strength, this much we know. Yet, if we wait four or five turns of the Two-Moons, we will be able to surprise them." Isicaranon held up a parchment scroll. "They made it clear they know your plans." He handed the scroll to Barnabus.

Barnabus' hand snatched the scroll out of Isicaranon's hand, and then threw it into the nearby fire. "That's what I think of them and their supposed knowledge." Barnabus walked toward the window. "Do you really think they know more than me? Me. Who knows when and where they lay in their beds this very night!" He turned and looked at Isicaranon. "We ride tonight. We'll show those Elderians who rules this land! Make plans to pull out before Two-Suns rising." Barnabus stormed out of the room.

Looking out the window, Isicaranon thought of his plan. He managed to sucker Barnabus into his snare. "I can't believe it."

Walking out from behind the curtain, Olaf said, "He is prime for the picking. We need only set the stage and he performs just as we knew he would."

"He will hoist with his own petard. It will be sweet revenge for what he has done to our people."

"It would be funny if it wasn't so sad. To be beaten with his own weapon *is* poetic justice for us all. I'll get word to our contacts. Stay safe, my liege."

Isicaranon watched Olaf leave the room. He picked up a piece of parchment, drew a few icons on its surface, rolled it into a tight, tiny tube. Walking over to a nearby perch, he held out his hand. The owl moved onto his gloved hand.

While placing the tiny tube on the owl's leg, Isicaranon said, "I'm entrusting you with this important message for the only beings in Eldershire that know the truth. It is imperative you make it to their camp. Do you understand?"

"I do. I will do honor for you." The owl moved to the window.

"Fly fast. Fly hard. Our lives depend on it!" Isicaranon opened the window. The owl lifted off. "Now, I must wait."

BARNABUS STOOD when Olaf walked through the door. "Well?"

"Isicaranon fell for my deception. Hook, line, and sinker. I should be a fisherman of thieves."

"That you already are, my comrade. That you are." Barnabus patted Olaf on the back and walked past him to the nearby table. "Come here. I want to show you our forces."

Olaf walked over to where Barnabus stood.

"We have an army of four Trebbians and four Grey Menace legions, the leftover of Nukpana's rule, under the command of Publius Scorpion and Tiberius "Ti" Cowardius Longus."

"I know the many conquests of General Scorpion, but I'm not familiar with Commander Longus." Olaf sat down at the table. He looked up to Barnabus.

"Ti, as he likes to be called, is a fool. But, he is ruthless. He will kill for the sake of killing. Right now, we need to inflict as much damage as possible to the resistance. If I could get my claws on that old, scruffy owl, and his company of ingrates, it would rid us of the blockage to my ultimate power." Barnabus stood tapping his finger on the battle plan map.

"You will succeed. You have the power and will of the Trebbians and the Grey Menace. No one has the power you have. No one ever has." Olaf exalted.

Barnabus agreed with his loyal servant. He walked over to the map of Eldershire on the wall, painted in the various colors highlighting the devastation each sector had suffered under his rule since he managed to knock Princess Istar out of her reign.

"It has been a long, hard, and well fought conquest to rule King Elder's Camp. I find it difficult to understand why the ingrates under Mr Scruffy's command don't realize their fate is in my hands. Their quest is futile. They will lose. I always win. The battle with Princess Istar and her weaklings is only the beginning. That successful skirmish proved that our superiority is eminent. We will win! We always win! We are winning!"

"You are right! Just! Powerful!" Olaf continued. "I've been waiting for a leader to come along that would prove that we lowly working beings of Eldershire, who gain nothing each time we work harder, would be rewarded by your presence. We are indeed justified to follow in your footsteps."

Barnabus looked with confidence toward Olaf, "Just as the famous Earth leader, Adolf once said, 'I go the way that Providence dictates with an assurance of a sleep walker.' I lead, Olaf, I lead, *and* I'll win."

KC WALKED UP to Mylo and they embraced. "It's been a while." Mylo stood back and motioned for the others to move in closer.

"It has, my friend. We need you desperately now. You learned of Princess Istar's fate?"

KC looked to the other Snowquidians standing around. "No. What has happened?"

"She is resting in my thípi. Barnabus and the Trebbians overcame her and King Elder's forces. This skirmish proves Barnabus was going to take over all of Eldershire."

KC's stared. "Was she hurt?"

"Not physically. She is distraught. Her grandfather is dying. He was taken captive." Mylo watched KC move away from her.

"I have so many questions. Who is Barnabus?" KC said.

"It's best you leave that for Mother Elder and Yggdrasil to fill you in. Are you fine with waiting?"

"I guess I must. I'm glad I will get to see Mother Elder and Yggdrasil." KC looked around. "Where are Mr Scruffy, Iolair, Gavin and the rest of his company? They are all right?"

Mylo smiled. "It's like you never left. You do have many questions." Mylo wondered why she felt KC was not the same. "We are to meet Mother Elder at early Two-Moons. Let's eat. You will need energy for the journey ahead of us. You can visit with the Snowquidians that found you. Come."

Mylo motioned for them to walk to the nearby thípi. KC was walking way behind her. She wondered why KC was acting distant and not warming up to her.

KC said, "Sure. I could use some water."

Mylo looked around to see to whom KC was talking and saw no one. *She has become rather bossy.* "KC, you can get your water over there," Mylo pointed to a table near the far wall.

"Mylo, you said Princess Istar is resting in your thípi. When may I see her?"

"How about now?" the voice came from behind KC. She turned.

"Oh, my! Look at you! Beautiful. I'm so sorry to see you again under these circumstances."

"They've filled you in, then?" Princess Istar said walking up to KC. They embraced.

"Yes." KC stood back from Princess Istar.

Mylo watched with a careful eye and noted how KC kept wringing her hands.

"You weren't hurt?" KC asked.

"No. But, I should have died saving my King. I'm a failure." Princess Istar bowed her head.

KC raised her chin up. "Don't you *ever* hang your head. You have nothing to be ashamed of. Nothing! Have I made myself clear?"

Princess Istar stared at KC. "Yes." She put her arm on KC's shoulder. "You sounded like my King. Those were his words the last time I saw him."

"Good. It means he's channeling through me and he is still alive. We will find him. You can believe that with all of your being." KC turned to Mylo. "Let's go get some food. You can fill me in on what has been going on around here."

Mylo smiled while inside she felt tightness in her chest. She didn't have a desire to eat, only a need to speak with Mr Scruffy.

CHAPTER 16
MR SCRUFFY & CO

"He is a hubris nincompoop. Evil personified!" Mr Scruffy raised his wings and a scowl came across his face. Iolair took a step back.

"Whoa! Mr Scruffy, what has gotten you so riled?" Iolair looked to Gavin in hopes he would aid him in calming down Mr Scruffy. Gavin shook his head. "Why are you spreading your wings in a threatening stance? You do realize you are among friends?"

Mr Scruffy strutted across the room, made a hissing sound, and flashed his wings showing off the pure white undersides. "You are right that I'm angry. I'm as angry as any one should be under the circumstances we've been placed in. To be ostracized, shunned, by the very beings we've risked life and limb for. How dare those pompous Elderians call us traitors? It is enough to cause me to want to strangle each and every one of them." Mr Scruffy let out a long hissing sound.

"Gavin, can you help me here?" Iolair pleaded. "I'm so glad this part of you is here with us, while your split part is on Earth."

"What can I do? He's an owl—a Great Horned Owl at that. You know how they show anger. It's best we stay back and let him work through it."

Mr Scruffy turned and gave off a rapid fire clacking of his bill. The high-pitched sound caused his friends to cover their ears with their wings.

"Mr Scruffy!" Iolair bellowed. "Please stop!"

Sudden silence caused Gavin and Iolair to lower their wings and look for what silenced Mr Scruffy. Standing in the doorway was KC.

A SURGE of tension seemed to fill the room. Nukpana sat at the end of the marble top table tapping her forefinger ever so lightly. Barnabus walked over to the far end of the table and began to organize his latest report of his progress at disrupting King Elder's world. A Trebbian had walked in behind Barnabus and stood waiting.

"Sit there, to my right," Barnabus said to him. "I'll be ready in only a moment."

He stepped forward and moved to the right. I've been brought here for a specific reason, the being thought. How am I going to get through this? Why did I agree to be his Trebbian General? Only days before I was a roustabout screaming chants at the top of my lungs. I wanted revenge. I wanted to destroy the weaklings of King Elder. Not sitting here, before her, staring into *her* face.

"Do you know whom you are staring at?" Nukpana broke the silence.

"Yes," the Trebbian replied.

"Tell me what you've heard. Be forewarned, I'll know when you lie."

"As a sapling, I learned of your dealings with Elderians all through Eldershire. You were the one that killed my parents during the Great War when the Drakein roamed. I'm here to serve you."

"You are wise. Barnabus, you chose well. He will do. He appears to learn quick too." An evil laugh emerged from her throat in a low rumble.

Barnabus stood and walked toward Nukpana. "Thank you, your Treoraí." He bowed low. "Let me introduce to you Shis Kin Wu, my General of the Trebbians."

"Shis Kin Wu? What happened to Olaf?"

"Let's say he no longer is with us," Barnabus replied. "May we now strategize our next steps?"

"You may. But, first, I think I want to hear more from Shis Kin Wu. Tell me why you hate me too?"

Shis Kin Wu swallowed hard. A lump caught in his throat. "I mean no harm. I'm a full fledged Trebbian doing the bidding of Barnabus at your service." Shis Kin Wu lowered his eyes and diverted his desire to strike a kill.

"Your eyes belie your intent," Nukpana stood, flipped her long tailed dress behind her and strutted toward where Shis Kin Wu sat. "Tell me why you are trying to hide your true feelings?"

Nukpana raised Blazewing. The crystal began to glow. Barnabus stood back against the wall.

Shis Kin Wu stood. "I tell you no lies. I hold back no feelings. I share all truths."

"Falsehoods you share!" Nukpana was standing beside him. Her eyes seemed to slide into slits on the side of her face. Shis Kin Wu wondered if she was transforming before him. "Tell me now what you are thinking!"

"I wondered if you were beginning to transform before me." Shis Kin Wu diverted his eyes once more.

"Good." Nukpana lowered Blazewing and the glow of the crystal subdued. "Tell me why you are here?"

"I was hired by Barnabus to serve as his general of the Trebbians."

"What does a general of the Trebbians do?"

"I don't know. I was told by Barnabus I'd learn while I'm here with you."

"Have you fought in many wars?"

"Only the one when you scorched our encampment. I'm willing to do what needs to be done to overthrow the weaklings of Eldershire. Without their indecisiveness, we wouldn't be overtaken."

"You believe you are being overtaken?" Nukpana lifted Blazewing a little higher.

"No. But, many do. I believe you want to make Eldershire great again. I want that too. That is why I'm willing to do what I need to do to help you and Barnabus.

"Help me *and* Barnabus?" Nukpana turned and looked back at Barnabus.

Shis Kin Wu looked down. He knew he may have laid Barnabus open, but he no longer cared. It was clear to him that Barnabus had lied about his goal for the people of Eldershire. Had he known that Barnabus was working for Nukpana, he would have joined forces with Scruffy. Now, it looked like he was stuck. What could he do?

"Indeed, what can you do?" Nukpana raised Blazewing; its sphere began to glow.

"Wait!" Barnabus raised his hand. "He will be useful to us."

MYLO WALKED around the corner of her cabin and saw a figure lurking around. It couldn't be, she thought. "KC? Is that you?"

"Hi," KC said. "Yes."

"Where have you been? Seborn and the rest of the pack have looked everywhere for you. How did you get here?"

"I found myself here and I wasn't sure if you were alone. I didn't mean to look like I was being a peeping tom." KC smiled.

"A what?"

"Sneaking around, looking into your cabin. I'm hungry. Do you think we can get some food?"

"Sure. Where are my manners?" Mylo smiled. "Come on in. We will join Seborn and the others soon."

KC WALKED into the room followed by Mylo, Seborn, and the other three Snowquidians who took care of KC when she first appeared in Snowboro.

"Seems I arrived just in time," KC smiled.

Mr Scruffy returned to his normal size, sat back on his haunches, and then used his wings to flatten down his feathers and preen himself.

"Well, is that all you three are going to do to greet me back in Eldershire?" KC walked over to Gavin and Iolair. "I understand Mr Scruffy is angry, but what about the two of you?"

Iolair extended his wing toward KC. "If I could wrap my wings around you, I would. It is good to see you. When did you return?"

"Thank you, Iolair. It is good to be here, at least I hope it will be." KC turned to Gavin and said while reaching out to him, "It is good to see you both." Gavin extended his wing. She turned back toward Mr Scruffy. "And, what do you have to say for yourself?"

Mr Scruffy replied, "You didn't answer when you returned."

"I will. But, first, what is happening with you?"

He paced around the room while he related the events in Eldershire since KC left them. "And, since that time, Barnabus and his mindless followers have turned our existence into pure unadulterated terror. He is a menace. Evil. Personified. Pure and simple." Mr Scruffy kept pacing the room.

KC moved to a nearby table, sat down in a chair, and then looked around the room. Mr Scruffy tried to figure out how he could calm down. He couldn't help how he felt seeing KC here when she was supposed to be with Mother Elder. Besides, something was off. He knew she wouldn't like him testing her, but until he knew more, there was no choice.

"Mr Scruffy!" He turned and looked at KC. "Sit down! Let someone else talk." Her face was stern. *She is staring at me. Why?*

"Let's see how she reacts with my territorial call," Mr Scruffy telepathically said to Mylo. He hoped he would be able to reach KC's better instincts without raising his claws. He turned, walked toward KC while making a loud, low in pitch, sound. "Hoo-hoo-hooooo."

KC shuffled her feet and looked to the others.

Mr Scruffy sat down beside her, and then moved his wing over onto her knee.

"As you have told me," KC said. "Half of the beings of King Elder's Camp that fought against Nukpana when I was last here are now working in cahoots with Barnabus."

"One could say they were blindsided by his charm, charisma, and the various promises he made. His lies will not be a benefit to anyone but Barnabus and his minions. Those minions have adopted a name," Gavin chimed in. "They call themselves the Trebbians. Barnabus has a few of the Atcenians from Nukpana's reign helping him too. There is also a pack of wights we are not fully informed about."

"Very good information, Gavin," KC replied. "We should pool all of our knowledge of Barnabus and determine what kind of hold he has over Eldershire before we can right the wrongs. So, who would like to go first? I'll make note of what we learn."

"Do you not think we haven't already done this?" Iolair said standing up and beginning to pace.

"Why are all of you so nervous? First, it was Mr Scruffy pacing. Now, it is you, Iolair. Each of you seem to be on edge. What is going on here?"

"We're fugitives on the run in our own land," Gavin exclaimed. "This has never been the case for any of us. We don't know what to do."

"That is understandable," Seborn said. "My companions and I have lived your life for many years. We know what it is like to be falsely accused and hunted like an animal for the slaughter. May I give you some advice?"

"Forgive me, Seborn. I failed to properly introduce you and your Snowquidian Pack. Let me do that first please," Mylo said, stepping forward.

Seborn motioned to the other Snowquidians to join him standing beside Mylo.

"Mr Scruffy, Gavin, Iolair, and the rest of you, I'm honored to present to you Seborn Armenius, Snowquidian Pack Leader. With him are the members of his pack. They serve as outlook and centurions for Snowboro."

"Thank you, Mylo," Seborn said. "Beside me is Arrington Balam."

He nodded, and then bowed. "It is an honor to serve you. My friends call me Arrington."

Iolair nodded. Seborn pointed to the next Snowquidian.

"Eri," Eri bowed. "He doesn't use a family name nor does he know much about his family, but he is observant."

"And, last but not least, Larissa Mar."

She stepped forward and said, "Most call me by my full name, Larissa Mar. And, I am at your service."

Mr Scruffy said, "We are glad you are here. Can you possibly give us some insights into what happened when you found KC when she first arrived?"

"We hope we can. We'll tell you what we know. We do not know when she first arrived. From the time we found her, she was with us six full Two-Moons. Then, she disappeared before our eyes." Seborn looked to his companions. "Any of you want to offer information?"

Arrington said, "When we found KC, we didn't know who she was. And, she was in what we thought was a deep sleep. We couldn't ask her where she came from or how long she had lain in the snow."

KC said. "I had no idea when you found me, and I didn't get the chance to thank you for caring for me. From what I've heard today." KC looked around the room. "All of you are in a bit of a quandary. Based on what I know about Barnabus, are you sure he is not working with Nukpana?"

"What?" Mr Scruffy grew to the size of a human. He faced KC directly. "What are you talking about? Whoooo are you?" His anger was on display. "You can't be KC and speak her name so freely!"

KC reacted by looking to Mr Scruffy with her mouth open, and then she felt something at her side. She slowly reached back and felt her sword—the Sword of Fea.

Holding Fea up, KC said, "Would this glow yellow if it were not I?" KC stared.

Mr Scruffy reduced in size. "You have the sword." He moved closer to her and raised his wing to touch it. "Where was it?"

"It does not matter now." KC ruffled the top of Mr Scruffy's head. "What matters is what we do next." Mr Scruffy began to click his beak, his breathing was loud, and he flexed his wings.

"And, just what will we do next?" Iolair asked, his voice rising with passion. "We're ostracized by our own. How can we possibly fight the likes of Barnabus and his evil doers?"

A murmur rose of agreement.

KC stood before the provoked group. "You choose to fight?" She looked to each of them. Each nodded. "Then, you find those like-minded souls that are willing to help you move forward. United under one strong belief—you are better than your adversaries! You must not allow their lies, their evil ways, their disregard for all beings to beat you down."

The band of rebels looked to each other, and then broke into separate groups. A couple talked to each other, while the others looked to Mr Scruffy.

Mr Scruffy said, "Here now. This is good for us to remember." He hoped he could keep the leaders rallied, but he wondered. "We are beginning to sound like our old selves. But, we must know what is going on in King Elder's Camp before we can make a plan to strike. KC, you said you came from there?"

"No. I didn't. And, it is time you know the truth. I have been in Eldershire about one full season or three months Earth time."

"What?" Iolair stood up. "Where? We heard you might be back, but we found no one that could tell us where you were."

"When I was transported, I was incapacitated."

"Who?" Mr Scruffy stood up. "Took care of you? Why weren't we told this before?"

"No worries. I was taken care of properly. But, those who cared for me decided not to reveal my whereabouts to protect me until I was well." The group was quiet.

"Not even to us?" Iolair asked.

"No. To no one." KC shook her head while she crossed and uncrossed her arms. "You must now be told. Nukpana is not dead!"

CHAPTER 17
A NEW VIEW

That night the rain stopped, the skies cleared. For the first time since returning to Eldershire, KC looked out through the cave opening and saw through the tree canopy the Two-Moons. A part of her felt at home. The rain soaked forest gave off the sweet smell she loved when she walked in the forest near her son's cabin. The light of the moon caused her to wonder how Bill and Marie were doing. She hoped they were well. Marie should be beginning her third trimester of pregnancy by now. Mr Scruffy approached KC.

"Do you ever get tired of looking at them?" KC pointed up to the moons.

"No. There are times they are too bright though when I'm looking for food at night," Mr Scruffy said.

"You sound like you are not happy with me?"

"What makes you say that?"

"Oh, I don't know. It's not so much your words." KC looked at him. "Maybe your tone!" She walked away from the cave entrance and into the forest.

"Where are you going?" Mr Scruffy called as he followed her.

KC turned around. "Why do you care?"

"KC wait. Don't walk away. We need to talk this out." Mr Scruffy flew over to her and took her hand in his wing. "Come. Sit over here on this tree stump. I can perch on the branch there."

They sat down and KC picked a twig up off the ground. She began to fiddle with it. They sat in silence for a while.

"Okay. You win," Mr Scruffy said. "I'm sorry. I shouldn't have taken it out on you that no one told us you were back. We are glad you are here."

"Really? If I didn't know better, I'd almost believe you think I'm not real."

"You wouldn't be too wrong." Mr Scruffy said. He struggled with the idea that she was KC. Yet, he had no major reason to believe otherwise, only his gut feeling and the little quirky things she had been doing. "I didn't believe it was you at first. I never thought you would return."

"I had no idea where I was until about a month ago."

"Mylo told you?"

"No. She didn't know I had arrived until after Seborn and his pack found me. Then, when she found out, she was thwarted by her own people. Some of the Snowquidians wanted to turn me over to that Barnabus character for the reward. Other Snowquidians—those who go about their daily lives and don't think about how their lives work—when they learned of me, they thought I'd bring all manner of evil to them. Still more wanted to follow Mylo's lead. It was a mess."

Mr Scruffy tapped his right front talon, "It sounds like it. So, you have an idea what Iolair, Gavin, and the rest of us have gone through with Barnabus and his approach to creating discontent."

"Yes, I guess so. And after talking with you, Iolair, and Gavin, I understand you believe that Barnabus has all this power to brainwash the Elderians against the resistance."

"Many of those same Elderians do not harbor ill will against King Elder or Princess Istar. It is a puzzle. It is as if the fools want to have their cake and eat it too, and aren't ashamed to tell you so."

"Nukpana's magic is stronger than you realized." KC shook her head. "She caused this."

"Don't! Do not allow Nukpana to get into your head."

KC got up and walked over to a nearby tree. "You see. She's already here."

Mr Scruffy tilted his head as though confused. *Is she going to reveal Nukpana?*

KC pointed to her head. "Here. In my head. I'm not sure how to get her out." KC's body crumbled to the forest floor and she began to sob.

Mr Scruffy was relieved, yet concerned. He moved swiftly to her side.

"How could I have known what you are going through?"

After crying a few minutes, KC said, "I wish I could have told you where I was or that I was even in Eldershire. By the time I came out of my deep sleep, you and the others were in hiding. No one dared try to contact you. I was still so weak, I had no way to know how to find you."

"And, today? How did you find us?" Mr Scruffy said. *How have you learned all you know?*

"I remembered this cave from when we had one of our last stands."

"Why else do you think you have come to us?"

"I think it was Nukpana. She went with me when I went home. I know that now. I wasn't sure what was happening to me. Jack and my children insisted I get some tests. They thought I might have had a brain tumor or even cancer. It was a cancer of sorts. It was Nukpana."

Mr Scruffy made a mental note of her words. "But how? I thought when you used Fea, the Hat, and the Efil Stone, you could destroy her?"

"As did Drakania. We were wrong. Nukpana's magic had grown stronger than anyone understood. She was able to split a portion of herself away and reside with me. It wasn't until I went through the MRI machine that I was able to split us apart again."

"An MRI? Really?"

KC nodded. "Why?"

"I was on Earth when the idea of designing an MRI machine was first discussed."

"What? Who were you with?"

"Raymond Damadian, a doctor and medical practitioner. When you get back home, you can read all about him."

"Funny. You make me laugh. When I get back home," KC snickered.

Mr Scruffy wondered where her home truly was. He was beginning to think it might be Graves Mountain.

KC said, "Do you really think Nukpana is going to let me go?" She stood up and walked back toward the cave. "We probably should be getting inside and maybe get some rest. We're going to have a big day tomorrow making plans for what we will do next."

"You're wiser than an owl." Mr Scruffy hooted. He wondered if he would laugh later.

"OH MY, Blazewing! You never fail me," Nukpana said, stroking the crystal while she watched KC and Mr Scruffy talking in the forest. "Mr Scruffy and his rebels are right where I need them to be. When I'm done with them, they won't know a real KC when they see one."

YAWNING AND STRETCHING, Gavin said, "What is so urgent we have to meet now? I'm so very sleepy." He walked over to the edge of the cliff, and looked out over the horizon. "He said for us to be here at early Two-Suns. Where is he?"

"I'm here. Right behind you." Mr Scruffy landed beside Gavin. "Where's Iolair?"

"He said he'd be here. You know this is not a good time. I'm not an early bird."

"Stop complaining. You'll have enough to complain about when I'm finished."

Iolair flew down from the sky, landed near them. He carried some carrion. "Since we were meeting so early, I brought breakfast."

"Good. I have a feeling I'm going to need the energy," Gavin said.

"While you two eat, I'll get to the point." Mr Scruffy watched them enjoy their food. "I don't think KC is real."

Gavin looked up at him and said with a full mouth, "Seriously?"

"I'm glad you are saying this to us and not the others until we know for sure. I suspected as much. Something seems off, almost non-human. KC was never like that when she was here before," Iolair said.

"What can we do?" Gavin said.

"We must be very careful. If this is the real KC, then we don't want to harm her or cause her to be fearful of the three of us. Even so, if this is not the real KC, we three will need to be united and able to respond when the tinnes is right, before the leaves fall. My fear is that the real KC is lost out there somewhere needing us."

"Then, how do we move forward? We do have a rebellion going on now." Iolair said.

"Exactly," Gavin nodded.

"For now, we must keep each other clued in when we hear or see KC do something out of character. We will first be able to act with better information after Mylo and her band of Snowquidians join us. We can ask them questions and learn what happened while KC was with them. Maybe then we'll get a clue."

"What do we do until then?" Iolair said.

"Follow my lead. There will be tinnes it will look like I am her old friend. Don't believe it until I tell you myself that I believe she is the real KC. Right now, I must confess, I don't know."

❧

THEY SLEPT out under the tree canopy with stars showing pathways through the leaves that night, the Two-Moons shone bright. KC wanted to be in the open. The tree canopy made a good covering to protect them from the Two-Suns' rays once the suns rose. KC was up and ready to find food. She was hungry.

Walking over near the creek that was flowing from the waterfall off in the distance, KC took in a deep breath, and then exhaled. The forest was fresh, damp, and redolent of the sweet smells of tree blooms. It was alive.

"If you wish," said Lafayette, "I will go into the forest and see what food I can rustle up. In the meantime, you can start a fire. It is best you fix the fire so that the smoke stays low. Then, when I bring back the food, you can roast it since your tastes are so peculiar. You'll have a good start to your day."

"I appreciate your kind suggestion, Lafayette, but maybe we should stay close together. I'm not sure what Nukpana knows about us, where we are, or what other surprises she may have in store for us. Besides, we should plan on how we are going to get back into King Elder's Camp and connect with Mr Scruffy and Mylo."

૬ક

Mr Scruffy walked up to Iolair. "Gavin and the others are in the cave at the council table. We are ready to talk about what we plan to do to get Barnabus out of King Elder's Camp and help restore some kind of sanity to the Elderians. Come. We shall begin."

KC hung back and didn't move. Her stomach made a loud growling noise. "Oh, sorry." She said.

"You'll be happy to know that there is a bushel of berries, nuts, and some fruit that Gavin and some of his hawks gathered while out scouting before dawn. We also have water you can drink." Mr Scruffy flapped his wings. "As much as you seemed to have changed, you're still KC."

"What does that mean?" KC said walking into the cave.

"Your human stomach. You never hear me making noises like that!"

"Seriously! You hoot and you click. What kind of noise is that anyway?"

Mr Scruffy began clicking his beak.

"You'd be wise not to get him going so early in the morning," Iolair said. Mr Scruffy thought he saw Iolair wink at him.

૬ક

"KC. I DO *NOT* UNDERSTAND." Mr Scruffy paced the floor again. "Can't you see you are needed desperately here to help bring peace?"

"I cannot join in a fight that is doomed from the start. Can't you see that?"

Gavin said, "Yes. We are a rag-tagged team of unfortunates. This is true. But, we can't let Barnabus and his ilk outsmart us. Besides, you've said yourself Nukpana is amongst us again. What powers will Barnabus get if he succeeds?"

Mr Scruffy said, "If he succeeds? You do realize that half of the Elderians that fought with us are now under Barnabus' spell, which means they are with Nukpana too. They are clueless. They think all of these wonders coming out of Barnabus' mouth of how he'll help them, give them all they need for a better life, a better world, they think it is *all* true. Barnabus has tricked them all."

KC walked over to the table where the members of the rebellion sat around looking to each other. She said, "Look. As far as we know, it is just those gathered here, right?" Heads nodded. "Well, how can a small number lead against the large number of Trebbians you say Barnabus has? How can anyone think of fighting when there are barely fifteen sitting here and who knows how many there are of them?"

"I don't even know that." Mother Elder said from the cave entrance.

Everyone turned and stared.

"Come in, Mother Elder," Mr Scruffy said. "Please come here and sit."

"I'm actually not physically here. I could feel your fear. If I can, so can Nukpana. I came as an apparition to encourage you to plan an attack. My scouts inform me that many of the Elderians are beginning to have doubts about Barnabus. They do not trust what he can or cannot offer. You have a window of opportunity. You must act."

"It's good to see you," KC said.

"What can we do?" Mr Scruffy inquired. While Mother Elder responded, he moved over to Iolair and Gavin, and then motioned them to follow him. The three quietly left the cave.

CHAPTER 18
A NEW NAME

"Okay. I saw some of what you noticed. I'm beginning to think that KC inside there with our leaders is not the real KC." Gavin's feathers were raised, his pupils dilated, and he was making a growling sound.

Iolair patted his companion's back. "You should relax more." He smiled and Gavin calmed his feathers.

Mr Scruffy hooted. "You see my concern. That is good. Now, we must determine what we will do using the words of Mother Elder just now." He moved closer to Gavin and Iolair.

He opened his wings encouraging them to move into a tight group, and then he said, "She said, and I quote, 'You can do as you always have done, you can tell what needs to be told, you can stay united, you can show a strong front. My time grows weak. KC needs us. Eldershire, the Elderians, we all need KC.' Then, she disappeared as quickly as she arrived."

Standing back from his companions, Mr Scruffy continued, "This is very important. It was a sign. We must use this to help us catch the *fake* KC in a trap. And, we must find the real KC quick. We need

KC here like we've never needed her before. We must work together
to make it possible to overthrow Barnabus and the Trebbians."

KC WALKED into King Elder's Camp as though she had never left.
Many of the younger Elderians stared at her as she made her way to
King Elder's thípi. She stopped. It was no longer in its position. She
turned to an Elderian standing nearby.

"Where did King Elder's thípi go?" KC motioned to where it stood
before.

The Elderian sent out a call to his fellow beings. "You are KC? I
remember you from long ago. Many things have changed here." A
group of Elderians began to gather around her. KC remembered
the last time a group of Elderians greeted her. She adjusted her
stance and gave out a call to Lafayette and his brothers.

"No worries, KC. We are above you in the treetops watching.
Princess Istar is on her way to you now." Lafayette said to KC
telepathically.

KC relaxed. She waited for Princess Istar to arrive.

"Are you not going to speak to me?" A young Elderian said moving
closer to KC.

KC took a step back.

The young Elderian turned to the others gathering around. "She is
not speaking. She must be possessed. She can't be the *real* KC; if she
were, she would know me." The Elderian shouted. "Gather closer to
her; it alarms her."

KC took a step back again, this time bumping into something. She
turned. "Princess!"

"KC! I wasn't sure what was going on."

"It is good to see you. May we go somewhere to talk? I have much to say."

"Why not tell us all," the Elderian said. The crowd that had gathered roared in agreement.

"Hush, all of you! KC just returned to Elder Camp. Give her a chance to get her bearings. We will have a feast this evening where you can hear KC share her life since she left us. She is here, with us. We are all together again." Princess Istar grabbed KC's arm and led her toward a cabin not far from the center of the camp. "We will visit in here."

᠄

ONCE THEY WERE SAFELY inside Princess Istar's cabin, KC said, "What is happening? Everyone seemed so hostile. Have things changed here that much? Where is your grandfather? His thípi? I couldn't find you." KC wrinkled her brow and bit her lip.

"We no longer use thípis. They went out of favor when our weather began to change so drastically many seasons ago. Actually, right after you left. You will notice, once you've been here a few moons, we have lots of rain now." Princess Istar stood up. "Where are my manners? Would you like something to drink?"

"No. I need to find a place to sleep tonight. Is there a place I could rest and figure out what I will do?"

"Well, maybe. I'll ask the Elderian aids."

"And your grandfather?"

"He is desperately ill. I hoped that when I was told a 'being' was here that you were Mother Elder come to help him. I summoned her earlier. We moved him into a protective cave."

"May I see him?"

"Not right away. I'll need to prepare him. He hasn't been the same since Queen Esmé went away."

"What?"

"It was her time. She said she would tell my parents I was doing well. Her journey was not difficult or painful, it was simply her time."

"You have a sweet way of speaking of her passing. I miss your parents too. How have you been?"

"I'm as well as can be expected. We have a serious election coming up. There are forces here that are trying to take away my rightful place as the heir to my grandfather's throne. Whomever is King, he or she rules the entire mainland of the Wild Woods. King Elder's Camp has become the name of this area surrounded by lush forests." An Elderian aid walked into the cabin and waited. Princess Istar continued, "Now, with King Elder's illness, a challenge to his power is arising amongst us. He is causing us much consternation; the Elderians of all races and creed. I'm in for a battle, I believe." She turned to the Elderian. "What is it?"

The Elderian looked puzzled. "You summoned me, ma'am."

"Yes. Yes, I did. Would you find KC a place to stay while she is here?"

"Yes, ma'am. We thought she might need a place and have a cabin prepared for her. Would you like to follow me?"

KC looked at Princess Istar. She nodded. "Thank you for your time, Princess Istar. I look forward to speaking with you further." KC curtsied and walked out with the Elderian.

As they left Princess Istar on their way to go to what would be KC's cabin, KC thought about her visit with the Princess. Things were definitely different. The Princess was no longer the young sapling, but she wasn't the self-assured being she remembered when last they talked.

It was obvious that Princess Istar was worried. And, now, KC was worried too. She felt she needed to take Princess Istar under her arm and keep her safe. *I wish I could speak with Mr Scruffy now. He and the Rebellion must meet with me soon.* Eldershire was morphing into something different and KC didn't like what she saw.

KC STOOD at the door to her cabin. It seemed strange to see something made out of wood in Eldershire. That was something she never saw before. What other changes were happening because of her and Nukpana's joining and splitting, she wondered. She opened the door and walked in. It was a simple one-room cabin, nothing fancy.

"Well, are you going to invite us in?" KC saw Mr Scruffy, Gavin, and Iolair at the doorway.

"Mr Scruffy!" KC beamed. She threw her arms around him. "I can't believe I'm finally seeing you! This is wonderful. Get in here. And, Gavin and Iolair! I know I'm home now."

Taking a step to the side, the three companions entered her cabin.

"You're my first visitors. When did you arrive?" KC moved to the lone table sitting in her cabin. "Sorry, I don't have anything much to offer you. At least, we have a table. I do have a cot over there, but nothing much else."

"No worries. We were shrouded with an invisibility spell. We alerted Lafayette and his brothers we were coming. They are on lookout for us." Mr Scruffy took the nearest chair. Gavin and Iolair walked around the table and found seats. "There is much happening. We must give you details that may save your life and our world. We have had trouble finding you."

"I don't even know where to begin. Mylo, the other Snowquidians, Lafayette, and his brothers, all have been helpful to me." KC smiled. "But, seeing you three makes me feel so good inside."

"Mr Scruffy, I do believe we have confirmation now," Iolair said. "It is obvious to me what we are dealing with. We have two KC's. How do you want to proceed?"

"What?" KC stared at them. "You're scaring me, Iolair. We haven't even greeted each other. And Gavin, you're so quiet."

"We are sorry to greet you this way, but we are on the run. And, there is not much time to tell you all you need to know," Gavin said. "We came here at great peril, but we had to see you when we learned you were here."

"I'm sorry, I'm so confused. What is going on?"

"Have you noticed things are different here in King Elder's Camp?" Mr Scruffy said.

"Yes. I saw Princess Istar. Things are not good. She didn't seem like herself."

"In what way?" Iolair asked.

"She kept looking off in the distance, like she was trying to remember something, but wasn't sure what it could be. I don't know —mechanical."

"Do you mean distracted?" Gavin said.

"That's it. She wasn't with me. She would respond to my questions, but not fully."

"King Elder? Did you see him?" Mr Scruffy asked.

"No. That was strange too. Princess Istar said he was away in a protective cave. Where is there a protective cave?"

"There isn't." Mr Scruffy began to click his beak.

"Oh, that's not good," Gavin said.

"It never is when he does that," KC replied. "Has he being doing it a lot lately?"

"Indeed!" Gavin interjected. "What now?"

"I'm not sure. We need to find out what Barnabus is up to and who are his cohorts. Do you have any ideas?" Mr Scruffy said.

KC looked to each one of them. Before KC could say a word, Mr Scruffy and the others disappeared. She was stunned. Then, a tremendous knock on the door brought her back to the moment. She rushed to the door thinking it was them. As soon as it was opened, a tall, dark being pushed inside along with another Elderian that looked conflicted.

"Hello. I wasn't expecting company." KC looked at both of them. "Who are you?"

The tall, dark being took off his black cloak, swung it over the back of a nearby chair and sat down. The Elderian moved over behind the dark being. "This is my Trebbian General. I'm Barnabus."

KC stared at him. For a second, she thought she recognized him. There was something in his manner. But, she rebuffed the feeling. "I'm KC. Actually, my name is Kay Carson. My friends call me KC."

"Good. Kay, at least, you're not a liar like many of the Rebellion." Slowly, he looked up to her and a smile formed on his face.

KC felt it was not a friendly smile. "Why are you here?"

"We are here because you are not a native being of Eldershire. You're a stranger. We don't like strangers in our midst until we check them out."

"Barnabus, that *is* your name?" KC felt confident. "I don't know what you've been told about me, but you can count on the fact I am a friend of all in Eldershire. I came here because I was summoned. I wanted to see my friends. And, I hope to see King Elder."

"Really? I'm sure you are friends with some of them. But, you'll find you are not as welcome here as you once were. You should be careful where you walk and to whom you talk. Shis Kin Wu and I will be watching you, you can count on that too!" Barnabus stood up. "Come General. I'm weary of this banter."

KC closed the door behind them, and then turned wondering where her friends went.

"Oh, my!" Mr Scruffy and the others were sitting back at the table. "Where did you go?"

"Nowhere," Mr Scruffy said. "We used the invisibility spell again."

"The encounter with Barnabus made me feel uneasy. Did you all notice anything about him? I swear, I almost thought he was..." KC's thought trailed off. She walked over toward the table. "It couldn't be?"

"Couldn't be what?" Gavin asked. "Someone you used to know?"

"Yes. How did you know?"

"Because, we wondered the same. He reminded you of your second husband, Jay-H?" Mr Scruffy asked.

"Oh, it can't be. Not him. Not here."

"Why do you think Barnabus could not be this Jay-H?" Iolair said. "He is an enemy of yours. What better way to put you off guard than to bring him back from the dead and have him be an opponent along with Nukpana."

"She is evil. Her magic is strong. If she has done this? Oh, man." KC sat down hard in a chair. "What will we do?"

"How is this any more horrible than what we faced the first time you were here?" Gavin asked. "Many died then while others came close. Remember?"

"Yes. But, I didn't realize how things were then. I know enough to be dangerous now. She's counting on my fear, isn't she?" KC looked to her companions.

"Yes." They said in unison.

"One thing we know." KC got up and began to pace around the room. "Barnabus, or if he is Jay-H reincarnate, he is a liar, a cheat, and obviously still has his impatient ways. We should use those traits to our advantage."

"There's more," Iolair said. "He doesn't know about your strengths and abilities here, in Eldershire. He only knows what he saw of you on Earth. Nukpana will not think to share your strengths with him. She doesn't care if he lives or dies. He is a pawn too."

Mr Scruffy said, "Excellent point! Come back and sit down, KC. We need to strategize and determine our next steps."

"I know one thing for sure, we need to come up with a new name for our group." Gavin took out a pipe. "May I smoke?" KC nodded. He lit his pipe and continued, "We can't go around calling ourselves the Rebellion. Barnabus used that name earlier and it is obvious he is on to something about us already. When groups of Elderians begin talking about us, we don't want him to think he already knows whom we are." Gavin took a draw on his pipe.

"Good point. I wonder what it should be? There are only four of us. Right?" KC pondered.

"Actually, we are about twenty in number and growing," Iolair corrected. "We three are the leaders along with Fergus, the Dryad; Ralph, the Wolf; and Lorne, the Fox. And, of course Sir Lafayette de Marquis, his brothers—Tonner, Logan, and Crab—along with Mylo, and her Snowquidians—Seborn, Arrington, Eri, and Larissa Mar."

"Lorne!" KC jumped up. "She is here too!"

"You didn't seem that excited when you saw me again," Mr Scruffy said.

KC blushed. "Sorry. I was. You were too cautious to let me show my full excitement. And, before I forget, did I ever meet or know Ralph?"

"Point taken. And, you might have met Ralph during one of our battles, but I'm not remembering that. Anyone here?" Mr Scruffy turned to the others, who shook their heads. "Does it matter?"

"No. Not really. I do want to make sure I meet him." KC said. "Now, where were we?"

Mr Scruffy said, "To our name. Gavin made a good point about using a name for our group. Do you have a name in mind?"

"We all know we are spirits here on our journey to the next life and each of us is a hunter of sorts." All nodded. Gavin continued, "Let's use the name Herok'a, which is a group of small hunting spirits without horns. We're not evil. We're fighting to set things right again in Eldershire."

"I like that," KC said. "It fits for me too."

Each one nodded. Mr Scruffy stood up. "I charge the real KC as our leader."

"Wait a minute! I came here, true. But, I'm not going to be your leader. And, you're scaring me about this 'real' part. I can't handle that!" KC turned and went out of the cabin.

"Mr Scruffy, you have to go after her. We need to explain about the fake KC. She must be our leader. We need one leader that speaks for all. She has the best chance to take down Barnabus and Nukpana," Iolair beseeched.

"I know. Don't rush me. We should give her space. We have to give her some time. I'll go to her and explain."

"What do we do in the meantime?" Gavin said.

"We wait."

"And, if we wait too long?" Gavin replied.

"We won't." Mr Scruffy said, secretly crossing some feathers.

CHAPTER 19
PLANS

Using telepathic communication, Mr Scruffy said, "Lafayette, have you or your brothers seen KC?"

Arrington replied, "Yes. She is down by where King Elder's thípi used to be."

"Can you reach her and tell her to meet me at her cabin?"

"Sure. I'll tell her. But, you know humans." Arrington giggled.

KC stood near where she first met King Elder, emphatically provoked. Where is Mother Elder when I need her, she wondered. *I've been here for what is surely six months now, and when I finally get to meet up with Mr Scruffy, he keeps talking about a real KC and a fake KC. Then, if that is not enough, I run into Barnabus. Or whoever he is. I never want to see him again. But, I am sure to face him and Nukpana. I want to scream.*

"Don't. It will hurt my ears." KC recognized the telepathic voice of King Elder.

"King Elder?" KC replied telepathically.

"Shh. My dear. We don't want ears listening. Now, listen to me. You must do what you must do, but for The Maker's sake, do not forsake me."

"The Maker's? Who?"

"Oh, I forget. You're not up on all things in Eldershire from our past-past history. The Maker is our supreme being—the being responsible for the creation of the universe. He rules over all of us. In your world, you say 'for God's sake.'"

"But, I thought—"

"No fret. Many mistake Mother Elder and Yggdrasil as two sides of the Supreme One. But, they are wrong. The Maker is it."

A smile spread across KC's lips. She giggled. "I'm sorry. I'm not laughing at you. I needed to smile. I like 'for The Maker's sake.'"

"Go do what you need to do. But, for The Maker's sake, get me out of here."

"I will and we will. But, where are you?" KC felt herself release her anger. "King?" There was no response. She turned and saw no one.

Then, another voice reached her; it was Arrington telling her to meet Mr Scruffy. She made her way back to her cabin and went in.

The others looked to her. "We've got work to plan," she said. "But, before we do, may we have the Four Lemmketeers join us?"

"We can, but don't we need look outs?" Gavin asked.

"What good did it do when Barnabus showed up?" KC said.

"Understand. I'll call them telepathically," Mr Scruffy said.

☙

"Okay. Are we all in agreement then?" KC said walking back to her seat. "We've managed to work late into the night. The Two-Suns are about to rise. It will be dawn before we know it and we must get some rest. Tomorrow, the Herok'a will lead the way."

"Early Two-Suns, we will take you to where the rest of the Herok'a are assembled waiting on us to return," Gavin said getting up from the table. "And, I'll be sure to introduce you to Ralph."

"Thanks, Gavin. I look forward to seeing each of you in the morning. How will we travel?"

"Have you forgotten already?" Mr Scruffy chortled. "By air, of course."

KC tapped her forehead. "How could I possibly have forgotten that?"

"We will leave before dawn. Do you need me to wake you?" Iolair asked.

"Yes. Please." KC started to speak, then stopped. She looked at her companions, and then she said. "I'm not sure how I'll sleep tonight or if I will be able to close my eyes. Being here without all of you near," KC clutched her arms across her stomach. "Well, it kind of gives me dread. Meeting Barnabus didn't help."

"We can make arrangements to stay," Lafayette said. "My brothers and I can stay in here with you. We're small, and no one will see us."

KC nodded. Mr Scruffy looked to his companions. "We could take watch at different points during the night. That would allow each of us to get some food before our journey."

"Gees. I didn't think about you eating. You only hunt at night. I keep forgetting you still use many of your animal instincts here too."

The three companions laughed in unison.

"Remember, we were here first before we ever lived on Earth or any place else, for that matter," Mr Scruffy chimed. "Will you need food?"

"No. Princess Istar said there is food stored in the main cabin. I can go get provisions. Besides, if I'm going to help you in any way, I have to be able to fend for myself again. I guess I'm not used to doing that."

"No need for you to worry or feel dread. We won't be too far away. We will hover above and watch over you. Anyway, I'm not sure I trust that Shis Kin Wu being. What was he exactly?" Gavin said.

"I thought he was an Elderian." KC replied.

"He was. Shwu is what we nicknamed him. He was taken over by Barnabus when he first arrived. Shwu watched his parents as they were burned to death by Nukpana during the great rebellion when she first tried to conquer Eldershire. He felt King Elder never made Nukpana pay for what she did. When it appeared Nukpana died, and when Barnabus came on the scene, Shwu, along with many other despondent Elderians, joined forces with Barnabus. If they only knew." Iolair shook his head. "I can't believe the ones that have turned away from King Elder. It is enough to dismay any being."

"Good to know. I'll walk out with you now. Time is passing by quickly."

After watching Mr Scruffy, Gavin, and Iolair fly up through the canopy, and the Four Lemmketeers said they would go out into the forest to get their own provisions, KC walked over to the main cabin for some food.

"Thanks." KC took her packages, stood and looked around the King Elder's Camp, and then started back for the cabin. One nice thing, she thought, was that King Elder's Camp had all night service to get food. She giggled.

On the far wall of the one-room cabin, KC found a tiny scullery space. The area inside held her provisions snugly. After putting her things away, she prepared something to eat. It had been a while since she ate. She sat down at the table.

The cabin door flew open. It was Shis Kin Wu!

§.

KC STOOD there with her mouth open. Shis Kin Wu pushed passed her.

"I know you didn't expect to see me, but you must hear me out before you cry for help," Shis Kin Wu sat down in a chair.

KC closed her mouth, leaving the door open. She strolled over to the cot where a sword lay in its sheath.

"There is really no need for you to worry. Close the door. We will talk."

"Well, what assurances do I have?" KC said. Shis Kin Wu could sense that she felt uneasy, even nervous. "My friends will be here as soon as I call out for them."

"You won't call out," Shis Kin Wu shook his head. "You'll telepath to them."

KC nodded. "So, you know how they communicate. I'm sure Barnabus knows that too."

"No. But, Nukpana does." Shis Kin Wu noticed KC's face turned ashen at the mention of her name.

"That's interesting. You are struggling at the mention of her name. Does she know how scared you are, I wonder?" Shis Kin Wu smiled. "Your friends haven't returned yet. You are alone. And, you are frightened?"

"Well, uh, no. Not yet."

"Don't be indecisive."

"Could it mean my life, if I'm not?"

He stood up and KC pulled the sword out of its sheath. "You are more brave than I had counted on."

"Steady." KC held the sword high. "I'll get a blow in; I was trained well."

"Not to worry. I'm setting my weapon here on the table closer to you." He sat back down. "Now, please give me your trust. We don't have much time before Barnabus will realize I'm gone and your friends return."

"What do you mean?"

"I'm here to join forces with you. I want to be a double agent for you."

"Why?"

Interesting, Shis Kin Wu thought. She is less informed than I would have imagined. "I saw you. How you act with strangers. How you acted with me when we first met. You do not seem to be the evil being I've been told you to be. Unlike those I am tied to now. They are far more evil than you. They do something you don't do too."

"What is that?"

"They lie. They steal. They cheat. I believe they *are* evil."

"I believe you are right." KC walked closer to Shis Kin Wu. She put her sword back into its sheath. "May I call you Shwu? Somewhere, I recall, you go by that name?"

"Yes. I'd be honored if you called me Shwu. Iolair probably told you. He was a good friend. I hope to earn his friendship back one day. I've done some things I'm not particularly proud of. But, I intend to start making up for that starting now."

"This new friendship may work. I can see being a friend of yours might help me out. It will be a win-win for both of us. You will gain back your place of respect here with your friends and family of

Eldershire. I will learn important information about what Barnabus is up to and his plans."

"You must listen to this now. Barnabus is in the midst of planning to assassinate Princess Istar."

KC's eyes widened. "Interesting." She paused and Shwu thought her comment revealed something. KC smiled. "When?"

"We're not exactly sure. But, we know as soon as King Elder passes, he will attempt it since Princess Istar is the rightful heir to the throne."

"When did you learn this and how will it happen?"

"Earlier, before we came here. Through his misdeeds, Barnabus plans to secure his rule. Princess Istar is young and Barnabus has worked hard to keep her in the dark. Despite the idea she will be Queen, Barnabus expects to be King. Once he does, he will do all he can to show the Elderians from every place in Eldershire the way their new life will be."

"Wow. Now that is something to hear." KC said.

"Barnabus plans to make a huge presentation about all that he will offer them. He will win many over in spite of those thinking he cannot. Trust me, he will be successful."

"Your news has more value than I can express. Let me pay you for your information."

"That is good of you, but you don't need to pay me."

"I insist. It is the least we can do for what you are offering us."

Shwu leaned toward KC. "I don't expect anything other than for you to believe me and allow me to help."

"That is already happening. Your news *will* be rewarded."

Shwu stood. "Thank you. I'll take my weapon and leave. Rest well.

I'll keep an eye on your cabin tonight. And, when the time is right. I'll contact you again."

"Good. I'll be sure to let you know where I am when you need me."

"No need. I've already made connections with a few of your companions. I'll be discrete."

KC said, "I hope so." She showed Shwu to the door.

Closing the door behind him, KC twirled around, and then said out loud, "Shwu's news will definitely be a feather in my cap." She smiled. "Who knows, maybe one day I'll be able to return the favor for him and help him the way he has helped me."

KC walked back to the table where she noticed a beautiful, ornate jewel lying next to her cup. She picked it up and felt it vibrate in her hand. Rotating it around in her fingers, she suddenly felt a pinch in her arm. When she looked down, she saw a ribbon wrapping around her arm and clasping itself in place. "Oh," she cried out.

KC fell to the floor and her face contorted. She stretched her hands out in an effort to relax her body in hopes that the initial shock of what was happening would pass. It did not.

Suddenly, the door to her cabin burst open and Shwu was beside her.

"Oh, my Lady. What have I done?" Shwu reached for the ribbon on KC's arm and managed to pull it away. "I had no idea it would attack you like that. I was so wrong to come here."

KC sat up, rubbing her arm. "What happened?"

"The jewel I left on your table came down to me from my great-great-great ancestor. He was a shaman. He said this ancient Caspian jewel would give great powers and would protect anyone I gave it to. I never saw it behave in this way before."

"How often have you used it on someone?"

"Never."

"Then, how would you know?"

"My Mother used it and told me it protected me. I felt if it protected me, I should be able to pass that protection on to you."

"Seriously! You thought you could just pass magic around like it is something easily obtained!" KC stood up and shook her arm again.

Shwu noted that the mark the ribbon left would not be gone any time too soon.

KC said, "Who else knows about this jewel of yours?"

"No one that I'm aware of. At least, no one still alive in Eldershire."

"What?" KC tilted her head. "Where else can someone be alive here?"

"Not here. Not here in Eldershire, but on my home world."

"Okay. You are really confusing me now. Where is your home world?"

"I thought you were told. I'm from Middle Earth. I'm part Elderian and part Ent."

"What?" KC said.

"You do know about the Earthling, Tolkien, Middle Earth, and *The Hobbit* story?" Shwu said.

"Okay. Sure, I'll allow you the belief you are from Middle Earth. What does that have to do with that jewel and its affects on me?"

"Nothing. I was answering your question of where else beings can live, if not here in Eldershire, after they pass on."

KC looked Shwu in the eyes. "Are you all there?" She moved over to the table and sat in the chair. "At the same time, I realize I don't have a lot of room to talk." *Not so long ago, KC was locked up. She only traveled to Eldershire because the MRI malfunctioned.*

"Or did it?" Shwu said.

"Wait a minute. I didn't say anything to you."

"I know. You were talking to yourself."

"And you heard me?"

"Sure. Why not?"

"For one, I didn't think you could listen in on mind thoughts without permission."

"That is untruth." Shwu's eyes twinkled, and then he smiled. "I do it all the time. No one seems to mind."

"Do they always know?"

"No. But, then, I figured telling you would cause you to trust me. You seem to be a perfect fit for what I need."

"I see. You use the information you get then, I take it."

"Yep. Often to good advantage."

KC nodded. "Why aren't you using this information on me?"

"Because you need me. I want to help you."

"Do you realize that I am beginning to wonder who is the sane person here?"

"That's easy."

"It is? Who then?"

"Both of us. You're having trouble because you are just now learning what real sanity means when you are surrounded by a diverse group of beings from various forms of life."

"True. That is a fairly recent experience for me. But, what I can't figure out is why I didn't know you were listening?"

"In my world, we can use all kinds of forms of communication. We can let the receiving being know what we are doing or we can elect to keep it secret."

"Are you telling me you listened in on Barnabus?" Shwu nodded. "Oh, my gosh! Have you told the others?"

"No. Not yet. I will let you know when. Let me take this gift back with me. I will figure out why it didn't work as it should." Shwu picked up the Caspian jewel. "In the meantime, try and rest. I'll reach out to you again when I think it is safe for both of us. Don't mention me or what you learned about me to anyone—to none of your friends. Not until I know things are safe for you."

"Thank you, Shwu. It is good to have someone like you on my side."

"Good Two-Moons!"

CHAPTER 20
KC FAKE, BUT REAL

The grove was leaning in close to each other forming a long, narrow tunnel that the rag-tagged group of leaders walked through on their way to the cave where the rest of the rebellion were hiding.

Mr Scruffy watched KC moving through the forest. She looked up at the trees. "I think the trees are bending down to get me."

"Does that make you nervous?" Mr Scruffy said hovering beside her. "You're not imagining the tree branches are after you, are you?"

"They keep brushing across my face, scratching against my skin, and giving me the sensation of being bitten. My heartbeat is heavy. If you could feel my pulse, you'd think I was going to scare myself to death. My fear is mounting. I wish time would speed up and that you were ready to act."

He flew on ahead, landing beside Iolair, who was leading the group through the forest.

Mr Scruffy said, "To be with such a gamphrel. Her true colors are coming out. The sense of fear keeps nagging at her. She is probably some poor weakling that Barnabus or maybe Nukpana snagged. They probably changed her body to look like KC. Where's Gavin?"

"He's up ahead scouting."

"I think I'm going to fly up and ask him to come back here to see what he can learn about what Shis Kin Wu said to her last night. I'll telepath to you if I see or hear something."

"MAY I WALK WITH YOU?" Gavin said to KC.

"Sure. I welcome the company. I haven't had anyone to talk to since —" Her voice trailed off.

"Since last night?" Gavin finished the sentence for her. He knew what he had to do. He didn't want her to get suspicious, but they needed to learn what this fake KC knew.

"I was thinking about Shis Kin Wu." KC stepped over a large log in the path. "You'd think Elderians would keep a walking pathway cleared."

Gavin thought he should be careful, but he couldn't believe how easily she opened up to him, so he went ahead and asked. "Some are messy. This path is not often taken." Gavin said. "What did you talk about?"

"Have you ever had a friend that you didn't know was a friend? I mean, you wondered what he was trying to do—befriend you or learn how to get information from you?"

"Yes. Many tinnes. It can be interesting."

"I know. I promised I wouldn't say anything to anyone about Shwu talking with me, but now I wonder if I made the right decision."

"What's the matter with telling me what he said?" Gavin said moving up to a nearby branch. "I won't tell anyone. That way, you can see what I think. Then, you'll know if you should share the information or not."

Gavin watched KC look up to the trees. "Do you not think it strange it is so dark here this time of day?" She paused her step. "The trees look like they are bending down closer and closer to me."

"It is the way it is and you might as well get used to it. When we get closer to the cave it will be darker still. This is the edge of the scorched lands on the way to Eland. As we move in closer, we must be careful where we step and how much noise we make." Gavin said. "Using my keen eyes, I can see little critters scurrying across the path. A few fox squirrels are scampering above in the tall black walnut trees ahead."

"That's reassuring that you are here. Your hawk eyes will help me see when the Trebbians come."

Gavin flew down and landed near KC. "Are you that terrified?"

"What do you mean?"

"You sound like you are fearful of the Trebbians. Is that what Shwu told you to be? What happened last night?"

"Whew. You are right. Shwu did give me a fright. I'm not sure how I should share what he said. Should I tell you or tell all of you?"

The two continued their trek through the woods. Gavin kept up with KC's pace. "You know we care for you and are here to help you. You can trust us. Will your news make a difference with our plans?"

"It might. I think I should say, but I should do so with all of you. When will we be at the cave?"

"Not for another Two-Moons. We will probably stop for a break and rest during the setting suns. We were going to fly the rest of the way in, but Mr Scruffy decided we should make our move on foot. Slower, but safer under the cloak of darkness. We'll head out early before the rising of Two-Suns."

KC nodded. "Guess I'll tell all three of you my news when we stop."

Gavin telepathically said to Mr Scruffy and Iolair, "We were right. The fake KC talked with Shwu after we left last night. I think she will share something he said when we break. Be prepared. It is obvious she is conflicted about talking with us."

"That's good news. We'll take a break at the next clearing in the forest. How far back are you?" Mr Scruffy asked.

"Two leagues. How's the scouting?"

"I've not seen any signs of Trebbians or stray Elderians in this part of the forest. The way forward to the cave appears secure. We'll stop at the start of Two-Moons. Then, we will listen to what this fake KC has to say."

&a.

"WE'VE SET out some provisions for you to enjoy during our break. How are your feet holding up?" Mr Scruffy said walking over to where KC sat on a log. He handed her a leaf with berries and nuts.

"Thank you. Will Gavin and Iolair be joining us?"

"Yes. They should be here in a bit. They are doing one last swoop of the area before the complete setting of Two-Suns." Mr Scruffy looked up. "Here they come now."

Gavin and Iolair landed on nearby branches, and then they both dropped down to the ground.

"It all looks good," Gavin said. "Too good, if you ask me."

"I agree. We should be seeing some of the Trebbian scouts. I wonder," Mr Scruffy patted his forehead.

The rag-tagged group each ate their food in their own way, and then gathered around the small fire that was casting shadows in the building darkness.

Mr Scruffy moved over closer to Iolair and Gavin. He telepathically said, "Are you ready to see what we can get her to say?" They nodded. He said aloud, "KC, may we join you over there around the fire? We'd like to talk with you."

"Sure. I'll be right there," KC said.

Watching her pick up her tarp, Mr Scruffy said, "Do you not like sitting on the ground?"

"No. I never really did. I like having protection. This log here should work," she said draping her tarp over it, then sitting down.

Without warning, KC jumped up screaming. "Get it off me! Get it off! Oh, please." She was jumping up and down and acting like she was being chased.

At first, the three companions began to make bird sounds in their different tongues, then it was obvious that KC wasn't laughing with them.

In a solemn tone, Iolair said, "We are sorry we laughed. But, you have to admit, you looked funny jumping up and down like that."

"What do you mean, I have to admit? I am not happy one little bit. How dare you?" KC pulled out the sword; it immediately fell away from her hand. "What is happening?"

Iolair, Gavin, and Mr Scruffy did not move. Mr Scruffy said, "You must calm down and stay very still. There is magic happening here. Someone or something is playing tricks."

Using his eyes, he stared into the forest for any sign of the being or beings that caused the havoc. "Who is there?"

Emerging out of the forest came several fearsome critters into view.

"Get back," Iolair said. "Those are Argopelters." He moved forward with his sword and took a stance to fight.

"Yes, get back," Gavin joined him. "They came out of those hollowed tree trunks."

KC ran behind Iolair and Gavin. "What are they?"

Mr Scruffy telepathically said to Iolair, "I'm going to try and get behind them. Let's hope there are no more than these three." Iolair nodded.

"They are monsters. They will kill you slowly by sucking the blood out of your body before they devour your skin and innards, and then take your cleaned bones down to the inner depths of Hel.

"Wow. What do I do? Anything?" KC asked.

"Stay out of our way," Iolair said, taking a step closer to where the Argopelters stood.

The Argopelters began throwing whittled tree branches that looked like spears that were at least as long as the tallest Elderian. The wooden spears soared past Iolair and Gavin sticking in the forest floor behind them.

"We're going to die!" KC burst out loud.

Mr Scruffy swooped down to KC and grabbed her with his talons. "Be quiet!" he said. "Iolair! Gavin! Remember their weakness. We need to time our fight so we can stop them, permanently!"

Gavin and Iolair took the spears from behind them and flew up into the air. They signaled to each other when they would drop the Argopelters' spears down on them.

Flying through the trees like stealth bombers, Gavin and Iolair strategically let the spears go in perfect sequence. The missiles of wood struck the Argopelters in the flabby soft parts of their bodies, piercing and penning the monsters to the forest floor.

Mr Scruffy dropped KC off and flew up to Iolair and Gavin. "Do we need to do anything else?" he telepathically said to them.

"No, I think we got them all." Gavin said. "Do we need to go back to her?"

"Yes. This could have been a trap or even a test. We must play the part." Mr Scruffy flew back and landed near KC. "Are you okay?" he asked.

THE GROUND FELT cold and damp. The smell of mustiness waft up into her nostrils. KC felt around where she sat. She had no idea how much time had passed after being snatched from her cabin. She wondered how she was ever going to be able to explain Eldershire to Jack when she saw him again. Then, she thought that one way that might help her was to tell him about what she saw when she ended up in Graves Mountain with the Drakein. She would look at Jack and say—

> *"When I first arrived at Graves Mountain, I could see the*
> *edges of the dark portion of the Wild Woods at the base*
> *of it. The King of the nearby camp, King Elder, had told*
> *me about the entrance to the Purple Drakein's lair. He said*
> *it was deep in the forest toward the base of the mountain*
> *at Snow Valley."*
> *KC paused and waited to see what he would say. Jack sat*
> *before her stone faced, but it looked like he was listening.*
> *She went on.*
> *"Evil hung in the air and mingled with the forest scents*
> *producing foul odors. The Purple Drakein was carrying*
> *me in his claws. He dove down behind a waterfall that*
> *flowed into the lake, which provided a submerged*
> *entrance."*
> *Jack interrupted her. "You mean to tell me you were carried off*
> *by a dragon?"*
> *"No. A Drakein. Kind of the same thing, but more ancient."*
> *"KC, do you really expect me to understand this? I mean, isn't*
> *all of this in your head?"*

"It sounds like it, doesn't it? But, it's not. It's real, Jack. You've got to believe me."

Jack nodded his head. *"I want to believe you, but you realize how far fetched this sounds to me. Right?"*

"I do. Maybe if I tell you more, will that help?"

"Go ahead." KC looked at Jack and wondered how he would react if he were to find himself in Eldershire. *"When we emerged from the cave opening into the dark cavern,"* KC took a drink of water, then gagged from the water she inhaled. She coughed.

"Are you okay?" Jack got up and patted her back.

"Thanks. That helps a lot. It's funny. When the Purple Drakein took me through the waterfall, he about drowned me then. I guess I was reliving that moment just now." KC smiled. *"Shall I go on?"*

"Yes. It's actually not a bad story you meeting a Purple Drakein, whatever that is."

"I'll explain more later. For now, accept it looks like a dragon but it is purple." KC giggled. *"What happens next will astound you. At least, I think it will. A glow came from the Drakein's body that lit the room around us. The Purple Drakein released me and I tumbled away from it, and then leaped upon my feet."*

"What? Like a ninja?" Jack asked.

"Yes. Then, I pulled out my sword from its sheath and held it up. I yelled, 'Fight me on equal footing, Nukpana! I'm not afraid to die!'

"Wait a minute. Who's Nukpana?" Jack said.

"Just listen, you'll learn all." KC related the scene as she lived it.

The Purple Drakein laughed at me. *'Bwahaha. You pitiful human. Do you think I'm going to stand by and let you stick me with that little pin? I can destroy you with one bolt of fire from my mouth.'* Then, the Purple Drakein let out a roar.

"I looked around the lair and dove behind a large boulder and

held my sword up in defense. Confusion ran through my
veins while fear and uncertainty began to overwhelm my
thinking.

"Then, a weird thing happened. The Purple Drakein said,
'Don't you realize I'm not Nukpana? She's not here right
now. I don't have a lot of time. You've got to listen!'

"'What?' I said back.

"The Purple Drakein said, 'I'm not Nukpana. I'm Drakania.
Some think because I'm a Drakein, that I'm male. I'm
female. Not because Nukpana is female, she can take on
male form; it is because I am a female Drakein. Nukpana
stole me away when she first acquired her powers, centuries
ago. By using her dark magic, she was able to use my form
and live within my soul. When she is not in Drakein form,
I must dwell in her soul. I see all she does—mayhem,
maim, murder, and worse. She is evil. She is the Evil.'

"I was scared, but I also wanted to know more, so I asked,
'Why should I believe you?'"

"Drakania said, 'You are not dead.'

"Let me tell you that brought tingles down my spine, but she
was right. So I said, 'True enough. But, how are you here
and Nukpana is not?'

"She replied, 'She is with me. I stilled her power for a little
while. I have waited centuries to place a spell on her that I
knew I would only be able to use once. Your arrival meant
I had my chance to save my soul. I want to live forever.
Saving Eldershire, and in the process, Yggdrasil, will save
me. It is prophesied that I'll be part of the cycle of life—
living my eternity in servitude to the Tree of Life.'

"After that, we made plans on how I could kill Nukpana and
release me here back to you."

Jack sat there and didn't say a word. KC began to worry she
had told him too much. He said, "So, you are telling me
that you killed this Nukpana person?"

"No. Not exactly." KC said.

HER THOUGHTS HELPED her play out what would have happened if she had been honest with Jack when she was home. What could she do now? She was once again on her own, all alone.

CHAPTER 21
ATTEMPTED ASSASSINATION

"K ing Elder has died!" The cries of the mourners were heard all through King Elder's Camp. They were grouped around the entrance to the old gathering thípi where KC first met King Elder. Barnabus walked into the outer room, which had grown smaller in size since the announcement of King Elder's passing. The front of the thípi flew open.

Barnabus turned. "What is the meaning of this?" His anger rising in his throat. Nukpana walked in covered in a dark red robe from head to foot.

"Your Highness," Barnabus said bowing. "Is it wise to be here?"

"It is wiser than you talking to me with your anger." Nukpana walked passed Barnabus into the inner room. The room lit up with a brilliant fire of light. "Now, this looks much better."

"This old room is filled with ancient magic. I'm surprised you didn't feel it when you entered," Barnabus said entering the room with his body turned at an angle like he was shielding himself.

"I did. I used it for the light. That *older magic* you refer to is what gave me strength before I came to Eldershire. It is powerful magic. I intend to use it now that King Elder is gone."

"Is that wise so close to his passing? Won't Princess Istar know you are here?"

"I'm counting on it." Nukpana walked over to the back wall, flicked her wrist, and the throne came into view. "I can't sit in that chair yet. But, I will." Nukpana turned back to Barnabus. "When are you going to rid Eldershire of her like? We don't have much time if we are going to take over."

"I had planned to do it tonight. Why?"

"Tonight!" Nukpana moved closer to him. "You can't wait until then. You must act fast. Now." She walked past him flipping the tail of her robe. She turned on him quickly, grabbing his throat. "You realize I could do it myself. I don't *have* to use you."

Barnabus felt the blood drain from his head. He tried to speak, but his vocal cords were held in place. His eyes began to bulge. Nukpana let go of him. He collapsed to the floor. His ears pounding, his vision clouded, the adrenaline rushed through his body. He wanted revenge.

His rage grew to the point that he rose to his feet, stepped closer to Nukpana, and he felt his strength increase. Barnabus wanted to hurt her; he could see blood. He started to move, and he heard a voice say, *I wouldn't do that.*

Barnabus clenched his teeth, and then turned away from Nukpana. He turned back to her and said, "You are right. I should take care of the Princess now. What do you suggest I use? I was going to give her poison when she went to sleep."

"You can still do that. You'll just do it now instead of tonight. Go see her. Give your condolences. Slip the poison in her drink. Better yet. Take her some apples with the poison laced inside. That should make you feel useful." Nukpana let out a blood-curdling laugh.

Barnabus stared at her; he rubbed his cheek where he felt a pain in his jaw. He backed out of the room, and went to find Princess Istar.

෨

"BARNABUS." Princess Istar said answering her cabin door. "Come in. It is good of you to visit. Have you seen Grandfather?"

Barnabus stepped across the threshold carrying a basket of food and a container of liquid. "Thank you for allowing me in, Princess Istar. Our hearts are heavy in the passing of King Elder. I have not been to see him yet. I didn't know if you wanted to go sit with him. I thought maybe I could join you and sit with you, if you liked."

"Oh. Thank you. That is kind." Looking down at the basket Barnabus held, Princess Istar said, "What's this?"

"It is not much, but I brought you a few provisions. I wasn't sure if you had thought of eating. You will need your strength for the days ahead."

He sat the basket on a nearby table. When he turned to her, Princess Istar collapsed in his arms sobbing.

Barnabus held her a few moments giving her comfort. Then, he took her chin in his hand and held her head up, when he said, "Come now. You should sit. Here, I can fix you something to eat. Then, we can go visit the King. That is what is best for you to do right now."

Princess Istar nodded. "You are right. I need my strength. I am weak."

After fixing each a plate, Barnabus asked, "Would you like some of this ale?" He held up a decanter. "I brought it special to honor your grandfather. I believe you will enjoy how it helps you relax and feel at ease."

"Sure. I've heard your ale has a taste of ginger. It will be good to drink something gingery. I could use a lift."

Barnabus poured a small amount into a wooden bowl. It sizzled. She took the container, but before she could move it to her lips, it was knocked out of her hand.

"Shis Kin Wu! What are you doing, you fool?" Barnabus was in a rage. Shwu pulled his sword and Barnabus pulled his. The swords clashed as Princess Istar tried to get out of the way knocking over the decanter. It shattered onto the cabin floor spilling its contents, which burst into flames at the same time, the apples in the basket rotted straight away.

Barnabus fled out of the cabin. Shwu grabbed Princess Istar. "Are you okay?"

"Yes. I think so. What was in that drink and those apples?"

"It was a substance that was filled with a magical potion of death. When found, you would have been thought of as dying from a broken heart, but no one here in King Elder's Camp would have known the truth. You would have been a zombie, in limbo, between here and purgatory."

Princess Istar shrieked in fear. "Oh, my poor Grandfather. Has it?" She swallowed hard. "Has the same happened to him?"

"I'm not sure. It may have. I wouldn't put it past Barnabus. He is evil. That is not all. He is working for Nukpana."

Princess Istar fainted.

"Now, you sure you have everything you need?" Shwu asked while he gathered his belongings. "I haven't got much time before I must leave."

"Yes. We should be good here," Mylo said. "No need to fear. We have her protected. We have King Elder's body secured. It will take Barnabus and Nukpana at least a season or two to find us. You go on. We have all we need here to be safe for many moons, if need be."

"I will tell the resistance what all you have done to help us. You are a true patriot." Shwu saluted Mylo. "Before I go, I want to be sure I can say good bye to Princess Istar. May I?"

"Of course. She is resting in the other room. I'll stay out here and wait for you."

Shwu knocked on the door to the next room. "It is Shwu. May I come in?"

"Yes," Princess Istar said. "Please."

"I'm sorry to disturb you, but I must leave. It will take me several hours to reach KC and her team. I must warn them of the latest events."

"I am very thankful for you. Without you, I'm not sure what would have happened to me, my Grandfather, King Elder's Camp, or all of Eldershire. You saved us all."

"Not so fast. Not yet. We only stopped Barnabus from assassinating you. He still got away. And he managed to harm your grandfather. That means that Nukpana knows we know. I must leave quickly, but before I go, I wanted you to have this gift. It is an ancient Caspian stone."

Shwu handed the stone to Princess Istar. "Keep it close to you at all times. Use it when the need is great. Hold it close to your heart." Shwu demonstrated by moving his own hands to where a heart would be if he were human. "When you do this, the Caspian stone gives you the protection of a legion of forces at your side until I or someone else can come to your rescue. Do you understand?"

"I do. But, do you have to go now?" Princess Istar held the Caspian stone in her hand. "I would like to talk with you more."

"When I return. For now, rest. Mylo and the others are here to keep you safe. We have your Grandfather well protected. Mother Elder and Yggdrasil will be here to aid you. I will see you again." Shwu signaled his good bye and left the room.

"When may we hear from you again?" Mylo asked handing him a pouch. "I fixed some provisions for you until you reach the resistance. They will be glad to hear what you have done. My only fear is that Nukpana finds us before Mother Elder and Yggdrasil can get here."

"Mother Elder will arrive soon, Yggdrasil assured me. Thank you for this," Shwu held up the pouch. "Please know I do this not just for Eldershire, but for my homeland too."

"I look forward to celebrating with you when this is all over. I have a feeling you have much to tell us all."

"Good day." Shwu closed the door.

SHWU FLED DEEP into the Wild Woods and traveled for several Two-Moons. On the morning of the third day, he managed to reach the edge of the scorched lands of Eland. Standing beside a tree that was gnarled, bent, and all of its branches had been stripped, he bent to see if he could read the marking on the side of its trunk when he felt a heavy object come down on his head.

A TROOP of sentinels of the resistance were walking along the edge of their encampment's perimeter when they spotted a body face down at the edge of a burned out wooded area.

One of the sentinels rolled the body over. "I know him. That's Shis Kin Wu. He was a General of the Trebbian for Barnabus. Why is he here?"

"Kill him," Another sentinel said. "We can't let him find where we are camped."

"No!" The first sentinel blocked the sword before it connected with Shwu's neck. "We can't make that assumption. We must tell KC or Mr Scruffy first." He turned to another. "Run to the encampment and tell them what we've found. We'll stand here guarding him until someone comes back. Make haste!"

MR SCRUFFY FLEW DOWN to where the troop stood over the injured Shis Kin Wu. "Is he still alive?"

"Yes. We weren't sure if we should finish him off or wait."

"I'm glad you waited. He may prove to be more important than any of us may realize. Can you carry him over to me? I'm going to grow and you can strap him on me. I'll take him to the camp."

SAFELY BACK IN THE ENCAMPMENT, Mr Scruffy went about finding the necessary aids to help him bandage Shwu's head. He was putting the finishing touches on Shwu when he woke up.

"Ah, there you are." Mr Scruffy laid the patch of basil paste aside. "How are you feeling?"

"Where am I?" Shwu tried to rise up, but lay back down. "Oh, my head." Shwu moved his hand to his forehead.

"Can you drink something?"

"Yes. That may help. My mouth is dry. What happened to me?"

"We're not sure. The sentinel troop out on duty checking the perimeter of the encampment found you lying face down. Do you have any memory of where you were headed?"

"Yes. I was coming to see you. I have news. KC told you about us, right?"

Mr Scruffy's beak began to click as though it was jumping uncontrollably. "We've not talked yet."

Shwu knew that KC would not say a word until she received her orders. "Where is she?"

"She is in her thípi. I'll get her."

"No need. I have summoned her." Shwu watched Mr Scruffy's brows knit together. "You doubt me."

"I do."

"I have an ability to telepathically speak to a being without allowing other beings to know. It is a trait my family has perfected and shared for generations."

"Just where do you come from, if you're not a native Elderian?"

"Why don't we wait for KC? We will see what she has to say. It will make it easier if you listen to what she has to say. And, I won't have to explain myself."

Moments later, KC walked into the thípi. "I can't believe you are here. When did you arrive?"

"Sometime before the Two-Moons set. I would have called out to you, but my head was bashed in. It happened when I wasn't looking. It is good to be here, I have so much to share."

KC looked at Mr Scruffy. He wanted her to know he was disappointed, holding his head tilted down and giving her his best frown.

"What?" KC asked.

"You know very well *what*," Mr Scruffy replied.

"You two can figure out who believes me and who doesn't later.

Right now, I need to tell you why I'm here." Shwu looked at them and waited. Mr Scruffy motioned for him to continue.

"It's been reported King Elder was murdered. It is not in the sense you'd normally think. He's really not dead. He's actually in a deep state of unconsciousness that gives the appearance of death, a zombie, if you will. Princess Istar would be in the same shape, if I hadn't been there to foil Barnabus."

"That changes everything," Mr Scruffy said. "But, we thought you were in league with Barnabus?"

"I was. But, then, I read KC's mind when we first met. I realized then that Nukpana was in the mix. She would try to destroy all of the good of Eldershire. And, I was with Barnabus making plans with Nukpana to make sure that happened.

Shwu paused. "Then, Barnabus talked with me about how he wanted to double cross Nukpana. You beings of the resistance are the only ones that have the best interests of Eldershire as your main focus. You don't plan to use the madness to help you get what you want and desire."

KC interjected, "But you said you were going to work with Barnabus."

"True," Shwu said.

"We appreciate you coming to us like this. This information is very important. But, before we embrace you within our group, the leaders of the resistance will need to discuss your appearance here. You understand?" Mr Scruffy said.

"Most definitely. You should scrutinize me. You have no idea if I am a plant of Barnabus' diabolical plans. I welcome your investigation into me, my past, and my intent." Shwu repositioned himself on the cot. "In the meantime, do you think I might be able to have something to eat? I may get my strength back quicker with some food."

"Of course," Mr Scruffy said, and then looked at KC. "You haven't fed him yet?" KC stood and stared back at him. "Shwu, what will you eat?"

"At this point, I'll take whatever you can give me. I'm hungry."

Mr Scruffy went to the doorway of the thípi. "I'll go share Shwu's news with Iolair, Gavin, and the other leaders. KC, will you join us after you get him some food? If all of this proves to be as Shwu said, we will need to put a plan into action sooner than later."

After Mr Scruffy left the thípi, Shwu said, "I hope my being here has not caused you problems."

"Why do you say that?"

"I got the distinct impression you had not told Mr Scruffy about us."

"Us? What *us* do you mean?"

"That we are friends and you trust me."

Shwu watched KC's expression change.

KC turned away and said, "Um, I'll go get, uh, that food now."

Watching her walk out of the thípi, he worried if KC was a friend or foe. He wondered how much she knew or why she seemed confused. Worse, he worried if he had made a wrong decision; it could mean life or death.

CHAPTER 22
FOILING THE IMPOSTOR

Shwu's had brought Mr Scruffy news that none of the Rebellion were prepared to hear so soon—the apparent death of King Elder. It has changed things. Unthinkable. Yet, here he stood, deep on the outskirts of Eland, in the scorched land, getting ready to make plans to lead a small band of rebels against Barnabus and Nukpana and their armies. What was he thinking? To top it off, he had a fake KC on his hands, and he wasn't sure how he'd get the real KC back into the fight.

Iolair paced back and forth in the thípi. "Where did you say Mr Scruffy went?" he said to Gavin.

"I think someone said Mr Scruffy was seen taking flight into the canopy of trees out past the cave entrance after he finished talking with Shwu."

"Great." Iolair walked to the doorway of the thípi. "I'll be back." He walked to the edge of the encampment outside the cave entrance and looked up. He couldn't see far. The Two-Suns had set and the Two-Moons had not risen yet. The sky was dark.

Deciding to send out a telepathic call to Mr Scruffy, Iolair waited. Just then he heard the rustle of twigs and leaves on the forest floor behind him. He turned, and saw Shwu.

"You startled me," Iolair said.

"That's not like you to have someone come up behind you without you allowing it. I remember our games at King Elder's Camp when we were young." Shwu walked up beside Iolair. "May I join you?"

"Yes. We must talk. Your presence here has caused great strife amongst us. There are those that believe you are an agent for Barnabus and bring us harm. The fact you saved Princess Istar from Barnabus is good news to us. We are pleased to know you did that good deed—"

"I know what you will say. It was only one good deed out of many bad ones lately." Shwu looked to the eagle that at one time was his friend. "What do you believe about why I'm here?"

"We know Barnabus is out to kill us for Nukpana. We know you were the General of the Trebbians. Yet, here you are. We are not sure of you, as you can understand. What do you want?"

"I want to change what I have helped start. I want to make my bad deeds as right as I can. I want to be an Elderian again—proud and brave."

Iolair looked to his old friend and wondered. He said, "Why should I believe you?"

"You remember that time we were caught in the terrible fire storm after the Drakein had killed my parents?" Iolair nodded. "You saved me that night. You pointed out what I needed to do to face my enemy to get out of that horrifying time. I'm standing here before you and am asking you to trust me as you asked me to trust you that night. I am Shis Kin Wu, the same you knew before. Your friend, Shwu." He stared into Iolair's eyes.

Iolair bowed his head. "You will need to prove yourself to me, but I respect your effort just now. And, I am willing to give you a chance. How do you propose to help right the wrongs you've done?"

"I have news about Princess Istar and how Barnabus tried to assassinate her. And, I must share what I've been told and have seen. I'd like to share it with the entire leadership of the resistance. Will you stand up for me and ask for me to be accepted?"

"You never cease to amaze me. You have information about Barnabus' attempted assassination of Princess Istar. Really?"

"Yes. I was there. And, you can discuss what I told KC before she came to meet you. You might find what she says to you very useful."

"Very well. I will do as you advise. I will speak with KC. Now, can you tell me what you know about Barnabus and how he tried to assassinate Princess Istar?"

THE TWO-SUNS SET EARLY, Mr Scruffy thought. It was dark. Darker than he remembered, and definitely darker than it had been since KC's return.

"May I enter?" Mr Scruffy said.

KC was sitting across the room with her back to the door. She jumped.

"Oh, ah, yes!" KC turned around. "Mr Scruffy! Come in."

KC got up and walked over toward him and motioned for him to enter.

"I didn't hear you come to the entrance. I was thinking about . . .Well, I was thinking."

"Time moves slow, doesn't it?" Mr Scruffy said. He walked into her thípi and motioned for her to sit back down. He flew up to the tabletop, and maneuvered his body to sit down.

Mr Scruffy said, "Think of me as a barrister complete with a black robe embellished with gold, a peruke, and bespeckled glasses with a professor's cap. Besides, it will help you as I ask some serious questions—"

"What?"

"You do know how British lawyers dress, right?"

"I'm not sure." KC said.

Mr Scruffy said, "We need to talk. You need to tell me everything." He settled down on his haunches, and folded his wings politely in front of himself, and then looked at KC.

She burst out with laughter.

The owl was not amused.

"I am so sorry," KC said—his shoulders dropped down and his posture took a hunched shape—"Have I let you down?"

The sound of Mr Scruffy's beak clicking echoed within the small thípi.

"Please forgive me, Mr Scruffy. I shouldn't have laughed at you like that. But, you have to admit; you are acting like you're ready to give me a lesson. I mean you truly did look like my Zen master. I felt like I was your newly minted magical apprentice. You have to admit that is funny considering what we are doing here."

"Enough of this chatter. I need to know what you know about Shis Kin Wu, Barnabus, and Nukpana. Everything. Do you understand?" He tried to control the tone of his voice, but felt it no longer mattered to be polite. He needed to know what they were facing.

KC shared what Shwu told her when they were in King Elder's

Camp. Further, she shared what Shwu knew about Barnabus, how he thought Barnabus was going to try to assassinate Princess Istar, and what he thought he could do about it.

The entire time that KC was sharing her encounter with Shwu, Mr Scruffy sat still, his ears pointed in her direction, his eyes focused. He was paying very close attention to each word.

"And, so that is it," KC said. "Do you have any questions?"

"What about Nukpana?"

KC looked down at her hands. "I don't have anything to say about her?"

"I thank you for sharing what you have. Did you not think it was important that you tell us about Shwu's telepathic abilities sooner than waiting until I asked you?"

"Yes, I guess so, now that you mention it. But, things happened so fast. I never had a chance to talk with you before he showed up."

"You could have telepathically told me, you know?"

"Yes. That is something I could have done. I'll be honest though. I didn't even think about it. All I could think about was getting to sleep so that I could make the journey here. I actually thought I'd have time before now to tell you. I've had a lot on my mind. I'm still adjusting to this new me. Besides, the pressure has ratcheted up quite a bit since the mention of Nukpana."

"You're right. I am not aware of what you've been through. Things are different." Mr Scruffy paused. He thought about what he would say next to not alarm her. "We all are on our game, you seem to be less so. You shouldn't be standing back without sharing what you know as though it will work out. With Nukpana orchestrating things, it won't."

"You don't think I know that!" KC stood up, then paced around the room.

Mr Scruffy recognized the signs of a squirm. She was caught, and she knew it. Her face was reddened and she walked with stiltedness.

"I can't believe this," she said, her arms and hands moving up and down in jerks. "I'm the bad guy because I failed to inform you about a being that all of you knew long before I met him. Why is this all on me?" KC adjusted her clothing. "We've got to begin making decisions and we shouldn't waste any more time on what I did or didn't do. What is your decision about Shwu and how we're going to proceed? I need to know."

"I'm not sure. But, you are right about one thing—we do need to move on and make our plans. We can continue this discussion later." Mr Scruffy looked to KC. He knew he had her caught with a cord around her neck; he needed to decide how tight he wanted to twist it.

Iolair, Gavin, and Mr Scruffy flew almost soundlessly through the trees. Mr Scruffy telepathically said to his companions, "Join me on that top tree branch that clears the canopy."

The three landed at different points, then moved together where they talked without fear of being overheard.

"I think it is time," Mr Scruffy said while listening carefully to the forest sounds below. His companions moved closer to him. "We will reveal the fake KC at our first meeting of the Herok'a. We must find out what we can about what she knows of Nukpana. She lied to me earlier. She is aware we might know; she is no fool."

"It concerns me that we can't sequester her now pending interrogation. What if she sends a warning to Barnabus or Nukpana?" Gavin said while scanning the forest with his eyes. "I feel like we are already in a battle."

"We are," Iolair agreed. "We might as well realize that Nukpana, through the help of Barnabus, took KC and replaced her with this fake one to learn our plans. Before we make plans for the battle, we must get rid of the fake one."

"What I don't get is when were they able to switch them out?" Gavin shook his feathers. "At least one of us was with her at all times."

"No, not exactly. There were a few clicks or two when she was alone," Mr Scruffy said. "When we left to go eat that night before we started out for the cave. Remember?"

"Ah," Iolair said. "You are right. She went to get her provisions. We took off to get food and get back to sit outside her cabin."

"Yes. By then, the switch had already happened."

"But how?" Gavin asked. "Weren't the Four Lemmketeers there?"

"No. They went to get food too. It was the perfect moment for Nukpana and Barnabus to act."

"Feathers! I can't believe we dropped our guard like that." Gavin fluffed up his feathers making him seem twice as large.

"Wow, Gavin," Mr Scruffy said. "Stop acting like you're a young'un. You're at least as old as me. Settle down. We will find the real KC."

"I hope you are right," Iolair said. "Let's go and foil the plans of an impostor."

THE THREE COMPANIONS motioned the other leaders to move on into the inner cave without delay.

Mr Scruffy nodded to Iolair and Gavin, "Let's do this!"

The assembled gathering was lively talking amongst their selves. Mr Scruffy sat at one end of the table with the leaders of the different

Eldershire beings seated around. To his left sat Iolair, leader of the Eagles; Gavin, leader of the Hawks; Fergus, leader of the Dryads; Lorne, leader of the Foxes; Ralph, leader of the Wolves, and then there was an empty seat. Next, was KC, who was not the real KC. All of their faces looked to Mr Scruffy, leader of the Owls to begin. The cave had grown darker since they had taken their respective seats.

"Should we have light?" KC asked.

"We must talk in darkness. Dark does not cast a shadow. We never know who may be lurking nearby," Iolair said. He looked to Mr Scruffy, "Would you like to begin?"

Mr Scruffy stood. "We are here to discuss our plans, our approach to what all of us are fully aware—the overthrow of Barnabus and Nukpana, and the taking back of King Elder's Camp."

The leaders all cried together, "Bravo! We will!"

"Settle down. First, before we begin our planning, I need you to know that when the time is right, I will introduce you to someone some of you know, others of you have only heard about. We will welcome him into our leadership group, and we will listen to him as he is very wise, knows much, and can help us in ways we cannot imagine."

"Who is he?" Lorne asked. "Will we meet him now?"

"In a bit. KC knows most of you, but one she has not met is Ralph, the Alpha of Wolves. Ralph, this is KC, our leader." Mr Scruffy telepathically said to Ralph, "Be cautious."

KC nodded to Ralph. "Good to meet you."

Ralph let out a long howl. "I just told my pack that you are amongst us. They will know who you are."

Mr Scruffy thought he saw a slight expression of disgust on Ralph's face when he raised his upper lip, the bridge of his nose wrinkled with his cheeks rising up.

He telepathically said to Ralph, "Easy. We will deal with her." Ralph's face relaxed. Being a wolf, Mr Scruffy was glad to calm him down.

"Now, to the business at hand," Mr Scruffy said. "I am about to introduce to you, Shis Kin Wu, an Elderian that is also a descendant of the Ents from Middle Earth. You know him as Shwu." The group began to murmur. "He is not what he seems. Many of you were told he is the General of the Trebbian and in cahoots with Barnabus. He is not. And, you need to know what we are facing. Barnabus is in cahoots with Nukpana."

The resistance leaders all stood up in unison when they heard Nukpana's name. "Is that true?" they asked. "What is Shwu doing here? Can we trust him? Can you explain this?"—and so on.

"Yes it is true! He brings us important news of King Elder! You can trust him and you better do so! I am explaining this. Now, if you would sit back down, wait, and listen, I'll continue." Mr Scruffy said, exasperated.

He held his wings behind his back and began to pace around the table while the leaders sat down. Mr Scruffy looked around the table to each leader and noted that they were not as agitated. They appeared to be giving him their attention.

"Good. It is best you let me tell you what you need to know before you jump to conclusions. The most important thing you need to know is that he is a friend. We don't need any misconceptions, lies, or misunderstandings causing us to fight amongst ourselves." The leaders nodded their heads. "Two-Moons ago, he visited with KC. He told her things that we need to know. He is willing to stand before you tonight to share his information. I ask of you to welcome him, give him your attention, and then we will decide how to move forward."

Gavin said, "Before we invite Shwu into the meeting, may we share what we know of him and what he has done for us?"

"Yes. I think that is a good idea, thank you," Mr Scruffy said.

Iolair raised his wing to speak. Mr Scruffy nodded.

"Thank you, Mr Scruffy. Before you introduce Shwu to the group, I think it important that I share with you what I know about him too." Iolair shared what Shwu had told KC about the planned assassination of Princess Istar and his encounter with Shwu the prior Two-Moons.

When Iolair finished, Ralph asked, "Since when do you believe a traitor, such as him?"

"You're right to be suspicious. I was. But, there is a piece of his news I could not overlook. He saved Princess Istar. He risked his life to do so. He then made his way here to warn us. And, he willingly shared Barnabus' plans of how he will fight us. That, in and of itself alone, is important."

"Maybe. Or, he has lied about saving Princess Istar and all the rest of it. I sent a select pack from my wolves to investigate," Ralph interjected. "I am to hear word from the main scout soon. We will see if what Shwu has told you and KC is true, and then I'll tell you my—" Ralph was interrupted.

In the distance the sounds of a pack of wolves howling made its way to the group. Ralph moved to the entrance of the thípi. He replied with an ear-piercing howl. The response was quick. Ralph moved back inside and took his seat.

"Well?" Mr Scruffy said.

"Shwu speaks the truth. My vote is to hear him out. Princess Istar is safe. Shwu took her to Mylo in Snowboro. Things in King Elder's Camp are in great disarray. It is also true that King Elder is not dead, but was put into a death-like coma. Shwu saved him too. I will be honored to meet him."

"Now, we should have Shwu join the meeting," Mr Scruffy said. "He can tell you why he risked coming here two Two-Moons ago.

But, before he joins us, I must ask you to be patient. Do not interrupt him and ask questions. He has come a long way at great risk to his life. He will serve us well; you must be careful not to annoy him. His anger could lead to our undoing. Is that clear?"

Each leader nodded.

CHAPTER 23
SHWU AND BATTLE PLANS

Ralph walked over to the entrance to the thípi. He lowered his tail, sat back on his haunches, and bent his front paws in greeting to Shwu. "I give you my allegiance," Ralph said, and then returned to his seat.

Shwu nodded toward Ralph offering his acceptance of his offer. He then looked to Mr Scruffy. "Where may I stand?"

"No need to stand," Mr Scruffy said. "Here is a seat for you." Mr Scruffy pointed to the empty chair. "I honor you and your rebellious work. Before we formally introduce you, I've asked Gavin to explain the name he, Iolair, and I have adopted for our group."

"I gladly share with you that from this time forward we will be known as the Herok'a." Gavin smiled. "Herok'a is a group of small hunting spirits without horns. We, as a rebellious group, are not evil. We're fighting to set things right again in Eldershire."

The leaders applauded and many said, "A good name."

Iolair stood before the Herok'a. "I'm here to introduce to you a new member of our fighting spirits, Shis Kin Wu, who is an Elderian. He goes by the name of Shwu."

"It is an honor to be introduced by a friend. Your rebellion name of Herok'a is fitting. I am ready to serve you as you deem necessary," Shwu said, making a reverent bow.

"Good." Iolair stood up and moved closer to Shwu. "Before we have you tell us what you know about Barnabus and his plans, we'd like for you to know we need you to serve as a leader of the Elderians that have joined the resistance. Will you take this lead?"

"Yes, with honor. Thank you."

"It is time we begin our plans in earnest," Mr Scruffy said. "Shwu, share what you know of Barnabus and his effort to over take all of Eldershire with Nukpana."

Mr Scruffy moved to his seat ready to listen. Shwu shared what he had learned and how he learned it. Many heads turned in shock when he told the leaders that he could listen into their thinking without them knowing he was listening.

"I assure you, I will not use that skill on you. Not now, not ever. But, you need to understand how I'm able to know what I do about Barnabus and still sit here before you alive. He has no idea and neither does Nukpana. She suspects something is up with me. That much I gathered while in her presence. I made sure I was never in her presence again. The situation with Princess Istar and King Elder hastened my departure from King Elder's Camp. I do not think I'll be able to return as long as Barnabus is ruler and Nukpana is alive."

"You suspect he has already taken over?" Gavin asked.

Shwu nodded. "Yes. I'm afraid so."

"How did King Elder's sentinels allow this to happen?" Lorne said. "I mean, weren't they guarding him?"

"They were. But, they were convinced Barnabus would not harm the King. When I overheard Barnabus' plans for Princess Istar, I knew I had to make haste. I couldn't get to King Elder before he was taken. And, telling the sentinels was a waste of time. I had to help the Princess."

"Of course. I saw first hand how Barnabus used his ability to make the Elderians think he was only working to help them. He has the knack of a wolf in sheep's clothing," KC said.

"Hold on there, young human." Ralph growled. "That story of a wolf dressing in sheep's clothing has misrepresented my kind for centuries. We never would stoop so low. We are proud of our abilities and strengths and have no need to act less than the strong beings we are."

"You'll be alright. It is only something I heard from someone else," KC said.

Ralph tilted his head. "Let's hear more of what Shwu has to say. Just remember you are in the midst of a diverse group of beings."

Mr Scruffy wondered, if when KC spoke up, she was under some kind of control from forces outside their group.

"Shwu, do you have more you need to explain before we begin considering our plans of attack?" Mr Scruffy said pointing to the map of Eldershire he placed on the table. Shwu shook his head. "Very good. Now, looking over the map, you will see I've stuck seeds on the map where different groups of the Herok'a are in place around King Elder's Camp."

"What about groups around Graves Mountain or Emerald Mountain? Should we not have scouts there?" KC inquired. "I seem to remember Nukpana held those close to her."

"Interesting you would mention those two sites. Gavin, share what you and your hawks have learned."

"We have, over the past six seasons, flown reconnaissance of both mountain areas, not knowing until this time that Nukpana was alive. We began those missions for the single goal to learn the fate of The Grey Menace and the size of Barnabus' Trebbian armies. Hearing about Nukpana being back amongst us, it makes what I thought was a mistake in our findings all the more correct now."

Gavin stood up and leaned over the table. He pointed to several locations while he continued. "We had seen activities in this area near Graves Mountain, but thought it strange that the beings we saw were not The Grey Menace. We expected to see them at Emerald Mountain, but as we learned they had fled into further regions of the vast lands to the west across the Bay of Styks."

"Gavin, may I ask a question?" Shwu said.

"Yes, of course."

"Did you fly up near Stone's River?"

"Yes. Once. We felt we should keep close to the areas we knew The Grey Menace tended to congregate. There was a report of the Trebbians near Stone's River, but we knew nothing of their strengths or of Barnabus' intent. Now, we need to scout that area with keen eyes."

"You should indeed," Shwu said. "I'd like to tell you about a battle I learned about regarding a river during the ancient time on Earth." He looked to the leaders and Mr Scruffy nodded.

Shwu said, "The battle was held across a river, a main tributary across the top section of this land called Italy. The cavalry and light troops were concealed by a ravine. The command of the losing army didn't think much about it. But, two-thirds of the losing army was lost, with many killed as they tried to escape back across the river. Most of the losing army that managed to survive were in small groups, and thus easily captured." Shwu paused.

"Are you suggesting that we setup a similar fight?" Iolair asked.

"Yes."

KC snickered. "Sorry, Shwu, but we used this very battle attack with our last encounter of Nukpana and The Grey Menace. They would see us coming."

"I don't think the Trebbians, and I'm sure Barnabus neither, would think you would try to use a similar attack. They are fools at heart. The Trebbians are also very rash and overly confident. Barnabus is sure he will overtake you. He is blind to his own counsel and seeks glory. The forest blinds him to the individual trees."

"That's a good point," Ralph said.

"I agree." Mr Scruffy got up and walked on the table to the map and placed his right claw near Stone's River north of Emerald Mountain. "Look at this map carefully. Gavin, you said your scouts saw a band of Trebbians here, correct?"

"Yes. About a season or so ago."

"Good. That means they have set up an encampment there. Where else have you seen them?"

Gavin pointed out on the map two additional locations—one at Reed Creek, north of the Fields of MaryJane, and the other at Stone's River south of King Elder's Camp and east of Grave's Mountain.

"This is looking promising. What if we set up a trap for Barnabus and his Trebbians at all three locations?" Mr Scruffy looked to the leaders and began to click his beak.

"It looks to me like we have a plan in the making," Iolair said.

Mr Scruffy, KC, and the leaders of Herok'a were standing before the various beings that served under the Herok'a leaders. They gathered outside the thípi where the leaders had held their meeting. Mr Scruffy stepped forward.

"Hello to each of you. The news we bring to you is that we have made our initial plans for our offense to attack the Trebbians in secret. We need each of you to listen to your respective leaders and what your individual troops will do to aid us with the surprise attack. It is critical that each of you learn your duties and those of the troops to your left and right. This is important in case you need to close ranks. We will make our first attack in four two-moons. You have until then to ready yourselves and give peace to your supreme being. May peace be with you and yours."

KC turned to Mr Scruffy, "What happens now?"

"We go through the training, we also speak with our scouts to verify the Trebbians are moving toward Graves Mountain like we suspect. If they are headed in a different direction, we'll need to adjust our attack plans."

"Are you sure she cannot hear us?" Iolair asked Shwu.

"I've placed a block on her ability to listen in," Shwu said. "What do we do?"

"First, we must find out where the real KC is being held. We also need to be sure we know that when we take out the fake KC, we are not tripping up our efforts for the surprise attack," Mr Scruffy said while walking in a circle, his wings behind his back, his face solemn. "This is hard for me. I look at the fake KC and all I see *is* KC, until she speaks. Then, I am stabbed to my core with the sickness of Nukpana. We must not fail."

Mr Scruffy walked along the banks of the Reed Creek, a short flight west of the encampment. He looked south, the direction from which it flowed. It was one of the only rivers that flowed north. He knew exactly where it began—just a little north of King Elder's Camp—along the Fields of MaryJane. He looked up into the night's sky. The Two-Moons had not yet risen. He wondered if Iolair and Gavin received his message he'd sent to them when the meeting ended. He had flown to Reed Creek in haste.

The silent whirl of wings beating fast, and then slowing caused Mr Scruffy to look to his left side. Gliding to the ground he saw Iolair's broad, strong wings moving in perfect timing with the wide surface of his wings causing a drag on the air. Iolair landed gently on the ground nearby. Not long after Iolair landed, Mr Scruffy saw Gavin in flight. His wings, broad, and rounded, shorter than Iolair's, were held at a shallow V-shape and his tail fanned out during flight. Gavin made a slight noise while moving in closer, slowly turning in circles to make his descent.

Iolair walked over to Mr Scruffy, "He is such a funny flier. Have you noticed how Gavin always has to do those endless circles? I think it's because his wings are so short. Mine are huge compared to his. I'm also a much better flier than he, don't you think?" Iolair grinned.

"Seriously. You want me to compare the two of you. I can't believe you're asking that of me, at a time like this." Mr Scruffy watched Gavin complete his landing. "Good. Now, we can get down to business."

Gavin walked up to his companions using a quick step. "Hope I'm not too late. I had to drop down for some carrion on the way over. It had been since early Two-Suns since I last ate. Because your message was unexpected, I didn't know when I'd have a chance to get some food again. What's up?"

"Too much information. I have been waiting a short time," Iolair said. "Scruffy, what *is* it? Your message sounded urgent."

"It is dire, I'm afraid. Let's move over here near the water. Reed Creek seems to be flowing full. It rained somewhere this night. The forest received a nice bath."

"Scruffy, what are you talking about?" Iolair looked to Gavin. The three moved nearer the water.

"I'm talking idle talk for a reason. Do you see that being over there?" His companions nodded. "That is the Little Washer of Sorrow. I knew she might be near. I wanted you here to witness this with me. We'll need more than this for proof, but I needed you to be with me before I make this accusation known to the other leaders."

"Little Washer of Sorrow?" Gavin said. "I'm not familiar with that being. What is she?"

"This particular being is a female spirit that when she appears by the side of a stream, you will notice she is washing clothes. Look closely at those things she is washing. Do you recognize them?"

Iolair said, "Why don't I go grab them? We can look at them closer."

"No! Don't. It is imperative you don't disturb this being. She is here for one purpose."

"And, what is that?" Gavin asked.

"To wail and weep for the coming death of someone close and important to us. Do you see the fabric, the colors, and the patterns? Do you recognize them?

Gavin stared. "They look like, but it can't be. How is this possible?"

"The being that this particular banshee is connected to is that of KC. It is her clothes. This spirit is telling us she is soon to be departed."

"What?" Iolair looked to Gavin. "That's impossible? How does it know? There are two KC's, right?"

"Yes." Mr Scruffy moved over to the edge of the woods. "We have much to discuss. I'm fearful that things are not as they appear. The evil one has worked her magic in ways I don't even think Mother Elder or Yggdrasil are prepared to encounter."

"Can we speak here secretly?" Iolair asked.

"No. We must make our way to The Land of Promise. But, we must go separately. Make haste. It is early Two-Moons now. We must meet up before early Two-Suns."

*

SCRUFFY, Iolair, and Gavin all landed within inches of each other. Waiting for them was Mother Elder and Yggdrasil.

"We got your urgent message," Mother Elder said. "Follow me. We've no time to lose."

They moved quickly to Mother Elder's special meeting room. Mr Scruffy waited until everyone was seated.

"I never thought I'd ever be saying this to you. The *real* KC is in mortal danger."

The group of leaders sat there in stunned silence. Mr Scruffy folded his wings behind his back, and began to pace back-and-forth.

"This is just as hard on me. We three have been dealing with the fact we have a fake KC amongst us."

"What?" Mother Elder sighed. "Are you sure?"

"We just left the fake KC not long before we flew here. She looks exactly like the real one. She is a little more stressed than I remember the real KC being."

"But that isn't the only thing you are going on to think she is fake, is it?" Yggdrasil said.

"No. Things she doesn't remember, things she acts like she remembers, but doesn't. And, things she should remember yet gets the details jumbled," Gavin said. "Worse. She is different. She reacts to different animals and strange beings with contempt or she doesn't want to be bothered. It is as if she has something on her mind or in it."

"Her arrival to Eldershire this second time, we were hoping she'd be our companion again. But that changed," Mr Scruffy lowered his head.

"When did you notice the change in her?" Mother Elder asked.

"For me, I noticed some things right after we met up with her in King Elder's Camp before we traveled to the encampment in the cave," Iolair said.

"Me too," said Mr Scruffy.

"And me," Gavin joined in, and then got up. "You know, it was about the time we all separated for dinner, wasn't it?"

"Yes. That's it. We went for our food. But weren't the Four Lemmketeers with KC?" Iolair said.

"I don't think so. I recall them saying they were going to get their food too," Mr Scruffy said.

Yggdrasil said, "That means KC was alone while she gathered her own food."

"They replaced her then with the fake KC, right?"

"Gavin, you're probably right," Mr Scruffy shook his head. "My question is if we kill the fake KC do we doom the *real* KC to death at Nukpana's hand?"

"Maybe. Unless we plan otherwise," Gavin said.

"What do you mean?" Mother Elder said.

"Suppose we work hard to find the real KC. Then, rescue her at the same time that we sacrifice the fake KC."

Mr Scruffy shared he wasn't happy with where any of their discussion was going. "What galls me most, though, is that she came back here and none of us thought we'd ever need her again."

"That's not exactly true," Mother Elder said standing up and motioning for Mr Scruffy to take her seat. "I have a story I need to tell you. Something in hindsight, I probably should have told you long before now." She walked around the group, and then stopping to stand behind Mr Scruffy. "KC is our Savior, which is true. But, she must die. If she does not, Eldershire will not survive."

The three companions gasped in surprise.

Mr Scruffy turned his head away and covered his mouth. Then, he said, "If she dies here, there is no returning to Earth. Is that truly her destiny?" His voice cracked.

"Yes. I'm saddened to have to confirm what Mother Elder says is true." Yggdrasil walked over to Mr Scruffy and patted his shoulder. "There is a reason this must happen. The blood Nukpana shed here must be paid for in sacrifice. Her evilness makes it too ugly to be received. By using the blood of an innocent—KC—we can appease the rule of life here in Eldershire."

"Did Nukpana know that this would happen when KC was here before?" Gavin asked.

"We do not believe so. Not even after KC was able to retrieve the Efil Stone."

"But that means we can sacrifice the fake KC in her place!" Gavin was elated.

Mother Elder said, "It is a good thought, but I'm not sure it will work. It is best we are prepared for the worst and hope for the best regardless of what we try."

"You're saying that because she was able to return the Efil Stone, she sealed her fate at dying during this dark time we are living now?" Iolair's eyes widened. "Are you sure?"

"Yes. We are sure," Mother Elder looked to each of them. "Each of you. Listen. Look at me. It is important we don't lose sight of our duties. We *can* make a difference."

"Can we save her?" Mr Scruffy interrupted. "Can we?"

"Yes. We believe you can, but you must listen. You must not interject. You must follow our directions to the last step." Yggdrasil said.

Mother Elder raised her chin high. Her neck became exposed.

Mr Scruffy noticed the spot below her neck where the Efil Stone was made. He knew she was baring her soul to them. "I'm ready to hear your words," he said.

Mother Elder looked to the others. "And, what about each of you?"

"I'm ready," Iolair said.

"As, am I," Gavin replied.

CHAPTER 24
NUKPANA'S REVENGE

"Gather around. All Elderians! Come One, Come All! Join us at half-night, here in front of Barnabus' cabin. We will learn of his plans for our future. You want to bring your entire family with you, as many of you that can come. Come One, Come All!" The voice boomed throughout King Elder's Camp through the echoing chambers made of hollowed tree trunks that were placed by Barnabus' Trebbians.

Barnabus walked up to the short statured Elderian standing beside the machine that played the voice in a loop making the announcement. The Elderian looked up, and then smiled.

"Willie. Good to see you up and about working again. Thank you for bringing this machine from Earth." Barnabus patted him on the back. "It looks like you've got good color back in you. Are you feeling better?"

"Yes. Thank you, sir. It is good to be back helping you again. Thank you, sir." Willie said. "I had no idea how long I was gone. It's very good to be back in Eldershire. How are things going with your preparations for tonight?"

"We're all set. We will want as many of the families gathered together this evening promptly at half-night. Will you and your Trebbians be able to make sure that happens?"

"You can count on it. They will be rounded up and moved here to the stage at the appointed hour. Will you want to use any guards around the camp area?"

"Yes. I believe that the rebellion members will try and break in this night to get to our little captive. We were able to get this far without them realizing what we have done. Those beings are so foolish and clueless. It was so easy to lie to them and to trick them into believing whatever we wanted them to believe. Clueless. They are so clueless."

"Barnabus, before you go, may I say thank you for all you've done for me through the years. You've been a trusted master to me. I hope I repay you with my work and deeds." Willie smiled.

"You will, as long as all the preparations make me look good this night." Barnabus turned and left.

"ENTER," the voice called from deep within the room in response to the knock on the door. "I've been waiting for you. What is your report?"

"The brain washing is working. All is going as planned. It was pure genius. Absolutely, genius. If you hadn't convinced me, I never would have thought we could have tricked her so easily. The time you spent in her body paid off for us. You understand that human better than any magic alone could do. Well done, My Treoraí."

The voice walked out of the shadows and smiled. "None of them have any idea, do they?"

"No. They look at the KC that is with them, and have no idea that she is not the real one. Their KC is a ghost of you. I want to learn how you did it. You are the master! The greatest Crone ever the way you created the fake KC. How much longer can you linger in this split state? Aren't you draining your life's blood to keep both of you breathing and walking?"

"Barnabus, you have much to learn. Much. Patience is not one of your virtues. I will teach you when the time is right. As for the fate of KC, in time, the magic will work that will enable her to be more me than I am myself. It is a sweet plan. One of pure revenge. She took the essence of my old body away. What better way to make things right again than for me to take the essence of her life force away. She will then walk as a dark shadow too."

"When do we begin?"

"Soon. Very soon. Your Trebbians, they are ready for the performance this night?"

"Yes. We have the area all prepared. Each Elderian family that attends will be reduced to a small pile of ash. All you have to do is have Blazewing at the ready."

"Perfect. We will then need the ash gathered. It will be necessary to have the ash ready in order to complete the last of the spell. Then, when the Rebellion least expects it, we'll drop the big bomb on them. Where is your loyal servant Shis Kin Wu, or should I say traitor?"

"He is staying by the fake KC's side. He said if he stayed there, she would not be the wiser to what has happened to her or will happen to the beings of King Elder's Camp."

"And, Princess Istar? Where is she?"

"Locked away in her cabin. She has no idea what is about to befall her precious Elderians. This, of course, could never have happened if King Elder were still alive. You were wise to get rid of him when you did."

"Barnabus, you are *wise* to praise me now. If things go badly—if things do not work out as I have planned—you realize you will receive the blame." Nukpana moved past Barnabus. He caught a whiff of a foul smell. He wondered if her body was deteriorating.

"Of course. As it should be, My Treoraí!" Barnabus took a deep bow in tribute to his leader. He stood back up, and then said, "Why would I not expect that? You are the Supreme Being of all of Eldershire. Only you can lead this vast place to the next level of winning we need. You are the only one to know the best for all of us. No one, and I do mean no one, is as smart and as intelligent as you!"

Laughter came into the room as a huge sound that vibrated in all directions. Barnabus looked around the room. Nowhere was Nukpana. He was alone. It angered him that she had laughed at his praises. I don't like that, he thought. She knows it too. She is tormenting me. There will be time sometime soon when I will be able to tell her that her approach to me was evil. She will learn that I, too, have power. I may not be as powerful as she; howbeit, I can make her life uncomfortable.

"Really? What makes you think I need you anymore?"

The voice ricocheted across the room, bouncing off the walls, and sounding like huge bells ringing in a big church. The pain from the loud sound caused Barnabus to fall to his knees. He grabbed his ears and began to cry out in pain.

"Oh, Nukpana, My Treoraí! Please, I beg of you!"

"You should have thought of the possibility of my anger taking revenge on you. My need for you is no more. Be gone!"

Blazewing's light shone throughout the room, the light grew in intensity, and then everything seemed to sizzle. Barnabus felt his adrenaline surge. His lips and chin trembled, and he pressed his elbows into his sides, thinking he could make his body as small as possible when the awful sound of the light beams searing his surroundings seemed to engulf him.

❧

THEN, it was quiet. Barnabus looked around. Shaking uncontrollably, he tried to straighten up. Could it be true? Did he survive? He didn't see Nukpana. The room was empty. All that was left was the dust that was settling around him, and the walls. Even the windows no longer held glass. How did I survive, he wondered? His knees were locked in place when he tried to take a step.

"I've got to get out of here," he said aloud. Or, he thought he did, but then he realized he couldn't speak. His fear had gripped him. He wanted to flee, but he had no idea where he could go.

He managed to move closer to the window that looked out over Graves Mountain. His eyes bulged; he couldn't blink. His body shook with tremors. He wrapped his arms around his belly squeezing his eyes shut, and then moaned. "I survived. I survived."

KC FELT a hand on her chin. Her head was pushed back and she could see the outline of a figure before her. She wasn't sure, but it looked like Shwu. She mouthed the words, but she wasn't sure if he could hear her.

"She's trying to speak, Master." Willie said.

"Good. Where did you say Barnabus went?" Shwu said. He walked over toward where KC was tied up on the cot in the cabin.

"He didn't tell me. He said he would be back in time for the announcement. Do you know what he is planning?"

"Now, why would he have told me anything? He hasn't trusted me since I went to this human's encampment and convinced them that I was on their side. The fools."

"They are dumb. I didn't believe it. I'd heard so much about how smart they were. Who would have thought any being could be so gullible?"

"It's not hard to imagine," Shwu said, a smile eased on his face. He had witnessed some beings that were not bright, like the one before him that moment. In contrast, KC was one of the brighter ones. She figured out something wasn't right. Otherwise, she wouldn't be here waiting for her fate now. He couldn't let her tell the others what he had done. Their future depended on their ignorance.

ॐ

A SOFT KNOCK was heard at Mylo's cabin door. Gavin stepped in, "Hello?" He looked around. Then, he walked over to the door to where KC was resting. He tapped on the door with a light touch. The door opened.

"Gavin, glad you could be here. We need to talk," KC said, and then walked away toward the cot. "I hoped you would come without anyone else."

"Is there a reason you are not talking with Mr Scruffy and Iolair too?"

"Yes. I don't trust them. I don't think they believe I am me. I am worried they will do something heinous to me. I am frightened that I won't be able to reach Shwu before he must do his part in helping to stop Nukpana. Why won't you say something? You just stare at me."

Gavin walked closer to her. "May I sit down?" KC nodded. "I am not sure what I can do. I'm only a red-tailed hawk. How can I possibly fight a great bald eagle like Iolair or a powerful horned owl, such as Mr Scruffy? After all, you've not given me much to go on to believe you are the *real* KC. What kind of sign can you give me?"

"That's the problem. There isn't a sign. I can only tell you I am me. The REAL me. Can you not see it in my eyes?"

Gavin looked into her eyes. "I trust you. I will go now to Mr Scruffy and Iolair and let them know they are making a grave mistake. Will that help you?"

KC nodded. "It will be a start. I must get to King Elder's Camp before dark, before it is too late. You remember Shwu told us he would be setting up a plan. We must be ready or Nukpana will win. She will get Barnabus to do her bidding. You do know that, right?"

Gavin stood up. "Yes, I know. You told us many times. You've made us listen to you and to repeat what you said. We are aware of Shwu and what he is trying to do." He walked toward the door. "I will go tell them now so that we might come back and help you."

KC looked at Gavin and began to sob. Gavin shook his head, and closed the door behind him.

SHE CRANED HER NECK; it hurt to move it. She had been in the cramped position too long. The blood in her legs seemed to have stopped flowing. Her arms were asleep from being held behind her for at least Two-Moons. That is, if watching the night sky through the window above her head was real.

She no longer knew what she could believe. Slowly, she moved her head back down and rested her chin on her chest. Her weakness seemed to be worse. How can I even think about fighting my way out of here, she thought? *Oh, where are you Mr Scruffy?*

"THE PLAN we've derived is all well and good, still, how will we know it has worked? Shouldn't we have a test of some kind that helps us know we did get the right KC?" Gavin asked.

"We are all who we are now, not what we thought we were, what we wanted to be, or what we will be," Mr Scruffy said. He looked to his friend. "We will need to find some kind of questions to ask her or derive something she needs to do to prove she is not the real KC. Maybe Shwu will have an idea."

"Why not something regarding the Elderians? They are tree

beings," Iolair shared. "A trivia question or challenge asking her to prove her muster."

"Those are good ideas, but a trivia question? Really?" Mr Scruffy snickered. "Let's be more focused on KC. What is one thing we know for sure about KC that no one knows, but maybe Nukpana?"

"That her husband Jay-H was not real, but a plant by Nukpana," Gavin said.

"Good one," Mr Scruffy said. "You know what makes it even better?" His companions shook their heads. "That the fake KC would not have been schooled on Jay-H."

"You do know that the *real* KC thinks Barnabus is Jay-H?" Shwu said walking up to the group. "She told me the last time we spoke."

"When was that?" Mr Scruffy asked.

"You think she was abducted right after we all split from her, correct?" Mr Scruffy nodded. "Then, it would have been that night before she went for her provisions, and we separated."

"Interesting. That means the real KC did think Barnabus was Jay-H, and if the fake KC is working in cahoots with Nukpana and Barnabus, why would she know about Jay-H?" Gavin said.

"We have our test. We'll ask her to tell us about her husband, and see what she says. If she never mentions Jay-H or that she was married more than once, we'll know we have the right one."

"Perfect. When we will do this? Our time is running out. We don't know how much time KC has left," Shwu said.

"What's wrong with tonight?" Iolair looked around to his friends. "We know where the real KC is now, yes?"

"I came here to tell you we got word that it is confirmed, the real KC is being held in King Elder's Camp, in a dungeon. We need to time this down perfectly, or else our plan could be doomed," Shwu said. "I'm heading there now. I should be in place by the time you are ready to destroy the fake KC. Send me a telepathic message with one word. I'll know to strike."

"What is the word?" Gavin asked.

"How about marplot? We are working to break up or destroy Nukpana's plot to take over King Elder's Camp. Seems a fitting word, don't you think?" Shwu said.

"Marplot it is. I'll telepathy you when all is ready here. You send me the word back if you are ready to go. If not, no reply in a few clicks will mean to abandon our plans. Will that work for you?" Mr Scruffy said.

"Yes. It will be a perfect fitting end for the fellifluous being that is Nukpana!" Shwu said. "The only part we are not prepared for is what will happen to the real KC when we destroy the fake one."

"We can't wait to find out, can we?" Gavin asked.

"No. Any waiting will risk the real KC being killed by Nukpana." Iolair said.

Shwu said, "Worse. If we don't act this night, the KC you all know and love will be no more."

CHAPTER 25
NOW, IT BEGINS

Willie stepped up to the platform, signaled the band to begin playing. The crowd moved closer and the noise settled to silence. Willie nodded to the bandleader for a softer sound. The band played a low tune that would remind one of a lullaby.

Barnabus made a hand signal for Willie to speed up the opening. He then said to Shwu, "Well, my friend. We are about to make history, if there is such a thing, here in Eldershire. Mind you, be prepared."

Shwu looked out at the crowd. He knew many would die that day—die before their appointed time like his parents did so long ago. He hoped that all the groundwork they had laid would pay off when it was needed most.

The symbols clanged, the trumpets blared, and Barnabus took to the stage. Shwu moved behind the stage toward the opening that he had carefully fixed. It would be his escape route when the time came.

"Elderians! Elderians! Thank you for your kind applause." Barnabus clapped at the crowd. He stood there watching and showing his appreciation by raising his fists in salute. The crowd's roar reduced to a slight whimper.

"This is it," Shwu said, and then ducked in between the folds of the back curtain.

"My fellow Elderians, I am here to bring you news of great things to come. I am here to share with you the whereabouts of King Elder, Princess Istar, and the decision of your Great Council. I bring to you news of the destruction of those rebellious members of your clan that when seen should be killed on sight."

The crowd roared to life. They began to chant a mixture of slogans they heard Barnabus spout while he traveled around making plans for his takeover. Shwu jostled his way through the brush to his cabin where he picked up his things. He could hear Barnabus' bluster. His words repeating the very thoughts he encouraged Barnabus to say. Shwu hoped it would buy him the time he needed to make his getaway. He peered out the cabin door. He saw no one approaching. He turned to pick up his belongings, when he met her standing there in all of her glory.

"And, where, may I ask are you going?" Nukpana said. "You are supposed to be with Barnabus. Has something changed I should know about?"

"No, My Treoraí." Shwu bowed in reverence. "I came to get my belongings as Barnabus instructed me to do. He said I should be ready to help him move with you. Is there something else I am to be doing at this moment? Aren't you supposed to be ready to go on stage?"

"No worries about me, Shis Kin Wu. I am standing on stage with Barnabus too while I'm here with you, playing the fake KC, and my last essence is hidden away. My powers have grown exponentially since we last met. I knew you would betray us. You have, haven't you?"

"If I have, you would know. There would be no need for questions. To answer you. No. I have not betrayed you. I have done all the things you asked of me. I am loyal to you and to Barnabus."

In the background, the voice of Barnabus echoed through. "I ask you Elderians, why give your allegiance to an elderly old fool. King Elder has died. Princess Istar is not here. Why not give your allegiance to me? I will take care of you as I always have done. And, to prove it, I have something of a surprise for you. Someone I know you will be surprised to see. Listen, my Elderians. Listen to *her* words!"

The crowd cheered for the excitement of a surprise. The pure joy of a surprise caused the crowd to act as though they were being saved from death's very door.

Shwu waited for Nukpana to finish, but then she was gone. He looked around the cabin and saw the blood stain on the floor. "She is weakening. The strain of playing four different beings at the same time is taking its toll on her. Her weakening is greater than anyone determined would be possible." Shwu smiled. My plan may work after all, he thought walking out of his cabin.

"THAT's all she said this time. I'm worried. It is as if she is weakening. Are you sure she is not the *real* KC?" Gavin sat down after he finished giving a report of his visit with her.

"Think about it Gavin. It is so obvious she is not real. After all, the KC we all know would not argue with any of us, most importantly Mr Scruffy." Iolair got up and walked over to the nearby table and picked up a couple of pieces of carrion. "When do we head out," he said to Mr Scruffy.

"You both are right. Gavin, she is weak," Mr Scruffy said, "I think. Actually, I hope it is because Nukpana is weak from splitting herself into different beings. Make no mistake, this is the fake KC, and she is being made to do what she is doing because part of Nukpana is inside her."

"You believe the fake KC is possessed by Nukpana? Why did we allow her to hear our plans?" Mylo said.

Nodding his head Mr Scruffy said, "We know she is playing the part of KC here, she must be herself somewhere in Eldershire, and she is playing yet another part to help Barnabus. It wouldn't surprise me that she has a portion of herself safely tucked away in case her plans fail. How else will she be able to survive if something goes wrong?" Mr Scruffy looked to his companions.

"Besides," he continued. "Iolair, you are right too. We can count on the fact this is not the real KC because she is too shallow, too smug, and definitely not the KC we've come to know." Mr Scruffy pointed toward his heart. "And. I don't feel the connection I had with her here. That means a lot to me."

Mother Elder walked over to them. "Yggdrasil and I are continuing to make this impostor think she is in Mylo's cabin. If Nukpana was to learn she was actually in the Land of Promise, I'm not sure how her magic would strengthen."

"Very good." Mr Scruffy got up and walked over to the table. He could feel hunger growing. "I know I should eat your provisions here, but I wonder if you would mind if I flew out for a while. My need to feel the wind on my face, my wings to fly through the air, will go a long way to help me learn how to deal with what we must do next."

"How long will you be?" Mother Elder asked.

"Not long. I will need to be refreshed before we make our next move. Shwu told us that Nukpana plans to use Blazewing during the rally. If she does, it will be her weakest point, and our only chance to destroy the fake KC, and release the real KC with Shwu." The group nodded in agreement. "I'll be back soon."

"THERE YOU ARE," Iolair said to Mr Scruffy as he landed and

moved toward the leaders of the Herok'a. "We were about ready to leave without you. Are you ready?"

"I am now. But, before we go, we must act," Mr Scruffy held the BlueStone for all to see. A gasp came across the group. "It is time."

Mother Elder stepped forward. "We will use as much of its power as we deem necessary. No more."

⁊▪

"YOU KNOW, I learned a long time ago that my world, the world of Earth, was made by a God that was very creative. When I learned that through reading works by writers of my world, like C. S. Lewis, I became aware that my world was enchanted. Yet, I seem to know without a shadow of doubt that Eldershire is the essence of all creativity and enchantment. If that is so, you don't hold as much power over me as you believe you do," KC said to Nukpana.

KC stared at the evil witch with an intensity she felt in her bones. The bitter taste in her mouth echoed the taste of the bead of sweat that fell on her lips. The feeling of anger had left her. She was being engulfed with rage and vengeance to the point she smelt sulfur like that when a match is first struck.

"When you or I make a choice, there are consequences. Pure. Simple. I chose not to believe you. Mr Scruffy, Iolair, Gavin, Mother Elder, Yggdrasil, none of the rebels are in danger. You are the one. You are on the verge of defeat. It panics you, doesn't it?"

A large grin spread across her face. Then, deep, down in her gut, a belly laugh began to form. She started laughing and continued while tears flowed down her cheeks.

Nukpana turned in a huff.

KC stopped laughing. "You will *never* beat us," she said. "Never."

Nukpana walked out.

"You hear me?" KC called after her. **"Never!"** KC laughed hysterically.

&

Nukpana walked up to Barnabus. "I asked you to wait before you called me out to the crowd. You needed to see she was here. Why did you not come to me immediately?"

"I came as soon as I could get off the stage without it looking ridiculous. Where is Shwu? I thought he was with you."

"He left by the back getaway route."

"What?" Barnabus starred at Nukpana. What has the fool done now, he wondered. "When?"

"Evidently, while you were on stage. I followed him, but then I lost him."

"You lost him? How is that even possible?"

"I am split into four beings now. My strength is not where it should be for me to strike. If I use Blazewing now, without Shwu here to aid in my energy replacement, I will surely die. At least, this being of me will. Is that what you both were counting on?" Nukpana raised her hand prepared to strike.

"Are you mad? Now, when we are so close? Of course not," Barnabus stepped back from Nukpana. "Let me contact Shwu. I'll find out where he is and what he is doing."

"No need. I found him. He is in there, the cell beside KC. He is half dead; he won't last much longer. If you want to avoid the same, you will get him to confide in you."

Barnabus nodded. "How soon may I see him?"

"You better see him now. I feel his life force waning."

Barnabus walked into Shwu's cell. His body—battered and bruised

—lay against the stone wall, his head slumped over. When Barnabus touched him, Shwu groaned.

"It is me," Barnabus said. "What have you done? Why did you leave me?"

Shwu lifted his head a bit. He mouthed something.

Barnabus said, "I don't understand. Do you need water?"

Barnabus reached for a cup near a bucket. He dipped the cup into the water only to see a lizard crawl out. Dropping the cup, he left the room. He searched the dungeon for Nukpana; she was nowhere to be found. He saw a shadow moving away from the cell that held KC. He walked toward it, then heard the horrifying laughter of madness.

"Has she won?" Barnabus said.

He felt a shudder move down his spine. It was like the unnerving tingling he felt when he awoke inside the crypt; he thought he was buried alive. He knew he was going to die. And then, he saw her—standing there before him. Beckoning him to join her.

He had united with her and now, here he was. Lost in a dungeon. Searching for her, she was nowhere. Fear began to grip him. He shook his shoulders in hopes he could calm himself.

KC's cell was behind him. He turned and walked over, looking in; he could not make out what shape he saw. The laughter had subsided. His eyes adjusted to the darkness. What he saw horrified him as much as the sounds he heard earlier.

KC's body was stretched into a perfect pentagon shape—her arms, legs, and head each was one of five points. Blood drained from her body down to the floor. The smell was rancid and rotten. Parts of her body had been skinned, other parts lashed and cut. She was near death too.

"What have I done?" Barnabus reached to open the cell door.

"You help her, you seal your fate," Nukpana said behind him.

He turned toward her. "You said you were going to capture her. You never said anything about murder. Why are you killing them both? Shwu was to be your vessel. How can you transport into him in his weak state? You can't go back to her now either. Are you insane?"

"Of course!"

•

WHEN THE LEADERS of the Herok'a found the dirt path that might lead them to the entrance to the dungeon where Shwu and KC were rumored to be held, the group moved through the forest like they owned the land, the trees, and were well prepared to take no prisoners.

Mr Scruffy found a sentry at the dungeon's entrance. He was asleep on his watch. Iolair moved quietly up behind him; grabbed him by the throat, and used his hallux talon to finish him off. The sentry's body slumped over to the side. Iolair motioned for the leaders to follow him inside the dungeon.

Moving to the entrance, Mr Scruffy said telepathically to all, "From this point forward, we will only talk amongst ourselves telepathically." They all nodded. Then, Mr Scruffy said to Iolair, "Where do you think they may be?"

"I have sense of Shwu in this direction," Iolair pointed straight ahead. He walked with steady steps forward, looking out for where another sentry might be stationed. He stopped and replied to Mr Scruffy, "Wait there. I'm not sure what is happening. There is a wall in front of me. No exit to the left or right."

Mr Scruffy said, "Let me come up to where you are. Maybe together we can see what is before us but appears hidden in the darkness. My eyes are better than yours in the dark."

Reaching where Iolair stood, Mr Scruffy scanned the area. He saw, what looked like a handle made out of a boulder embedded in the wall. "What is this?" he said telepathically. "I wonder." He pulled on the handle and a secret passageway opened before them."

"What should we do now?" Gavin said walking up behind them.

"We should give it a try. The worse that will happen is we'll be in hand-to-hand combat with our enemy." Iolair moved into the passageway. He turned back and motioned for the others to follow.

The group worked their way into the next corridor, all the time looking for a cell that might be keeping KC or Shwu. Suddenly, they heard a loud burst of wicked laughter. The sound came from deep within the dungeon down the corridor. Gavin started to make his way toward the sound when Mr Scruffy held him back.

"We don't know for sure if that is KC or the evil witch playing a trick on us. We must be careful and take our time. Nod to me if you understand." Gavin nodded, as did the others. "Good. We will continue down this corridor, but we'll advance with great care. The Evil One can jump out on us at any moment. Be prepared."

It seemed like an eternity to Mr Scruffy when they found the cell that held KC. He was appalled at what he saw. The pain he cried was sent like a shock wave of sound hitting those who could hear him telepathically. He knew he had to control his anger. He wasn't sure how well that would work if Nukpana walked in on them at that moment. His blood pressure climbing, he hoped his companions were keeping themselves together.

Moving up beside KC, he saw she was still breathing, though barely. He reached out to Iolair, who stood beside him shaking. He knew that shake. Iolair was ready to kill. He turned and found Gavin rocking back and forth as though he were arguing with himself about what to do next.

"Iolair and Gavin, I need you to control your tempers. Now, more than ever, we need to be in control if we're going to be able to save her."

Mr Scruffy hoped he could control his own anger. He was having difficulty swallowing, and couldn't help but fixate on what he saw. Nukpana had mangled KC in ways he had not seen since the time of the rampage of the Drakein. Thanks to Yggdrasil, Nukpana didn't have fire as a weapon this time.

"How will we get her out of here? She can't walk. It looks like they broke both of her knee caps." Iolair said examining her.

"Can we pour some of the BlueStone water on strategic places to help those areas heal enough she can be moved?" Gavin asked.

KC let out a wail. The three friends realized the horrible noise they had heard earlier was KC.

CHAPTER 26
THE HEROK'A

It was hard not to feel her pain, to smell the rancid odor of old, dried blood, to imagine what she was going through, to succumb to the darkness that emerged with the black procession of phantoms that haunted his eyes as he looked at KC's unconscious ones. The dark shadow that was cast over her was like a ghost lurking around in pursuit of all souls and betraying them too.

Mr Scruffy said, "Our acts our angels are, for good or ill, are our fatal shadows that walk by us still," He looked to his companions. "Her pain must be great. She was tormented until she surrendered her sanity. Mother Elder said that if we found her incapacitated, to feed her the water. Help me hold her head up so we can give her droplets."

"She'll need more than droplets," Iolair said.

"Yes. But, for now, we want to only be able to get her awake enough she won't scream and we can get her out of here." Mr Scruffy lifted her chin, KC moaned. Gavin, with care, administered the water.

"Good. I think you managed to get a fair amount into her. Mother Elder said it wouldn't take long. While we wait, can the two of you look for Shwu?" Mr Scruffy said holding KC's head with tenderness.

"No need," Ralph said. "We found him not far from here. He is very weak. We are not sure how he is still alive. As bad as KC looks, he is in much worse shape. They had to have used him as a punching bag. It also appears that she used her weapon on him."

"Let's hope she didn't find out what he was doing for us. If so, we may not be able to get out of here." Iolair said. "Should we move him in here?"

"Ralph, you and Lorne, see if you can give him some of the water. Then, we'll determine what we can do to help him out while we also try and get KC out." Mr Scruffy said. "It's a good thing we didn't expect him to be okay. I'm not sure we could have gotten him out and KC if it had been only the three of us." He saw Iolair pacing while rubbing his wings together while Gavin's gaze flitted around the room, never settling on a single object.

Mr Scruffy said, "You two can't be Worry Birds—"

KC started to laugh, and then she said, "Worry Birds. Is that anything like the Angry Bird game I played back home?"

Mr Scruffy and his companions began to talk at once. "We are pleased to see you out of your stupor." "Your wounds, they are all but healed?" "How do you feel? Are you still weak?"

"Hold on. Give me a chance. Where am I?"

Before Mr Scruffy could answer, Ralph and Lorne came into the room helping Shwu.

"He is awake, but clearly in much pain from the grimace on his face," Lorne said.

"Seeing you alive, means we have succeeded," Shwu said to KC. "I'm very happy to see you again."

"As am I," KC replied.

"We can continue this reunion once we are safely out of here," Mr Scruffy said. "Let's see if we can make it outside, and then we'll take flight."

After getting Shwu situated with enough of the healing water—his external wounds were not as severe—the Herok'a moved their friends to the exit of the dungeon.

Right at the moment KC took a step to enter the forest, KC saw Nukpana standing before them.

"Watch—"

Nukpana summoned Blazewing with a strike toward KC, but Shwu lunged in front of the light, taking the brunt of the weapon's discharge. He dropped at KC's feet.

"Nooooo!" KC's anger boiled over. Fea magically appeared in her hand. She wielded her sword, and slashed several Trebbians that stood beside Nukpana. Then, she made a connecting blow to Nukpana, who was weak after using Blazewing.

The blow from KC was not fatal, but it hit its mark. Blood oozed out of Nukpana's left arm. She disappeared in a cloud of red vapor. The remaining Trebbians fell to their deaths when the Herok'a took their revenge, but not without Iolair receiving a crippling blow to his wing.

WHEN THE HEROK'A arrived back in the Land of Promise, Mother Elder and Yggdrasil awaited them at the cabin they had set up to house the wounded. Iolair was bandaged and given some of the healing water, while Shwu and KC were taken to Mother Elder's cabin to be treated due to the severity of their wounds.

It seemed as though it took KC a long while to come out of her stupor. Mr Scruffy waited by her side. The other Herok'a waited outside Mother Elder's cabin for word of how KC and Shwu were progressing.

"You realize we now have to deal with the fake KC before Two-Suns. If the real KC sees her, or if Nukpana is aware of either KC being here, we could be doomed," Fergus said to Ralph and Iolair.

"You are right. We must have Mr Scruffy make a decision about how to finish our plan for the fake KC," Iolair said. "I'll see if he will speak with me."

"And, if he doesn't?" Fergus inquired.

"Then, we will need to make a decision without him." Iolair turned and went into Mother Elder's cabin.

"Mr Scruffy, thank you for seeing me. I didn't want to disturb you, but you understand, we must act now," Iolair said.

"You are right to force my thoughts on this manner. Fergus is able to do the test of the fake KC. Have him, you, Gavin, Ralph, and Lorne confront her. Be on your guard as we now know Nukpana is making this poor creature serve her evil deeds. Nukpana may be weak, but her magic is strong."

"We will go complete the plan to destroy the fake KC," Iolair said. "It is best you stay with KC now. She may wake and will want to see you."

"Two-Moons have been risen for many clicks and you are now coming to see me. I told you I was supposed to be at King Elder's Camp and not stuck here in Snowboro," Fake KC said. She turned to Mylo. "Sorry. Your hospitality has been good. I am supposed to be helping Shwu. Why won't you let me go to him?"

"There is no need," Fergus said. "We are here to award you with our highest honor by offering you a test of sorts, and then bestowing on you the laurels of the forest."

"Really? Well, now that is more like it. What kind of test?"

"You will need to answer a question or two," Fergus said.

"Ask away. I've learned well while here. I can help you with what you need." KC smiled.

"Tell us about your husband. He is still on Earth, right?" Fergus said —she is so brainwashed, she will stumble in her effort to show how smart she is to her detriment.

Fake KC stood before the assembled Herok'a and shared what she knew of the real KC's husband Jack. Not once did she mention Jay-H. Fergus knew she was trapped.

"You failed to tell us about your second husband, and how he was a pawn of Nukpana," Fergus said.

Fake KC took a step back. Her face showed she realized her error. Pulling her sword, she began to swing violently at those standing in the cabin. While exerting her energy wielding the sword, for a few clicks, Nukpana appeared.

"Danger! Protect yourselves, she is here!" Iolair said.

A battle ensued with Iolair and Fergus both fighting with the fake KC. The swords clashing and moving through the air gave a swishing sound mingled with metal clanging.

Fergus tripped over an uneven spot on the floor causing him to fall and drop his sword. Iolair noticed Fergus searching for it with fear marked on his face. The fake KC moved over to strike him while he tried to get to his feet.

She raised her sword to strike Fergus while Iolair stepped over to give him a chance to move. Iolair swung his sword connecting with precision, lopping the fake KC's head away from her body. Her head rolled up into the air, and then vaporized.

At that same moment, the darkness of the cabin grew in intensity as though being swallowed up by night. The room trembled, and then a light began to grow as Early Two-Suns rose.

AFTER THE DESTRUCTION of the fake KC, Mr Scruffy, along with Iolair and Gavin, visited with KC in the Land of Promise to let her know she was protected by them.

"What can you tell us about what Shwu did for you and how this all came to be that you were captured by Nukpana," Mr Scruffy asked. Iolair and Gavin stood nearby.

"Shwu actually saved me from certain death by Nukpana's hand by sacrificing himself to be her vessel." KC said. She got up from the cot and walked over to the table. Her thirst was great. She had not had good, clean water for a long time. She took a drink. "That tasted wonderful. How long was I gone?"

Mr Scruffy walked over to the table and sat nearby, "At least one full cycle of the Two-Moons, which to your Earth time would be a month. Tell me what did he do?"

"He did what any good blooded secret agent would do. He lied to Nukpana. He lied about how I was not willing to help after he tried to persuade me to serve Nukpana as her vessel. In reality, we had come up with a plan to switch places. He would be the vessel; I would destroy her when she went to morph into his body. We did not plan to be caught."

Mr Scruffy cocked his head to the side, pursed his lips, and lowered his eyebrows. "How can that be? He was going to rescue you, and then the two of you together would meet us here, in the Land of Promise."

"True. That was the plan. Shwu learned that Willie got wind somehow of what we planned regarding trading places. He told Nukpana while not telling Barnabus. Barnabus was thrown to the wolves by Willie, as we say in the mountains of Appalachia."

Mother Elder and Yggdrasil walked in. "We're here to tend to your wounds. How are you feeling?"

"I'm still very weak and I hurt."

"That is to be expected."

"How is Shwu doing? I see Iolair here." KC looked to Iolair. "You look no worse for the wear."

"Thanks, KC. You will be up and about before you know it too," Iolair said.

Yggdrasil moved over to remove a bandage and pour more of the healing water over KC. "Iolair is all but healed. I think he is enjoying the attention." Everyone giggled.

"I'm sure he is," Mr Scruffy said.

"Shwu is improving a little slower than you. The Blazewing attack damaged his insides," Yggdrasil said. "The acid bubbles ate deep into him. We are hopeful."

"You will keep me apprised of his condition, right?"

"Of course. Come Mother Elder, we must see Shwu now." They left the room.

"May we continue?" Mr Scruffy asked.

"Sure." KC said. "I, too, have things I need to know. Most importantly, why was Barnabus not killed as planned by Nukpana? From what Shwu told me, Barnabus was to be sacrificed in front of the Elderians when Nukpana used Blazewing on him first, and then she would turn it on all of those in the crowd."

"That is a puzzle. What else—"

"KC," Gavin was at her doorway. "You must come. Shwu has turned for the worst."

"It is not clear to me why he is not responding," Mother Elder said to KC when she walked into the sick room. "Shwu is strong, an Elderian. These waters should heal the damage done."

"He is not a full blooded Elderian," KC said. Mother Elder, Yggdrasil, and Mr Scruffy looked to each other, and then to her to continue. "Remember, he is part Ent and part Elderian. His parents were killed by Nukpana during the first uprising when the Drakein roamed. He thought you had not done your due diligence in trying to circumvent their death and destruction to this place he called home. When Barnabus arrived, he fell prey to his diabolical ways."

"If he is of Ent descent, then he is even more a tree being than many who live as Elderians now. That doesn't explain why the waters are not healing him," Yggdrasil said.

"True. But, Ents are part tree and part human. It is his human part that is causing his being to fight back. His anger was aroused when he went after Nukpana. At that moment, his Elderian spirit was at its weakest. I seem to recall when Nukpana and I were joined, she felt confident that she would be able to strike me down once I was on Elderian soil. I believe that Shwu's Ent heritage is what weakens him now, his human portion."

"If that is true, why did the healing water help you?"

"I wasn't struck by Blazewing and the full evil of Nukpana herself."

Shwu moaned. KC moved closer to him.

"Can you talk?" Mr Scruffy said while KC wiped the liquid that had formed around his mouth. Shwu nodded. "Please tell us what happened when you went to get KC?"

Shwu struggled with a cough. Gasping, he said, "Barnabus began to develop powers he didn't know he acquired. In confidence he said that Nukpana found him near death in a crypt. Since that time, he felt something changing within him."

Shwu's voice was growing weaker. Mr Scruffy, Iolair, and Gavin moved closer to hear him.

"Not long after he began working with Nukpana, she poured some of her elixir into Barnabus to help him in order to use him. What she didn't know was she inadvertently gave him some of her power when she shared her powerful liquid."

Mother Elder's mouth fell open.

KC said, "What?"

"Yes. I had not told you this before KC. You know, I shared with you that there is a secret place in Graves Mountain that would enable you to get the elixir. This elixir KC could use to destroy the remaining three-forms of Nukpana. KC's timing will need to be exact and it would require her to maybe sacrifice herself." Shwu gagged. KC reached for some of the healing waters and offered him more. He shook his head.

"You must hear me out. You must know, so you can decide what you will do next." He swallowed. "A part of you might die when you touch the elixir. KC, you will need to be careful. But, since you were possessed with a part of Nukpana, there is the chance you will have some protection from the liquid's power—its harm to you. You won't know until you pick up the vial."

The leaders stood around Shwu. No one said a word. KC felt tears fall onto her cheeks. "Thank you, Shwu." KC shook her head. "This is important to know. I have a lot to consider," she said in a monotone voice.

Shwu reached for KC's hand. He smiled at her, then with a voice that sounded as though his essence was leaving him, Shwu said, "This is only the life of my shadow. Real life hasn't started for me yet. It will, and when it does, we will meet again." He smiled, took a last breath, and then died.

After the many deaths KC saw on Earth and in Eldershire, watching

Shwu die, KC's chest felt like it caved in. She dropped to her knees sobbing.

&

"WHAT?" Gavin cried out after KC. "Come back here, KC!"

KC walked out of the room that held Shwu's lifeless body. She walked toward the open space of Mother Elder's meeting area. Looking down, and then out into the sky before her, she was at a loss for words, for reason, for understanding. She rubbed her arms absent-mindedly, pacing the area trying to make sense of what had just happened. *Why am I here? Why do I care?*

She turned around, then looked up, dropped her hands to her side, and cried, "What have I done to deserve this?"

Yggdrasil walked up to her. "Nothing, my child. You are here to take on the quest to save Eldershire once more. This is your destiny."

KC jerked her head back, looked at him with widening eyes. "That's what you have to say—my destiny—really? At least, Shwu gave me more than that. Look where it got him." KC turned her back on Yggdrasil.

Mr Scruffy flew over to KC's side. "May I talk with you?"

"What are you going to say that will make any of this right?"

"I don't know that I can, but I know this." Mr Scruffy paused.

KC said, "What? Get it over with."

"Your sword, Fea." KC nodded. "It is the anathema to Nukpana. You and Fea together are a force for good."

"You can't be serious?" KC shrugged. "You are wrong!"

"Think about it. I've noticed each time Nukpana uses Blazewing since she came back, you also held Fea in your hands. She appeared to lose power and control, whereas, you, wielding Fea were in control and your strength seemed to improve."

KC thought of their fight in the dungeon. Could Mr Scruffy be right? She turned to him and at the same time pulled Fea from its sheath.

"Could it be that simple?" Fea glowed with a bright light. KC smiled at Mr Scruffy. "Thank you, my friend. I should never doubt you."

CHAPTER 27
STEALTH MODE

The growl that grew within took even her by surprise, her eyes popped with anger; her hands trembled as the insane cry came from her throat.

"I'll destroy them all!" Nukpana screamed.

She slumped down in the Throne chair; weak from the destruction of the fake KC and her replicated self in the dungeon. She could feel her blood boiling as the wrath grew. She didn't want to hide her shock and rage. She wanted the Trebbians standing around her in the Throne room at Graves Mountain to see and realize she could get worse.

Jerking to her feet, Blazewing in her fingers, Nukpana didn't care how weak she already was, she would use it. She needed to destroy something.

"My Treoraí!" Olaf called to her.

Nukpana turned and saw Olaf, the Flashy, standing before her. He was the reason she knew of Shwu's betrayal and Barnabus' clumsiness. She would not let her plans to take over Eldershire fail.

A chant began down in her gut. She was ready to use the deep, dark magic of Amon, her ruthless mentor, and a powerful demon. He told her to use the Alp chant only when she felt trapped. Turning toward Olaf, her chanting changed to a choral tone. She would release the Alp within her.

"We are here to serve. How would you want us to help?" Olaf said.

Nukpana's pointed, dark-black hat turned into a Tarnkappe—a hat Amon gave her to use to conjure her power. She would use it to turn into the mist. The Tarnkappe, colored a blend of deep purple, black, and gray sat high on her head, like a top hat with a purple veil wrapped around her face and neck giving the illusion of the mist she would become.

Her eyes grew large while she continued to chant; her body started twisting and turning. She transformed into a mist that moved through the air as a ghostly apparition enveloping Olaf, the Tarnkappe still visible floating along.

"What—" His voice muffled when the mist moved into his body.

Olaf jerked, squirmed, and then straightened. He stood tall. The Tarnkappe returned to the shape of Nukpana's pointed hat. He picked up Blazewing, and then turned to the Trebbians.

In a deep voice he said, "I am ready to rule now."

"Do you have your weapon?" Mr Scruffy asked KC moving closer where she stood at the entrance to her thípi in the Land of Promise.

"Yes. Fea is in my thípi. Any news? Isicaranon along with Seborn and his squad should have arrived at King Elder's Camp by now. Barnabus, or worse, Nukpana, might trick us once she learns I'm with you."

"Most likely one of them will, especially, once Barnabus learns Shwu betrayed him. To your question, there's been no word."

"You're not worried?"

"No. Owls never worry. I leave that to you."

"Thanks. I appreciate your willingness to leave it to me," KC said, ribbing him. "I'm going to my thípi and try to get myself used to holding Fea like a weapon again. It's been awhile. See you at early Two-Moons."

"It will come back to you like magic."

Mr Scruffy flew off toward Mother Elder. KC walked into her thípi. She felt herself begin to brood. She couldn't help worrying about Seborn and thinking about their loss of Shwu. *Seborn said he'd contact us when he got to King Elder's Camp,* she pondered. KC decided to walk to the mesa that stretched to the horizon. It gave her a beautiful view of the Land of Promise. Peace and tranquility made it feel like a safe place to think. *I want to stare up at the sky.*

When her foot stepped passed the threshold of her thípi, KC felt strange. A chemical smell—a mix of smoke and sulfur—wafted past KC's nose. She shook it off, and then a surge of energy came over her. She looked down at her hands and couldn't see them. Her heart started to race.

"Nukpana?" KC looked to her left and right. She couldn't see the horizon. "Nukpana?" Her voice was louder. "I know you can hear me. Face me. Or, are you more of a coward than I thought you were?"

"I'm not Nukpana. But, I'll allow you to see me. I won't be there with you; it is a projection of me."

"Drakania? Is that really you?" KC remembered her reptilian form. She was a beautiful dragon. The scales of her skin shimmered like iridescence multi-colored stained glass when the Two-Suns' rays shined upon her. Her eyes sparkled like new diamonds accented by her aquamarine pupils.

"It's true! I learned you were free from Nukpana. I had to see you. I wanted to verify it was true. How are you?"

"Right now, I'm a little scared."

"You can relax. I won't harm you. You saved me, after all." Drakania said.

KC smiled, yet she wished that Fea was with her.

Drakania said, "No need to worry about me. I know things because I've passed on to the next realm in Eldershire. Mother Elder has kept me informed about you."

"I'm surprised I can see you. How is it possible?"

"Eldershire. Remember. It's a byway on our journey of life; it is where one goes after dying while waiting to go to the next part of one's journey. I'm still waiting."

"How long has it been?"

"Many seasons. As part of my penance, I must repay those who helped me. I have done so for all those who helped me after I was free of her dreadful spirit—all, that is, except you. I couldn't help you while you were in the Earth place. Now, that you are here, and no longer held prisoner by Nukpana, I can help you. I'm ready to be at your service."

KC shook her head in disbelief. "Each time I've come to Eldershire, I marvel at the ways of this world. What do you know about Nukpana taking me?"

"Only that Nukpana split herself into four beings. You've managed to rid Eldershire of two of them—the fake KC and the Nukpana of the dungeon. There are two more out there. You must remove them from Eldershire as well before you can return home. But, her magic is growing in power."

"It is manna you've come to me this night. We are preparing to make our first strike against the Trebbians. Can you help us?"

"I'll do better than that. I can have an army of beings to help, if you like?"

"We need to tell Mr Scruffy. We'll want to bring you and your army of beings up to speed on our plans. Can you come with me?"

"No. I am breaking the rules of Eldershire speaking with you now. I was able to do this because you were open to hearing me. I'll need to ask Mother Elder if I might rejoin you for this battle. Then, I can hear Mr Scruffy's plans and let you know what we can do to help you."

"Your abilities are limited, then?"

"Yes. I am pleased that I get to help you after you saved me. It makes me happy. It will enable me go to the next phase of my journey."

KC thought a moment, and then she said, "You wait right here. I'll be back with Mr Scruffy."

KC turned, walked toward her thípi, and stepped back over the threshold. She turned to look back, and could no longer see Drakania.

She found Mr Scruffy and shared what Drakania said. She watched him pace back and forth.

"Isn't this amazing? Drakania here. How did she find us? I'm not sure how much I should trust her. I mean after all, she was possessed by Nukpana before."

"Don't go back," Mr Scruffy grew to his flying size. "You must get on my back now. Where's Fea?"

KC felt a feeling of uncertainty sweep over her. "In my thípi, it's Nukpana. Isn't it? "

"It might be. Or, it might be something else. Hang on." Mr Scruffy took flight.

He flew KC over to her thípi where she got Fea. She climbed back upon his back, and he telepathically said, "We're heading to Snowboro as fast as the wind. I've let Iolair and Gavin know. We have no time to lose."

KC wondered how getting to Snowboro would allow her to break the spell, or if it was Nukpana, break that connection, but she trusted him. She held on. Before she realized it, they were landing next to Mylo's hut.

Mylo came out to greet them. "I got your message loud and clear. We cast the protection spell; my home and the surrounding area is covered in a secure bubble."

KC got down off Mr Scruffy's back. "I didn't think I'd be seeing you here this soon."

"Neither did we." Mylo turned and out of her hut walked the Four Lemmketeers.

In a fashion similar to a fine choreographed dance movement, the Four Lemmketeers together said, "We are at your service."

All four of them bowed to her, with their heads bent showing respect and their right hands moved their hats in a graceful arch across their bodies. Landing their hats on their heads, they came to attention with a perfectly timed salute.

KC was overcome with pride. She clapped enthusiastically. "Thank you. It's good to see you all."

"Let's get inside," Mr Scruffy said after reducing in size. "We'll be able to talk in private, but I have a feeling she may have spies aware of our new location."

"You are probably right," Mylo said. "Go on. All of you get inside. We can discuss what we will do next while we break open some ale."

KC smiled at them all. She wasn't as uncertain about her future as she was after considering that Drakania was actually Nukpana. Walking into Mylo's cabin, she caught a glimpse of Mr Scruffy. *What am I doing?*

How foolish to think she was protected from Nukpana now that she was in Snowboro. *It is such a waste.* I'm such a fool, KC thought.

"Nukpana knows exactly where I am, what I am doing, and when she plans to get me. I need to figure out how she plans to do it, if I'm going to stop her," She said telepathically to Mr Scruffy.

"Come sit here with me," Mylo said motioning to KC to join her in the center of her hut. "There is room here." Mylo patted the seat beside her. "I want you to know we will do everything we can to keep you protected. As my old mum used to say to me, 'you are wealthy when you sip a cup of tea with a friend.' So, sit here, and let's have tea or would you prefer ale like the Lemmketeers?"

Moving over toward Mylo, KC looked to Mr Scruffy for an indication about what they were going to do. He was in conversation with the Four Lemmketeers. Watching Crab, KC could see him becoming agitated. Was his anger growing? She wondered. Then, when she saw him pull his sword, KC stood up, and pulled out Fea.

"What are you doing?" Mylo stood up between Crab and KC. "We don't need bloodshed here. Your anger should be saved for the battle field."

KC replaced her sword, and Crab put his down as well. "I'm not sure what is happening." KC pressed her lips together forming a slight grimace. "I guess," she paused. "I don't know." She stood there and tried to think. She felt her anger subside, and rubbed a hand through her hair.

She said, "I'm sorry. I don't seem to know what to feel at this moment. I didn't mean to react so strongly toward you, Crab."

Crab covered his mouth with his paw, shook his head, and then closed his eyes. A slow smile formed on his face. "I think I could have taken you, if I wasn't so sure you were conflicted with what you were going to do."

Lafayette giggled. "Sure. Sure, you would have." Lafayette turned to

Mr Scruffy. "I guess we should make sure Crab doesn't get itchy fingers around KC in the future."

"I would like to lie down for a bit instead of sipping tea or ale. May I?" KC said to Mylo.

"Sure, dear. You can use my room. Come with me."

KC walked with Mylo to the door of her room and said, "I believe I'm going to rest for a little while. Would you wake me before later day? And, if Mr Scruffy needs me before then, come get me."

"Surely. Enjoy your rest." KC closed the door to the room. She walked over toward the cot, and stood there lost in thought.

She stared while she watched on the dirt floor the letters forming. Then, she read the words plainly written—HELP ME!

"I'M TELLING YOU ALL. I know what I saw. It was written right there as plain as if I bent over and wrote it myself. Can't you see? It confirms my suspicions. I am right. Something is wrong at King Elder's Camp. Isicaranon and Seborn are in danger."

"You do realize this is a trap. Pure. Simple." Mr Scruffy said. He walked over to where the words were supposed to have been scrawled in the dirt floor. "The words you saw are gone."

KC paced around the room. "How did they disappear so quickly? I wasn't away from this room more than five minutes. I don't get it." KC kept rubbing her chin, moving her hand to the back of her neck. "What's the matter with me, my mind keeps freezing up?"

"What?" Crab said. "What is five minutes?"

"Sorry. It is time passing. In my world, not very much time."

"Time? What language are you speaking?" Crab said.

KC looked to Mr Scruffy. "Help Me!"

"Just like what you saw?" Lafayette said.

Slumping down on the cot, KC put her hands to her forehead and rested her head in them. She said, "I can see his face. He's in pain. Great anguish."

"Who?" Lafayette said.

"Isicaranon!" KC jumped up and turned toward them. "What is the matter with you? He came to us to help us. He took a chance, a big chance. He told us what we needed to know in order to get Nukpana. Then, he gave his body for us, for me!" She talked fast. "Something is not right! Can't you tell that something is not right? It's not right anywhere I go. It hasn't been for some time. What is happening to me?" KC slumped to the floor and began to sob.

"KC, drink this." Mylo handed to her a cup of tea. "It will soothe you. You need to calm down; you need to get some rest. We're worried about you. Here, dear."

KC knocked the tea out of Mylo's hands. "Get away from me. All of you! I don't believe you are who you claim to be! Nukpana! I've figured you out. You won't win. NEVER!" Fea started to glow, and as it glowed brighter, KC felt a surge of energy.

❧

"How are you feeling," Mr Scruffy said walking over to KC. "We've been worried about you?"

"What happened?" KC said while looking around the room. "Where am I now?"

"You are in Mylo's hut. We brought you here upon realizing you were possessed by some form of evil after you talked with Drakania."

"I am in Mylo's hut? Did I fight with you and Mylo?"

"No. We heard you, telepathically, screaming. Once we found you,

you were acting as though you were trying to find someone in the forest. After we subdued you, we brought you here."

"Where's Fea?" KC said as she scanned her cot.

"It is there, beside you."

KC's hand fell on the cold, metal of the sheath and picked it up. She pulled the sword out of its sheath, and held Fea up before her. The sword shone brightly when the Two-Suns' rays bounced off its surface. KC smiled.

"I'm safe, aren't I?" KC said.

"As you should be. Mylo and her team of Snowquidians have made every effort to blanket the area with a protective bubble. It is our hope you will remain safe."

"Thank you. And give my thanks to all those that have helped you and me."

"When we found you, you were speaking incoherently about Isicaranon and Seborn. We want you to know we've talked with them. They are safe."

"Good. That makes me feel some better. Do you know what possessed me?"

He shook his head, and then handed KC her locket, a red plaid collar, and the bowler hat. "We felt you should have these and keep them close along with Fea."

"My Mother's locket. Where did you find it? I thought I lost it after I transported here."

"Seborn had it and kept it safe. After we rescued you from Nukpana, we got Seborn to bring your locket to us at Mother Elder's. We planned to give it to you then, but you were obviously ill."

"I appreciate your care of this locket for me. And the red plaid collar? It reminds me of Boomer. Why is this significant? I thought I had it on me too." KC reached in her pocket and pulled out a red plaid cloth. "This is what Dr. Crowell placed on my head."

"Yggdrasil gave it to me before you transported. I was to get it to you through Gavin when he was serving with Dr. Crowell. You transported before we could do so. Yggdrasil said the collar must be with you. We believe because you did not have this particular plaid collar with you, it was why you landed in Snowboro away from anyone that knew whom you were or the importance of your returning."

"That explains it then. But, why are you giving it to me now?"

"Somehow, the one Dr. Crowell gave you in the hospital, did not help you as was hoped. Mother Elder and Yggdrasil believe you need this too on your quest."

"I feel like I have a trove of things I need to use to protect me."

"You do. Nukpana's magic is dark and strong. You need all of the talismans you can gather."

"Agreed. We know the value of the bowler hat from my last visit. I will wear it too. Are you thinking that together these items will give me protection?"

"Yes. Your Mother's locket, the red plaid collar, the bowler hat, and Fea are all needed as we move forward to stop Barnabus and Nukpana from succeeding with their plans to take over King Elder's Camp and all of Eldershire."

"Do you know what she plans to do next?" KC asked while biting the inside of her cheek. She looked down at her hands and cleared her throat.

"You are uncertain as to what you are to do, right?" Mr Scruffy said. "I understand that uncertainty more than you know. You have every right to be confused, which would result in your being unsure. What we know is that Nukpana must have split herself into four beings—forming herself as a fake KC, forming herself into a double of herself that you interacted with in the dungeon and others encountered around Eldershire and leaving a portion of herself hidden. But most importantly, we believe she has hidden away a part of her essence to keep it safe if her plans were to fail."

"There is another portion she must've split herself into." KC looked to her companions. "When I met Drakania, she spoke to me as Drakania, but she was Nukpana, wasn't she? It is amazing the lengths Nukpana has taken to gain control of Eldershire." KC shook her head. "What do we do now?"

"We are not sure. And, we don't know that she *was* Drakania. We believe there could be another force at work, but we are not sure. We need to determine whom we can use in King Elder's Camp that is still connected with Barnabus now that Shwu is gone. I would have said Isicaranon, but now I'm afraid he is known as working with the Herok'a."

"I'd be lying to you if I told you I understand why Shwu died. And, finding the right Elderian to aid us will not be easy. Something I just remembered is Shwu said there were two others that worked with Barnabus. I'm not sure what they do, but one is Olaf and the other is Willie."

"Willie? I don't believe I know him. Our latest word is Olaf has been overtaken by Nukpana, so we must be weary of him." Mr Scruffy said.

"Could Iolair or Gavin know anything about Willie? I know Shwu said Willie was working with someone, maybe someone with the Herok'a."

Mr Scruffy said. "I'll go check with them now. You get some rest and we'll see what we can find out about Willie."

"From our underground work, we know that Barnabus uses jerkdomism. His series of behaviors were staged to gain control of the Elderians and keep them in line. To help him, we've learned he had three supporters. Olaf, the Flashy, Isicaranon, his counselor, and Shis Kin Wu, his Trebbian General," Iolair said while moving over to the Eldershire map that hung on the nearby wall. "What we found is that it is not clear what part Willie played for or against Barnabus. He seems to have been his personal aide, a 'go-to' when he needed someone to do something secretly. Willie is being protected by a group of Elderians in this part of Eldershire. We do not know where Olaf is at this point. And of course, Isicaranon is helping us here with his disguise."

"Of the five, Barnabus and Olaf are still working together?" Mr Scruffy said.

"Yes. Based on what we know now," Gavin said. "We know how valuable Isicaranon is to us. We have learned and believe Willie was also working on his own to stop Barnabus."

"That is remarkable. I wonder why we didn't know of him. Based on what we've learned, he might be a good one to join with us."

"Let me see what my scouts can find out," Gavin said. "I'll send our questions to them telepathically."

"Good. In the meantime, we need to plan our next steps." Mr Scruffy said.

"Yes," Iolair said and Gavin nodded. "I suggest that the role of Willie should be investigated in detail before we move forward. I fear he may be a pawn of Nukpana."

CHAPTER 28
MAGIC ABOUNDS

The BlueStone, lying on the altar behind the Elder Tree in the Land of Promise, began to glow. Simultaneously, a low and subtle tone was emitted like the ringing of a bell. A silence filled the air after each tone completed its vibration. Then, another tone was emitted. With each ring of the stone, the tone grew incrementally in strength and duration.

Mother Elder and Yggdrasil appeared in the sacred room, but the brightness of the beam from the BlueStone caused a glare. The sound of the tone was deafening.

"We must go to them," Mother Elder said. "KC, Mr Scruffy, and the Herok'a must hear of this from us immediately."

KC WATCHED Mr Scruffy walking toward where she stood near the entrance to her cabin in Snowboro.

"It was so nice of Mylo to arrange for my own cabin. I feel like I belong here. Have you heard from Seborn or Isicaranon?"

"You look like you do belong here. Snowboro suits you. The cold, I could do without, but the landscape is perfect for owls," Mr Scruffy said. "We've not heard any news yet."

KC said, "I was just thinking about the last time I saw Graves Mountain. That was not a particularly fun time. Will you walk with me?" They moved along together.

"Not a fun time, but you managed to finish your quest. You will finish this one too."

"Whoa!" KC stopped walking. She turned to Mr Scruffy. "You wait right there." She called out to Gavin and Iolair. They flew over to where KC and Mr Scruffy were standing.

"Are you okay?" Gavin hawked.

"Yes," KC replied. "I want the three of you to hear me and hear me clearly. I am *not* going on a quest for you or anyone else. Do you understand me?" KC looked to each of them. Iolair and Gavin looked to Mr Scruffy. "Don't expect him to answer for you. Each of you will answer me. Gavin?"

Gavin used his right claws to scratch at the ground. He looked up to KC. "Yes. I understand."

Iolair flew up to a nearby branch. "I understand, but I don't like it."

Mr Scruffy looked to KC. "You've got to understand our point of view. Eldershire needs you. We need you in ways you cannot begin to understand. You can't make this decision now. First, you must remember what the Elderians said, hear their voices, and understand their need. Then, if you decide you still will not go forward and help us, we will understand."

"I'm willing to compromise. I'll listen. You'll have to set it up for them to talk with me. I'm not going begging or telling them what they need to do. They've had enough of that kind of stuff from Barnabus and Nukpana. And, you'll be with me when you take me.

Besides, I don't know how to get back to King Elder's Camp from here. But, no promises. Okay?"

"Sure," Gavin said.

Iolair flew down to the ground. He took his right wing and patted Mr Scruffy. "I think KC is wise to give us her time. I understand there are no promises."

Mr Scruffy thought a moment, and then looked to KC. "I accept your compromise. I understand there are no promises.

"This pleases me that you are willing to let me move at my pace."

"It is slower than we *need* to move, but you *must* accept this challenge. You must help. Your future depends on it."

"What do you mean?" KC looked toward Iolair and Gavin with her head steady, her eyes strong. She leaned forward to hear their replies.

"It's important you know what is before you," Mr Scruffy stopped talking.

"What is it?" KC said. She watched Mother Elder and Yggdrasil come into view as they appeared before them. "What has happened?"

"We came to tell you there is a disturbance in the life force. The BlueStone is glowing. We needed to tell each of you that your life depends on how you go forth. The way your encounter with Nukpana plays out will determine the future of your existence and that of Eldershire."

Mother Elder paused. Yggdrasil said, "It was hoped that when we destroyed the fake KC that your debt, KC, to Eldershire was paid." Iolair looked down to the ground.

KC rubbed her hands against her pants to free them of sweat. "My *debt* is paid? What debt?" She felt a strong desire to run. With a sharp intake of breath, she felt her face blush. "What are you saying exactly?"

"It's complicated," Yggdrasil said. "Before your return, Mother Elder explained that with your last encounter with Nukpana, because a portion of her died, you owe Eldershire for the loss of that portion of her being."

"What?" KC's face reddened, she felt sweat on her cheeks and forehead. Rubbing the back of her neck, she began to pace. "I don't understand why I should have to pay a debt after all the souls Nukpana destroyed. I am mazed like you often say."

Mr Scruffy stepped forward. "Mazed is a good word. Let's go back to your cabin. We can discuss what Mother Elder and Yggdrasil are trying to explain. And, we can plan what we must do with the news of the BlueStone. You need to know what is in front of you," Mr Scruffy said.

KC's lips began to tremble, fear was beginning to engulf her soul. "I can't do this. This is not something I asked to do. Don't you understand? I'm not strong enough. I don't want to be. I want to go home!" She collapsed on the ground and began to sob.

Mr Scruffy reached out to KC and put his wing on her shoulder.

KC was unable to speak; she felt a surge of anger begin to build. "Why? What have I done?" She cried.

Mother Elder and Yggdrasil motioned to Iolair and Gavin. The four went away and left Mr Scruffy and KC alone.

KC CRIED until she could cry no more. She looked up to Mr Scruffy. He had not left her side; he stood patiently by, waiting for her to work through her shock and anger. She smiled at him.

"Thanks for letting me get that out. I needed to let it go. I felt as though I was going to explode."

"Fighting this evil that has taken up residence in Eldershire is not an easy task for any of us. But, we need to use our collective strengths and wisdom to overcome Nukpana if Eldershire is to survive. Want to walk back to your cabin?"

KC nodded. They did not speak along the way. KC thought through what she heard and wondered what it all would mean in the end. Would she ever go home again?

Sitting in her cabin, KC looked to Mother Elder and Yggdrasil. She nodded to them, and then walked over to her cot and sat down. "What now?" she said.

After a long discussion, KC knew the path forward was riddled with the potential of failure in more ways than she could count. Her fate was out of her hands and she felt weak.

She stood up, then said to the group, "Okay. So, I think I have a handle on what must happen." She looked to Mr Scruffy. "I will take on this quest. I really don't have a choice, do I?"

"No. You don't," he replied. He motioned for everyone to leave the room. KC walked over and sat down at the nearby table, placed her head in her hands, and continued to worry. Her thoughts were interrupted by a noise. She looked up and saw Mr Scruffy was still standing in her cabin.

"Would you like to sit here beside me?" KC said.

"Will you tell me what you are thinking and how I might help you?"

"I will. Will you?"

"Yes. You go first," Mr Scruffy said. He landed softly on the tabletop and walked over closer to KC. Once again, he placed his wing on her shoulder.

"What has happened to us?" KC said and looked over at Mr Scruffy.

Mr Scruffy said, "I like perching here beside you."

"It's not that I don't trust you. I don't trust myself. What if I make a mistake? Suppose Willie is a plant, or Olaf, or someone else we don't know? Suppose Barnabus knows all, which means Nukpana knows too. What if Drakania was actually Nukpana in disguise?"

"Speculation. All speculation. Asking 'What ifs' gets us nowhere." Mr Scruffy jumped down to the floor. "Come outside with me. We need our private time. We need to bond again."

Outside in the clearing near the center of their encampment, Mr Scruffy grew to a size that allowed KC to climb on his back. He put his wing down and winked at her. She felt giddy at the thought of flying with him again. It was when she felt free, yet protected; the single greatest thing she enjoyed doing in Eldershire.

"I know," Mr Scruffy telepathically said to KC. "We can talk and express what we need like old times."

"I so need this time with you." KC climbed upon his back, wrapped her hands in the deep feathers of his neck, and Mr Scruffy soared up into the evening sky.

Within seconds, KC felt like she did the very first time Mr Scruffy took her for a flight. She could feel the air whipping her hair, her skin felt tingly. She was free.

TWO-MOONS WERE RISING when they returned to their encampment in Snowboro.

KC got down off of Mr Scruffy's back. She said, "Earlier, when we first started out the Two-Suns were bright, golden yellow. Now, the Two-Moons are before us for the evening. I am pleased to be beside you once again."

Mr Scruffy smiled. He then telepathically said to Iolair and Gavin, "The team is together, for now. We will need to continue to help KC know things will work out. They *always* do in Eldershire."

"WE HAVE DISCUSSED every aspect of how we will go about our offensive attack of the Trebbians, Barnabus, and whatever Nukpana throws at us. Are we all in agreement?" Mr Scruffy looked to his companions.

"I am always in agreement, but what can we do?" Lafayette said with his brothers beside him.

"The Four Lemmketeers! Lafayette, Logan, Tonner, and Crab. Come! Please come in," KC said. She walked over to greet and hug each of them. "I am so glad you are back with us after you went to King Elder's Camp. How are Seborn, Arrington, Eri, and Isicaranon?"

"We're right here," Seborn said. Arrington, Eri, and Isicaranon stood behind him.

"Welcome! We are in the midst of discussing our plans," Mr Scruffy said. "Sit here with us. We will fill you in."

"Where are the other Herok'a leaders? Will they be joining us too?" Seborn asked.

"We thought we'd have you brief us. Lorne and Fergus won't be back until much later. We hope to connect with the remaining Herok'a in the next two Two-Moons. Our plan is to arrive in King Elder's Camp as soon as possible. Isicaranon, will you give us your report?"

"Before we do that," KC said. "May I ask something since many of the Herok'a leaders are here?" KC felt a lump grow in her throat while holding back tears.

"Of course," Mr Scruffy said.

"There is a secret location somewhere in Graves Mountain that holds an elixir. Shwu told me that this elixir could be used to destroy the remaining forms of Nukpana, whatever they may be. Do any of you know about this elixir?"

No one made a move or said anything. KC said, "Shwu told me that when and if I find this elixir, I might also be offering myself in sacrifice. He said a part of me might die when I touch the vial. There is hope, though, since Nukpana was in my body, a part of her possessed me, that I might have some immunity to the poison of the elixir."

"KC, your concern about the elixir may be right. I've heard from my scouts. May I share their news?" Gavin said stepping forward.

"By all means," KC said.

"My scouts have found Willie. He is alive and well, and he is in hiding. We believe we will be able to get him to join us. I'll keep you posted on where and when we may determine what he can do for us."

"Excellent," Mr Scruffy said. "KC, we'll come back to the elixir question. For now, let's talk about our plan of attack against Barnabus and his Trebbians." Mr Scruffy looked to each of the leaders.

"KC, we will get the elixir. I know where it is and how to get it," Isicaranon said.

CHAPTER 29
A RIPPLE IN THE FORCE

King Elder's Camp was wrapped in tenebrosity. KC, with cautious movement, maneuvered around the varied trees scattered between her and Princess Istar's cabin. Mr Scruffy and the remaining Herok'a, except the Four Lemmketeers, were hiding in strategic outlooks along the boundary of the camp. The Lemmketeers were KC's scouts while she planned her moves with the Elderians; the ones Mr Scruffy told her she could trust.

Reaching Princess Istar's cabin, KC knocked softly on her door.

The door opened, KC felt a lump rise in her throat as a moment of fear gripped her. With Princess Istar still hidden away after coming out of Barnabus' spell, the Herok'a was not sure who would be in Princess Istar's cabin. KC wanted to make contact anyway. Now, she questioned if she was too hasty.

Standing before her was an Elderian she did not know. "May I come in?" she said.

Stepping aside, the Elderian looked out the door in both directions and closed it quickly. "How did you know I was here?"

"I didn't," KC said. "Who are you?"

"Oh, I figured you would have recognized me. You don't remember meeting me?"

"No. Should I?"

"Probably not. You were being tortured by Nukpana. I'm Willie."

"This indeed is a surprise. I've heard of you. But, you are right. We've not met. Can we talk here?" KC said. She sent a message to Mr Scruffy telepathically letting him know whom she found in Princess Istar's cabin.

"Yes," Willie said. "Come with me over here. Would you like something to drink?"

"No. I have my pouch. How did you get here? And, more importantly, how did you know it would be me at the door?"

"Gavin's scouts brought me here. I'd been hiding near the Bay of Styks. I figured Nukpana would avoid that area. I'm sorry I could not help you and Shwu in time to prevent his murder."

"You helped us?"

"I tried. I got news to several of the rebellion by sending Vivette Chouette to them with a note from me."

"Vivette Chouette?"

"Yes, she is a friend, an owl. I've not seen her since my return. Are you aware of where she might be?"

"No. I'm sorry. I'll ask Mr Scruffy to see if he can find her. We are pleased to learn you are willing to help us. Shwu spoke of you and said you would be a loyal Elderian."

"I had hoped I could have saved you both. I was a double spy with Shwu. We were working together and Barnabus and Olaf learned of my cloak-and-dagger activities."

KC grinned. "I'm sorry for smiling. It is only you talk like some of the spy novels I used to read when I was home. I hadn't thought of home in a long while."

"That makes me happy. I loved my time on Earth."

"You lived on Earth too?"

"Most Elderians have had a chance at least once, even if they were only there as infants. It is a beautiful planet."

"We must talk when this is all over. I'd love to hear your opinion on a few things." KC paused, and then shook her head. "What am I doing talking about home like all is well here? We must get down to business. Do you think you can tell me about the other Elderians here in King Elder's Camp we might count on to help us?"

"Yes. As a matter of fact, we have a large group we can depend upon. Gavin's scouts told me that the Herok'a have a good group of leaders. Where may we all meet?"

"I'm not sure where, but I do know we are hoping to begin planning a serious offensive attack in three Two-Moons. We decided it would take us that long to make sure those who will help us are fully trained and prepared to fight."

"Good. When will Mr Scruffy and the rest of the leaders arrive?"

"They are strategically stationed around here now. Before we connect with him, I need to find out something from you," KC said looking around Princess Istar's cabin. "What do you know about getting into Graves Mountain?"

"I know how to get in and out without anyone ever seeing me. You'd call me a 'stealth' Elderian." Willie smiled. "Why? Do you hope to acquire something when you are there?"

"Before Shwu passed on, he told me about an elixir and he said that I will need it. He said he learned it was hidden somewhere in the depths of Graves Mountain. Have you heard of such a thing?"

"Yes. I have seen the vial."

"What?" KC was pleased. "When?"

"While I was working with Barnabus as his personal aide. I had plans to use the elixir on him before I learned about Nukpana. Then, I realized she was controlling him. I figured I'd need to learn more about how to use the elixir before I'd know if it would work on her."

"It will work on her. It might work on me, if I'm not careful."

"Want to go there tonight? We could get it and be back before Early Two-Suns."

KC was excited by his proposal, but a strange feeling came over her. She felt she should not trust him so willingly. Willie was acting too eager, too sure of himself. I've been tricked by Nukpana before, she thought.

"I tell you what," she said standing up and walking to the door. "Let me go find Mr Scruffy and talk with him and the other Herok'a leaders to let them know what you said about the Elderians we can trust. I'll be back in a few clicks. We'll bring a few of the Herok'a leaders here. Then, we can make an accord with them."

KC walked to the door, opened it, and walked out into the night. She telepathically called to Mr Scruffy. "Where are you?"

"I'm in the tree tops above you. Are you okay?"

"Yes. I wasn't sure if I should trust Willie. He wants to head to Graves Mountain tonight while Two-Moons are high. What do you think?"

"I think I need to go with you. Wait where you are and I'll come to you."

KC stood there looking around when she thought she saw Lafayette in the under brush across from where she stood. She called to him telepathically, "Is that you, Lafayette?"

There was no answer. She looked down at her locket; the BlueStone was glowing. KC was not alone.

BARNABUS ARRIVED at Graves Mountain right after word reached him that KC and Shwu had escaped. The last time he talked with Nukpana was at the Elderian Camp gathering. He hoped to return to her in full triumph after taking over King Elder's Camp. He had even had a new thípi and cabin erected with the name emblazoned on the threshold—Barnabus' Camp—he knew she wouldn't like that, but he felt emboldened.

Walking up to the Trebbian guard Barnabus said, "Stand aside. I must enter."

The Trebbian guard did not move.

"I'm here to see Nukpana! Don't you know who I am?" The guard looked at Barnabus with a blank stare. "You fool!" Barnabus struck him down with his stare.

Barnabus knew he failed when he came to Nukpana without full control of King Elder's Camp. But, what he had was all he needed —he had control of the main body of the camp. And, he was feeling strong, stronger than he had in many years. Nukpana's strength was becoming his own; he could feel it.

When I confront her with my plans, he thought, I'd be able to spin things to her favor. Nukpana will never be the wiser. He walked up to her door and knocked.

The door creaked open moving slowly. Barnabus was shocked by what he saw. "Olaf, what are you doing here?"

"I'm in charge now, Barnabus!" Olaf laughed a wicked laugh that sent chills down Barnabus' spine. That laugh was familiar. *It couldn't be?*

"It's you, isn't it, Nukpana?" Barnabus said.

"What was your first clue?" Olaf danced around the room. "I have successfully used the magic of Alf. You, my silly Barnabus, are a total idiot. You have no idea how you've been played by KC and her toons. I will win no matter what you try to do!"

Barnabus was stunned by her change. He stood before Nukpana in total disbelief realizing she used the darkest of magic to take over Olaf's body. Shwu was supposed to be the vessel, but she chose Olaf. She will be surprised.

In Olaf's deep voice, Nukpana said, "What do you think of me and my strength, my power? It grew exponentially stronger since King Elder's death. And, I've managed to learn how to control its power."

"King Elder's death? When did that happen? And, how do you have Olaf's body? I killed him after I locked him away in the dungeon."

Olaf slowly returned back into Nukpana. She twirled around in a tight circle, like a ballerina, and then looked toward Barnabus under her raised arm. Her face was uglier than he remembered. She'd done something to herself using that dark magic.

"Well?" she said. "What do you think of me now?"

"Do you want the truth?" Barnabus knew she didn't have long in Olaf's body. "How long have you been in his body?"

"What difference does that make?"

"I said I killed him when I locked him away. Maybe when you moved into his body, he had not completely passed. You are on borrowed time, My Queen."

"Your failure comes at a cost to me and my magic," Nukpana slammed the bottom of her scepter on the throne room floor. An echo reverberated through the mountain sending waves through the air ruffling everyone in attendance. Nukpana's anger overwhelmed her. She twirled Blazewing and pointed it to destroy Barnabus.

"Wait, My Queen!"

"Why?"

"Because, when you found me and gave me your elixir, I believe a part of you came into me. I have a part of you with me!"

"What?" Nukpana lowered Blazewing. "How do you know?"

"I felt your surge of power earlier. I knew something had changed in you."

Nukpana walked over to the large window. She turned and looked back at Barnabus. She smiled. "Then, it is true. You do have a part of me in you."

Holding up Blazewing, Nukpana stepped toward Barnabus. The Alp chant began down in her gut. She would use the deep, dark magic of Amon, again. Turning toward Barnabus, her chanting changed to a choral tone. The Alp was released. Nukpana reached down on her chair and placed the Tarnkappe hat on her head.

"Are you sure you want to—" Barnabus said.

Her eyes grew large; the chant grew louder. Her body twisted and moved into a contorted shape. The mist engulfed her, and then covered Barnabus. He stood frozen as Nukpana's ghostly apparition moved into his body through its orifices.

Barnabus stood still. His left arm jerked. The only sign his body was being taken over by Nukpana. Calmly, Barnabus moved over to the throne chair, placed Blazewing in its holder, and then looked out over Snow Valley and, on into the distance, the Atcenian Hills.

In a deep voice he said, "It is done. It **all** belongs to me."

AT KING ELDER'S CAMP, KC felt an overwhelming surge of power that wrapped her with fear. She looked around and could not see anyone near that would cause her to have such a feeling. She looked down at her necklace; the BlueStone was not glowing.

I wonder, she thought. She walked over to her cot, picked up her bowler hat, Fea, and then placed the plaid collar in her pocket. She called to Mr Scruffy telepathically, "I must see you. There is a ripple in Eldershire that I feel is growing."

"Go to the center of King Elder's Camp. I'll be there in a few clicks."

KC walked out into the opening and looked up. She wondered why Mr Scruffy hadn't already arrived. She turned and saw Isicaranon walking toward her.

"What's going on?" KC said while being prepared for something unexpected. "Where are Mr Scruffy and the Herok'a?"

"They are at the meeting center, King Elder's throne room. They were called there just now. Mr Scruffy asked me to come get you. You were right." Isicaranon took KC by the arm and began to lead her toward King Elder's cabin. "There is a ripple in the essence of Eldershire. Come," Isicaranon said.

KC walked in to King Elder's throne room with Isicaranon following.

"What is going on?" KC said placing her knapsack down on the nearby table. She motioned to Mr Scruffy to climb up on her shoulder. "Having you close calms my fears." Mr Scruffy flew up to her shoulder and landed softly. She petted his head. "It's good to have you close."

"We have much to discuss," Mr Scruffy said, and then he clicked his beak at Iolair, who was wearing a bowler hat with a red plaid hatband. "You're looking dapper!"

KC felt a surge of determination—her muscles tightened, her lips pressed together, standing before them, she said, "I'm aware of how bad things are amongst the Elderians and their faith in Princes Istar as their leader. Barnabus and Nukpana have brought mortal danger to all of us by sowing discontent. We are facing greater peril than when Nukpana was here as the fire-breathing Purple Drakein."

At the mentioning of the Purple Drakein, a rumbling of discontent moved through the Herok'a leaders.

"Each of you understands how serious Barnabus is in threatening to take over King Elder's Camp with the goal of becoming the supreme ruler of Eldershire. We must be prepared to fight."

KC walked over to her knapsack, opened it, and placed an old book she had found when she first returned to King Elder's Camp.

"This book," she said, pointing to it. "Is a very old record of the Land of Eldershire. I do not know how it came into my possession, but I have read it. It is a record of all of the lives that have passed through this land. Mother Elder and Yggdrasil told me I would learn much from the book. I have." KC handed the book to Iolair sitting beside her. "Pass the book around. Each of you look in the book and find your family's linkage."

KC waited while the book moved around the room. Each of the Herok'a leaders looked in it. "It seems all of you feel as I did when I read the names or saw the marks of each of the many families that have crossed over into Eldershire. Your melancholy is noted and understood."

"Strange and terrifying is what I'd call what is happening to us now. As horrible as the death and destruction of the Purple Drakein was to us all—I lost many members of my families clan—the ripping apart of the various clans of Eldershire through hatred, distrust, and discontent is far more evil than anything I would have imagined could be done here. What are Mother Elder and Yggdrasil doing to work against Nukpana and Barnabus?" Ralph said.

"You are right to feel the way you do," Iolair said. "My encounters with Nukpana have cost me and my clan as well. I recently suffered physically and know the pain and discomfort first hand. Yet, we must be careful we do not harbor anger to those who were once our friends. They have been led astray by untruths and innuendo. We must help them understand what Nukpana and Barnabus are doing. We must remember who we are—Elderians, united together."

"Thank you, Iolair. You said what I've been thinking. We must not fight each other. The failure to overcome Nukpana and Barnabus could result in the destruction of Eldershire, as we know it. Already, there are signs mounting that a ripple is in the force of the goodness here in Eldershire," Mr Scruffy said.

"What kind of ripple?" KC asked.

"One that isn't obvious but comes in waves. We have learned there is a large portion of the Elderians of King Elder's Camp that is in full support of Barnabus. Note that I say in support of Barnabus. This means that Barnabus must have used some of Nukpana's magic to position himself as the leader of King Elder's Camp. That is why he planned for Princess Istar to be taken away in secret after he poisoned her."

"Mr Scruffy, what do you suggest we do next since this is happening?" KC said while moving him down to stand on the tabletop.

"You must hear this now. Princess Istar's grandfather, King Elder, is alive. He has not died as was reported by Barnabus at his last gathering. King Elder was revived when we got him to safety, but he is still very weak. He passed his crown to Princess Istar."

All of the leaders of the Herok'a stood and gave cheer. "Princess! Princess! Princess!" they chanted.

Moving his wings up and down, Mr Scruffy motioned for the leaders to retake their seats to listen to him.

"I share in your excitement, but we must not forget what we must do and what we still face. First, we'll need to install Princess Istar as the new and rightful leader." Mr Scruffy was interrupted again with cheers. He hooted along with his companions.

"Okay. Now that our celebration is out of the way, we need to make plans for our next steps. This means ferreting about to determine who our enemies are amongst us. We will do this on this night, and then install Princess Istar at Two-Suns light.

"And then, what will we do after that?" KC said.

"We will meet back here where we will put into action our offensive siege." Mr Scruffy winked at KC. At least, she thought that was what she saw her friend do.

"An offensive siege? What is that?" KC said.

"You'll soon find out. First, we need to make plans to get Princess Istar crowned Queen of Elder's Camp." Mr Scruffy walked over to Iolair and Gavin. "Will the two of you make the preparations for the coronation? KC, Fergus, and I will see what we can do in preparing the decorations."

Mr Scruffy turned to the other Herok'a. "This night we prepare to celebrate the new Queen of Elder's Camp. Let us go together in pride."

KC moved over to Mr Scruffy. "Before we go to celebrate, I need to talk with you. Can we meet at my cabin?"

"Sure. I'll see you there."

CHAPTER 30
DARKNESS DESCENDS

Princess Istar paced in her cabin. She was weary of all of the changes happening around her. King Elder had summoned her after he was returned to King Elder's Camp. She was pleased to see him, but not sure if he was real. She needed to know who was on her side. Since Barnabus betrayed her, she had not trusted anyone. He was a coward using her as a shield.

Stopping in her steps, Princess Istar said telepathically to Mylo, "I need you here. KC and Mr Scruffy are readying things to crown me Queen Elder of King Elder's Camp. I need you!"

There was a knock at her cabin door. Princess Istar opened it to see Mylo standing before her. "I'm so glad you are here. When did you arrive?"

"I was here when you telepathically called me. I have KC and Mr Scruffy here too. Will you see them?" Mylo said stepping aside to let KC and Mr Scruffy walk in.

"I don't know. I know you want to do what is right for me, but I am not trusting anyone. How do I know you *are* who you say you are?"

KC smiled. "I understand your concern, but you should not worry.

Nukpana and Barnabus have done their best to stop us. They have failed. Your grandfather's survival and your safety should be proof for you."

"You are wise, KC. Thank you for pointing out what I have overlooked." Princess Istar continued to pace. "What will we do now?"

"We will bring all of the Elderians who reside in King Elder's Camp together at the meeting central place. There, we will perform the crowning ceremony. We must work to unite the different groups— those who believe Barnabus, those who believe King Elder, and those who believe Nukpana."

"Must we?" Princess Istar said wringing her hands together.

"Yes. It is the only way. It is our destiny to unite King Elder's Camp. We might need to bring your grandfather out to greet all of the beings too."

"You can't." Princess Istar stood before them. She was angry and was not going to relinquish her rule back to her grandfather. "He will not take back his rule. He said he was done."

"We won't be giving the rule back to him. You are the rightful ruler. We will crown you. No fears there," Mr Scruffy said. "Are we ready to go forward?"

Princess Istar nodded.

Mr Scruffy and KC were standing near the platform that was setup by Barnabus when he gathered the Elderians of King Elder's Camp to hear him speak.

"Are you sure you want to use this platform? Will it not cause those who are believing Barnabus to question us and our intentions?" KC asked. She picked up a chair and moved it onto the platform.

"We will be fine. Once they see Princess Istar and learn of King Elder's health, the Elderians will be respectful." Mr Scruffy stopped what he was doing. He let out a shriek.

"What's wrong?"

"There," he pointed. "Do you see that owl there?"

"Yes. You don't know him?"

"It's not a him. That's Isicaranon's owl friend, Vivette."

"Vivette? I was supposed to ask you about her for Willie when we met in Princess Istar's cabin. He said he used her to get messages out to the rebellion."

"Willie said that?" Mr Scruffy shook his head. "I don't believe him. She isn't answering my call. Something is not right here." Mr Scruffy flew off toward where Vivette was perched in a tree.

KC watched but couldn't make out what was happening.

AFTER A WHILE, KC decided she needed to find where Mr Scruffy went when she saw him and Vivette fly off into the forest. When Mr Scruffy flew off, she called to him telepathically, but he did not respond. He had not responded to her for too long of a time now. Elderians were starting to gather around the platform.

KC reached down and picked up her bowler hat, put it on, and turned to walk over to Princess Istar's cabin when she was hit with an apple.

"What is going on?" She looked around and saw the Four Lemmketeers and at the same time, she saw another apple coming at her forehead. She ducked.

"Logan? What are you doing?"

"We've come to get you, but we didn't want to draw attention to us. Follow us through the forest. Mr Scruffy sent for you," Logan said.

After a few clicks, they arrived in a clearing not far from the platform in King Elder's Camp. KC looked around, but didn't see anyone. She looked; her necklace wasn't glowing. She pulled Fea out of its sheath; it too was not glowing.

"What's going on?" She asked Logan who was no longer by her side. She telepathically called to Mr Scruffy, "Where are you? Do you need my help?"

"No, not yet," Mr Scruffy said walking up behind KC. "Sorry about the mystery, but Vivette revealed information that is rather disturbing. KC, I'd like to introduce you to Vivette."

Vivette materialized before KC. "Wow. That's magical. How come you can't do that Mr Scruffy?" KC smiled. "Glad to meet you, Vivette." KC studied Vivette's downy white feathers with flecks of black plumage. The yellow-eyed, black-beaked charmer had thick plumage with heavily feathered taloned feet. She was the most beautiful snowy owl KC had seen in person.

"I can do it, I choose not to do it," Mr Scruffy said.

"What news do you bring?" KC said to Vivette.

"Isicaranon has gone missing. We are not sure why or how. Also, things are different with Nukpana and Barnabus. You need to be prepared for something happening. With Isicaranon gone, we do not know what to expect. I must join my clan. We are hoping to find Isicaranon before it is too late for him." Vivette disappeared.

KC looked to Mr Scruffy. "What do we do now?"

"We go on with the ceremony. We have no choice if we are to beat Nukpana at her own game. Be ever ready for a battle is upon us, I fear."

❧

THE ELDERIANS of King Elder's Camp crowded closer to the platform.

They stood in distinct groups. It was clear to KC that some of them were not happy standing near others. She did not remember the Elderians acting so divisive when she saw them the first time she arrived with Ish. They had worked in unison to protect their camp. Watching how they were treating each other, she clearly saw them acting as though certain Elderians were not worthy of being in the same place.

There was a rumbling of discontent moving through the Elderians. KC was beginning to think that the group that trusted Barnabus was suspicious of anyone who did not support him.

"Mr Scruffy," KC telepathically called. "I think we have an altercation brewing here amongst some of the Elderians. Do we have any of the Herok'a nearby?"

"Yes," Mr Scruffy replied telepathically. "We are about to start the ceremony. We'll do our best to get through the crowning before trouble breaks out."

"I hope you are right," KC responded.

Princess Istar walked out onto the platform. The crowd erupted into cheers with an occasional booing heard mingled within. KC scanned the crowd hoping to see when something started she might be able to stop it.

Iolair, Gavin, Mylo, and Ralph all walked up behind Princess Istar. They stood in a semi-circle behind her on the platform.

Mr Scruffy walked up to the microphone, grew to a reasonable size for all to see him, and then said, "Welcome, Elderians! We are here to celebrate King Elder's reign!"

The crowd erupted into cheers. KC noticed a few younger Elderians poking at each other; at first she thought it was in jest. Then, she noticed a knife come out and it was being wielded around. KC took a step closer to the group.

"Elderians! Come closer as we crown Princess Istar, King Elder's granddaughter as the Queen of Elder's Camp!"

Mylo placed the crown on Princess Istar's head, and then the crowd erupted into fervent cheers.

As Princess Istar bowed, several of the unruly group KC was watching began to argue with some of the Elderians in clear support of Princess Istar. Those who supported Barnabus carried a different looking sword; it was curved in a funky manner from what KC was familiar. The blade had a large, curled cross-guard, with an elaborate miniature sword on each side. The fairly large, wide, curved blade made of bronze is held by a grip wrapped in gilded, maroon Trebbian leather. She noticed a grey bearded Elderian walk over to the raucous young Elderians. It appeared he was trying to reason with them, when she saw the knife cut into his face.

KC felt herself turning into a character she could only think reminded her of female warriors of old. She wielded her sword like Achilles going into furious battle. She went into the craziness of the group, kicking, screaming, and flaying her sword in hopes of scaring the young Elderians into stopping.

Sweat poured down her spine as fear began to engulf her. She wasn't sure if what she was doing would help or hinder their efforts to keep peace during the ceremony. All she knew was that she had to make an impression on those young beings before they turned vile and ugly.

KC saw Mr Scruffy looking out into the crowd. She telepathically said to him that a group of young Elderians was stirring up trouble.

"KC needs our help," Mr Scruffy said to the Herok'a leaders on stage. He then telepathically called out to the Four Lemmketeers.

"We are here," Lafayette said, his three brothers charged into the crowd with him.

Before KC knew it, a battle began. Some of Barnabus' soldiers were killed and KC realized what she tried to stop escalated before she knew it. Looking up to the stage, she saw Princess Istar signal Mylo, and both of them joined KC in the fight.

THE SKIRMISH OVER, KC turned her attention to how her companions muddled through. She learned talking with some of the spectators that Barnabus was not at the ceremony. She was told by one Elderian that he thought Barnabus was still at Graves Mountain.

KC walked over to Princess Istar and Mylo. "Are you both okay?"

"Yes. No worse for the wear." Princess Istar removed her sword from her sheath and wiped it clean. "It is a shame I had to use this while being crowned Queen. I guess it is official now. I did earn my right."

"That you did," Mylo said. "I, too, connected with a few of those young fools. When will they learn that evil begets evil?"

"I'm not sure they will learn as long as Barnabus is their savor. Or, so they think." KC said. "I plan to go to Graves Mountain to find Barnabus. This won't be over until I confront him and Nukpana."

"We will come with you," Mylo said.

"No. You need to stay here with Princess Istar. Help her set up her reign. Her Grandfather will help, but he is weak. I'll take a few of the Herok'a leaders with me, but most will stay here to keep peace. It is best not too many travel with me. I fear Nukpana is behind all of this in ways we have yet to understand."

KC INFORMED Mr Scruffy telepathically about the battle in the crowd. She shared she'd meet him in her cabin to discuss their next steps.

Reaching her cabin, KC walked through it to make sure it was not occupied by an evil spirit. She used her necklace and Fea to check for any spirits that would cause the stones to glow. Neither did. She waited.

There was a soft knock at her door; KC rose and opened it. Mr Scruffy, Iolair, and Gavin walked in.

"We are ready. What do you need?" Mr Scruffy said.

KC explained her theory of what was happening based on her interviewing several of the disruptive young Elderians. They told her that they didn't really know why they got so angry. That clued KC in that there was magic at work tricking them into misbehaving during the ceremony.

"You are right," Mr Scruffy said. "It appears that Nukpana has begun to use her dark magic in very diabolical ways. Elderians pitted against each other; yet they don't know why or what they are doing. That is a sure sign that Nukpana is involved."

"My plan is that we travel to Graves Mountain, where Barnabus was last seen. We track him down and we make him tell us what he knows about Nukpana and her evil magic."

"I like that plan, except for one point," Iolair said. "What happens if Nukpana has taken over Barnabus' body too?"

"We can't believe she hasn't done so, but we must work as though we are early enough to stop her," KC said. "Are we ready to go?"

"Yes. I think so. Do you want more of the Herok'a with us?" Gavin asked.

"No. I think the smaller the group, the better chances we may have. Let's go!"

৪৯

THE TREK through the forest to Graves Mountain was uneventful. KC and the Herok'a leaders with her traveled with their keen sense of awareness at its peak, but they did not encounter any Trebbians along the way, which caused them to be even more on guard.

The team moved quickly and as quietly as possible through the entrance to the dungeon, the vast tunnels, and up into the living chambers of Nukpana's portion of the internal castle.

When KC stepped into the main chamber, her memory of the pain Nukpana inflicted on her came rushing back. Her steps faltered.

"Are you okay?" Mr Scruffy telepathically asked KC.

"Yes. I will be fine."

She studied the room and noticed laying on the floor, near the steps going up to the throne, the crown she once saw Barnabus boast about wearing one day. Not far away, there were several pieces of clothing scattered near the window giving the impression the clothes were cast off in a frenzy.

"What do you imagine happened here?" KC asked Mr Scruffy telepathically.

"This looks to me like what you would see after a helpless prey is devoured by a predator and the feathers are left over. Maybe, Nukpana killed her pawn?"

KC said to her companions, "Let's see what else we can find. Spread out, but keep each other in sight. Speak only telepathically. I'm going to search for signs of where Nukpana might have gone."

❧

THE TWO-MOONS WERE STARTING to rise when KC and the Herok'a leaders regrouped in the throne room.

"We didn't find any signs of Nukpana," Mr Scruffy said. "It is necessary that—"

Standing before them in the archway of the throne room stood Willie.

"It's about time you appeared," Gavin said moving over to Willie. "Come, share what you know happened here."

Willie walked over to where Mr Scruffy and KC stood. He held out his hand to Mr Scruffy. "Hello. I don't think I've met you before."

Mr Scruffy said, "I'm sure you'll understand if I don't shake your hand. Especially me. What information do you have for us?"

Looking him over, KC noticed Willie was standing bent, almost twisted. He appeared spineless to her. She could tell from the way he held his hands—folded and close to his body—he was nervous. But, why? She wondered about his real intent.

"It is important you tell us what you know, Willie. We will not harm you, if that is what is making you nervous?" KC said stepping closer to him. Willie took a step back.

"I'm a lowly servant of Barnabus, and now Nukpana. My intent is only to let you know that Barnabus is gone. Nukpana said you'd be here and I was to greet you."

"Gone? What do you mean by that? Is Barnabus at King Elder's Camp? Or, is he dead?"

Willie's face looked to be reddening. His gaze jumped from each of the Herok'a leaders and back to KC. He cleared his throat. "No. No, Barnabus is not dead. He is back. He is not at King Elder's Camp either. He is back." He rolled his eyes, and then said, "I am not sure when he will return here. But, he is back."

"Willie, I'm confused. You keep saying, 'he is back.' What exactly do you mean?" KC said, stepping closer to Willie.

Willie twisted his fingers. He started to tap his right foot. He grimaced while he said, "Well, uh, Barnabus is back means just that. He is back. He is back to life."

"Back to life?"

"Yes. Barnabus died a while ago. I found him after he said he was saved by Nukpana. I've been in his service ever since. He is her magic in living form." Willie turned and ran from the room.

Mr Scruffy and the other Herok'a leaders gathered around KC.

"What do we do now?" Gavin said.

"Not panic." KC held up Fea. It was not glowing. "Willie was not possessed, but he was definitely scared. I don't blame him. I'm beginning to think that Barnabus was never dead. Not really. I'm afraid Barnabus is more powerful now."

Ralph walked into the Throne Room.

"Why are you here? Has something happened at King Elder's Camp?" Iolair said.

"No. I was told to come. I, and the rest of the Herok'a leaders are here."

The Four Lemmketeers, Lorne, Fergus, Mylo, and Seborn entered.

Mr Scruffy, Iolair, Gavin, and KC formed into a circle with their backs to each other, their weapons raised.

"Wait!" Ralph said. "We are *not* the enemy."

Princess Istar stepped out from behind the Herok'a leaders. "What Ralph says is true. We are not possessed."

"Why are you here? We don't know where Nukpana is. She could be controlling all of us at this very moment."

Princess Istar bowed her head. "We know. We felt we had to come. Our scouts have been everywhere in the land of Eldershire. Even Mother Elder and Yggdrasil used their powers. King Elder said that we should tell you face to face that Nukpana is *nowhere* to be found."

KC embraced Princess Istar. "It is fine. We don't need to focus on where she is. We need to focus on what we will do next." KC pushed back from her embrace.

"We are at the mercy of the essence of Eldershire. Grandfather said that Nukpana's power is greater than any of us can imagine."

KC nodded. "I'm afraid he is right. Darkness descends upon us."

CHAPTER 31
FLOWERS FOR KC

After scouting and verifying they could leave Graves Mountain, Mr Scruffy and KC led the Herok'a to the nearby cave and encampment they used before.

Mr Scruffy said, "I think the Herok'a should plan their offense with the news that Nukpana and Barnabus were not found in all of Eldershire."

"That is wise. We are still close to Graves Mountain to react quickly if they reappeared." KC nodded to her friend.

IN THE MEETING room of the deep cave, the table was prepared with six seats around the perimeter. KC stopped at each one while walking around the table, and then said, "Is it necessary we have assigned seating for this meeting?"

"Yes." Mr Scruffy flew into the room, landed on the table, and let the gathered flowers fall to the tabletop. "Would you put the flowers at each place I tell you?"

"Sure. But, how will each leader know who sits in which seat?"

"Each flower was assigned to a specific clan many eons ago. The leaders will know.'"

KC picked up the flowers, and waited for Mr Scruffy to tell her where to place each one. She hoped she remembered the names of the flowers. Four of them she felt confident, but the remaining two, she wasn't positive what kind they were.

Mr Scruffy said, "Those three yellow-orange daffodils are to go here. This will be Iolair's seat."

"Why does he receive three?" KC said while placing the three daffodils on the table in front of the chair.

"Lore says that if you receive a single daffodil, it is foretelling misfortune. So, Iolair receives three daffodils. We don't need to setup this meeting for failure before it ever gets started." Mr Scruffy clicked his beak. "The daffodil symbolizes rebirth and new beginnings. Both things we need desperately now." Mr Scruffy pointed to the next place.

KC moved to it and waited.

"Place the purple aster there. It is for Gavin and represents his and the Hawks' loyalty, royalty, and wisdom."

KC thought how regal Gavin looked when he flew. The purple aster was well assigned. She moved to the next seat and waited. She thought a second, and then she said, "May I select the flower for here?"

Mr Scruffy tilted his head. "Sure. Why not? Put down the flower for whom you think sits there."

KC looked at the remaining flowers in her hand and picked the red rose. She laid it on the table. "Did I pick correctly?"

"You did. Nicely done. It is the flower that should go there for Fergus, the leader of the Dryads. The red rose symbolizes love and romance, but most importantly it is the prefect way to say 'I Love You.' And, what do we need more right now as we prepare for battle than love. Fergus and his Dryads bring us calm and love."

Moving to the next chair, KC placed the ruffled deep pink with white edged carnation. "How'd I do this time?"

"You got close, but not exactly right. That flower belongs to Lorne and should be in the next seat after this one. The flower that goes here is the yellow begonia for Ralph, leader of the wolves."

"That explains it."

"What?"

"I haven't gotten to know Ralph that well yet. So, his aura wasn't as strong as Lorne's. And, she is a fox while he is a wolf. They aren't that different, are they?"

"Wise to say that," Mr Scruffy said. "The yellow begonia symbolizes wealth and happiness and brings joy to any who receive it. Having the wolves with us will enhance our chances of success. When you see Ralph later, make sure you let him know how happy you are to work with him. He will howl for you."

"Wonderful. I have always thought the sound of wolves howling was a beautiful song." KC moved to Lorne's seat and placed the carnation. What does this flower symbolize?"

"This flower symbolizes the tears of The Maker, which makes the pink carnation a symbol of a parent's undying love."

"I wasn't sure what type of flower the yellow begonia was. And, the second you said its name I remembered it. But, this last one, the one that goes in this seat is for me or you?" KC held the flower up. "And, why don't we have a seventh flower? There are seven of us."

"That is a petunia, a purple petunia at that. It is for me. First, the traditional meaning behind the petunia can be one of three—anger, resentment, or being comfortable with someone. For purposes of this meeting, the purple petunia means that I am in a serious relationship with the Herok'a and that each member of this group is close to me in a special way. This is my seat."

KC placed the purple petunia on the table. "Do I receive one?"

"You do."

"When will I learn what it is?"

"Right now," Iolair said walking into the thípi with a white flower. As he walked up to KC, the perfume of the flower filled the room.

"What is it?" KC said taking the flower that Iolair handed her. "I've smelled that before, but I can't place it."

"It is a white gardenia." Iolair walked over to the other side of the table and sat in his respective chair. "Mr Scruffy, you can tell her about it." KC thought Iolair had a blush to his feathered face, if that was possible.

"The gardenia is a most beautiful flower, but hard to grow. Its aroma can spread for miles and it is one of the most aromatic flowers in existence. The beauty of the flower means that its meaning is central to its lore. When this flower is given, it means the giver is saying to the recipient that 'you are lovely,' and it is actually a symbol of secret love. In your world, KC, it is the flower associated with the love story of Romeo and Juliet."

KC took a large, deep, savoring breath. She cleared her throat, and felt her knees grow weak. She wondered if it was obvious to Iolair what she was feeling. She knew this was not a normal experience for him or her, but she realized her suspicion that he was actually her Jack made her heart soar with deep love. She walked over, picked up the gardenia, and held it close to her heart, and then smiled at Iolair.

"Okay. Enough of this trip down flower lane. We must prepare for our meeting. The others will be arriving soon. Are we ready?" Mr Scruffy said.

"No, not yet," Gavin said. He held a beautiful bouquet.

"What are those?" KC asked.

"This flower bouquet of Edelweiss is in honor of all those who came before—a symbol of their courage and devotion to Eldershire. We thank them all for their service and their support of our cause." Gavin placed the bouquet in a vase and placed it on the mantle behind the table.

Relaxing her posture, KC moved to her seat, to sit down, but there was no chair. She looked to Mr Scruffy. Magically, a chair appeared. She sat down and leaned back.

"How much time do we have?" She felt her body relax.

"A few clicks at best." Gavin sat down in his chair.

"Good. I'm going to enjoy this feeling right now. The scents of all these flowers have brought a feeling of calm over me." KC wanted to savor the moment.

THE HEROK'A LEADERS ASSEMBLED, each sitting in their respective chair. No one mentioned or questioned the flower before them.

Without fanfare, Mr Scruffy called the meeting to order.

KC knew without a signal from Mr Scruffy regarding what they were going to discuss and plan to do could mean the future of Eldershire and all of its inhabitants. Something terrible was going to happen, only thing was, she wasn't sure how soon.

THE MEETING COMPLETED, many of the Herok'a leaders went back to their respective packs to explain what their part in the siege would be. KC walked into the meeting room and saw Iolair sitting in the chair he occupied during the meeting.

"May I come in?" KC said.

Iolair looked up. He then stood up and moved upon the tabletop. He knew his place, but he also knew as a Bald Eagle, he should display a sense of respect. He did so out of more than respect for this particular human.

"Please. I welcome your company." Iolair motioned for KC to sit in the chair next to him. "I welcome a chance to speak with you alone."

"I've come to you because I feel I need to explain," KC stumbled on her words. "I'm sorry. I'm a little nervous. I want to tell you what I've felt for some time now." Iolair nodded. "Do you mind if I blurt it out?"

"I've always felt that the more direct beings are with each other, the less likely there is a misunderstanding of intent." Iolair moved back into his chair.

"You realize how strange this is for me?"

"I do. As it is for me too."

"Iolair. I have no way of knowing what you feel or think. But, my heart tells me I must speak my mind or die trying."

"Die trying?" Iolair shook his head. "I worry you overreact to life here in Eldershire."

"I do, but then, again, none of this is something I've grown accustom to experiencing. But, I find that if I don't tell you how I feel, I may never have the chance."

"KC," Iolair paused. "Are you sure you need to say what you are going to say? I will be leaving this area in a few clicks. My assignment is Emerald Mountain."

"Emerald Mountain?" KC's eyes flutter. Iolair wondered how she would react when she heard. "Will I see you again?"

"Yes. In a way." Iolair moved his wing up to her shoulder. "We will always be together."

"There is peace within me," KC said. "I am changed. I went far away—and, I will do so again. My hope is that one day I'll go away with you." KC stood up. She touched Iolair's shoulder, caressing it slightly. "You are indeed more important to me than I ever knew. Be safe!" KC left the room.

Iolair looked down. A tear fell onto his face. He looked up, and then said, "Your Jack will be with you soon." He smiled.

☙

LOGAN KEPT PACING back and forth. His brothers watched him.

"What are you so worried about?" Crab asked him, letting out a sigh.

"I'm not sure," Logan said. "Things are not right. That's all I know."

"You are always paranoid when it comes to ALL things," Tonner said. "Relax, Logan. Everyone is concerned about the fight ahead of us."

"As they should be. Nothing feels right. I can feel the mists of Eldershire shifting." Logan's face had a wide-eyed look; his hands were fidgety.

"Have you rested any since we broke from the Herok'a meeting?" Lafayette asked.

"No. I can't sit still long enough to close my eyes."

"You realize we will be heading out for the first leg of the siege soon. You should rest."

"You are right to warn me, Lafayette. I'll try. But, when I lay my head down, my mind is racing. I can't seem to keep my eyes closed. I'm too restless."

"You will be too tired to help any of us," Crab said. "Want me to knock you out? You'll rest then." Crab smiled.

"No. I appreciate the thought, brother. I can't help but see signs of danger all around me. I keep seeing a bloody sword, a torn hat, a lost necklace. These things worry me as they are all what KC carries with her."

"You are right to be worried. You've shared what you keep seeing. Your paranoia is valid. Tonner, would you tell Mr Scruffy what Logan keeps seeing? He will find this important to note," Lafayette said.

Tonner saluted his brother and scurried away. Logan looked to Crab and Lafayette, and then said, "Thank you, brothers. I do feel a little less worried. But, I'll remain wary. We all need to be alert to possible danger."

TONNER FINISHED EXPLAINING to Mr Scruffy what Logan had seen.

"Thank you for telling me," Mr Scruffy said. "I'll be sure to let Iolair and Gavin know too. Tell Logan he can relax. We agree with him that being on guard for what Nukpana and Barnabus might do is important to keeping KC safe."

"I'll report back to my brothers. The Four Lemmketeers are at your service," Tonner bowed gracefully and left.

Mr Scruffy turned to Lorne and Gavin. "The Four Lemmketeers are faithful servants. KC is well protected with them around." Mr Scruffy looked down at his wings. "We must continue our plans regarding that portion of KC left on Earth. You understand, when you go to Earth to talk with Jack, the two of you can't reveal anything to KC when you return."

Lorne and Gavin nodded. "KC's family will recognize me from when I was with KC when she went into the coma," Gavin said. "That is something I can explain. How do we explain Lorne?"

"It won't be easy, but Lorne has a plan," Mr Scruffy said.

Lorne smiled. "Thanks, Mr Scruffy for saying it is my plan. It's not, but I'll take credit. I will explain to the family that I am a researcher that has conducted many studies on the cause and effects to humans when they have an MRI." Lorne stood up and stretched her back. "We're going to have to prevail on Jack to bring KC's comatose body here—to Eldershire." She paused for effect. "The reason will be for me to conduct further studies. The act of getting Jack to allow her body to come here should then be easy."

"How do you propose convincing him?" Gavin said.

"The family realizes things aren't right with KC in a coma after the MRI. This almost never happens, unless the patient has a trauma of some sort that went undetected prior to the test."

"Okay, that I can follow," Gavin said.

"If we walk in with confidence, we should be able to talk with Jack in a serious tone in such a manner he'll come to believe we are who we say we are. That our research in the Dølerud, The Fairytale Forest of Norway, will be a good camouflage for when we move her body out of the hospital. Then, he'll be willing to allow us to take her."

"That sounds workable," Mr Scruffy said. "What about the actual moving of her comatose body?"

"We will move her in a private jet. We'll tell Jack that he and his children can follow us in a commercial airliner. This will give us the cover we need to then transport her to Eldershire."

"What happens if that fails?"

"Then, we will need to reveal that if Jack doesn't allow KC's comatose body to travel to Eldershire, then the KC we know and love will be in dire straits."

"Sure." Gavin smirked. "That should work."

CHAPTER 32
FLIGHT AND FIGHT

"Thank you, Mr. Carson for agreeing to speak to us," Lorne said walking over extending her hand. "Dr. Crowell said you would be willing to hear our proposal for the future care of Mrs. Carson. May we sit?"

"Yes. Please do," Jack said. "This is our son, Bill, and our daughter-in-law, Marie. I'm not sure I heard your names?"

"I'm Dr. Lorne and this is my aid, Gavin. We've heard about Mrs. Carson's case. We talked with Dr. Crowell and are interested because we think we can help Mrs. Carson."

Jack looked to Bill and Marie. He turned and smiled at Lorne. "This pleases me. We weren't sure what steps we could take to help my wife, Kay. We call her 'KC.'

"Dr. Crowell allowed us to examine her before we came to you to make our offer of service. May we call your wife, KC, too?"

Jack nodded. "We have a research facility located in the Norwegian forest. The particular forest area where our research facility is hidden is called Dølerud. It is also known at 'the fairytale forest,' which has protected status—no motorized vehicles are allowed."

"Then, how will we get there?" Jack asked.

"Our research facility, Eldershire, is on the northern edges of this forest. This means that unless you know it is there, you can't find it. We do this to keep our patients safe and undisturbed. We find it helps us do the research we need to do safely and accurately."

"That's interesting," Bill said. "But, I've never heard of you or this research facility?"

"Dr. Crowell is very knowledgeable of our program. We have written many journal articles and have presented at a multitude of conferences. The communication of our findings is what helps to keep us funded."

"And, how will you transport KC there?" Jack said.

"The facility is serviced by our private landing area. We will use a private jet. This means we will have all the equipment necessary to safely transport KC in her comatose state. Gavin and I will be on the plane along with our skilled pilots and nurses. They will provide KC with the proper care. You, and if your son and daughter-in-law want to join, can come to our facility using a commercial airliner."

"You give me hope," Jack said. "What do we need to do now?"

"You only need to sign this form," Lorne handed Jack the waiver.

Jack looked it over, and then Bill read it. He nodded to his father. Jack took the form and signed it.

"Thank you, Mr. Carson," Lorne said.

"I guess you should call me Jack," he smiled. "No need for formality since we will talk with each other often while KC is in a coma."

"Very well, Jack," Lorne smiled. "Let me say that it is hard to explain the essence of the souls that work in Eldershire. There are many invisible threads of luck woven into a sparkling web of life so fragile and unnoticed. Yet, when one thread is pulled, the entire web falters. We want to help prevent that happening with KC and your family."

"Good." Jack looked to Bill. He shrugged. "I'm willing to go along with this, as it seems nothing is helping us here. I appreciate Dr. Crowell and you for stepping forward to give us something to try to help KC."

"We will ready her for transport. You should plan to get your tickets for travel. Because you are going by commercial flight, we will arrive several hours prior to you. This will give us time to prepare KC for you to see her in her room. What is KC's favorite color? We like to make the room seem as though she is awake and aware."

"She loves blue and green. We will be able to stay in touch with you as she is moved?"

"Oh, yes. Let me give you my card," Lorne said. "We will be leaving here in the next few hours. It will take us a little bit to prepare her for the trip."

"There isn't anyway I can ride with her?" Jack said.

"Sadly, no. There is not enough room."

"Well, then we will get our tickets on the commercial airliner. Should we go and make arrangements and meet you back here?"

"That will work best. We may leave before you get back, will that be an issue?"

"Yes. It will be. You are leaving from the main airport, right?"

"We will be in the air in probably an hour at best. Does that help you?"

"Thank you. We'll look forward to seeing you in Dølerud, if not before," Jack said.

&

JACK WAS NOT FULLY ACCEPTING that he could not fly with KC on the private jet. He asked Bill to go and get their tickets. On his drive home, he could hear KC's voice talking about Eldershire. He knew that the Eldershire Dr. Lorne talked about could be the very Eldershire that KC had mentioned before she went into her coma. He was going to be on that plane with KC if it was the last thing he did.

Arriving home, Jack put on his pilots uniform, gathered his pilot credentials, and left a note for Bill and Marie. He would use his knowledge of airports and security to stow away on the plane. He told Bill not to worry that he'd contact him once he was sure KC was okay and settled into her room in Dølerud.

THE PRIVATE JET took off toward Norway. The plane reached cruising altitude. Gavin walked over to Lorne.

"I can't believe how well this worked out. Mr Scruffy will be pleased we were able to acquire KC's comatose body. Now, what I don't get is why Jack didn't ever come back to the hospital or even meet us at the airport."

"I know. That concerns me too," Lorne said. "I hope he didn't accidentally miss us. It will be hard enough on KC when she learns later that we talked with Jack and her children. She must miss them terribly."

The pilot came over the intercom. "Lorne and Gavin, we are making our descent. We have flown off radar. The plane has now been reported as going down and missing. We should transport to Eldershire in a few clicks where Mother Elder and Yggdrasil will rejoin KC's body."

"I knew it!" Jack said standing at the portal near the back kitchen area.

"Jack!" Lorne said. "You shouldn't be on this plane."

Right as Lorne saw Jack, the plane began to dissolve away from them. Jack staggered, and hit his head and was knocked unconscious.

❧

LORNE AND GAVIN telepathically called to Mr Scruffy. He met them at Princess Istar's cabin when they were safely in King Elder's Camp.

"What do we do?" Lorne asked when a few of the Elderians brought Jack into the cabin.

"He was standing in the doorway to the kitchen when the plane started its entrance into Eldershire. He stumbled and must have hit his head. He hasn't regained consciousness since we materialized here. Are we sure he is okay?"

Checking him over, Mr Scruffy turned to them. He said, "You don't need to worry. He is fine. He should wake soon. We'll place him in another cabin and have Larissa Mar and Eri watch over him."

Mr Scruffy turned to the Elderians. He told them what he wanted them to do. They picked up Jack and moved him to the nearby cabin.

"When he wakes, we'll signal for you to be in his cabin when we must explain to him where he is and what is going on. In the meantime, don't let anyone know you brought him here. Now, we need to have Mother Elder and Yggdrasil rejoin KC's comatose body with her other half that is here. And then, we will prepare KC. She will be more than shocked upon seeing Jack."

❧

GAVIN AND LORNE walked into the cabin. Mr Scruffy stood off to one side of the doorway.

"Thank you for agreeing to stay in your Earth form. When Jack awakes and sees you as you were when you were on Earth, he will be more than likely to remain calm," Mr Scruffy said stepping back into the shadows. "After we explain where he is, you will need to transform to your true appearance here in Eldershire. He might as well get used to the idea of his new home."

Lorne moved over to where Jack slept on the cot. She touched his forehead. "He doesn't appear to be awake yet. When should we see some kind of reaction from him?"

Gavin looked to Mr Scruffy. "Everything I know about humans is limited to my encounters with KC when she traveled here. Mr Scruffy?"

"I'm not sure myself. Mother Elder said he should wake in a short time when she checked on him earlier. Are you *sure* he hit his head?"

"Yes," Lorne said. She started to step away and she felt Jack grab her hand.

"What is going on?" Jack said sitting up with a wild look in his eyes.

"You hit your head when the plane went into descent. How are you feeling?" Lorne said. "May I check your vitals?"

"Are you kidding me? I know we are **not** on Earth. Who was that talking with you?"

"You were awake?" Gavin asked.

"The two of you have tried to pull a fast one. You forgot that I was a soldier. Where is KC?" Jack sat up, swung his legs over the edge of the cot, and tried to stand, but faltered.

"Steady," Gavin said, holding onto his arm to help Jack keep from falling.

"I guess I am more dizzy than I thought," he said sitting down. "That doesn't change things. Where is KC?"

"Would you like to go to her?" Gavin asked matter-of-factly.

"What?" Jack said with incredulous laughter. "Just like that?"

"We know this sounds impossible to you. But, it is not. We know that KC would be happy to have you with us, here, in our home world of Eldershire."

Jack stood up. "Are you all crazy? My wife is missing. Her body disappeared before my very eyes. What is going on here? Why are you not doing something?"

Gavin stood up beside Jack. He looked him in the eyes. "KC is the bravest human I've ever met. She saved our world once. We will take you to her, but we need you to calm down and listen to us, willingly. This is a hard thing to do right now, but you must trust us."

Jack slumped down on the cot. He looked to Lorne and Gavin. "KC?"

"Do you feel up to going to her now?" Gavin said looking at Jack.

"I'd like to see her."

"Before we take you to her, we will need to prepare you for what you are about to see."

Gavin turned to Lorne. "Are you ready to change?" She nodded. "Jack, it is important you try to remain calm. As when you see us as we are here in Eldershire, you are likely to be shocked. You might want to sit back down on the cot."

"I think I'll stand."

"Very well. Most humans have never seen the likes of us. Besides, they don't know what all this means." Lorne looked at Gavin.

She gradually shed her look of a doctor in a white lab coat into the grayish white fur on her throat, chin, and belly with striking red fur across her face, back, sides and tail—except for the fluffy white tip of her tail. She stood before Jack as a proud red fox.

Gavin simultaneously metamorphosed from wearing an aide's

hospital blue scrubs into a red-tailed hawk with a whitish underbelly highlighted with a dark brown band across his belly caused by the feather patterning. The white enhanced the dark brown along his nape and under his head giving him the look of wearing a hood. His back became a slightly darker brown, again his feathers casting the look of stippling from the Two-Suns' rays striking his back. Gavin's tail fluttered out into a rufous brick-red with a band of black. He fluffed his feathers, and settled down on a nearby table.

Jack stood staring. He slowly sat down. Then, Mr Scruffy stepped out of the shadows.

"Welcome to Eldershire, Jack," Mr Scruffy said.

It was obvious from watching Jack trying to determine what to do next that he must have wanted to run.

"It's okay," Lorne said. She moved toward him. "We won't hurt you."

Jack leaned back and sat down hard on the cot. He covered his head acting fearful they would attack.

"You do realize that if we wanted to hurt you, we would have done so before now," Mr Scruffy said. Jack looked up with wide eyes.

"You all can speak English?" Jack said.

"Yes. We can speak many languages. But, don't let that scare you," Gavin said with a smirk.

Jack smiled. "I guess I have been scared for no reason. Where is KC and how did we get here?"

"Can we all sit? Maybe if I explain a little more about what we know happened to KC, it will help you understand what is going on here," Gavin said.

"I would like to see KC. How soon is that possible?" Jack repositioned himself on the cot. "I don't want to be bossy, but I am worried about her."

"There is no need to worry. We have some of our friends explaining to her that you are here."

"Really? She didn't know I was coming here?"

Mr Scruffy moved over and stood beside Jack. "No. We weren't sure how you would react at learning you were in Eldershire. We believe you will be able to help KC and she can help you."

"How did KC get here in the first place?" Jack said.

"Similar to how you arrived. Except, she came through the MRI, and we flew through the portal with the plane. When KC was about to have the test, it had not begun at the time of her disappearance. However, the magnetic field in the MRI was beginning to build. Due to an MRI's magnetic field being at least 140,000 times stronger than the Earth's magnetic field, a portal was opened. That portal allowed for the existence of a doorway to Eldershire. KC went through that doorway."

"And we went through that same door?" Jack asked.

"Yes."

"What now?"

"Now, we go see KC. Are you ready?"

"I think. Whom else will I see on my way to see KC?"

"There are many diverse beings in Eldershire. In time, you will learn about us all. For now, look around you as we go to her. Recognize that KC came here before. She has learned many things about the Land of Eldershire. There is much you can learn from her. You need to listen and to be patient." Mr Scruffy motioned for Jack to follow him. Lorne and Gavin followed behind.

§&

AT KC's CABIN DOOR, Mylo opened it. Jack gasped.

"Mylo, this is Jack, KC's husband. Jack, this is Mylo. She is a Snowquidian. You will learn more about her and her people. They are good friends to KC. They have taken care of her these last months while she has been here," Mr Scruffy said.

Mylo curtsied. "Please come in. KC is expecting you."

Jack stepped across the threshold and KC ran into his arms.

"Jack! Jack, I can't believe you're here!" KC cried.

Upon their embrace, the Two-Suns brightened to a glow that lit all of Eldershire. Nukpana noticed the light in the dark dungeon of Graves Mountain.

Lorne, Gavin, Mylo, and Mr Scruffy left KC and Jack alone in the cabin. Mr Scruffy closed the door behind them.

"What happens now?" Gavin said.

"We give KC time to explain to Jack what is going on. She will explain how he can help in our fight. He was a good soldier on Earth. He'll understand our needs. While they catch up, we need to make preparations for our siege. Two-Moons will be rising soon. We will need to get everyone prepared for what is to happen at early Two-Suns."

"Will we need to prepare Jack to fight?" Lorne said pulling her bow and arrow from behind the bushes next to KC's cabin. "I put these here in case we had trouble when Jack came here."

"You thought Jack would give us trouble?" Mr Scruffy said.

"No. I didn't know what surprises we might have from those in Barnabus' and Nukpana's clutches."

"Good thought. Wish I'd thought of it," Gavin said.

"KC said Jack was a skilled soldier in his world. We might be able to use him with the Snowquidians, if you think that fits with your plans," Mylo said.

"That might work," Mr Scruffy replied. "Let me see how well Jack adapts to his new surroundings. You remember how frightened KC was the first time she met the Elderians." The others nodded.

"It wasn't too pretty," Gavin said. "When will Iolair be allowed to rejoin us?"

"Not anytime soon," Mr Scruffy said. "He and his scouts are making sure Emerald Mountain is safe. It might be we will retreat there if this siege doesn't go as planned."

"Let's go see what we can do about equipping Jack with some weapons and getting him and KC some provisions. He's likely to be hungry."

"No need about food," Mylo said tapping Mr Scruffy on the shoulder. "Seborn and Arrington brought plenty for them to eat and drink."

"Good. We'll check back here when the Two-Moons are high in the night sky."

CHAPTER 33
BARNABUS

"My Treoraí," the Trebbian guard stood before Barnabus. "Here is the book." The Trebbian handed the leather bound book to Barnabus.

Barnabus moved it back and forth between his hands, and then motioned for the Trebbian guard to leave the room.

Waiting until he was sure the guard had left. He listened for the dull sound of the large door shutting. Barnabus moved over to his throne chair where he sat down. Opening the book, he moved his hands gingerly over the pages. He flipped through each page taking a solemn moment to read.

Upon turning to the page that contained the Alp chant that Nukpana had said while absorbing his body. Barnabus paused, letting out a heavy sigh he looked out the window.

"So, that is what happened?" he said out loud. "It makes sense to me now. Why did I not remember this?" He tapped his fingers on the page.

There is a sudden, sharp knock at his door.

"What do you want?" Barnabus felt the sweat roll down his cheeks. Looking around the room, he looked at the window, back at the far point of the room, and back at the door. "Well?"

The Trebbian guard peaked around the door as it slowly opened.

"What do you want?" Barnabus stood slamming the book down on the nearby table.

"Willie is here and would like to speak with you. You said you didn't want to be disturbed, but he said—"

"Bring him in, you fool! Of course, I'll see Willie. He is my eyes and ears in King Elder's Camp." Barnabus put the book behind a cushion of the throne chair. Then, he skipped down the steps to greet Willie coming in the door. "It is good to see you. What news have you?"

"My Treoraí," Willie made a deep bow. "I bring news of the Trebbian armies stationed at different points around the Wild Woods and in Snow Valley."

"And, what is happening?" Barnabus cleared his throat. "Um, well?" Barnabus had a sensation of being overheated.

"It appears the rebellion is making a move, but it is not clear in which direction they will attack. It seems as though they have learned how to move through the forest without being seen. It is puzzling to the Trebbians. They've not encountered this type of attack before."

Barnabus' mounting frustration was causing his thoughts to go blank.

"My Treoraí?"

"Yes. I know. I have many things on my mind. No need to worry." Barnabus wondered if Willie noticed his lack of command. *I need to be careful. I've stretched myself too thin. I'm feeling the effects of Barnabus fighting my possession of him.*

"Yes, My Treoraí. What would you like for me to do?"

"Nothing. Go back to the Trebbians. Tell them I'll lead them to the rebellion shortly. I must go and prepare myself for battle."

"You have no orders?" Willie said.

The hair on the back of Barnabus' neck bristled. "Get out!" Barnabus began to pace around the room. He needed to calm down and not allow his frustration to mount, not now. Not while he has a chance to beat the rebellion.

Barnabus walked back over to the throne, removed the book, and opened it to the page he needed. Written across the top were the words he needed to memorize.

THE USE of the dark magic—the Alp—gave Barnabus a way to leave Graves Mountain without being seen by anyone. He stood off to the left side of the mountain, not far from the entrance to the secret dungeon. When Barnabus completed reciting the chant, his soul dissolved away. It caused his body to transfer back into Nukpana.

She made her way to where she marked a spot that she was preparing to use. Her mentor, Amon, told her that if she ever needed to put a protective spell over her body, it was best to remove a part of her heart and bury it in close proximity to where her body would be located, leaving her with a partial heart to function.

Since she split her body into four beings, she decided earlier that she should place a protective spell over the hidden portion of her body. With the destruction of two of the three, she needed to be sure she completed the protective spell before she encountered the rebellion or fought KC.

Taking the vial from her waistcoat, she drank the concoction she made earlier. Then, Nukpana reached into her chest and pulled out her partial heart. With slow and determined movements and easy breaths, she placed the half of her heart into a box made from black ironwood and glass sides. She closed the lid and lowered the box into the small hole she dug.

Her plan was now in play. When the time is right, Nukpana thought, I will bring KC here where we will have our final battle, and then I can make my escape.

JACK WAS CONFUSED. "Mylo, what are you saying?"

"We are in Snowboro, a country north of King Elder's Camp and very far away from Graves Mountain where KC and Mr Scruffy are heading to take on Nukpana and her armies." Mylo walked over to the cell door, slammed it shut, and walked away.

"You can't leave me here! I need to go to KC!" Jack began to manically pace around his cell. Jack's voice resonated when he said, "What am I going to do?"

"You're going to sit down and listen, assuming you want some help," Vivette Chouette said.

Jack looked around his cell and couldn't tell from which direction the voice was coming.

"I'm down here," Vivette said.

"Another talking owl?"

"Actually, I'm a talking owlette," Vivette said with a twinkle in her voice. "I heard your anger, and I understand it. Do you understand why you were brought here instead of taken to KC's side where the siege will be?"

"No. That is why I'm angry."

"KC needs to do this fight at Graves Mountain on her own without your help. She needs to face her enemy head on; no one needs to fight her battles." Vivette agitated her feathers, and then flattened them down. "Do you understand now?"

"Yes, I believe I do." Jack looked down at his hands. "I need to go to her. Do you understand me?"

"We do," Larissa Mar and Arrington said walking up to Jack's cell door.

"We've come to break you out," Arrington said.

"Great!"

"Hold on," Vivette said. "There's no need to break him out. I have the key right here. I only wanted to make sure he was going for the right reason." Vivette hooted.

"WE'RE HONORED to help KC's husband. We're planning to secretly marry," Larissa Mar said while handing Jack a sword, a shield, and a horn. "We would want to be together if we were going into battle."

Jack shook Arrington's hand. "Congratulations, to you both." He looked at the horn. "What is it?"

"It is to call for aid when you need it. Put it to your lips and breath in normally. Don't blow hard. It sends out a silent sound that only Snowquidians can hear. We will come to help." Larissa Mar smiled.

Arrington's hand went up and stopped Jack from trying out the horn. "Don't do it now. You'll bring all of Mylo's guards down on us."

"No he won't," Mylo said. "We're here already."

"Now, Mylo," Jack said. "You've got to understand. They are here to help me, nothing more."

Mylo smiled. "I know. I was coming to break you out myself. Come. We've got a journey ahead of us."

"Can't we transport there?" Larissa Mar asked.

"Under normal situations, I'd say yes. But, Jack hasn't even been trained yet on how to use his sword and fight. We must protect him too." Mylo turned to Jack. "If you die here, you will cease to exist on Earth. We don't want that to happen until we are sure you have been protected by Mother Elder and Yggdrasil too."

"I understand," Jack said.

Yggdrasil and Mother Elder appeared in the cell.

"What?" Jack said.

Mylo touched Jack's hand. "No worries. May I present to you Mother Elder and Yggdrasil, the Tree of Life." Mylo and the others bowed in respect.

Jack tilted his head and at the same time caught a hat falling down into his hands. "Where did—"

"It is a very special and magical hat," Mother Elder said. "It is the bowler hat that KC first used to come to Eldershire. It will bring protection to you as well as aid you when you protect KC. Go now, my son. Be safe."

"Yes, we must march in haste," Mylo said. "It will take the full setting of Two-Moons once more before we reach where KC and Mr Scruffy will be camping."

"Wait," Vivette said. "Let me grow to travel size. Jack can ride on my back. Then, you and your fellow Snowquidians can transport there. We'll be fine and not far behind you."

Jack said, "I don't care how I get there. Or how long it takes. I need to go to my bride."

"And so you shall. Let's walk outside this cell into the open. Mylo, will you and the others help Jack get strapped onto my back? Will one of you give Jack the gift of telepathically speaking?" Vivette looked at Mother Elder and Yggdrasil.

"Jack, can you hear me?" Mother Elder said to Jack telepathically.

"What?" Jack looked around. "Who said that?"

"It was I, Mother Elder. Look at me. You'll see my lips are not moving."

Jack stared. "I can hear you," he said aloud.

"Good. You give it a try. Say what you are thinking, but only to yourself. Do not speak the words."

"You mean like this?" Jack said.

"Yes, exactly like that," Vivette said. "Good. When we fly, I can tell you things to do and help you stay on my back."

"But, you are so small. Will they shrink me?" Jack said telepathically.

"No. You can speak out loud again. Remember, to speak to Vivette telepathically, think of her, and then think of the words you would say to her. She will hear you." Mother Elder smiled. "Vivette will grow in size so that you can ride on her back."

"This is amazing to me. I've been a pilot on Earth. Now, I'll be able to fly with an owl."

Jack watched Vivette grow in size. His eyes seemed to grow as she grew.

"Amazing," Jack said looking to Mylo. "KC loves owls. She shared with me about her friendship with Mr Scruffy. Have you ridden on an owl?"

"No. There's no need with our ability to transport in seconds to anywhere in Eldershire."

"No wonder KC marveled at what she saw here. It had to be hard for her to know what she saw; yet she couldn't share it with me. I know how she feels in a small way. I never could explain what it felt like to fly an airplane."

"KC has ridden on Mr Scruffy's back. The two of you will have much to talk about. Come, now. You can climb upon my back." Vivette laid her wing down for Jack to step upon. "Use my wing to help you climb up."

Jack settled on Vivette's back. "I can't believe this is happening."

"Remember, talk to me telepathically. Give it a try now," Vivette said.

"Like this?" Jack asked telepathically.

"Yes. Good."

Vivette signaled to Mylo. Then, she took flight. Jack felt the air upon his face, his hair blew back away, he could feel the bowler hat flap, but it stayed in place. He smiled. He was going to see his beloved KC.

CHAPTER 34
NUKPANA'S DARK SHADOW

"**A**re you ready?" Mr Scruffy asked KC. "What are you searching for?"

"As best as I can be. I'm fully outfitted. I have Fea, my necklace, and the plaid collar. But, I can't find the bowler hat. Have you seen it?"

"Not recently. Where were you the last time you wore it?"

"At the Herok'a leaders meeting. I set it down on the table. I wonder." KC put her finger to her chin. "Did you see Iolair take it?"

"No, why would he do that?"

"I'm not sure, but it seems logical, for some reason. Where is he, anyway?" KC moved over to her cot, lifted a pillow, and found nothing there.

"He is at Emerald Mountain with his scouts getting ready for us when we do the siege. We thought it best that we group there, in case Nukpana escapes us."

"That makes sense. I wonder how I missed that discussion?"

"We didn't discuss it as a group," Mr Scruffy said. "Come, we can't hang around here much longer." He led KC out of the door. "You will be fine without the bowler hat during this fight. We don't expect to deal with Nukpana during our first attempt. She always likes making an entrance."

"Before you ask, Mylo took Jack over to meet Seborn, Arrington, Eri, and Larissa Mar. She said she'd bring him to our position after he was fully fitted with protection."

"He knows what he is about to get into, then?"

"Yes, as best I could prepare him," KC said looking grave. "I'm scared for him, and for me."

"We all are," Mr Scruffy said.

Together, they continued over to the central portion of the encampment. KC looked around and noticed many of the Herok'a leaders and their band of fighters were milling around in groups.

"I see the hawks, but I don't see Gavin. Over there are the eagles, but I don't see Iolair." KC pointed to the group of foxes. "Where is Lorne?" KC stood still trying to determine what was going on.

"You are worrying again," Mr Scruffy said. "A portion of Iolair's team stayed behind to help Gavin. Both Gavin and Lorne are old hands at fighting. They will take their respective places when the time is right. Come with me. We need to meet with Princess Istar."

THE TWO-SUNS WERE DIRECTLY OVERHEAD when Mr Scruffy turned to KC and said, "It is time."

"Mylo has come with Jack?" KC said.

"No. I'm sure they will join us. Our plan to make our siege at the base of Graves Mountain is our only chance to fight the Trebbians, Barnabus, *and* Nukpana. The spot we selected will give us an upper hand. We can't wait for them. If we stay here much longer, we could lose the chance of surprise. Are you ready?"

"Let's go!" KC said.

§⃝

KC SAW Mr Scruffy standing off at a distance from the other Herok'a leaders. She motioned for him to move over to her.

Landing next to her, he said telepathically, "Are you ready, my friend?"

"With you by my side, I'm as ready as I can be," KC said. She looked up at the sky. The sunlight flickered through the leaves of the trees as the Two-Suns began to set. The dappled sunlight brought a feeling she hadn't noticed in a long time. "Nothing happened today. Maybe it will be Two-Moons," KC giggled.

"What's funny," Mr Scruffy said.

"I'm feeling rather peaceful. Seems strange when we're preparing to siege Graves Mountain, don't you think?"

"Not really. There are many that speak of the old adage, 'the quiet before the storm.'" Mr Scruffy smiled.

"Come, get on my shoulder," KC lifted Mr Scruffy up. His wings opened as though hugging her. "You make me feel loved." The tension in KC's body left her, she took a deeper breath, and then slowly released it.

"Think of me as your soul angel. I will be with you always, by your side, holding your hand. I am your spirit guide." Mr Scruffy's wings continued to hug KC.

"You know I'll be fighting beside you."

"Yes. We've not had much time to prepare you for this siege or the battles to come. From what Princess Istar told us she learned from her scouts, Nukpana is getting stronger using dark magic. I feel I need to share with you my devotion, to give you my vow, I'll be there for you."

"Thank you, Mr Scruffy. Your support of me, your friendship, and your love of Eldershire will help me be strong when I need to be."

Together, they stood looking out at the setting Two-Suns as the rays of light made an interplay between the leaves of the trees. The late evening air cooled, and the sweet smells of forest trees in bloom with the scents of flowers growing under the canopy mingled with the settling dew.

"Look," KC pointed. "Do you see?"

"I have been watching Vivette flying toward us for a few clicks. You realize who is on her back?"

"Oh, my! Jack!" KC waved. "Do you think she will land near?"

"She'll crash into us, if we're not careful," Mr Scruffy said moving back. "Move out of her way."

Vivette touched down near KC and Mr Scruffy. She moved her wing for Jack to step off. He ran into KC's arms.

"I can't believe I just did that. Can you?" KC smiled at Jack. He quickly told her about the flight. She moved her hand up to his lips and used her fingers to quiet his chatter. "I'm talking too much, aren't I?"

KC nodded. "It's all right. I know how you feel. After the many times I've flown with Mr Scruffy, I never tire of the sensation of freedom it gives."

"What exactly is going on here? Mylo, Mother Elder, and Yggdrasil tried—" Jack said.

"What do you think of Mother Elder and Yggdrasil?"

"It was like meeting a deity. My fears and tension left me the second I saw them. I found myself staring at them as goose bumps slid along the back of my neck. I was giddy."

A smile swept across KC's face. Her heart warmed with compassion. She was pleased Jack was with her, but their existence in Eldershire was dependent on how well he would listen to her now. She had to be sure he understood what was going to happen.

"Jack, you know what we are going to do, right?"

"Yes. I am a soldier. I recognize the preparation for an attack."

"Not an attack, a siege. It will be difficult, but we hope to cause Barnabus, a companion to Nukpana Fraener, to surrender."

"From what Mother Elder and Yggdrasil explained to me, do you think it will work?"

Taking in a cleansing breath, KC sighed. "To be honest, no."

"Then, why?"

"We need to give Iolair the time necessary to prepare Emerald Mountain. We think if we can cut off Nukpana's escape, we can corner her here at Graves Mountain and use our collective powers against her."

"You do realize that I probably can help you?"

"Yes, but you must know that here you are not a leader, you are—"

"A soldier." Jack smiled. "I am a good soldier too. What do you need me to do?"

KC explained the various groups of the Herok'a and what each group would be responsible for doing during the siege at the hidden entrance to Graves Mountain.

Moving closer to KC, Jack took her in his arms. They embraced.

"I'm sorry. I probably shouldn't have kissed you like that here on what is a battlefield. I've never done something like that before. I was overcome with your strength and fortitude," Jack said.

"It's okay. I've missed you too. And, I'm glad to know you've not kissed someone on a battlefield like that before." KC winked at him.

"There will be plenty of time for us to catch up after this is all over. I'll keep my place until it is done."

"Good." KC looked pensive. "You realize I'm the leader of this entire pack along with Mr Scruffy. You will have to listen to my orders and do as I say?"

"I *am* a good soldier."

"Mr Scruffy!" Isicaranon called, stumbling into the encampment. "Mr Scruffy." He fell to the ground and moaned.

"What's going on here?" Ralph said while others gathered around.

Isicaranon raised his head, "Get word to Mr Scruffy." His head fell back. He was in a stupor. Ralph looked him over and saw where he was stabbed.

"Several of you, pick Isicaranon up and carry him to my thípi. We will need to tend to his wound, if it is not too late." Two of the Herok'a picked him up. "Fergus, find Mr Scruffy and bring him to my thípi."

"I got here as soon as I could," Mr Scruffy said. "Is he dying?"

"Yes. He managed to wake once and said he was shanked by a Trebbian as he was leaving the secret dungeon of Graves Mountain. I fear he saw something we should know, but he hasn't been conscious again," Ralph said while using a wad of wet moss to wipe Isicaranon's forehead. "We managed to stop the bleeding, but I'm not sure how severe the damage."

Mr Scruffy moved closer to Isicaranon. "I'm here. Can you speak?"

Isicaranon opened his eyes. "I've been saving my energy to tell you. I saw Nukpana. She shed Barnabus' skin, like a snake does. First, I saw Barnabus, and then in the next moment, Nukpana stood before me. Then, she did something strange. She drank a potion, took her heart out of her body, and then buried it in some sort of box." Isicaranon coughed, and lay back down.

"Where did this happen?" Fergus asked.

"Near the secret dungeon entrance to Graves Mountain. I'm fearful for what this means. Her dark magic is stronger than even I imagined." He took a deep breath releasing his soul. "I leave you now. My time in Eldershire is over. Peace be with you." Isicaranon was gone.

THE SIEGE RAGED on after what seemed like hours of fighting as the Herok'a fought to take control. They were near the secret dungeon entrance to Grave's Mountain. The shouts and shrieks could be heard without much effort—the sounds of metal clashing on metal, the grunts, and the cries of pain. Trebbians and Herok'a intertwined in a dance of death and destruction.

As beings were struck down, they fell, and then they would dissolve away. The sight brought tears to KC's eyes while she scanned the area for Nukpana. She should be here, KC thought.

The Two-Suns were high in the sky, their rays shining down with intense heat, much like the heat in the hearts of those fighting to win.

KC, Mr Scruffy, and all of the Herok'a fought valiantly against the Trebbians. KC looked for Jack. He was not far from her left side, using his sword, which Mylo gave him, with skill. She marveled at his agility. He was giving the fight his best against a tall, giant of a Trebbian. Their swords flashed moving through the air when the Two-Suns rays bounced off them causing the swords to look alive.

Off to the other side, Mr Scruffy and his owls were battling with another group of Trebbians. The space between them narrowed while the fight continued edging closer to the base of Graves Mountain.

KC managed to fend off a charge to her with the help of Ralph and his fierce pack of wolves by his side. She had grown to love Ralph like a brother. His loyalty seemed to have no bounds. A recognition of her love for dogs bled over into her compassion for Ralph.

The Lemmketeers came up and stood close by fighting an attack from behind. The forest seemed to darken.

Logan said, "KC, be careful. I don't trust what is happening in the sky. It is darkening too early."

"We're deeper into the forest. It is hard for the light to shine through," KC said.

"No. It is something else. I don't like it!" Logan shouted as he fought off an attacker. "Be careful!"

They continued to fight hand-to-hand, trading barbs, and escalating their swings. The smell and sounds of war wafted out around them —sweat stung their eyes, gore sprayed their faces, metal clashed against metal, cries of pain and death—disorder and violence were all around them.

KC CAUGHT a glimpse of her BlueStone locket glowing bright blue. Nukpana appeared in front of her. She stepped back. Crab took a step forward when Nukpana's sword came slashing forth connecting with his arm, slashing it off. He cried out in pain and fell to the ground.

Enraged with fear, KC stepped forward using Fea to slash at Nukpana.

"My Pitiful One. How good of you to come visit me. You are out of practice," Nukpana said raising her sword and cutting down the front of KC causing her to drop Fea.

Jack screamed in anger, "I'll kill you!" His adrenaline coursing through his bloodstream, he ran to KC, picked up her sword lying on the ground, and threw it at Nukpana.

Fea soared past Nukpana and landed in the soft forest floor, sinking downward up to its hilt. The force of the sword striking the ground lifted the ironwood box partially out of the soil. The sword had pierced through the top. The BlueStone on the sword turned white.

Nukpana grabbed at her heart. "You've killed me!" Her body vaporized.

KC, lying on the ground, raised her arm and pointed to the purple cloud floating above her head. She was mortally wounded.

The battle was over a few clicks after Nukpana screamed out in pain. The Herok'a rushed over to where KC lay in Jack's arms. Tears flowed down his face.

Mr Scruffy stepped forward and placed his wing on Jack's shoulder.

"She's gone," Jack said. "I've lost my sweetness."

Ralph and his wolf pack let out the howls of the ages. The other creatures of Eldershire began to mourn.

Mother Elder and Yggdrasil stood before Jack. He looked up to them, his tear stained eyes showed his pain.

"Why?"

"It was foretold. Life in Eldershire will now continue. We will revenge her death," Yggdrasil said.

"The prophecy?" Jack said. His anger beginning to boil. "You used my wife to save your world. And, I'm supposed to accept this and go on?"

"No. We don't expect you to accept this event. We will have trouble acknowledging it. This is a great loss to our world too," Mr Scruffy said.

He bowed his head; a tear fell from his eye, dropping on the ground near KC. A rumbling began; Graves Mountain shook and trembled.

"We must move quickly," Mother Elder said.

How Mother Elder transported the Herok'a with Jack and KC to King Elder's Camp, no one seemed to know, but they were away from Graves Mountain and its falling boulders. There was food and drink provided for them and they all sat down to a meal. All that is except for Jack. He refused to eat.

"You must keep up your strength," Mr Scruffy said handing Jack a plate of food—berries, nuts, and some cakes apparently made from ground leaves.

"No. I can't eat. KC just died before my eyes. I couldn't save her. I should not be alive."

"Are you sure she is gone?" Mr Scruffy said.

"She's not breathing."

"Are you sure she is not?" Mr Scruffy looked at Jack. "You are not on Earth anymore. Life here is different. Magic is part of this world. Nukpana was using dark magic. Anything is possible, including the fact that KC is back in a coma, here, now."

Jack's eyes widened. "I hadn't thought of that at all. What can we do?"

"We must wait. Iolair will be returning at high Two-Moons. He will be bringing to us information he telepathically told me he found in Emerald Mountain."

"Emerald Mountain?" Jack looked confused. "What is it?"

"The sister mountain to Graves Mountain. When Nukpana first came to Eldershire, she lived in Emerald Mountain and used Graves Mountain for when she became the Purple Drakein."

"I remember some of what KC told me about that time."

"When Iolair arrives, we'll have information that will help us locate KC."

"Her body lies in that chamber there," Jack pointed to the ceremonial thípi that was erected by the Elderians to celebrate KC's death. "We don't need to locate her."

"Don't we?" Mr Scruffy smiled.

TO THE READER

This book chronicles a second visit to Eldershire and KC's encounters with many inhabitants. After this letter, there is a concordance, *Words of Eldershire*, to help you with pronunciations and meanings of terms, names, and places. As the series grows, words will be added. A complete concordance will be on my website.

The Chronicles of Eldershire is a long adventure that is over forty-five years in the making. I put it away right after I graduated from high school, and then worked on it again around the time I found out I was pregnant with our daughter, Julie. Then, in 2005 or so, I became friends with a special writing colleague. In 2009, Rosa and I attended a writing conference where I shared the early chapters of this story. It failed drastically. My writing and creativity came to a halt. Rosa encouraged me to trudge forward. After writing four books (a memoir and a thriller trilogy), I decided I'd think about writing KC's story once more.

During the winter of December 2017, I was able to publish the first book of The Chronicles—*The Owl, the Sword, & the Efil Stone*. This book, *DarkShadow*, has proven to be harder to write than I anticipated. But, patience, tenacity, and a little ole elbow grease helped me get this book ready for you to enjoy. It is hoped you will.

Thank you, readers, for your support, for reading my words, and for sharing my story with others.

Read on!
Pam

WORDS OF ELDERSHIRE

There is an internal language of the tree spirits that can only be understood by those who are of Elder decent. A common language is used amongst all beings of Eldershire to aid in communicating. This common language is also known as English on Earth. The following listing of words used is provided to aid the reader's understanding. As the series grows, new words with their meanings will be added to a complete concordance on my website. Due to space limitations, the listing in this book is not extensive. Names are in bold-italics while places and things are bold.

Drakein (syll. drake-in)—origin is Greek. The first type of Greek dragon was the Dracon whose name was derived from the Greek words "drakein" and "derkomai" meaning "to see clearly" or "gaze sharply." The English word, dragon, is derived from drakein.

Eldershire—the world of the Elders and other magical beings. For more details, see *Where is the Land of Eldershire?* in the front of this book.

Fraener (syll. fray-ner)—a variant form of Fafnir (Old Norse). An Old Norse myth name of a dwarf who transformed into a dragon, the symbol of greed. Also called Fáfnir.

Mother Elder—associated closely with Celtic faerie lands, sacred to the goddesses Venus and Holle. The Myth is that of a spirit who inhabits the Elder tree, holds the power to work a variety of magics on Earth and in Eldershire; her skin, bark, and outer wood are strong and hard, offering protection against witches and the sap is the blood of life and the dwelling place of the spirit.

Nukpana (syll. nuk-pa-na)—origin is Native American and means evil one. Nukpana is a mythological hybrid and the offspring of the union between descendants of Anzû and Lilith with Drakein ancestry. Nukpana is a 'Blender'—half witch and half Drakein. She can transform between one or the other at will. When angry, both come out of her.

Snowquids (alt. Snowquidians, Snowquid)—the beings of the Land of Snowboro. Snowquids cherish life but realize everything is subject to change.

Treorai (syll. tre-o-ray)—Irish for leader or navigator.

Yggdrasil (syll. ig-dra-sil)—in Norse mythology, Yggdrasil is the holy Ash World Tree surrounded by nine worlds. It is said to connect the Underworld to Heaven with its branches and roots. From the symbol of the tree flows human awareness and consciousness.

Visit https://pambnewberry.com for a complete concordance.

ACKNOWLEDGMENTS

The continuation of a dream is magical. For you, my devoted readers, who have stuck with me during my writing journey, thank you. You make it possible. Your steadfast encouragement, your devotion to follow my writing, and your desire to connect with me are key to giving me the courage and aspiration to use my pen to produce another story. There are those people in my world who are critical to the successful completion of any goal.

My husband, Albert, is my best friend. He helps me look at life through "happy" glasses, and to sit back and smell the flowers. Thank you, with all my love. Your encouragement never ceases to inspire me. I love you!

Julie, our daughter, continues her magic designing another beautiful cover. Her ability to pull out nuances that I imagine and put them into an image is a joy to see. Thank you! Daddy and I love you, dearly.

How does one capture in a short sentence or two the value of friends—Rosa Lee Jude, the alpha reader, thank you! If you've not enjoyed Rosa's stories, find her stories through her website: RosaLeeJude.com.

The VIP Squad—Patrick Downes, Linda Eisenhauer, Glo Frye, Bonita Jones, Diane Kitts, Barbara Lambert, Tammie Lowry, and Marcella Taylor, and the gamma reader and final eyes, Jodie Huff— all of these readers helped to make this story stellar!

Each VIP offered suggestions, questions, and eagle eyes that propelled me forward, and it is hoped, helping me to become a better writer. I am grateful! I salute each of you for being my cheering squad and for reminding me that a dream is only a dream if you let it stay in your mind.

To my friends and friends to be, thank you for being readers of my words. Moreover, thank you for writing to let me know if I've touched your life in some small way, and for sharing my work with others. There are so many who offer support, please know I thank you much.

I Write On!

ABOUT THE AUTHOR

Pam B. Newberry lives in the mountains of Southwest Virginia with her husband where she is at work on her next book. She is the author of *The Letter: A Page of My Life*, The Marine Letsco Trilogy —*The Fire Within*, *The Fire of Revenge*, and *A Time for Fire*, and The Chronicles of Eldershire— *The Owl, the Sword, & the Efil Stone* and *DarkShadow*. She enjoys fun in the sun—gardening, fishing, and working with her husband on their hobby farm.

Connect with Pam through her website: https://pambnewberry.com

Follow Pam through her Amazon author page with Goodreads, Pinterest, and YouTube. Her YouTube channel offers a playlist of music she listened to while she wrote *The Sword, the Owl, & the Efil Stone* and *DarkShadow*. She loves hearing from readers regarding authors she should read and musicians she should listen to or follow.